Tom Holt was born in London in 1961. At Oxford he studied bar billiards, ancient Greek agriculture and the care and feeding of small, temperamental Japanese motorcycle engines; interests which led him, perhaps inevitably, to qualify as a solicitor and emigrate to Somerset, where he specialised in death and taxes for seven years before going straight in 1995. Now a full-time writer, he lives in Chard, Somerset, with his wife, one daughter and the unmistakable scent of blood, wafting in on the breeze from the local meat-packing plant.

Find out more about Tom Holt and other Orbit authors by registering for the free monthly newsletter at www.orbitbooks.co.uk

By Tom Holt

EXPECTING SOMEONE TALLER
WHO'S AFRAID OF BEOWULF?
FLYING DUTCH
YE GODS!
OVERTIME
HERE COMES THE SUN
GRAILBLAZERS
FAUST AMONG EQUALS
ODDS AND GODS
DJINN RUMMY
MY HERO
PAINT YOUR DRAGON
OPEN SESAME
WISH YOU WERE HERE
ONLY HUMAN
SNOW WHITE AND THE SEVEN SAMURAI
VALHALLA
NOTHING BUT BLUE SKIES
FALLING SIDEWAYS
LITTLE PEOPLE
THE PORTABLE DOOR
IN YOUR DREAMS

DEAD FUNNY: OMNIBUS 1
MIGHTIER THAN THE SWORD: OMNIBUS 2
DIVINE COMEDIES: OMNIBUS 3
FOR TWO NIGHTS ONLY: OMNIBUS 4
TALL STORIES: OMNIBUS 5
SAINTS AND SINNERS: OMNIBUS 6
FISHY WISHES: OMNIBUS 7

THE WALLED ORCHARD
ALEXANDER AT THE WORLD'S END
OLYMPIAD
A SONG FOR NERO

I, MARGARET

LUCIA TRIUMPHANT
LUCIA IN WARTIME

TOM HOLT

Tall Stories

Contains
Expecting Someone Taller
and Ye Gods!

www.orbitbooks.co.uk

An *Orbit* Book

First published in Great Britain by Orbit 2004
This omnibus edition © Tom Holt 2004

Expecting Someone Taller
First published in Great Britain in 1987 by
Macmillan (London) Limited
Copyright © 1987 by Tom Holt

Ye Gods!
First published in Great Britain by Orbit 1992

A CIP catalogue record for this book
is available from the British Library.

ISBN 1 84149 345 7

Typeset in Plantin by M Rules
Printed and bound in Great Britain by
Mackays of Chatham plc

Orbit
An imprint of
Time Warner Book Group UK
Brettenham House
Lancaster Place
London WC2E 7EN

CONTENTS

EXPECTING SOMEONE TALLER

To My Mother

CHAPTER ONE

After a particularly unrewarding interview with his beloved, Malcolm was driving home along a dark, winding country lane when he ran over a badger. He stopped the car and got out to inspect the damage to his paintwork and (largely from curiosity) to the badger. It was, he decided, all he needed, for there was a small but noticeable dent in his wing, and he had been hoping to sell the car.

'Damn,' he said aloud.

'So how do you think I feel?' said the badger.

Malcolm turned round quite slowly. He had had a bad day, but not so bad that he could face talking badgers – talking *dead* badgers – with equanimity. The badger was lying on its side, absolutely still. Malcolm relaxed; he must have imagined it, or perhaps the bump had accidentally switched on the car radio. Any connection was possible between the confused chow mein of wires under his dashboard.

'You're not the one who's been run over,' said the badger, bitterly.

This time, Malcolm turned round rather more quickly.

There was the black and white corpse, lying across the road like a dead zebra crossing; yet he could have sworn that human speech had come from it. Was some rustic ventriloquist, possibly a Friend of the Earth, playing tricks on him? He nerved himself to examine his victim. A dead badger, nothing more, nothing less; except that there was some sort of wire contraption wrapped round its muzzle – a homing device, perhaps, attached by a questing ecologist.

'Did you say something?' said Malcolm, nervously.

'So you're not deaf as well as blind,' said the badger. 'Yes, I did say something. Why don't you pay more attention when people talk to you?'

Malcolm felt rather embarrassed. His social equipment did not include formulae for talking to people he had just mortally wounded, or badgers, let alone a combination of the two. Nevertheless, he felt it incumbent upon him to say something, and his mind hit upon the word designed for unfamiliar situations.

'Sorry,' he said.

'You're sorry,' said the badger. 'The hell with you.'

There was a silence, broken only by the screech of a distant owl. After a while, Malcolm came to the conclusion that the badger *was* dead, and that during the collision he had somehow concussed himself without noticing it. Either that, or it was a dream. He had heard about people who fell asleep at the wheel, and remembered that they usually crashed and killed themselves. That did not cheer him up particularly.

'Anyway,' said the badger, 'what's your name?'

'Malcolm,' said Malcolm. 'Malcolm Fisher.'

'Say that again,' said the badger. 'Slowly.'

'Mal-colm Fi-sher.'

The badger was silent for a moment. 'Are you sure?' it said, sounding rather puzzled.

'Yes,' said Malcolm. 'Sorry.'

'Well, Malcolm Fisher, let's have a look at you.'

The badger twisted its head painfully round, and looked at him in silence for a while. 'You know,' it said at last, 'I was expecting someone rather taller.'

'Oh,' said Malcolm.

'Fair-haired, tall, muscular, athletic, without spectacles,' went on the badger. 'Younger, but also more mature, if you see what I mean. Someone with presence. Someone you'd notice if you walked into a room full of strangers. In fact, you're a bit of a disappointment.'

There was no answer to that, except Sorry again, and that would be a stupid thing to say. Nevertheless, it was irritating to have one's physical shortcomings pointed out quite so plainly twice in one evening, once by a beautiful girl and once by a dying badger. 'So what?' said Malcolm, uppishly.

'All right,' said the badger. 'Sorry I spoke, I'm sure. Well, now you're here, you might as well get it over with. Though I'm not sure it's not cheating hitting me with that thing.' And it waved a feeble paw at Malcolm's aged Renault.

'Get what over with?' asked Malcolm.

'Don't let's play games,' said the badger. 'You've killed me, you needn't mess me around as well. Take the Ring and the Tarnhelm and piss off.'

'I don't follow,' said Malcolm. 'What are you talking about?'

The badger jerked violently, and spasms of pain ran through its shattered body. 'You mean it was an *accident*?' it rasped. 'After nearly a thousand years, it's a bloody accident. Marvellous!' The dying animal made a faint gasping noise that might just have been the ghost of laughter.

'Now you have lost me,' said Malcolm.

3

'I'd better hurry up, then,' said the badger, with weary resignation in its voice. 'Unless you want me dying on you, that is, before I can tell you the story. Take that wire gadget off my nose.'

Gingerly, Malcolm stretched out his fingers, fully expecting the beast to snap at them. Badgers' jaws, he remembered, are immensely strong. But the animal lay still and patient, and he was able to pull the wire net free. At once the badger disappeared, and in its place there lay a huge, grey-haired man, at least seven feet tall, with cruel blue eyes and a long, tangled beard.

'That's better,' he said. 'I hated being a badger. Fleas.'

'I'd better get you to a hospital,' said Malcolm.

'Don't bother,' said the giant. 'Human medicine wouldn't work on me anyway. My heart is in my right foot, my spine is made of chalcedony, and my intestines are soluble in aspirin. I'm a Giant, you see. In fact I am – was – the last of the Giants.'

The Giant paused, like a television personality stepping out into the street and waiting for the first stare of recognition.

'How do you mean, Giant, exactly? You're very tall, but . . .'

The Giant closed his eyes and moaned softly.

'Come on,' said Malcolm, 'there's a casualty department in Taunton. We can get there in forty minutes.'

The Giant ignored him. 'Since you are totally ignorant of even basic theogony,' he said, 'I will explain. My name is Ingolf, and I am the last of the Frost-Giants of the Elder Age.'

'Pleased to meet you,' said Malcolm instinctively.

'Are you hell as like. I am the youngest brother of Fasolt and Fafner the castle-builders. Does that ring a bell? No?'

4

'No.'

'You didn't even see the opera?' said Ingolf despairingly.

'I'm afraid I'm not a great fan of opera,' said Malcolm, 'so it's unlikely.'

'I don't believe it. Well, let's not go into all that now. I'll be dead in about three minutes. When you get home, look up the Ring Cycle in your *Boy's Book of Knowledge*. My story starts with the last act of *Götterdämmerung*. The funeral pyre. Siegfried lying in state. On his belt, the Tarnhelm. On his finger, the Mbelung's Ring.' Ingolf paused. 'Sorry, am I boring you?'

'No,' Malcolm said. 'Go on, please.'

'Hagen snatches the Ring from Siegfried's hand as Brunnhilde plunges into the heart of the fire. At once, the Rhine bursts its banks – I'd been warning them about that embankment for years, but would they listen? – and the Rhinedaughters drag Hagen down into the depths of the river and drown him. For no readily apparent reason, Valhalla catches fire. Tableau. The End. Except,' and Ingolf chuckled hoarsely through his tattered lungs, 'the stupid tarts dropped the ring while they were drowning Hagen, and guess who was only a few feet away, clinging to a fallen tree, as I recall. Me. Ingolf. Ingolf the Neglected, Ingolf the Patient, Ingolf, Heir to the Ring! So I grabbed it, pulled the Tarnhelm from the ashes of the pyre, and escaped in the confusion. To here, in fact, the Vale of Taunton Deane. Last place God made, but never mind.'

'Fascinating,' said Malcolm after a while. 'That doesn't explain why you were a badger just now, and why you aren't one any longer.'

'Doesn't it?' Ingolf groaned again. 'The Tarnhelm, you ignorant child, is a magic cap made by Mime, the greatest craftsman in history. Whoever wears it can take any shape

5

or form he chooses, animate or inanimate, man, bird or beast, rock, tree or flower. Or he can be invisible, or transport himself instantaneously from one end of the earth to the other, just by thinking. And this idiot here thought, Who would come looking for a badger? So I turned myself into one and came to this godforsaken spot to hide.'

'Why?'

'Because it's godforsaken, and I'd had about as much of the Gods as I could take. They were after me, you see. In fact, they probably still are. Also the Volsungs. And the Rhinemaidens. And Alberich. The whole bloody lot of them. It hasn't been easy, I can tell you. Luckily, they're all so unbelievably *stupid*. They've spent the last thousand odd years searching high and low for a ninety-foot dragon with teeth like standing stones and an enormous tail. Just because my brother Fafner – a pleasant enough chap in his way, but scarcely imaginative – disguised *him*self as a dragon when he had the perishing thing. I could have told him that a ninety-foot dragon was scarcely inconspicuous, even in the Dawn of the World, but why should I help him? Anyway, I very sensibly became a badger and outsmarted them all.'

'Hang on,' said Malcolm, 'I'm a bit confused. Why did you have to hide?'

'Because,' said Ingolf, 'they wanted the Ring.'

'So why didn't you give it to them – whoever they were – and save yourself all the bother?'

'Whoever owns the ring is the master of the world,' said Ingolf, gravely.

'Oh,' said Malcolm. 'So you're . . .'

'And a fat lot of good it's done me, you might very well say. Who did you think ruled the world, anyway, the United bloody Nations?'

6

'I hadn't given it much thought, to be honest with you. But if you're the ruler of the world . . .'

'I know what you're thinking. If I'm master of the world, why should I have to hide in a copse in Somerset disguised as a badger?'

'More or less,' said Malcolm.

'Uneasy lies the head that wears a crown,' said the Giant sagely. 'Looking back, of course, I sometimes wonder whether it was all worth it. But you will learn by my mistakes.'

Malcolm furrowed his brow. 'You mean you're leaving them all to me?' he asked. 'The Ring and the – what did you say it was called?'

'Tarnhelm. It means helmet of darkness, though why they describe it as a helmet when it's just a little scrap of wire I couldn't tell you. Anyway, take them with my blessing, for what that's worth.'

Ingolf paused to catch his breath.

'To gain inexhaustible wealth,' he continued, 'just breathe on the Ring and rub it gently on your forehead. Go on, try it.'

Ingolf eased the plain gold ring off his finger and passed it to Malcolm, who accepted it rather as one might accept some delicacy made from the unspeakable parts of a rare amphibian at an embassy function. He did as Ingolf told him, and at once found himself knee-deep in gold. Gold cups, gold plates, gold brooches, pins, bracelets, anklets, pectorals, cruets and sauce-boats.

'Convinced?' said Ingolf. 'Or do you want a metallurgist's report?'

'I believe you,' said Malcolm, who was indeed firmly convinced that he was dreaming, and vowed never to eat Stilton cheese late at night again.

'Leave them,' said Ingolf. 'Plenty more where that came from. The Nibelungs make them in the bottomless caverns of Nibelheim, the Kingdom of the Mists. They'll be glad of the warehouse space.'

'And the Tarnhelm – that works too, does it?'

Ingolf finally seemed to lose patience. 'Of course it bloody works,' he shouted. 'Put it on and turn yourself into a human being.'

'Sorry,' said Malcolm. 'It's all been rather a shock.'

'Finally,' said Ingolf, 'cut my arm and lick some of the blood.'

'I'd rather not,' said Malcolm, firmly.

'If you do, you'll be able to understand the language of the birds.'

'I don't particularly want to be able to understand the language of the birds,' said Malcolm.

'You'll understand the language of the birds and like it, my lad,' said Ingolf severely. 'Now do as you are told. Use the pin on one of those brooches there.'

The blood tasted foul and was burning hot. For a second, Malcolm's brain clouded over; then, faintly in the distance, he heard the owl hoot again, and realised to his astonishment that he could understand what it was saying. Not that it was saying anything of any interest, of course.

'Oh,' said Malcolm. 'Oh, well, thank you.'

'Now then,' said the Giant. 'I am about to go on my last journey. Pile up that gold around my head. I must take it with me to pay the ferryman.'

'I thought it was just a coin on the eyes or something.'

'Inflation. Also, I'll take up rather a lot of room on the boat.' He scowled. 'Get on with it, will you?' he said. 'Or do you want a receipt?'

Malcolm did as he was told. After all, it wasn't as if it was real gold. Was it?

'Listen,' said Ingolf, 'listen carefully. I am dying now. When I am dead, my body will turn back into the living rock from which Lord Ymir moulded the race of the Frost-Giants when the world was young. Nothing will grow here for a thousand years, and horses will throw their riders when they pass the spot. Pity, really, it's a main road. Oh, well. Every year, on the anniversary of my death, fresh blood will well up out of the earth and the night air will be filled with uncanny cries. That is the Weird of the Ring-Bearer when his life is done. Be very careful, Malcolm Fisher. There is a curse on the Nibelung's Ring – the curse of Alberich, which brings all who wear it to a tragic and untimely death. Yet it is fated that when the Middle Age of the world is drawing to a close, a foolish, godlike boy who does not understand the nature of the Ring will break the power of Alberich's curse and thereby redeem the world. Then the Last Age of the world will begin, the Gods will go down for ever, and all things shall be well.' Ingolf's eyes were closing, his breath was faint, his words scarcely audible. But suddenly he started, and propped himself up on one elbow.

'Hold on a minute,' he gasped. 'A foolish, godlike boy who does not understand . . . who does not under-stand . . .' He sank down again, his strength exhausted. 'Still,' he said, 'I was expecting someone rather taller.'

He shuddered for the last time, and was as still as stone. The wind, which had been gathering during his last speech, started to scream, lashing the trees into a frenzy. The Giant was dead; already his shape was unrecognisable as his body turned back into grey stone, right in the middle of the Minehead to Bridgwater trunk road. All around him, Malcolm could hear a confused babble of voices, human and animal, living and dead, and, like the counterpoint to a vast fugue, the low, rumbling voices of the trees and the rocks. The entire earth was repeating the astonishing news: Ingolf was dead, the world had a new master.

Just then, two enormous ravens flapped slowly and lazily over Malcolm's head. He stood paralysed with inexplicable fear, but the ravens flew on. The voices died away, the wind dropped, the rain subsided. As soon as he was able to move, Malcolm jumped in his car and drove home as fast as the antiquated and ill-maintained engine would permit him to go. He undressed in the dark and fell into bed, and was soon fast asleep and dreaming a strange and terrible dream, all about being trapped in a crowded lift with no trousers on. Suddenly he woke up and sat bolt upright in the darkness. On his finger was the Ring. Beside his bed, between his watch and his key-chain, was the Tarnhelm. Outside his window, a nightingale was telling another nightingale what it had had for lunch.

'Oh my God,' said Malcolm, and went back to sleep.

The Oberkasseler Bridge over the Rhine has acquired a sinister reputation in recent years, and the two policemen who were patrolling it knew this only too well. They knew what to look for, and they seldom had to look far in this particular area.

A tall man with long grey hair falling untidily over the collar of his dark blue suit leaned against the parapet eating an ice cream. Although impeccably dressed, he was palpably all wrong, and the two policemen looked at each other with pleasant anticipation.

'Drugs?' suggested the first policeman.

'More like dirty books,' said the other. 'If he's armed, it's my turn.'

'It's always your turn,' grumbled his companion.

The first policeman shrugged his shoulders. 'Oh, all right then,' he said. 'But I get to drive back to the station.'

But as they approached their prey, they began to feel distinctly uncomfortable. It was not fear but a sort of awe or respect that caused them to hesitate as the tall man turned and stared at them calmly through his one eye. Suddenly, they found that they were having difficulty breathing.

'Excuse me, sir,' said the first policeman, gasping slightly, 'can you tell me the time?'

'Certainly,' said the tall man, without looking at his watch, 'it's just after half-past eleven.'

The two policemen turned and walked away quickly. As they did so, they both simultaneously looked at their own watches. Twenty-eight minutes to twelve.

'He must have been looking at the clock,' said the first policeman.

'What clock?' inquired his companion, puzzled.

'I don't know. Any bloody clock.'

The tall man turned and gazed down at the brown river for a while. Then he clicked his fingers, and a pair of enormous ravens floated down and landed on either side of him on the parapet. The tall man broke little pieces off the rim of his cornet and flicked them at the two birds as he questioned them.

'Any luck?' he asked.

'What do you think?' replied the smaller of the two.

'Keep trying,' said the tall man calmly. 'Have you done America today?'

The smaller raven's beak was full of cornet, so the larger raven, although unused to being the spokesman, said Yes, they had. No luck.

'We checked America,' said the smaller raven, 'and

11

Africa, and Asia, and Australasia, and Europe. Bugger all, same as always.'

'Maybe you were looking in the wrong place,' suggested the tall man.

'You don't understand,' said the smaller raven. 'It's like looking for . . .' the bird racked its brains for a suitably graphic simile '. . . for a needle in a haystack,' it concluded triumphantly.

'Well,' said the tall man, 'I suggest you go and look again. Carefully, this time. My patience is beginning to wear a little thin.'

Suddenly he closed his broad fist around the cornet, crushing it into flakes and dust.

'You've got ice cream all over your hand,' observed the larger raven.

'So I have,' said the tall man. 'Now get out, and this time concentrate.'

The ravens flapped their broad, drab wings and floated away. Frowning, the tall man clicked the fingers of his clean hand and took out his handkerchief.

'I've got a tissue if you'd rather use it,' said a nervous-looking thin man who had hurried up to him. The tall man waved it away.

'How about you?' he asked the thin man. 'Done any good?'

'Nothing. I did Toronto, Lusaka, and Brasilia. Have you ever been to Brasilia? Last place God made. Oh, I'm sorry. I didn't mean . . .'

'The more I think about it,' said the tall man, ignoring this gaffe, 'the more convinced I am that he's still in Europe. When Ingolf went to ground, the other continents hadn't even been discovered.'

The thin man looked puzzled. 'Ingolf?' he said. 'Haven't you heard?'

12

The tall man turned his head and fixed him with his one eye. The thin man started to tremble slightly, for he knew that expression well.

'Ingolf is dead,' continued the thin man. 'I thought you'd have known.'

The tall man was silent. Clouds, which had not been there a moment before, passed in front of the sun.

'I'm only the King of the Gods, nobody ever bothers to tell me anything,' said the tall man. 'So?'

'He died at a quarter to midnight last night, at a place called Ralegh's Cross in the West of England. He was knocked down by a car, and . . .'

Rain was falling now, hard and straight, but the thin man was sweating. Oddly enough, the tall man wasn't getting wet.

'No sign of the Ring,' said the thin man nervously. 'Or the helmet. I've checked all the usual suspects, but they don't seem to have heard or seen anything. In fact, they were as surprised as you were. I mean . . .'

Thunder now, and a flicker of distant lightning.

'I got there as quickly as I could,' said the thin man, desperately. 'As soon as I felt the shock. But I was in Brasilia, like I said, and it takes time . . .'

'All the usual suspects?'

'All of them. Every one.'

Suddenly, the tall man smiled. The rain stopped, and a rainbow flashed across the sky.

'I believe you,' said the tall man, 'thousands wouldn't. Right, so if it wasn't one of the usual suspects, it must have been an outsider, someone we haven't dealt with before. That should make it all much easier. So start searching.'

'Anywhere in particular?'

'Use your bloody imagination,' growled the tall man,

irritably, and the rainbow promptly faded away. The thin man smiled feebly, and soon was lost to sight among the passers-by. Wotan, the great Sky-God and King of all the Gods, put his handkerchief back in his pocket and gazed up into the sky, where the two enormous ravens were circling.

'Got all that?' Wotan murmured.

Thought, the elder and smaller of the two messenger ravens who are the God's eyes and ears on earth, dipped his wings to show that he had, and Wotan walked slowly away.

'Like looking for a needle in a haystack,' repeated Thought, sliding into a convenient thermal. His younger brother, Memory, banked steeply and followed him.

'This is true,' replied Memory, 'definitely.'

'You know the real trouble with this business?' said Memory, diving steeply after a large moth.

'What's that, then?'

'Bloody awful industrial relations, that's what. I mean, take Wotan. Thinks he's God almighty.'

'He is, isn't he?'

Memory hovered for a moment on a gust of air. 'I never thought of that,' he said at last.

'Well, you wouldn't,' said Thought, 'would you?'

CHAPTER TWO

The next morning, Malcolm thought long and hard before waking up, for he had come to recognise over the past quarter of a century that rather less can go wrong if you are asleep.

But the radiant light of a brilliant summer morning, shining in through the window in front of which he had neglected to draw the curtains, chased away all possibility of sleep, and Malcolm was left very much awake, although still rather confused. Such confusion was, however, his normal state of mind. Without it, he would feel rather lost.

Confusion is the only possible result of a lifetime of being asked unanswerable questions by one's parents and relatives, such as 'What *are* we going to do with you?' or 'Why can't you be more like your sister?' To judge by the frequency with which he encountered it, the latter problem was the truly significant one, to which not even the tremendous intellectual resources of his family had been able to find an answer. Malcolm himself had never made any sort of attempt to solve this problem; that was not his role in life. His role (if he had one, which he sometimes doubted) was to provide a comparison with his elder sister Bridget.

Rather like the control group in the testing process for a new medicine, Malcolm was there to ensure that his parents never took their exceptional daughter for granted. If ever they were misguided enough to doubt or underestimate that glorious creature, one look at Malcolm was enough to remind them how lucky they were, so it was Malcolm's calling to be a disappointment; he would be failing in his duty as a son and a brother if he was anything else.

When Bridget had married Timothy (a man who perfectly exemplified the old saying that all work and no play makes Jack a management consultant) and gone to turn the rays of her effulgence on Sydney, Australia, it was therefore natural that her parents, lured by the prospect of grandchildren to persecute, should sell all they had and follow her. They had muttered something about Malcolm presumably coming too, but their heart was not really in it; he was no longer needed, now that the lacklustre Timothy could take over the mantle of unworthiness. So Malcolm had decided that he would prefer to stay in England. He disliked bright sunlight, had no great interest in the cinema, opera, tennis or seafood, and didn't particularly want to go on getting under people's feet for the rest of his life. He was thus able to add ingratitude and lack of proper filial and brotherly affection to the already impressive list of things that were wrong with him but not with his sister.

After a great deal of enjoyable agonising, Mr and Mrs Fisher decided that Malcolm's only chance of ever amounting to anything was being made to stand on his own two feet, and allowed him to stay behind. Before they left, however, they went to an extraordinary amount of trouble and effort to find him a boring job and a perfectly horrible flat in a nasty village in the middle of nowhere. So it was that Malcolm had come to leave his native Derby, a place he had never greatly cared for, and go into the West, almost (but not quite) like King Arthur. Taking with him his good suit, his respectable shirts, his spongebag and his two A-levels, he had made his way to Somerset, where he had been greeted with a degree of enthusiasm usually reserved for the first drop of rain at a Wimbledon final by his parents' long-suffering contacts, whose tireless efforts had made his new life possible. Malcolm took to the trade of an auctioneer's clerk like a duck to petrol, found the local dialect almost as inscrutable as the locals found his own slight accent, and settled down, like Kent in *King Lear*, to shape his old course in a country new.

The fact that he hated and feared his new environment was largely beside the point, for he had been taught long ago that what he thought and felt about any given subject was without question the least important thing in the world. Indeed he had taken this lesson so much to heart that when the Government sent him little pieces of card apparently entitling him to vote in elections, he felt sure that they had intended them for somebody else. He told himself that he would soon get used to it, just as he had always been told that he would grow into the grotesquely outsized garments he was issued with as a child. Although two years had now passed since his arrival in the West Country, the sleeves of his new life, so to speak, still reached down to his fingernails. But that was presumably his fault for not growing. Needless to say, it was a remark of his sister Bridget's that best summed up his situation; to be precise, a joke she used to make at the age of seven. 'What is the difference,' she would ask, 'between Marmalade [the family cat] and Malcolm?' When no satisfactory answer could be provided by the admiring adults assembled to hear the joke, Bridget would smile and say, 'Daddy isn't allowed to shout at Marmalade.'

So it seemed rather strange (or counter-intuitive, as his sister would say) that Malcolm should have been chosen by the badger to be the new master of the world. Bridget, yes; she was very good indeed at organising things, and would doubtless make sure that the trains ran on time. But Malcolm – 'only Malcolm', as he was affectionately known to his family – that was a mistake, surely. Still, he reflected as he put the Ring back on his finger, since he was surely imagining the whole thing, what did it matter?

Without bothering to get out of bed, he breathed on the Ring and rubbed it on his forehead. At once, countless gold objects materialised in the air and fell heavily all around him, taking him so completely by surprise that all he could think was that this must be what the Americans mean by a shower. Gold cups, gold plates, gold chalices, torques, ashtrays, pipe-racks, cufflinks, bath-taps, and a few shapeless, unformed articles (presumably made by apprentice Nibelungs at evening classes under the general heading of paperweights) tumbled down on all sides, so that Malcolm had to snatch up a broad embossed dish and hold it over his head until the cascade had subsided in order to avoid serious injury.

Gathering the shreds of his incredulity around him, Malcolm tried to tell himself that it probably wasn't real or solid gold; but that was a hard hypothesis. Only a complete and utter cheapskate would go to the trouble of materialising copper or brass by supernatural means. No, it was real, it was solid, it existed, and it was making the place look like a scrapyard, as his mother would undoubtedly say were she present. Having wriggled out from under the hoard, Malcolm found some cardboard boxes and put it all neatly

18

away. That alone was hard work. Malcolm shook his head, yawned, and wiped the sweat from his forehead with the back of his hand, thus accidentally starting off the whole process all over again . . .

'For Christ's sake!' he shouted, as a solid gold ewer missed him by inches, 'will you stop that?'

The torrent ceased, and Malcolm sat down on the bed.

'Well, I'm damned,' he said aloud, as he removed a gold tie-pin that had fallen into his pyjama pocket. 'Ruler of the world . . .'

Try as he might, he couldn't get the concept to make sense, so he put it aside. There was also the Tarnhelm to consider. Very, very tentatively, he put it on and stood in front of the mirror. It covered his head – it seemed to have grown in the night, or did it expand and contract automatically to fit its owner? – and was fastened under the chin by a little buckle in the shape of a crouching gnome.

So far as he could remember, all he had to do was think of something he wanted to be, or a place he wanted to go to, and the magic cap did all the rest. As usual when asked to think of something, Malcolm's mind went completely blank. He stood for a while, perplexed, then recalled that the helmet could also make him invisible. He thought invisible. He was.

It was a strange sensation to look in the mirror and not see oneself, and Malcolm was not sure that he liked it. So he decided to reappear and was profoundly relieved when he saw his reflection in the glass once more. He repeated the process a couple of times, appearing and disappearing like a trafficator, now you see me, now you don't, and so on. Childish, he said to himself. We must take this thing seriously or else go stark staring mad.

Next, he must try shape-changing proper. He looked

19

round the room for inspiration, and his eye fell on an old newspaper with a photograph of the Chancellor of the Exchequer on the front page. The thought crossed his mind that his mother had always wanted him to make something of himself, and now if he wanted to, he could be a member of the Cabinet . . .

In the mirror, he caught sight of the Chancellor of the Exchequer, looking perhaps a trifle eccentric in blue pyjamas and a chain-mail cap, but nevertheless unmistakable. Even though he had done his best to prepare his mind for the experience of shape-changing, the shock was terrifying in its intensity. He looked frantically round the room to see if he could see himself anywhere, but no sign. He had actually changed shape.

He forced himself to look at the reflection in the mirror, and it occurred to him that if he was going to do this sort of thing at all, he might as well do it properly. He concentrated his mind and thought of the Chancellor in his customary dark grey suit. At once, the reflection changed, and now the only jarring note was the chain-mail cap. That might well be a problem if it insisted on remaining visible all the time. He could wear a hat over it, he supposed, but that would be tricky indoors, and so few people wore hats these days. Malcolm thought how nice it would be if the cap could make itself invisible. At once, it disappeared, giving an excellent view of the Chancellor's thinning grey hair. So the thing worked. Nevertheless, he reflected, it would be necessary to think with unaccustomed precision when using it.

Once he had overcome his initial fear of the Tarnhelm, Malcolm set about testing it thoroughly. Had anyone been sufficiently inquisitive, or sufficiently interested in Malcolm Fisher, to be spying on him with a pair of binoculars, they would have seen him change himself into the entire Cabinet, the King of Swaziland, Theseus, and Winston Churchill, all in under a minute. But it then occurred to him that he need not restrict himself to specific people. The only piece of equipment with similar potential he had ever encountered was a word-processor, and there was not even a manual he could consult. How would it be if the Tarnhelm could do Types?

'Make me,' he said aloud, 'as handsome as it is possible to be.'

He closed his eyes, not daring to look, then opened his right eye slowly. Then his left eye, rather more quickly. The result was pleasing, to say the least. For some reason best known to itself, the Tarnhelm had chosen to clothe this paradigm in some barbaric costume from an earlier era – probably to show the magnificent chest and shoulders off to their best advantage. But England is a cold place, even in what is supposed to be summer . . . 'Try that in a cream suit,' he suggested, 'and rather shorter hair. And lose the beard.'

He stood for a while and stared. The strange thing was that he felt completely comfortable with this remarkable new shape; in fact, he could not remember exactly what he actually looked like, himself, in propria persona. The first time he had ever been aware of his own appearance (so far as he could recall) was when he appeared in a school nativity play, typecast as Eighth Shepherd, at the age of five. He had had to stand in front of a mirror to do up his cloak, and had suddenly realised that the rather ordinary child in the glass was himself. Quite naturally, he had burst out crying, refusing to be comforted, so that the Second King had had to go on for him and say his one line (which was, he seemed to recall, 'Oh look!').

'I'll take it,' he said to the mirror, and nodded his head to make the reflection agree with him. He then hurried through every permutation of clothes and accessories, just to make sure. There was no doubt about it; the Tarnhelm had very good taste. 'We'll call that one Richard' (he had always wanted to be called Richard). He resumed his own shape (which came as a bitter disappointment) then said 'Richard', firmly. At once, the Most Handsome Man reappeared in the mirror, which proved that the Tarnhelm had a memory, like a pocket calculator.

'How about,' he said diffidently, 'the most beautiful *woman* in the world? Just for fun,' he added quickly.

Contrary to all his expectations, the Tarnhelm did as it was told, and the mirror was filled with a vision of exquisite loveliness, so that it took Malcolm some time to realise that it was him. In fact the extraordinary thing was that all this seemed perfectly natural. Why shouldn't he be what he wanted to be, and to hell with the laws of physics?

The next stage was to test the cap's travel mode. Ingolf had told him that he could enjoy instantaneous and unlimited travel, and although this sounded rather like a prize in a game show or an advertisement for a season ticket, he was fully prepared to believe that it was possible. If he was going out, however, he ought to get dressed, for he was still in his pyjamas. He looked around for some clean socks, then remembered that it wasn't necessary. He could simply think himself dressed, and no need to worry about clean shirts. In fact, he could now have that rather nice cashmere sweater he had seen in that shop in Bridgwater, and no problem about getting one in his size, either.

For his first journey it would be advisable not to be too ambitious, just in case there were complications. 'The bathroom,' he thought, and there he was. No sensation of rushing through the air or dissolving particle by particle; he was just there. Rather a disappointment, for Malcolm enjoyed travel, and it is better to travel hopefully than to arrive (or at least that had always been his experience). 'The High Street,' he commanded.

It was cold out in the street, and he had to call for an overcoat, which came at once, slipping imperceptibly over his shoulders and doing up its buttons of its own accord. 'Back,' he thought, and he was sitting on his bed once again. Suddenly, this too seemed intensely real, and it was the ease with which he managed it that made it seem so, no difficulty, as one might expect from a conjuring-trick or a sleight of hand. He transformed himself and travelled through space as easily as he moved the fingers of his hand, and by exactly the same process; he willed it to happen and it happened. In the same way, it seemed to lose its enchantment. Just because one is able to move one's arms simply by wanting to, it does not follow that one continually does so just for the fun of it. He felt somehow disillusioned, and had to make a conscious effort to continue with the experiment.

It occurred to him that he had not actually specified where he wanted to be put down in the High Street. This could lead to problems. If he were to say 'Jamaica' or 'Finland' without specifying where exactly in those particular countries he wished to end up, he might find himself standing on the surface of a lake or the fast lane of a motorway. He tried the High Street again, and found that he was exactly half-way up it, and standing safely on the pavement. He repeated the procedure three times, and each time ended up in the same spot. Then he tried a few of the neighbouring towns and villages. A distinct pattern emerged. The Tarnhelm put him as close as it reasonably could to the centre of the town, and in every instance in a place of safety where he could materialise without being noticed.

Could he combine shape-changing and travel? 'Bristol and a postman,' he cried, and a postman in the centre of Bristol he became. This was enjoyable. He rattled through the capital cities of the world (as many as he could remember; he had done badly at geography at school) in a variety of disguises, pausing only for a moment in each place to find a shop-window in which to see his reflection. The only failure – relative failure – in this procession was Washington, which he had elected to visit in the guise of a computer programmer. He forgot to specify which Washington, and the Tarnhelm, doubtless on the principle of *difficilior lectio*, had sent him to Tyne and Wear.

He had almost forgotten in all this excitement that he was also supposed to be able to understand the language of the birds. When he had returned to Nether Stowey, he overheard snatches of conversation outside the window, which worried him until he realised that it was in fact a pair of seriously-minded crows who were discussing the world situation, with special reference to the death of Ingolf. This reminded Malcolm that he really ought to find out a little more about the background to his new possessions. So he went, invisibly and instantaneously, to the library and spent an hour or so reading through the libretti of Wagner's operas.

Rather than wade through the text, which was German poetry translated into some obscure dialect of Middle English, he read through the synopses of the plot, and highly improbable he found it all. The fact that it was all (apparently) true did little to improve matters. Malcolm had never been greatly inclined to metaphysical or religious speculation, but he had hoped that if there was a supreme being or divine agency, it would at least show the elements of logic and common sense in its conduct. Seemingly, not so. On the other hand, the revelation that the destiny of the world had been shaped by a bunch of verbose idiots went some way towards explaining the problems of human existence.

For one could attribute any sort of illogical folly to a god who orders a castle to be built for him by a couple of Frost-Giants in the full knowledge that the price he is expected to pay for his new home is his sister-in-law. But this, apparently, was what Wotan, the great Sky-God and King of the Gods, had seen fit to do, promising his wife's sister Freia to the Giants Fasolt and Fafner. Arguably an arrangement by which one gains a castle and disposes of a relative by marriage at one and the same time is a bargain in anybody's terms; but Wotan, if this was at the back of his omniscient mind, had apparently overlooked the fact that this Freia was the guardian of the golden apples of youth, through whose power the Gods not only kept the doctor away but also maintained their immortality. Without Freia to supply them with golden apples, they would all dry up and perish, and the Giants, who appeared to have at least an elementary grounding in politics, philosophy and economics, were well aware of this when they struck the bargain.

Something of a dilemma for the everlasting Gods. But to their aid comes the clever Fire-God, Loge, who persuades the Giants that what they really need is not the most beautiful woman in the world, who also happens to be the guardian of the secret of eternal youth, but a small, plain gold ring that belongs to somebody else. The Ring is, in fact, the property of Alberich, a sulphur-dwarf from the underground caverns of Nibelheim.

Alberich had stolen some magic gold from the River Rhine, wherein dwelt (presumably before the river became polluted) three rather pretty girls, the Rhinedaughters, who owned the magic gold. This gold, if made into a ring by someone who vowed to do without Love (some of us, Malcolm reflected bitterly, have no choice in the matter), would confer upon its owner the control of the world, in some concrete but ill-defined way. Alberich had originally set out with the intention of chatting up one of the Rhinedaughters; having failed in this, he cursed Love, stole the gold, and made the Ring. By its power, he found that he was able to compel all his fellow sulphur-dwarves to mine and work gold for him in unlimited quantities, this apparently being what sulphur-dwarves do best. With this wealth, it was his intention to subvert the world and make himself its master.

Before he can get very far with this project, Wotan steals the Ring from him and uses it to pay off the Giants, who immediately start fighting over who should have it. Fafner kills Fasolt, and transforms himself into a dragon before retiring to a cave in a forest in the middle of nowhere, this apparently being preferable in his eyes to retiring to a cave in a forest with the Goddess Freia. It takes all sorts.

Wotan is understandably concerned to get hold of the Ring for himself. Once again, Malcolm was moved to wonder at the stupidity, or at least the obscurity, of the King of the Gods; evidently the sort of person who, if asked to rescue a cat from a roof, would tackle the problem by burning the house down. Wotan sets about securing the ring by having an affair with Mother Earth, the result of which is nine noisy daughters called Valkyries, and a son and a daughter called Volsungs. The latter obviously take after their father, for all they manage to do before meeting with horrible deaths is commit incest and produce a son.

This son is Siegfried, a muscular but stupid youth who kills the dragon Fafner. From the pile of gold on top of which the dragon has been sleeping for a hundred years (rather uncomfortable, Malcolm thought), Siegfried picks out the Ring and the Tarnhelm, not knowing what they are for. He only discovers the secret of these articles when, led by a woodbird, he wakes up the Number One Valkyrie, Brunnhilde, who has been sleeping on a fiery mountain for twenty years after a quarrel with her father.

Brunnhilde, who is of course Siegfried's *aunt*, is also the first woman he has ever seen, and the two of them fall in love at first sight. Brunnhilde tells Siegfried all about the Ring and the terrible curse that Alberich had placed on it which brings all who own it to a horrible and untimely death. Siegfried, not being a complete idiot, gives it to her as a present. This is, of course, all in accordance with Wotan's plan ('Sounds more like coincidence to me,' said Malcolm to himself, 'but never mind') since Brunnhilde is the embodiment of Wotan's will, and because Wotan is forbidden by his intermittent but ferocious conscience to touch the perishing thing himself, Brunnhilde getting it is the nearest he can come to controlling it.

In a logical world, that would be that. But Siegfried goes off into the world to continue his career as a professional Hero, and falls in with some very dubious people called the Gibichungs. They manage to persuade Siegfried to take the Ring back from Brunnhilde and marry their horse-faced sister Gutrune. Brunnhilde is naturally livid, and conspires with Hagen (a Gibichung and also, would you believe, Alberich's son) to kill Siegfried and get the Ring back. Hagen kills Siegfried, and Brunnhilde immediately changes her mind (so like a woman). She hurls herself onto Siegfried's funeral pyre, clutching the Ring, and is burnt to a crisp. As she does so, the Rhine fortuitously bursts its banks and floods Germany, allowing the Rhinedaughters to snatch the Ring from Brunnhilde's charred finger and drown Hagen. Meanwhile, the castle of the Gods (which had caused the whole mess in the first place) has caught fire and burns down, the Gods rather foolishly neglecting to leave it while it does so, and the curtain falls on a carbonised heaven and a flooded earth, or, in other words, a typical operatic Happy Ending. Or so Wagner thought . . .

Having finally come to the end of this narrative, Malcolm was left with two abiding impressions: first, that Fafner the dragon, instead of keeping his money under the mattress like everyone else, had kept his mattress under the money; second, that humanity generally gets the Gods it deserves. He shook his head sadly and transported himself to the pub.

Over a pint of beer and a chicken sandwich, he went over the story in his mind. The logical flaws and inconsistencies that riddled the tale, far from making him doubt its veracity, finally convinced him that it might indeed be true; for life is like that. He also wrote down on a beer-mat the names of all the Gods and monsters who might come looking for him, and turned his attention to more pressing matters.

First, there was the problem of turning the Nibelung's gold into folding money. He resolved to try the straightforward approach, and so transported himself to Bond Street, where he found an old-established jeweller's shop. He assumed a grave and respectable appearance and

28

approached the counter holding two heavy gold chalices selected at random from the gold he had materialised that morning. The jeweller studied them for a moment in silence.

'That's odd,' he said, turning one of them over in order to study the outlandish script on the rim, 'they aren't on the list.'

'What list?'

'The list of stolen gold and silver we get from the police each month. Or did you nick them recently?'

'I didn't steal them,' said Malcolm truthfully, 'they're mine.'

'Tell that to the inspector, chum,' said the jeweller. A burly assistant stood in front of the door, as the jeweller lifted the telephone and started to dial.

'You people never learn,' he said sadly. 'You come in off the street expecting me to buy five grand's worth of gold . . .'

'As much as that?'

'That's the value of the metal. Add a couple of grand for the workmanship, if it's genuine. I expect the owner will be glad to get them back.'

'Oh, that's all right, you can keep them,' Malcolm said, and vanished.

CHAPTER THREE

As he put the kettle on back in Nether Stowey, Malcolm worked out a way in which he could turn the Nibelung hoard into mastery of the world. First, he would have to find some way of contacting an unscrupulous gold dealer – not too difficult; all he need do would be to request the Tarnhelm, in its travel mode, to take him to an unscrupulous gold dealer's house and there he would be – and sell off a reasonable quantity of gold with no questions asked. With the money thus obtained, he could start buying shares – lots of shares in lots of big companies. Then sell more gold, then buy more shares. Sooner or later, he would flood the gold market, which would be a pity; but by then, he ought to have enough shares to enable him to do without the gold per se. After about a decade of buying as many shares as he could, he would be in a position to start seizing control of major international companies. Through these (and massive corruption) he could in turn gain influence over the Governments of the countries of the free world.

With the free world in his pocket, he could patch up a workable detente with the Communist bloc to the extent that he could start infiltrating them. By a combination of bribery, economic pressure and, where necessary, military force, he could in about thirty-five years gain unseen but effective control of the world, and probably about a hundred ulcers to go with it. It all sounded perfectly horrible and no fun at all, and Malcolm wanted no part of it. In a way he was relieved. Control of the world, as he had imagined it would be when Ingolf first mentioned the subject, would have entailed responsibilities as well as benefits. As it was, he could perfectly well throw the Ring away – back into the Rhine, if the Rhinedaughters had not long since died of sewage poisoning – and keep the Tarnhelm for his own amusement. He could get a job as an express messenger . . .

'Idiot,' said a voice.

He looked round, startled. There was nobody to be seen . . . then he remembered. The voice had come from a rather bedraggled pigeon perched on his window ledge.

'I beg your pardon?' he said.

'You're an idiot, Malcolm Fisher,' said the pigeon. 'Open the window and let me in.'

Although he was beginning to tire of being insulted and ordered about by dumb animals, Malcolm did as he was told.

'Sorry,' said the pigeon, 'it was rude of me. But I felt it was my duty to tell you. You see, I'm a woodbird, like the woodbird who advised Siegfried all those years ago.'

'No, you're not,' said Malcolm. 'You're a pigeon.'

'Correct. I'm a woodpigeon. And we care about things.'

That was presumably meant to be logical. Certainly, it made about as much sense as everything else Malcolm had heard during the past forty-eight hours. 'So why am I an idiot?' he asked. 'What have I done now?'

31

'The Ring you've got there,' said the pigeon, its beak full of crumbs from Malcolm's table, 'you don't understand what it is, do you? I mean, you've heard the story and you've read the book . . .'

'When do I get to see the film?'

'It's not a toy, you know,' said the pigeon, sternly, 'and before you ask, I know all this because I'm a bird.'

'Thank you.'

'You're welcome. You see,' continued the pigeon, preening its ruffled feathers, 'the Ring has other powers beyond creating wealth that were not even guessed at – good crumbs these, by the way. I'm into healthy scavenging – guessed at when it was forged. Have you heard today's news?'

Malcolm looked at his watch; it was five o'clock, and he leaned forward to switch on the radio. But even before he touched the set, the voice of the newsreader became clearly audible.

'That's handy,' said Malcolm.

'Giant's blood,' replied the pigeon. 'Of course, it's selective; you can only hear the broadcasts if you make a conscious decision to do so. Otherwise you'd go mad in a couple of minutes, with all those voices jabbering away in a hundred different languages. And yes, it does work with telephones.'

'Don't tell me,' said Malcolm, to whom a sudden revelation had been made, 'you birds can do it as well.'

The pigeon did not speak. Nevertheless Malcolm heard it clearly in his mind's ear. Although the bird did not open its beak, it was exactly the same as hearing a voice, rather like having a conversation with someone with their back to you. Even the pigeon's faint Midlands accent was preserved.

'And you can do everything that we can do, as well or even better. For instance you can read thoughts, like you're doing now – selectively, of course. But in your case, you can blot them out and hear nothing if you want to. We can't.'

One distinct advantage of this conversation without speech was that these communications, which would have taken several seconds to say out loud, flashed through Malcolm's mind in no time at all. To give an illustration: an actor reciting the whole of *Paradise Lost* by thought-transfer would detain his audience for no more than six minutes. As Malcolm opened his mind to the concept, he found that he could hear the pigeon's thoughts even when it wasn't trying to communicate them.

'Same to you,' he said (or thought) irritably.

'Sorry,' said the bird. 'I forgot you could hear. That's why we birds never evolved very far, I suppose, despite our considerable intelligence. We have to spend all our time and energy watching what we think, and so we can never get around to using our brains for anything useful. You humans only have to watch what you say. You're lucky.'

'Where was I?'

'Listening to the radio.'

'Oh, yes.'

This entire conversation had taken up the time between the second and third pips of the Greenwich time signal. Malcolm, whose mind had grown used to working at a faster speed, found the wait for the next pip unendurably dull, as whole seconds of inactivity ticked by. When the newsreader started speaking, her words were at first almost incomprehensible, like a recording slowed right down.

The announcer seemed rather harassed, for her beautiful BBC voice was distinctly strained as she went through the catalogue of natural and man-made disasters that had struck the planet since about one o'clock that morning.

'When you killed the Giant,' said the pigeon.

There had been earthquakes all across North and South America, a volcano had erupted in Italy, and a swarm of locusts bigger than any previously recorded had formed over North Africa. Seven Governments had been violently overthrown, the delicate peace negotiations in the Middle East had collapsed, the United States had broken off diplomatic relations with China, and England had lost the First Test by an innings and thirty-two runs.

'That's awful,' said Malcolm, aloud.

'Listen,' urged the pigeon.

Amazingly enough, said the announcer (and her voice palpably quavered) in all these disasters nobody had been killed or even seriously injured, anywhere in the world, although the damage to property had been incalculable. Meanwhile, at London Zoo Za-Za the Giant Panda . . .

Malcolm dismissed the voice from his mind. 'So what's going on?'

The pigeon was silent and its mind was blank. 'Is it my fault?' Malcolm demanded impatiently. 'Did I do all that?'

'No, not exactly. In fact, I would say it was sort of a tribute to your integrity, like.'

'My what?'

'Integrity. You see, because of the curse Alberich put on it, the Ring can't help causing destruction. Every day it continues to exist, it exercises power on the world, and unless this power is channelled deliberately into positive and constructive things, which is impossible anyway, it just sort of crashes about, causing damage and breaking things.'

'What sort of things?'

'The earth's crust. Governments. You name it. Why do

34

you think the world's been such a horrible place for the last thousand years? Ingolf couldn't care less what happened to the world so long as he was all right, and over the past century and a bit, when his temper wasn't improved by perpetual toothache, he actively encouraged the Ring by thinking unpleasant thoughts. Hence wars, progress and all the rest of it.'

Malcolm shook his head in disbelief. 'But . . . but what about the Gods, then? I mean, I've only just found out they exist. What do they do?'

'What they like, mostly. Wotan – he's the only one who matters – is omnipotent; well, omnipotent up to a point. The only thing he can't compete with is the Ring, which is far more powerful than he is. That's why he wants it so badly. But it doesn't really interfere with his being all-powerful. You see, no-one can control the Ring, or make it do what they want it to. That's the point . . .'

The pigeon's thought tailed off into a blank. Something had obviously occurred to it that it could not even put into thoughts, let alone words. It made an effort and continued.

'Needless to say,' said the pigeon, 'when the Ring changes hands, it gets very temperamental. Nobody likes being killed, and all the bad vibes that went through Ingolf's mind as he died last night won't have made things any better. You see, bad thoughts give the Ring something to get its teeth into. Hence all those earthquakes.'

Once again, the pigeon's thoughts tailed away. It walked round the table, pecked at a Biro, and then stopped dead in its tracks.

'And nobody got killed,' it said. 'That's strange, don't you think? Did you put the Ring on straight away?'

'Yes.'

'I don't know if this is even possible, but maybe you

35

were controlling the Ring in some way or other, stopping it from actually killing anyone. God knows how. I mean, even Siegfried couldn't control it, and he was much more . . .'

'I know, so everyone keeps telling me.'

'Anyway, he couldn't stop the curse, although he was probably the only one so far who had the potential – he was Wotan's grandson, but no longer in his power. But perhaps it's not the curse . . . Anyway, he couldn't do a thing with it. And look at you . . .'

'In that case,' said Malcolm, 'all I have to do to end this whole curse business and make the world safe, all I have to do is throw the Ring back into the Rhine. It was the Rhine, wasn't it?'

The pigeon flapped its wings and flew round the room to relieve its feelings. It didn't work.

'Idiot!' it shouted. 'You haven't been listening to a word I've thought, have you? That's the worst possible thing you could do.'

'But it said in the book. The waters of the Rhine will wash away Alberich's curse.'

'How quaintly you put it, I'm sure. You haven't grasped the point I've been trying to make. The curse isn't like that. In fact . . . Sorry.' The pigeon fluttered up from the table and perched forgivingly on Malcolm's head. 'I forgot, you aren't used to reading thoughts. Only it's just occurred to me that the curse is nothing to do with it. It's just a curse, that's all. It just brings all the owners of the Ring to a horrible and untimely death. But the Ring was powerful *before* Alberich put the curse on it. If you were to throw the Ring into the Rhine . . .'

'Would you please stop pecking at my head?'

'Sorry. It's instinct, I'm afraid. We birds are martyrs to instinct. Where was I? If you were to throw the Ring into

36

the Rhine, there's no guarantee that the Rhinedaughters would be able to control its nasty habits any more than Ingolf could. And even if they could and they wanted to, they can't be expected to be able to guard it properly against the bad guys – Wotan and Alberich and that lot. Let alone any new contenders. They have no power, you see, they can only offer an alternative.'

'What alternative?'

'Think about it.' The pigeon chuckled. 'In the Dark Ages, of course, it was inconceivable that anyone would prefer unlimited wealth to a bit of fun with a pretty Rhinedaughter – that's what all that stuff about forswearing Love was about – but that was a thousand years ago. What could you buy a thousand years ago that was worth having? The ultimate in consumer goods was a rowing-boat or a goatskin hat, and the ideal home was a damp log cabin with no chimney. These days, everything has changed. These days, most people would forswear Love for a new washing-machine, let alone the entire world. No, if you throw the Ring into the Rhine, you'll make everything much worse.'

Malcolm buried his head in his hands, causing the pigeon to lose its balance. 'Watch out,' it said.

'But Wagner said . . .'

'Forget Wagner, this is real life.'

'Where did he get the story from, by the way?'

'A little bird told him.'

Malcolm sat for a moment in silence, while the pigeon tried to eat his diary.

'This is terrible,' he said at last. 'Now I'm going to be personally responsible for every catastrophe in the world. And I thought it was only my mother who blamed me for everything.'

'Not necessarily,' said the pigeon, soothingly. 'Perhaps – I say perhaps – you can stop all these terrible things from happening. Don't ask me how, but you stopped I don't know how many people from being killed today.'

'Did I?'

'Well, if you didn't, then who the hell did? Let me put it to you this way.' The pigeon buried its beak in its feathers and thought hard for a moment. 'By and large, all things considered, you wouldn't actually want to kill anyone, now would you?'

'No,' replied Malcolm, 'certainly not.'

'But when you hear about disasters in other countries, it doesn't spoil your day. You think, Hard luck, poor devils, but you don't burst out crying all over the place.'

'True.'

'Whereas a disaster in this country would affect you rather more deeply, wouldn't it?'

'Yes, I suppose it would.'

'That follows. All these disasters, you see, happened abroad. The only bit of local disaster was that England lost a cricket match, and the way things are nowadays, that would probably have happened anyway. I remember when I was feeding in the outfield at Edgbaston in nineteen fifty-six . . .'

'Get on with it,' said Malcolm irritably.

'The way I see it,' said the pigeon, picking up a crumb of stale cheese it had previously overlooked, 'the Ring is being guided by your will. A certain number of momentous things have to happen when the Ring changes hands. It's like a volcano: all that force and violence has to go somewhere. But your will protected Britain . . .'

'Do you mind not using that word? It makes it sound like my last will and testament.'

38

'All right then, you protected Britain, because you care more about it than about other countries. All subconsciously, of course. And you refused to let the Ring kill anybody, because you instinctively don't approve of people being killed. When you think about it, that's pretty remarkable. Have you got any more of that cheese anywhere?'

Malcolm was rather taken aback. 'You mean I really can make the world do what I want?'

'Not in the way you think. The Ring won't take orders from your *conscious* mind. But you can prevent it from destroying the world, if you're sufficiently strong-minded.'

'But that can't be right.'

'It does seem odd, I agree. After all, Wotan couldn't do it. Fafner couldn't do it. Even Siegfried couldn't do it and he was much more . . .'

'Siegfried was an idiot. Or did Wagner get that wrong, too?'

'Yes, he did. Siegfried wasn't an idiot, not by a long way. He just didn't know what was going on. But then, neither did you.' The pigeon fell silent again.

'How come I can't read your thoughts?' Malcolm asked. 'You've done this two or three times now.'

'I'm not so much thinking as communing.'

'What with?'

'How should I know?' snapped the pigeon in a sudden flurry of bad temper. 'Mother Earth, I've always assumed. Go on, you try it.'

Malcolm tried it, opening his mind to everything in the world. There was a perfectly horrible noise and he switched it off. 'Nothing,' he said, 'just a lot of voices.'

'Oh,' said the pigeon, and Malcolm could sense unease, even awe, in its thoughts. 'Oh, I *see*.'

'You mean it's me you're communing with?' Malcolm

was so amazed that he turned himself into a stone without intending to.

'That's the way it's looking,' said the pigeon. 'Sir,' it added.

'Go ahead,' said Malcolm bitterly. 'You and my Immortal Soul have a nice chat, don't mind me.'

'I'm sorry,' said the pigeon, 'I suppose it must be very frustrating for you, especially since it's so good, you'd enjoy it if you could hear it, you really would.'

'What did it say last?'

'Well, it suggested that you may not be wise or noble or fearless or brave or cunning or anything like that . . .'

'That sounds like me talking.'

'. . . But you're probably the only *nice* person in history to own the wretched thing.'

'Nice?'

'Nice.'

'You really think I'm nice?' said Malcolm, blushing.

'Where I come from,' said the pigeon, 'that's not a compliment. Anyway, I didn't say it, you did, only you couldn't hear yourself think. But if by nice you mean decent, inoffensive, wouldn't hurt a fly, yes, I think you probably are. And all the other Ring-Bearers have been right bastards in one way or another.'

'Even Siegfried?'

'Siegfried had a wicked temper. If his porridge wasn't just right, he'd throw it all round the hall.'

Malcolm rubbed his eyes. 'And my niceness is going to save the world, is it?'

'Could do, who knows? Just try saying to yourself over and over again, I don't want anything bad to happen to anyone anywhere today. See if that makes any difference.' The pigeon turned its head and looked at the sun, which was starting to shine with the evening light. 'Time I was on my way,' it said. 'There's a field of oilseed rape out there I want to look in on as I go home. They've got one of those machines that go bang every ten minutes, but who cares? I like it round here. Always wanted to retire to the seaside.'

'So that's it, is it? Think nice thoughts?'

'Try it. If it doesn't work, try something else. Well, take care, won't you? It's been a privilege meeting you, I suppose. But watch out for the Gods and the Volsungs for a while. They'll be after you by now.'

'Can they read thoughts too?'

'No, but Wotan has a couple of clever ravens. I don't think they can find you easily, though. The Tarnhelm masks your thoughts, except at very short range, and the world's a very big place. You've got the advantage, having the Tarnhelm. But if I were you, I'd be a bit more discreet in future. It's not clever to go around looking like people who have been dead for a thousand years.'

'You mean Theseus?'

'Who's that? No, I mean Siegfried. And Brunnhilde, come to that.' The pigeon flapped its wings, said, 'Thanks for the crumbs,' and was gone.

For a moment, Malcolm did not understand what the pigeon had said about Siegfried and . . . He had only turned himself into one female character today. He stood in front of the mirror.

'Quick,' he ordered, 'Siegfried, then Brunnhilde.'

Once again, the images of the Most Handsome Man and the Most Beautiful Woman flashed across the glass. He sat down on the bed and, for some reason or other, began to cry.

CHAPTER FOUR

A potheosis can be rather unnerving. Even the most hardened and cynical Royal visitor to remote islands is taken aback to find the islanders worshipping his framed photograph, and he at least has the consolation of knowing that he isn't really a God. Malcolm had no such consolation as he faced up to the fact that his mind controlled the world.

'If only,' he kept on saying to himself, 'Mr Scanlon knew.' Mr Scanlon had tried to teach him Physics at school, and if his assessment of Malcolm's mental capacities had been correct, the world was in deep trouble. For his part, Malcolm had always been inclined to share his teacher's opinion; certainly, the weight of the evidence had always seemed to be on Mr Scanlon's side. Nevertheless, it was necessary to make the best of a bad job. Malcolm now had literally no-one to blame but himself, and the Daily Service on the radio seemed to be directly addressed to him. Especially one line, which Malcolm took it upon himself to paraphrase slightly:

'For there is none other that fighteth for us, but only thou. Oh, *God*!'

But the news from the outside world gave him grounds for cautious optimism. The disasters that had marked his accession cleared themselves up with embarrassing speed. The United Nations, for example, held a special session in New York and unanimously voted to levy an unprecedented contribution from all its members to relieve the suffering of the victims of the catastrophe. The various coups and revolutions resolved themselves into benign democracies as if that had been their intention all along. Peace negotiations in the Middle East were resumed, America and China started playing each other at ping-pong again, and the swarm of locusts was devoured by a huge flock of migrating birds. Admittedly, England lost the Second Test as well, but Malcolm knew that he could not be expected to work miracles. The only disaster that had been reported was the destruction by volcanic forces of a small, uninhabited atoll in the middle of the Pacific Ocean; and even that had its good side, as the residents of the neighbouring atoll had always complained that it was an eyesore and spoilt their view of the sunset.

It needed no ghost come from the grave, and no visitation of prophetic birds to tell Malcolm that this was all the result of being nice. He had rigorously excluded from his mind all unpleasant, spiteful or angry thoughts for the best part of a fortnight (the strain was beginning to show), and the result had been a quite unparalleled upturn in the fortunes of the human race. 'And all that,' Malcolm reflected smugly, 'was me.'

But it was extremely frustrating to have to keep all this to oneself. Malcolm had never achieved anything before, except third prize in a village flower show when he was nine (three people had entered that particular category), and the wish to be congratulated was very strong. His sister, for example, had achieved many things, but she had never stopped a war or disposed of a swarm of locusts. But the Ring seemed to cut him off from the rest of the human race. Although he was the master of the Tarnhelm, he scarcely went out at all. This was partly laziness, partly caution; for if he was to remain nice and keep his mind free of malice or resentment, it would not be advisable for him to see any of his friends or relatives. He was also beginning to feel extremely hungry. All the food lying about the flat (some of which had been there for a considerable time) was long since finished, he had no money left, and he could see little prospect of getting any more. Even if his job still existed (and after two weeks' unexplained absence, that seemed unlikely) he knew that for the sake of mankind he could not go back to it. One cannot work as a clerk in a provincial auction room without entertaining some fairly dark thoughts, any one of which, given his present position, could blot out a major city. The obvious alternative – theft, using the power of the Tarnhelm – was open to the same objection. If he were to start stealing things, who could tell what the consequences might be?

He contemplated the problem, turning himself into Aristotle in the hope that the transformation might assist his powers of reasoning. During the past two weeks, metamorphosis had been virtually his only occupation, and had kept him moderately amused. He had always rather wanted to know what various characters from history and fiction really looked like, especially the girls described by the poets. He also took the trouble to assume the shapes of all his likely assailants – Wotan and Alberich and Loge so as to be able to recognise them instantly, and had frightened himself half to death in the process.

The outward shape of Aristotle seemed to inspire him

and he went through the various ways in which he could sell gold for money without actually getting involved himself. Having dismissed the notion of putting an advertisement in the Classified section of the *Quantock Gazette*, he hit upon what seemed to be an acceptable notion. Armed with a large suitcase, he commanded the Tarnhelm to take him to some uninhabited vault in the Bank of England where he might find plenty of used banknotes. On arrival, he filled the suitcase (more of a small trunk) with ten- and twenty-pound notes, then started to materialise gold to a roughly equivalent value. By the time he had finished, his forehead was quite sore with rubbing and the floor of the vault was covered in exquisite treasures. He removed himself and the suitcase and tried the equivalent banks in France, America, Australia and other leading countries (for it would be unfair if only one or two countries suddenly found themselves linked to the gold standard). With the immense wealth he gathered in this way, he opened a large number of bank accounts in various names – a terrifying business, full of unforeseen complications – and bought himself the house he had always wanted, a huge and extremely attractive manor house near Taunton, which happened to be for sale.

As he had anticipated, no mention was made by any of the financial institutions with which he had done business of the sudden disappearance of large sums of money or the equally unexpected appearance of a fortune in gold. The price of the metal fluctuated wildly for a day or so, then went considerably higher than it had been for some time. Intrigued, Malcolm revisited his favourite banks, invisible and carrying two suitcases. All the gold had gone, and there were plenty more banknotes, neatly packaged up for ease of transportation. In the National Bank of Australia there was even a piece of card with 'Thanks; Please Call Again' written on it, propped up on a shelf.

Now that he was a multi-millionaire on both sides of the Iron Curtain, Malcolm turned his attention to furnishing his new house. It seemed likely that he would have to spend a great deal of time in it, on his own, and since money was no object, he decided to have the very best of everything. It was obvious that he could not risk appearing there in his own shape – what would Malcolm Fisher be doing buying Combe Hall? – and so he designed for himself a new persona to go with his new life. In doing so, he made a terrible mistake; but by the time he realised what he had done, it was too late.

It was simple carelessness on his part that caused the trouble. He had been so excited at the prospect of owning Combe Hall that he had gone to the estate agents who were handling the sale in his own shape. He was shown into an office and asked to wait while the senior partner came down to see him, and as the door opened to admit this gentleman, Malcolm caught sight of his own, original face in the mirror and realised his mistake. He commanded the Tarnhelm to change him into someone else, but did not have time to specify who. To his horror, he saw that the face in the mirror was that of the Most Handsome Man; but the estate agent had seen him now, so he could not change into anything less conspicuous. He had stuck like it, just as his mother had warned him he would.

Thus it was that Malcolm found himself condemned to embark on his new life with the face and body of Siegfried the Dragon-Slayer, also known as the Most Handsome Man. He could not help remembering the pigeon's warning about this, but it was too late now. Not that Malcolm objected in principle to being the most handsome man who had ever lived; but the sight of ravens (or crows, or blackbirds; he was no ornithologist) filled him with horror.

Meanwhile, he fleshed out his new character and by deviousness and contrivance of which he had not thought himself capable acquired the necessary documents and paperwork. In order to give his new self a history (multimillionaires do not simply appear from nowhere) he had to Tarnhelm himself at dead of night into the computer rooms of half the public records offices in the country, and since he knew next to nothing about twentieth-century machines, he accidentally erased the life histories of several hundred people before getting the result he wanted. Finally, however, he ended up with everything he needed to be Herr Manfred Finger of Dusseldorf, the name and identity he had chosen. Again, the German aspect was ill-advised and unintentional; he had wanted to be a foreigner of some sort (since in Somerset it is understood that all foreigners are mad, and allowances for eccentric or unusual behaviour are made accordingly) and had chosen a country at random. That he should have chosen Germany was either yet more carelessness or else the Ring trying to get its own back on him for making it do good in the world. He was not sure which, but was inclined to the first explanation, as being more in keeping with his own nature.

Herr Finger was soon familiar to all the inhabitants of Combe, who were naturally curious to know more about their new neighbour. As local custom demanded, they soon found a nickname for the new Lord of the Manor. The various members of the Booth family who had owned the Hall from the early Tudor period onwards had all been known by a variety of affectionate epithets – Mad Jack, or Drunken George – and the periphrasis bestowed on Malcolm was 'that rich foreign bastard'.

Such familiarity did not, however, imply acceptance. Although it was generally admitted that Herr Finger was not too bad on the surface and no worse than the last of the Booths (Sir William, or Daft Billy), it went without saying that there was something wrong about him. He was, it was agreed, a criminal of some sort; but whether he was an illegal arms dealer or a drug smuggler, the sages of Combe could not be certain. The only thing on which everyone was unanimous was that he had murdered his wife. After all, none of them had ever seen her in the village . . .

'And what time,' said Wotan, 'do you call this?'

Loge, his hands covered in oil, climbed wearily off his motorcycle and removed his helmet. 'It broke down again,' he said. 'Just outside Wuppertal. Plugs.'

Wotan shook his head sadly. Admittedly, it had been on his orders that the immortal Gods had traded in their eight-legged horses and chariots drawn by winged cats for forms of transport more suited to the twentieth century, but he expected his subordinates to be both punctual and properly turned out. Cleanliness, he was fond of asserting, is next to godliness.

'Well, you're here now,' he said. 'So what do you make of *that*?'

Loge looked about him. There was nothing to see except corn-fields. He said so.

'Well done,' growled Wotan. 'We are unusually observant this morning, are we not? And what do you find unusual about the corn in these corn-fields?'

Log scratched his head, getting oil on his hair. 'Dunno,' he said. 'It looks perfectly normal to me.'

'Normal for August?'

'Perfectly.'

'It's June.'

Loge, who had spent an hour wrestling with a motorcycle engine beside a busy autobahn, did not at first appreciate the significance of this remark. Then the pfennig dropped. 'It's two months in advance, you mean?'

'Precisely.' Wotan put his arm around Loge's shoulder. 'Good, wouldn't you say?'

'I suppose so.'

'It's bloody marvellous, considering the weather they've been having this year. And why do you suppose the crops are doing so very, very well? In fact, why is everything in the world doing so very, very well? Answer me that?'

Loge instinctively looked up at the sky. Thunder-clouds were beginning to form.

'Someone's been interfering?' he suggested.

'Correct!' Wotan shouted, and the first clap of thunder came in, dead on cue. 'Someone's been interfering. Now who could that be? Who on earth could be responsible for this new golden age?'

From his tone, Loge guessed that it couldn't have been Wotan himself. Which left only one candidate. 'You mean the Ring-Bearer?'

'Very good. The only force in the Universe capable of making things happen so quickly and so thoroughly. But isn't that a trifle strange in itself? Wouldn't you expect the Ring to do nasty things, not nice ones? Left to itself, I mean?'

Loge agreed that he would.

'So you would agree that anyone capable of making the Ring do what it doesn't want to do is likely to be a rather special person?'

Wotan had picked up this irritating habit of asking leading

49

questions from the late and unlamented Socrates. Loge hated it.

'In fact, someone so remarkable that even if he didn't have the Ring he would present a serious danger to our security. And since he does have the Ring . . .'

Wotan was trembling with rage, and the rain was falling fast, beating down the standing corn. 'We have to find him, quickly,' he roared. 'Otherwise, we are in grave danger. To be precise, *you* have to find him. Do you understand?'

Loge understood, but Wotan wanted to make his point. 'And if I were you, my friend, I would spare no effort in looking for him. I would leave no stone unturned and no avenue unexplored. And do you know why? Because if you don't, you might very well find yourself spending the rest of Eternity as a waterfall. You wouldn't like that, now would you?'

Loge agreed that he wouldn't, and Wotan was about to develop this theme further when it stopped raining. The clouds dispersed, and the sun shone brightly, pitching a vivid rainbow across the blue sky.

'Who said you could stop raining?' screamed Wotan. 'I want lightning. Now!'

The sky took no notice, and Loge went white with fear. Everyone has his own particular phobia, and Loge was terrified of fish. As a waterfall, he would have salmon jumping up him all day long. He would have prayed for rain if he wasn't a God himself. But the sky remained cloudless.

'That does it!' Wotan smashed his fist into the palm of his left hand. 'When I'm not even allowed to rain my own rain because it damages the crops, it's time for positive action.' He stood still for a moment, then turned to Loge.

'Are you still here?' he asked savagely.

'I'm on my way,' Loge replied, jumping desperately on

50

the kickstart of his motorcycle. 'I'll find him, don't you worry.'

Loge sped off into the distance, and Wotan was left alone, staring angrily at the sun. Two coal-black ravens floated down and settled on the fence.

'Nice weather we're having,' said Thought.

For some reason, this did not go down well. 'Any result?' Wotan snapped.

'Nothing so far, boss,' said Memory.

'Where have you been looking?'

'Everywhere, boss. But you know we can't find the Ring-Bearer. We can't see him, or read his thoughts, or anything like that.'

'God give me strength!' Wotan clenched his fist and made an effort to relax. 'Then what you do, you stupid bird, is go through all the people of the world, one by one, and when you find one whose thoughts you can't read and who you can't see, that's him. I'd have thought that was obvious.'

Thought looked at Memory. Memory looked at Thought. 'But that'll take weeks, boss,' said Memory.

'So what else were you planning to do?'

The two ravens flapped their wings and launched themselves into the air. They circled for a moment, then floated over the world. All day they flew, sweeping in wide circles across the continents, until Memory suddenly swooped down and landed beside the banks of the Rhine.

'Stuff this,' he said to Thought. 'Why don't we ask the girls?'

'Good idea,' said Memory. 'Wish I'd thought of that.'

'It must have slipped your mind.' The two birds took off again, but this time they flew only a mile or so, to a spot where, about a thousand years ago, a certain Alberich had stopped and watched three beautiful women swimming in the river. The ravens landed in a withered tree and folded their wings.

Under the tree, three young girls were sunbathing, and for them the Sun Goddess had saved the best of the evening light, for she was their friend.

'Flosshilde,' said one of the girls, 'there's a raven in that tree looking at you.'

'I hope he likes what he sees,' replied the Rhinedaughter lazily.

Wellgunde, the eldest and most serious of the three, rolled onto her stomach and lifted her designer sunglasses.

'Hello, Thought,' she said, 'hello, Memory. Found him yet, then?'

The ravens were silent, ruffling their coarse feathers with their beaks, and the girls giggled.

'But you've been looking for simply ages,' said Woglinde, the youngest and most frivolous of the three. 'It must be *somewhere*.'

'I'm always losing things,' said Flosshilde. 'Where do you last remember seeing it?'

'You sure it's not in your pocket?'

'You've put it somewhere safe and you can't remember where?'

Wotan's ravens had been putting up with this sort of thing for a thousand years, but it still irritated them. The girls laughed again, and Memory blushed under his feathers.

'If you don't find him soon,' yawned Flosshilde, combing her long, golden hair, 'he'll slip through your claws, just like clever old Ingolf did. By the way, fancy Ingolf being a badger!'

'He'll get the hang of the Tarnhelm and then no-one will ever find him,' purred Woglinde. 'What a shame that would be.'

'Good luck to him,' said Wellgunde. 'Who wants the boring old Ring, anyway?'

'Dunno what you're being so bloody funny about,' said Memory. 'Supposed to be your Ring we're looking for.'

'Forget it,' said Woglinde, waving her slender arms. 'It's a lovely day, the sun is shining, the crops are growing . . .'

Memory winced at this. Flosshilde giggled.

'. . . And it's been so long since Alberich took the beastly thing that we don't really care any more, do we?' Woglinde wiggled her toes attractively, in a way that had suggested something far nicer than measureless wealth for thousands of years. 'What do we want with gold when we have you to entertain us?'

'Save it for the human beings,' said Memory.

'I wonder what he looks like,' said Wellgunde. 'I bet you he's handsome.'

'And strong.'

'And noble. Don't forget noble.'

'I never could resist noble,' said Woglinde, watching the ravens carefully under her beautiful eyelashes.

'We came to tell you that we'd heard something,' said Thought. 'But since you're not interested any more . . .'

Wellgunde yawned, putting her hand daintily in front of her mouth. 'You're right,' she said. 'We're not.' She turned over onto her back and picked up a magazine.

'Something interesting, we've heard,' said Memory.

'Oh, all right,' said Flosshilde, smiling her most dazzling smile. 'Tell us if you must.'

Even Wotan's ravens, who are (firstly) immortal and (secondly) birds, cannot do much against the smiles of

Rhinedaughters. But since Memory was bluffing, there was nothing for him to do.

'I didn't say we were going to tell you what we'd heard,' he said, archly, 'only that we'd heard it.' It is not easy for a raven to be arch, but Memory had been practising.

'Oh go away,' said Flosshilde, throwing a piece of orange peel at the two messengers. 'You're teasing us, as usual.'

'You wait and see,' said Memory, lamely, but the three girls jumped up and dived into the water, as elegantly as the very best dolphins.

'We know something you don't know,' chanted Flosshilde, and the Sun-Goddess made the water sparkle around her floating hair. Then she disappeared, leaving behind only a stream of silver bubbles.

'I dunno,' said Thought. 'Women.'

The ravens flapped their heavy wings, circled morosely for a while, and flew away.

By a strange coincidence, a few moments after Flosshilde dived down to the bed of the Rhine, three identical girls hopped out of the muddy, fetid waters of the River Tone, at the point where it runs through the centre of Taunton. A few passers-by stopped and stared, for the three girls were far cleaner than anyone who has recently had anything to do with the Tone has any right to be. But the girls' smiles wiped such thoughts from their minds, and they went on their way whistling and wishing that they were twenty years younger. Had they realised that what they had just seen were the three Rhinedaughters, Flosshilde, Wellgunde and Woglinde, they might perhaps have taken a little more notice.

CHAPTER FIVE

One of the things that slightly worried Malcolm was the fact that he was becoming decidedly middle-aged. For example, the ritualised drinking of afternoon tea had come to mean a lot to him, not simply because it disposed of an hour's worth of daylight. He had chosen half-past four in the afternoon as the best time for reading the daily papers, and from half-past four to half-past five (occasionally a quarter to six) each day he almost made himself feel that he enjoyed being extremely nice and bored stiff, for he knew that all the good news that filled the papers was, in one way or another, his doing.

Today, there was any amount of good news from around the world. Malcolm could sense the frustration and despair of the editors and journalists as they forced themselves to report yet more bumper harvests, international accords and miraculous cures. Admittedly, there had been a freak storm in Germany (banner headlines in the tabloids) and some crops had been damaged in a few remote areas. Nevertheless, he noted with satisfaction, this minor disaster was not entirely a bad thing, since it had prompted the EEC to draft and sign a new agreement on compensating farmers for damage caused by acts of God. So every cloud, however small, had a silver lining, although these days it was beginning to look as though only a very few silver linings had clouds.

Malcolm tried to work out what could have caused the freak storm in the first place. He picked up the *Daily Mirror* ('German farmers in rain horror') and observed that the storm had started at three o'clock their time, which was two o'clock our time, which was when Malcolm's new secretary had finally managed to corner him and force him to sign five letters. He resolved to be more patient with her in future, and not call her a whatsisname under his breath.

His tea was stone cold, but that did not matter; it was after all, Only Him. That was a marvellous phrase, and one that he had come to treasure. When one has suddenly been forced into the role of the Man of Sorrows, self-pity is the only luxury that remains. In fact, Malcolm had no objection whatsoever to taking away the sins of the world, but it was useful to keep an option on self-pity just in case it came in useful later. He poured the cold tea onto the lawn and watched it soak into the ground. In the crab-apple tree behind him, a robin perched and sang excitedly, but he ignored it, closing his mind to its persistent chirping. He had found that the little birds liked to come up to him and confide their secrets that they could not share with other birds, and at first he had found this extremely flattering. But since the majority of these confidences were extremely personal and of interest only to a trained biologist, he had decided that it would be best not to encourage them. After a while, the robin stopped singing and went away. Malcolm rose to his feet and walked slowly into the house.

Combe Hall was undoubtedly very beautiful, but it was

also very big. It had been built in the days when a house-holder tended to feel claustrophobic if he could not accommodate at least one infantry regiment, including the band, in his country house. Its front pediment was world famous. Its windows had been praised and reviled in countless television series. Its kitchens were enormous and capable of being put to any use except the convenient preparation of food. It was very grand, very magnificent, and very empty.

Malcolm had always fancied living at Combe Hall on the strict understanding that his wish was never to come true. Now that he was its owner and (apart from the legion of staff) its only resident, he felt rather like a bewildered traveller at an international airport. The house was bad enough, but the staff were truly awful. There was no suave, articulate butler and no pretty parlourmaids; instead, Malcolm found himself employing an army of grimly professional contract cleaners and an incomprehensible Puerto Rican cook, whom he was sure he was shamelessly exploiting in some way he could not exactly understand. After a week, Malcolm left them all to it and retreated to one of the upstairs drawing-rooms, which he turned into a nicely squalid bedsit.

As a result, he felt under no obligation to assume the role of country gentleman. With the house had come an enormous park, some rather attractive gardens, into which Malcolm hardly dared go for fear of offending the gardeners, and the Home Farm. Ever since he could remember, Malcolm had listened to the Archers on the radio – not from choice, but because they had always been there in his childhood, and so had become surrogate relatives – and his mental picture of agriculture had been shaped by this influence. But the farm that he owned (now *there* was a thought!) whirred and purred with machines and clicked and ticked with computers, filling its owner with fear and amazement. Yet when he suggested to the farm manager that the whole thing might perhaps be rearranged on more picturesque lines and to hell with the profits, which nobody really needed, the farm manager stared at him as if he were mad. Since then, he had kept well away from it.

But with his new property came certain ineluctable responsibilities, the most arduous of which was coping with his new secretary. On the one hand, the woman was invaluable, for she ran the place and left him alone for most of the time. Without the irritations and petty nuisances of everyday life to contend with, he could keep his temper and make the maize grow tall all over Africa. But for this freedom from care he had to pay a severe price: his secretary, who was American and in her middle forties, had clearly made a resolution to be more English than anyone else in the history of the world. Her convert's passion for all things English gave her the zeal of a missionary, and it was obvious that she intended to Anglicise young Herr Finger if it killed her. And, like many missionaries, she was not above a little persecution in the cause of the communication of Enlightenment.

Apart from avoiding his staff and his secretary and anything else that might tend to irritate or annoy, however, Malcolm found that he had very little to do. Even as a small boy, he had never had a hobby of any kind, and he had always found making friends as difficult as doing jigsaw puzzles, and even less rewarding. As for the comfort and solace of his family, Malcolm knew only too well that that was out of the question. If, by some miracle, he could persuade his kin to believe this ludicrous tale of rings and badgers, he knew without having to think about it what their reaction would be. 'Malcolm,' his mother would say, 'give that ring back to Bridget this *instant*' – the implication being that it had been meant for her all along.

Not that the possibility had not crossed his mind. Surely, he had reflected, his talented and universally praised sister would make a far better job of all this than he would; she had five A-levels and had been to Warwick University. But somehow he felt sure that Bridget was not the right person for the job. For a start, she did not suffer fools gladly, and since a large percentage of the people of the world are fools, it was possible that she might not give them the care and consideration they needed. Throughout its history, Malcolm reflected, the Ring had been in the possession of gifted, talented, exceptional people, and look what had happened . . .

One morning, when Malcolm was listening (rather proudly) to the morning news, the English Rose, as he had mentally christened her, came hammering on his door. She seemed to have an uncanny knack of knowing where he was.

She informed him that the annual Combe Show was to be held in the grounds of the Hall in a fortnight's time. Malcolm, who loathed all such occasions from the bottom of his heart, tried to protest, but without success.

'Oh, but I've been talking to the folks from the village, and they all say that it's the social event of the year,' buzzed the Rose. 'It's one of the oldest surviving fairs in the country. According to the records I consulted . . .'

Malcolm saw that there was no hope of escape. His secretary, apart from having the persistence of a small child in pursuit of chocolate, was an outstanding example of true Ancestor Worship (although it was not her own ancestors that she worshipped; her name was Weinburger) and anything remotely traditional went to her head like wine. In fact, Malcolm was convinced, if she could revive the burning of witches, with all its attendant seventeenth-century pageantry, she probably would.

'But will it not be – how is it in English? – a great nuisance to arrange?' he suggested. That was, of course, the wrong thing to say. The Rose thrived on challenges.

'Herr Finger,' she said, looking at him belligerently over the top of her spectacles, 'that is not my attitude and well you know it. It will be truly rewarding for me to make all the necessary social arrangements for the proposed event, and Mr Ayres, who is the Chairman of the Show Committee, will be calling on you to discuss all the practicalities. There will be the usual livestock competition, of course, and I presume that the equestrian events will follow their customary pattern. I had hoped that we might prevail upon the Committee to revive the Jacobean Sheriff's Races, but Mr Ayres has, at my request, performed a feasibility study and feels that such a revival could not be satisfactorily arranged in the limited space of time left to us before the Show. So I fear that we will have to content ourselves with a gymkhana situation . . .'

Although Malcolm had acquired the gift of tongues from the blood of the Giant, he still had occasional difficulty in understanding his secretary's English. The name Ayres, however, was immediately recognisable. It was a name he was only too familiar with; indeed, he knew virtually all the words in the language that rhymed with it, for Liz Ayres was the girl he loved. Mr William Ayres, the Chairman of the Show Committee, was her father, and a nastier piece of work never read a Massey-Ferguson catalogue. But thoughts of malice or resentment were no longer available to Malcolm, and so finally he agreed. The English Rose scuttled away, no doubt to flick through Debrett (after Sir Walter Elliot, she was its most enthusiastic reader) and Malcolm resigned himself to another meeting with possibly his least favourite person in the world.

William Ayres could trace his ancestry back to the early fifteenth century; his namesake had won the respect of his betters at the battle of Agincourt by throwing down his longbow and pulling a fully armed French knight off his horse with his bare hands. The present William Ayres undoubtedly had the physical strength to emulate his ancestor's deed and, given his unbounded ferocity, would probably relish the opportunity to try. So massively built was he that people who met him for the first time often wondered why he bothered with tractors and the like on his sprawling farm at the top of the valley. Surely he could save both time and money by drawing the plough himself, if necessary with his teeth. Compared to his two sons, however, Mr Ayres was a puny but sunny-tempered dwarf, and Malcolm could at least console himself with the reflection that he would not be confronted with Joe or Mike Ayres at this unpleasant interview.

Malcolm decided that in order to face Mr Ayres it would be necessary for him to be extremely German, for his antagonist had strong views about rich foreigners who bought up fine old houses in England.

'It's a tremendously important occasion,' said Mr Ayres, 'one of the high points of the year in these parts. It's been going on for as long as I can remember, certainly. When Colonel Booth still had the Hall . . .'

Mr Ayres was a widower, and Malcolm toyed with the idea of introducing him to the English Rose. They would have so much in common . . .

61

'I am most keen on your English traditions, *naturlich*. Let us hope that we can make this a show to be remembered.'

Mr Ayres winced slightly. He disliked the German race, probably because they had thoughtlessly capitulated before he had been old enough to get at them during the War.

'Then perhaps you would care to invite some of the local people to the Hall,' he replied. 'It would be a splendid opportunity for you to get to know your neighbours.'

'Delighted, das *ist sehr gut*.' Mr Ayres did not like the German language, either. *'Aber* – who shall I invite? I am not yet well acquainted with the local folk.'

'Leave that to me,' said Mr Ayres. 'I'll send you a list, if you like.' He drank his tea brutally – everything he did, he seemed to do brutally. 'It should be a good show this year, especially the gymkhana.'

'What is gymkhana?' Malcolm asked innocently. 'In my country we have no such word.'

'So I believe,' said Mr Ayres, who had suspected as much from the start. He did his best to explain, but it was not easy; anyone would have difficulty in explaining such a basic and fundamental concept, just as it would be difficult to explain the sun to a blind man. In the end, he was forced to give up the struggle.

'I'll get my daughter to explain it to you,' he said brightly. 'She and her fiancé – they haven't announced it yet, but it'll be any day now – I expect they'll be taking part in the main competition. And far be it from me, but I think they're in with a good chance. Well, not Liz perhaps, but young Wilcox – that's her fiancé . . .'

Malcolm fought hard to retain his composure, and as he struggled, slight earth tremors were recorded in California. For all that he had never expected anything to come of his great love for Elizabeth Ayres, the news that she was soon to be engaged and married made him want to break something. Fortunately for the inhabitants of San Francisco he managed to get a grip on himself.

'Ah, that is good,' he said mildly. 'So you will make the necessary arrangements with my secretary, yes? So charmed to have met you. *Auf Wiedersehen.*'

'Good day, Mr Finger.' Mr Ayres stood up, for a moment blotting out the sun, and extended an enormous hand. Malcolm cringed as he met it with his own; he had shaken hands with Mr Ayres once before, and was convinced that the farmer's awesome grip had broken a small bone somewhere. To his surprise, however, he was able to meet the grip firmly and without serious injury, and he suddenly realised that his arm – the arm of Siegfried the Dragon-Slayer, give or take a bit – was as strong or possibly stronger. This made him feel a little better, but not much.

As soon as Mr Ayres had gone, Malcolm sat down heavily and relieved his feelings by tearing up a newspaper. They hadn't announced it yet, but it would be any day now. Soon there would be a coy paragraph in the local paper, followed by a ceremony at the beautiful church with the possibly Saxon font: then a reception at the Blue Boar – the car park full of Range-Rovers, champagne flowing freely (just this once) and minced-up fish on tiny biscuits – and so the line of the bowman of Agincourt would force its way on into the twenty-first century.

Fortune, Malcolm suddenly remembered, can make vile things precious. Like all her family, Liz was obsessed with horses. It might yet be a gymkhana to remember.

When the day came the drive of Combe Hall resembled a

plush armoured column, so crowded was it with luxury four-wheel drive vehicles. Large women in hats and large men in blazers, most of whom Malcolm had last seen making nuisances of themselves at the auction rooms in Taunton, strolled through the garden, apparently oblivious of the scowls of the gardeners, or peered through the windows of the house to see what atrocities its new, foreign owner had perpetrated. Malcolm, dressed impeccably and entirely unsuitably in a dark grey suit and crocodile shoes (courtesy of the Tarnhelm; Vorsprung durch Technik, as they say on the Rhine) was making the best job he could of being the shy, charming host, while the English Rose was having the time of her life introducing him to the local gentry. He had provided (rather generously, he thought) a cold collation on the lawn for all the guests on Mr Ayres' list, which they had devoured down to the last sprig of parsley, apparently unaware of the maxim that there is no free lunch.

When the last strand of flesh had been stripped off the last chicken leg, the guests swept like a tweed river into the Park, where the Show was in full swing. A talentless band made up of nasty old men and surly children were playing loudly, but not loudly enough to drown the high-pitched gabble of the Quality, as deafening and intimidating as the buzzing of angry bees. There were innumerable overweight farm animals in pens, inane sideshows, vintage traction engines, and a flock of sheep, who politely but firmly ignored the efforts of a number of sheepdogs to make them do illogical things. All as it should be, of course, and the centrepiece of this idyll was the showjumping.

As he surveyed his gentry-mottled grounds, Malcolm was ambushed by the Ayres clan: William, Michael, Joseph, and, of course, Elizabeth. He was introduced to the two terrifying brothers, who rarely made any sound in the presence of their father, and to the daughter of the family. A beautiful girl, Miss Ayres; about five feet three, light brown hair, very blue eyes and a smile you could read small print by. Malcolm, whose mind controlled the world, smiled back, displaying the Dragon-Slayer's geometrically perfect teeth. The two brightest smiles in the world, more dazzling than any toothpaste advertisement, and all this for politeness' sake. Malcolm managed to stop himself shouting, 'Look, Liz, it's me, only much better-looking', and listened attentively as the girl he loved desperately in his nebulous but whole-hearted way explained to him, as by rote, the principles of the gymkhana. To this explanation Malcolm did not listen, for he was using the power he had gained by drinking Giant's blood to read her thoughts. It was easily done and, with the exception of one or two of his school reports, Malcolm had never read anything so discouraging. For although the Tarnhelm had made him the most handsome man in the world, it was evident that Miss Ayres did not judge by appearances. For Liz was wondering who this boring foreigner reminded her of. Now, who was it? Ah, yes. That Malcolm Fisher . . .

He smiled, wished the family good luck in the arena, and walked swiftly away. When he was sure no-one was watching, he turned himself into an appletree and stood for a moment in one of his own hedges, secure in the knowledge that apple trees cannot weep. But even apple trees can have malicious thoughts (ask any botanist) and if the consequences for the world were unfortunate, then so be it. One of Malcolm's few remaining illusions had been shattered: he had always believed that his total lack of attractiveness to the opposite sex was due simply to his unprepossessing appearance, a shortcoming (as he argued) that was in no respect his fault, so that his failure in this field of human endeavour reflected badly not on him but on those who chose to make such shallow and superficial judgements.

The natural consequence of the destruction of this illusion was that Malcolm wanted very much to do something nasty and spiteful, and he wanted to do it to Philip Wilcox, preferably in front of a large number of malicious people. He shrugged his branches, dislodging a blackbird, and resumed his human shape.

Thanks to the blood of the Giant Ingolf, Malcolm could understand all languages and forms of speech, even the curious noises coming out of the tannoy. The competitors in the main event were being asked to assemble in the collecting ring. With the firm intention of turning himself into a horse-fly and stinging Philip Wilcox's horse at an appropriate moment, Malcolm made his way over to the arcade of horseboxes that formed a temporary mews under the shade of a little copse in the west corner of the Park. He recognised the Wilcox family horsebox, which was drawn up at the end of the row. There was the horse, just standing there.

An idea, sent no doubt by the Lord of the Flies, suddenly came into Malcolm's mind. How would it be if . . .? No-one was watching; the attention of the whole world seemed to be focused on a fat child in jodhpurs and his long-suffering pony. Malcolm made himself invisible, and with extreme apprehension (for he was terrified of horses) he led Philip Wilcox's steed out of its box and into the depths of the tangled copse, where he tied it securely to a tree. Then, with his nails pressed hard into the palms of his hands, he changed himself into an exact copy of the animal and transported himself back to the horsebox. This would be hard work, but never mind.

'And have you met the new owner?' asked Aunt Marjorie, settling herself comfortably on a straw bale. 'I never thought I'd live to see the day when a foreigner . . .'

'Just for a few minutes,' replied Liz Ayres. She had learnt over the years the art of separating the questions from the comments in her aunt's conversation, and slipping in answers to them during pauses for breath and other interruptions.

'What's he like? The trouble with most Germans . . .'

'I don't know. He seemed pleasant enough, in a gormless sort of way, but I only said a few words to him.'

'Well, I suppose we should all be very grateful to him for letting us put a waterjump in the middle of his Park, not that I imagine he minds anyway, or he wouldn't have. Colonel Booth never let us have one, but he was just plain difficult at times. I remember . . .'

'I don't think he's terribly interested in the Hall, actually.' Liz wondered if Aunt Marjorie had ever finished a sentence of her own free will in her life. Probably not. 'I'm told he doesn't *do* anything, just stays indoors all day. Daddy said . . . oh look, there's Joe.'

Elizabeth Ayres' loyalties were sadly divided in the jump-off for the main event, since the two competitors most likely to win it were her brother Joe and her fiancé. Joe was the better rider, but Philip's horse seemed to have found remarkable form just at the right moment. Only last week, Philip had been talking of selling it; perhaps it had been listening (at times, they seem almost human) for today it was sailing over the jumps like a Harrier. Even Aunt Marjorie, who in matters of showjumping was a firm believer in entropy, had admitted that the animal wasn't too bad.

67

'My money's on your boyfriend,' said Aunt Marjorie. 'What's that horse of his called? It's playing a blinder today. Almost as if it *understood*.'

She had a point there. Intelligence, so Philip had always maintained, had never been one of old Mayfair's attributes. Any animal capable of taking a paper bag or a rusting Mini for a pack of wolves and acting accordingly was unlikely ever to win Mastermind, and this lack of mental as opposed to physical agility had prompted one of Philip's brightest sayings. Even if you led Mayfair to water, he would say, it probably wouldn't even occur to him to drink. But today, Mayfair hadn't put a foot wrong, in any sense.

'Mr Joseph Ayres and Moonbeam,' said the tannoy. A hush fell over the crowd, for it seemed wrong that Joe should be riding the horse instead of the other way round. Joe was obviously the stronger of the two, just as Moonbeam was clearly the more intelligent. Aunt Marjorie, who was, like so many of her class, a sort of refined Centaur, leaned forward and fixed her round, bright eyes on horse and rider. 'Look at his knees,' she muttered. 'Just *look* at them.'

Joe did his best, but the consensus of opinion was that his best was not going to be good enough. 'Twelve faults,' said the tannoy, and Aunt Marjorie shook her head sadly. 'Why wasn't the idiot using a martingale?' she said. 'When I was a girl . . .'

'Excuse me,' said one of the three rather pretty girls who had just made their way to the front. 'You obviously know all about this sort of thing. Could you tell us what's going on? We're terribly ignorant about horse-racing.'

'It isn't racing, it's jumping,' said Aunt Marjorie, not looking round.

'Oh,' said the youngest of the three girls. 'Oh I *see*.'

'Haven't you been to a show before?' Liz asked, kindly.

'No,' chorused the girls, and this was true. There are no shows and very few gymkhanas at the bottom of the River Rhine, where these three girls, the Rhinedaughters Flosshilde, Wellgunde, and Woglinde, had spent the last two thousand years. They have trout races, but that is not quite the same.

'Well,' said Aunt Marjorie patiently, as if explaining to a Trobriand Islander how to use a fork, 'the idea is to make the horse jump over all the obstacles.'

'Why?' asked Flosshilde. Woglinde scowled at her.

'Because if you don't, you get faults,' said Aunt Marjorie, 'and if you get more faults than everyone else, you lose.'

'That explains a great deal,' said Flosshilde, brightly. 'Thank you.'

'Mr Philip Wilcox on Mayfair,' said the tannoy.

Aunt Marjorie turned to the Rhinemaidens, who were amusing themselves by making atrocious puns on the word 'fault'. 'Watch this,' she urged them. 'He's very good.'

The Rhinedaughters put on their most serious expressions (which were not very serious, in absolute terms) and paid the strictest attention as Philip Wilcox and his tired but determined horse entered the ring. As the horse went past her, Flosshilde suddenly started forward, but Wellgunde nudged her and she composed herself.

'You see,' said Aunt Marjorie, 'he's building up his speed nicely, he's timed it just right, and – oh.'

'Why's he stopped?' asked Woglinde. 'I thought you said he was going to jump over that fence thing.'

Aunt Marjorie, raising her voice above the gasps and whispers of the spectators, explained that that was called a refusal.

69

'Does he lose marks for that?'

'Yes,' said Liz, crisply.

'He's still got points in hand,' said Aunt Marjorie, trying to stay calm in this crisis. 'I expect he'll go round the other way now. Yes, I thought he would.'

'He's stopped again,' said Woglinde.

'So he has,' said Liz. 'I wonder why?'

'Is he allowed to hit his horse with that stick?' asked Flosshilde. 'It must hurt an awful lot.'

'I think it's cruel,' said Wellgunde.

'I think he's going to try the gate this time,' said Aunt Marjorie nervously. 'Oh dear, not *again* . . .'

'I think it's his fault for hitting the horse with that stick,' said Wellgunde. 'If I was the horse, I'd throw him off.'

'Thirty-three faults,' sniggered the tannoy.

'Is that a lot?' asked Flosshilde. Aunt Marjorie confirmed that it was, rather.

Philip Wilcox was obviously finding it hard to think straight through the buzz of malicious giggling that welled up all around him. About the only jump he hadn't tried yet was the water-jump. He pulled Mayfair's head round, promised him an apple if he made it and the glue factory if he didn't, and pressed with his heels in the approved manner. Mayfair began to move smoothly, rhythmically towards the obstacle.

'Come on, now,' Aunt Marjorie hissed under her breath, 'plenty of pace. Go on . . .'

There is nothing, nothing in the world that amuses human beings more than the sight of a fully grown, fully clothed man falling into water, and sooner or later the human race must come to terms with this fact. But, to the Rhinedaughters (who are not human, but were created by a unique and entirely accidental fusion of the life-forces) it seemed strange that this unfortunate accident should produce such gales of laughter from everyone present, including the tannoy. Even Wellgunde, who thought it served him right for hitting the horse with the stick, was moved to compassion. She looked round to see if she was the only person not laughing, and observed that at least the girl sitting next to the fat woman did not seem to be amused. In fact, she appeared to be perfectly calm, and her face was a picture of tranquillity, like some Renaissance Madonna. Perhaps, thought the Rhinedaughter, she's an immortal too. Or perhaps she's just annoyed.

'I'm so glad Joe won in the end,' said Liz, getting to her feet. 'Shall we go and find some tea?'

Restored to human shape once more, Malcolm crawled into the house and collapsed into a chair. He was utterly exhausted, his mouth was bruised and swollen, his back and sides were aching, and he had pulled a muscle in his neck when he had stopped so suddenly in front of the water-jump. The whole thing had probably hurt him just as much as it had hurt Philip Wilcox, and he had a terrible feeling that it hadn't been worth it. A minute or so of unbridled malice on his part was probably the worst thing that could happen to the universe, and his original argument, that anything that humiliated Philip Wilcox was bound to be good for the world, seemed rather flimsy in retrospect. He could only hope that the consequences would not be too dire.

With an effort, he rose to his feet and stumbled out into the grounds. The show was, mercifully, drawing to a close and, within an hour or so, all the cars that were hiding his grass from the sun would be winding their way home, probably, since this was Somerset, at fifteen miles an hour behind a milk tanker. All he had to do now was present the prizes. This would, of course, mean standing up in public and saying something coherent, and for a moment he stopped dead in his tracks. He should be feeling unmitigated terror at the prospect of this ordeal, but he wasn't. He tried to feel frightened, but the expected reaction refused to materialise. He raised his eyebrows and said 'Well, I'm damned' to himself several times.

As he stood on the platform handing out rosettes, the three Rhinedaughters studied him carefully through their designer sunglasses.

'No, don't tell me,' whispered Flosshilde, 'I'll remember in a minute.'

'Siegfried,' said Wellgunde. 'It's Siegfried. What a nerve!'

'Why shouldn't he be Siegfried if he wants to?' whispered Woglinde. 'I think it suits him.'

'Oh, well.' Flosshilde shrugged her slim shoulders. 'Here we go again.'

Malcolm was shaking Joe Ayres by the hand and saying 'Well done'. Joe Ayres winced as he withdrew his hand; he suspected that the German's ferocious grip had dislocated one of his knuckles.

'It could have been worse,' said Flosshilde, 'considering . . .' She stopped suddenly, and poked Wellgunde's arm. 'Look,' she hissed, 'over there, by the pear tree. Look who it is!'

'No!' Wellgunde's eyes were sparkling with excitement as she followed Flosshilde's pointing finger, and a pear on the tree ripened prematurely as a result. 'I don't believe it.'

'He doesn't look a day older,' said Woglinde, fondly.

The other two made faces at her.

Malcolm recognised Alberich at once. As the Prince of the Nibelungs approached him, Malcolm's heart seemed to collapse. Not that the Nibelung was a terrifying sight; a short, broad, grey-haired man in a dark overcoat, nothing more. There was no point in running away, and Malcolm stood his ground as Alberich approached and extended his hand for a handshake. Malcolm closed his fist around the Ring and put his hands behind his back.

'I'm sorry,' said Alberich in German. 'I thought you were someone else.'

'Oh, yes?'

'Someone I used to know in Germany, as a matter of fact. You look very like him, from a distance. But perhaps he was a little bit taller.'

'I don't think so,' said Malcolm without thinking.

Alberich laughed. 'How would you know? But you're right, actually. He wasn't.'

'My name is Manfred Finger,' Malcolm managed to say. 'I own the Hall.'

'Hans Albrecht.' Alberich smiled again. 'I'm afraid I don't know many people in England. But perhaps you know a friend of mine who lives near here.'

'I'm afraid I don't know many people either,' said Malcolm, forcing himself to smile. 'I've only been here a short while myself.'

'Well, this friend of mine is a very remarkable person, so perhaps you do know him. Malcolm Fisher. Familiar?'

'Any friend of Malcolm's is a friend of mine,' said Malcolm truthfully. 'But I don't remember him mentioning you.'

'That's so like him.' Alberich was massaging the fourth finger of his right hand as if it was hurting. 'Arthritis,' he explained. 'Anyway, if you see him before I do, you might remind him that he's got something of mine. A gold ring, and a hat. Both valueless, but I'd like them back.'

'I'm afraid Malcolm hasn't been quite himself lately,' said Malcolm. 'But I'll remind him if I see him before you do.'

'Would you? That's very kind. And do give him my best wishes.' Alberich turned to go, then stopped. 'Oh, and by the way,' he said in English. 'Well done. I liked your horse. Goodbye.'

As if that wasn't bad enough, Malcolm heard on the late news that two airliners had missed each other by inches over Manchester that afternoon. Had they collided, said the announcer, more than five hundred people would probably have lost their lives. An inquiry was being held, but the probable cause of the incident was human error.

CHAPTER SIX

Against the dark blue night sky above the Mendip Hills, someone with bright eyes might have been able to make out two tiny black dots, which could conceivably have been ravens, except of course that they were far too high up.

'It was around here somewhere,' said Thought.

'That's what you said last time,' said Memory. His pinions were aching, and he hadn't eaten for sixteen hours. During that time, he and his colleague had been round the world twenty-four times. Anything the sun could do, it seemed, they could do better.

'All right, then,' said Thought, 'don't believe me, see if I care. But he's down there somewhere, I know he is. I definitely heard the Ring calling.'

'That was probably Radio Bristol,' said Memory. Exhaustion had made him short-tempered.

They flew on in silence, completing a circuit of the counties of Somerset, Avon and Devon. Finally, they could go no further, and swooped down onto the roof of a thatched barn just outside Dulverton.

'How come you can hear the Ring, anyway?' said Memory. 'I can't.'

'Nor me, usually. It just sort of happens, once in a while. But it never lasts long enough for me to get an exact fix on it.'

A foolhardy bat fluttered towards them, curious to know who these strangers might be. The two ravens turned and stared at it, frightening it out of its wits.

'If it's about the radio licence,' said the bat, 'there's a cheque in the post.'

'Get lost,' said Memory, and the bat did its best to obey. Being gifted with natural radar, however, it did not find it easy.

'Wotan's in a terrible state these days,' said Thought. 'Not happy at all.'

'So what's new?'

'He's been all over the shop looking for clues. Went down a tin-mine in Bolivia the other day, came out all covered in dust.'

'I could have told him he'd do no good in Bolivia,' said Memory. 'Perhaps it would be better if we split up. That way we could cover more ground. You take one hemisphere, I take the other, sort of thing.'

Thought considered this for a moment. 'No, wouldn't work. You couldn't think where to go, and I couldn't remember where I'd been. Waste of everybody's time.'

'Please yourself.'

'You want to go off on your own then, or what?'

'Forget it.'

Thought was about to say something, but stopped. 'Listen,' he whispered. 'Did you hear that?'

'What?'

'It's the Ring again. Somewhere over there.' He pointed with his wing to the east. 'Not too far away, either.'

'How far?'

'Dunno, it's stopped again.'

Memory shook his head. 'I'm thinking of packing all this in,' he said.

'How do you mean?' said Thought.

'All this flying about, and that. I mean, where's it getting me?'

'It's a living, though.'

'Is it?' Memory leaned forward and snapped up a moth. It tasted sour. 'You take my brother-in-law. Talentless little git if you ask me. Used to run errands for the Moon-Goddess. Then they got one of those telexes, and he was out on his ear. So he set up this courier service – five years ago, give or take a bit – and look at him now. Nest in the tallest forest in Saxony, another in the Ardennes for the winter, and I bet he isn't eating moths.'

'Nests aren't everything,' said Thought. 'There's job satisfaction. There's travel. There's service to the community.'

'I know,' said Memory. 'Instead of all this fooling about, why don't we keep an eye on the girls, or Alberich? Maybe they know something we don't.'

Thought considered this. 'Could do,' he said, 'it's worth a try . . .' He stopped, and both birds were silent for a moment. 'There it goes again. Definitely over there somewhere.'

'Stuff it,' said Memory. 'Let's find the Rhinedaughters.'

Malcolm found it difficult to sleep that night. He had managed to get the thought of the two airliners out of his mind, but the meeting with Alberich was not so lightly dismissed. He had been afraid, more so than ever before, and the terrible thing was that he could not understand why. He was taller and stronger than the Nibelung, and he had the ability to make himself taller and stronger yet if the need arose. That was the whole point of the Tarnhelm. But the

Nibelung had something else that made his own magic powers seem irrelevant; he had authority, and that was not something Malcolm could afford to ignore.

He looked at his watch; it was half-past two in the morning. He toyed with the idea of transporting himself to Los Angeles or Adelaide, where it would be light and he could get a cup of coffee without waking up the housekeeper. He was on the point of doing this when he heard a noise in the corridor outside.

Combe Hall was full of unexplained noises, which everyone he asked attributed to the plumbing. But something told Malcolm that plumbing made gurgling noises, not stealthy creeping noises. Without understanding why, he knew that he was in danger, and something told him that it was probably the right time for him to become invisible.

His bedroom door was locked, and he stood beside it. Outside, he could hear footsteps, which stopped. There was a scrabbling sound, a click and the door opened gently. He recognised the face of Alberich, peering into the room, and for a moment was rooted to the spot. Then it occurred to him that he was considerably bigger than Alberich, and also invisible. The Nibelung crept into the room and tiptoed over to the bed. As he bent over it, Malcolm kicked him hard.

It would be unfair to Malcolm to say that he did not know his own strength. He knew his own strength very well (or rather his lack of it) but as yet he had not come to terms with the strength of Siegfried the Dragon-Slayer. As a result, he hit Alberich very hard indeed. The intruder uttered a loud yelp and fell over.

Malcolm was horrified. His first reaction was that he must have killed Alberich, but a loud and uncomplicated complaint from his victim convinced him that that was not so. His next reaction was to apologise.

'Sorry,' he said. 'What the hell do you think you're doing?'

'You clumsy idiot,' said the Prince of the Nibelungs, 'you've broken my leg.'

It occurred to Malcolm that this served Alberich right, and he said so. In fact, he suggested, Alberich was extremely lucky to get off so lightly, since presumably he had broken in with the intention of committing murder.

'Don't be stupid,' said Alberich. 'I only wanted the Ring.'

He made it sound as if he had just dropped by to borrow a bowl of sugar. 'Now, about my broken leg . . .'

'Never mind your broken leg.'

'I mind it a lot. Get a doctor.'

'You're taking a lot for granted, aren't you?' said Malcolm sternly. 'You're my deadliest enemy. Why shouldn't I . . . well, dispose of you, right now?'

Alberich laughed. 'You?' he said incredulously. 'Who do you think you are, Jack the Ripper?'

'I could be if I wanted to,' said Malcolm. The Nibelung ignored him.

'You wouldn't hurt a fly,' he sneered. 'That's your trouble. You'll never get anywhere in this world unless you improve your attitude. And did no-one ever tell you it's bad manners to be invisible when someone's talking to you?'

'You sound just like my mother,' said Malcolm.

He reappeared, and Alberich glowered at him. 'Still pretending to be who you aren't, I see,' he said.

'I'll be who I want to be. I'm not afraid of you any more.'

'Delighted to hear it. Perhaps you'll fetch a doctor now.'

'And the police,' said Malcolm, to frighten him. 'You're a burglar.'

'You wouldn't dare,' replied Alberich, but Malcolm could see he was worried. This was remarkable. A few minutes ago, he had been paralysed with fear. Now he found the whole thing vaguely comic. Still, it would be as well to call a doctor. He went to the telephone beside his bed.

'Not that sort of doctor,' said Alberich, irritably. 'What do you think I am, human?'

'So what sort of doctor do you want?' Malcolm asked.

'A proper doctor. A Nibelung.'

'Fine. And how do you suggest I set about finding one, look in the Yellow Pages?'

'Don't be facetious. Use the Ring.'

'Can I do that?' Malcolm was surprised by this.

'Of course you can. Just rub the Ring against your nose and call for a doctor.'

Feeling rather foolish, Malcolm did what he was told. At once, a short, stocky man with very pale skin materialised beside him, wearing what appeared to be a sack.

'You called?' said the Nibelung.

'Where did you come from?' Malcolm asked.

'Nibelheim, where do you think? So where's the patient?'

The doctor did something to Alberich's leg with a spanner and a jar of ointment, and disappeared as suddenly as he had come.

'That's handy,' Malcolm said. 'Can I just summon Nibelungs when I want to?'

'Of course,' said Alberich. 'Although why you should want to is another matter. By and large, they're incredibly boring people.'

Malcolm shrugged his shoulders. 'Anyway, how's your leg?' he asked.

'Very painful. But it's healed.'

'*Healed?* But I thought you said it was broken.'

'So it was,' replied Alberich, calmly. 'And now it's unbroken again. That's what the doctor was for. It'll be stiff for a day or so, of course, but that can't be helped. If you will go around kicking people, you must expect to cause anguish and suffering.'

Malcolm yawned. 'In that case, you can go away and leave me in peace,' he said. 'And don't let me catch you around here again, or there'll be trouble.'

This bravado didn't convince anyone. Alberich made no attempt to move, but sat on the floor rubbing his knee, until Malcolm, unable to think of anything else to do, offered him a drink.

'I thought you'd never ask,' said Alberich. 'I'll have a large schnapps, neat.'

'I don't think I've got any of that,' said Malcolm.

'You're supposed to be a German. Oh well, whatever comes to hand, so long as it isn't sherry. I don't like sherry.'

So it was that Malcolm found himself sharing a bottle of gin with the Prince of Nibelheim at three o'clock in the morning. It was not something he would have chosen to do, especially after a tiring day, but the mere fact that he was able to do it was remarkable enough. Alberich made no further attempt to relieve him of the Ring; he didn't even mention the subject until Malcolm himself raised it. Instead, he talked mostly about his health, or to be precise, his digestion.

'Lobster,' he remarked more than once, 'gives me the most appalling heartburn. And gooseberries . . .'

In short, there was nothing to fear from Alberich, and Malcolm found himself feeling rather sorry for the Nibelung, who, by his own account at least, had had rather a hard time.

'It wasn't the gold I wanted,' he said. 'I wanted to get my own back on those damned women.'

'Which women?'

'The Rhinedaughters. I won't bore you with all the

details. Not a nice story.' Alberich helped himself to some more gin. 'There I was, taking a stroll beside the Rhine on a pleasant summer evening, and these three girls, with no more clothes on than would keep a fly warm . . .'

'I know all that,' said Malcolm.

'Do you?' said Alberich, rather disappointed. 'Oh well, never mind. But it wasn't the power or the money I wanted – well, they would have been nice, I grant you, I'm not saying they wouldn't – but it's the principle of the thing. You know how it is when someone takes something away from you without any right to it at all. You feel angry. You feel hard done by. And if that thing is the control of the world, you feel very hard done by indeed. Not that I *want* to control the world particularly – I imagine I'd do it very badly. But it's like not being invited to a party, you feel hard done by even if you wouldn't have gone if they'd asked you. I know I'm not explaining this very well . . . You can get obsessive about it, you know? Especially if you've thought about nothing else for the last thousand years.'

'Couldn't you have done something else, to take your mind off it? Got a job, or something?'

'This may seem strange, but having been master of the world for forty-eight hours – that's how long they let me keep the Ring, you know – doesn't really qualify you for much. And they threw me out of Nibelheim.'

'Did they?'

'They did. You can't really blame them. I had enslaved them and made them mine gold for me. They weren't best pleased.'

'So what have you been doing ever since?'

'Moping about, mostly, feeling sorry for myself. And looking for the Ring, of course. And a bit of freelance met-allurgy, just to keep the wolf from the door. My card.'

He took a card from his wallet. 'Hans Albrecht and partners,' it read, 'Mining Engineers and Contractors, Est. AD 900.'

'Most people think the date's a misprint,' said Alberich, 'but it's not. Anyway, that's what I've been doing, and a thoroughly wretched time I've had, too.'

'Have another drink,' Malcolm suggested.

'You're too kind,' said Alberich. 'Mind you, if I have too much to drink these days, it plays hell with my digestion. Did I tell you about that?'

'Yes.'

Alberich shook his head sadly. 'I'm boring you, I can tell. But let me tell you something useful. Even if you won't give me the Ring, don't let Wotan get his hands on it.'

'I wasn't planning to,' said Malcolm. 'Another?'

'Why not? And then I must be going. It's late, and you've been a horse all afternoon. That's tiring, I know. Now, about Wotan. I don't know how you've managed it, but you've got the Ring to do what you want it to. Not what I had intended when I made it, let me say. In fact, I can't remember what I intended when I made it. It's been a long time. Anyway. Is there any tonic left?'

'No. Sorry.'

'Doesn't matter. About Wotan. He's devious, very devious, but if you've got the Ring on your side . . .'

Malcolm thought of something incredibly funny. 'I haven't got the Ring on my *side*,' he said, 'I've got it on my *finger*.'

They had a good laugh over that. 'No, but seriously,' said Alberich, 'if you can make the Ring do what you want it to, then there's nothing Wotan can do to you unless you want him to.'

'But I don't want him to do anything to me. I want him to go away.'

'That's what you think. Like I said, Wotan is devious. Devious devious *devious*. He'll get you exactly where he wants you unless you're very careful, I assure you.'

'How?'

'That, my friend, remains to be seen. The days of armed force and violence are long gone, I'm sorry to say. It's cleverness that gets results. It's the same in the mining industry. Did I tell you about that?'

'Yes,' Malcolm lied. 'Go on about Wotan.'

Alberich looked at the bottom of his glass. Unfortunately, there was nothing to obscure his view of it. He picked up the bottle, but it was empty.

'I am going to have raging indigestion all tomorrow,' he said sadly. 'Don't let them tell you there's no such thing as spontaneous combustion. I suffer from it continually. Wotan can't take the Ring from you, but he can make you give it to him of your own free will. And before you ask me, I don't know how he'll do it, but he'll think of something. Have you got any Bisodol?'

'I can get you a sandwich.'

'A sandwich? Do you want to kill me as well as breaking my leg? No, don't you let go of the Ring, Malcolm Fisher. If I can't have it, you might as well keep it. It'll be safe with you until you're ready to give it to me.'

Malcolm looked uncomfortable at this. Alberich laughed.

'Of your own free will, I mean. But that won't happen until it isn't a symbol of power any more, only a bit of old jewellery. It'll happen, though, you mark my words. See how it ends.'

'How do you know?'

'I don't.' Alberich rose unsteadily to his feet. 'Time I was going.'

'How's your leg?'

'My leg? Oh, that's fine, it's my stomach I'm worried about. I'm always worried about my stomach. We sulphur-dwarves were created out of the primal flux of the earth's core. We have always existed, and we will always exist, in some form or other. You can kill us, of course, but unless you do, we live for ever. The problem is, if you're made largely of sulphur, you are going to suffer from heartburn, and there's nothing at all you can do about it. Over the past however many it is million years, I have tried absolutely every remedy for dyspepsia that has ever been devised, and they're all use-less. All of them. In all the years I've been alive, there was only one time I didn't have indigestion. You know when that was? The forty-eight hours when I had the Ring. Good night.'

'You can stay here if you like,' said Malcolm.

'That's kind of you, but I've got a room over at the Blue Boar. The fresh air will clear my head. I'll see myself out.'

'That reminds me. How did you get in here?'

'Through the front door. I have a way with locks.'

'And how did you find me in the first place?'

'Easy. I smelt the Ring. Once you started using it, that was no problem.'

Alberich went to the door, then turned. 'Do you know something, Malcolm Fisher?' he said. 'It goes against the grain saying this, but I like you. In a way. Up to a point. You can keep the Ring for the time being. I like what you're doing with it.'

Malcolm wanted to say something but could think of nothing.

'And if ever there's anything . . . Oh, forget it. Good luck.'

A few minutes later, Malcolm heard the front door slam. He got back into bed and switched off the light. It was nearly morning, and he was very tired.

★

Two ravens were perched on the telegraph pole outside the Blue Boar in Combe.

'It's definitely coming from near here somewhere,' said Thought.

Memory had been listening for the Voice all day, and he no longer believed in it. 'You've been overdoing it,' he said. 'Maybe you should take a couple of days off. We can't hear the Ring, either of us. It's not possible.'

In the road below, a short, heavily-built man was waiting for the night porter to open the door of the hotel. Thought flapped his wings to attract his partner's attention.

'Look,' he whispered, 'down there.'

'It's Alberich,' replied Memory. 'What's he doing here?'

'I told you,' said Thought. 'I told you and you wouldn't . . .'

'All right, all right,' said Memory uneasily. 'Doesn't prove anything, does it? I mean, he could be here for some totally different reason.'

'Such as?'

Memory stared blankly at his claws. 'Dunno,' he said. 'But it still doesn't mean . . .'

'Come on,' said Thought, 'we've found him. He's somewhere in this village. We'd better tell Wotan.'

'Oh no.' Memory shook his head. 'You can if you like. If we're wrong, and Wotan comes flogging out here on a fool's errand . . .'

'So what do we do?'

They racked their brains for a moment, but in vain. Then Thought had a sudden inspiration. 'I know,' he said. 'We'll tell Loge. Then it'll be his duty to pass the message on to the Boss.'

The two ravens laughed, maliciously.

CHAPTER SEVEN

Alberich woke up next morning with a thick head, a weary heart, and indigestion. He took a taxi to Taunton, only to find that he had missed the London train, and was faced with an hour in one of the dreariest towns he had ever come across in the course of a very long life.

The only possible solution was a cup or two of strong, drinkable coffee, and he set off to find it. As he sat in a grimly coy coffee shop in Kingston Road, he tried to turn over in his mind the various courses of action still open to him, but found that rational thought was not possible in his state of health and the centre of Taunton. He gave it up, and as he did so became aware of a familiar voice behind him:

'Really,' it was saying, 'nobody's worn that shade of blue since the twelfth century. I *couldn't* go out looking like that.'

'You should have thought of that earlier,' said another voice, just as familiar. 'You're impossible sometimes.'

The last time Alberich had heard those two voices, and the third voice that broke in to contradict them both, was in the depths of the Rhine, about a thousand years ago. He turned round slowly.

'What are you three doing here?' he asked.

Flosshilde smiled sweetly at him, with the result that the milk in his coffee turned to cream. 'Hello, Alberich,' she said. 'How's the digestion?'

'Awful. What are you doing here?'

'Drinking coffee. What about you?'

'Don't be flippant.'

'But that's what we do best,' said Woglinde, also smiling. There was little point to this, except pure malice, for Alberich had forsworn Love and was therefore immune to all smiles, even those of Rhinedaughters. But Woglinde smiled anyway, as a sportsman who can find no pheasants will sometimes take a shot at a passing crow. 'We're too set in our ways to change now.'

'What are you doing here?' Alberich asked.

'That would be telling,' said Wellgunde, twitching her nose like a rabbit. 'How about you?'

'Tourism,' said Alberich with a shudder. 'I like grim, miserable places where there's nothing at all to do.'

'You would,' said Flosshilde. That, so far as she was concerned, closed the subject. But Wellgunde was rather more cautious.

'We're out shopping,' she said artlessly. 'Everyone's looking to Taunton for colours this season.'

'In fact,' said Flosshilde, 'Taunton is the place where it's all happening these days.' She giggled, and Wellgunde kicked her under the table.

Alberich shook his head, which was a rash move on his part. 'You'll find it harder than you imagine,' he said. 'You won't be able to trap him easily.'

'Trap who?'

Alberich ignored her. 'What you fail to take into account,' he continued, 'is his extreme lack of self-confidence. Even if he does fall in love with one or all of you, he's highly unlikely to feel up to doing anything about it. He'll just go home and feel miserable. And then what will you have achieved?'

'We're not like that,' said Woglinde. 'We're good at dealing with shy people.'

Alberich laughed and rose to his feet. 'I wish you luck,' he said.

'No, you don't,' said Wellgunde shrewdly.

'Let me rephrase that. You'll need luck. Lots of it. See you in another thousand years.'

'Not if we see you first,' said Flosshilde cheerfully. 'Have a nice day.'

One of the few luxuries that Malcolm had indulged in since his acquisition of limitless wealth was a brand new sports car. He had always wanted one, although now that he had it he found that he was rather unwilling to go above thirty miles an hour in it. The whole point of having a car, however, as any psychologist will tell you, is that it represents Defended Space, where no-one can get at you, and Malcolm always felt happier once he was behind the wheel. There were risks, of course; driving in Somerset, that county of narrow lanes and leisurely tractors, can cause impatience and bad temper, which Malcolm was in duty bound to avoid.

Once his headache had subsided, Malcolm thought it would make a change to go into Taunton and look at the shops. He had been an enthusiastic window-shopper all his life, and now that he could afford to buy not only the things in the shop-windows but the shops themselves if he wanted to, he enjoyed this activity even more. Not that he ever did buy anything, of course; the habits of a lifetime are not so easily broken.

For example, he stood for quite five minutes outside the fishing-tackle shop in Silver Street looking at all the elegant and attractive paraphernalia in the window. At least two rivers, possibly three, ran through the grounds of the Hall, and fishing was supposed to be a relaxing occupation which soothed the nerves and the temper. Not that he particularly wanted to catch or persecute fish; but it would at least be an interest, with things to learn and things to buy. For the same reason, he had a good look at the camera shop in St James Street, and he only stopped himself from going inside by reflecting that he had nobody to take pictures of, except perhaps the English Rose.

He walked by the auction-rooms, and wondered who was doing his old job now. Inside there would be Liz, cataloguing something or other, and Philip Wilcox, training, not very energetically, to be an auctioneer. Again, he felt a strong temptation to go inside and look at them, and that would be perfectly reasonable, since they both knew him only as the rich German who had bought the Hall. He could now afford to buy everything in the sale if he wanted to. But the sale today was of antique clocks, and he already knew only too well how slowly the time passed. Besides, there was no point in buying anything for himself (it was, after all, Only Him) and he had no-one else to buy things for.

As he walked down North Street towards what passes for a centre, he noticed a shop that he could not recall having seen before. It was one of those art and craft places, selling authentic pottery and ethnic clothes (hence no doubt its name, Earth 'n' Wear). But shops of that kind are always springing up and disappearing like mayflies in upwardly-mobile towns, and Taunton is nothing if not upwardly-mobile. In fact, as they will be delighted to tell you, Taunton is no longer a one-horse town; these days, they have a bicycle as well . . .

Entirely out of curiosity, since he was safe in the knowledge that there would not be anything in a shop of this sort that he could conceivably want to buy, Malcolm opened the door, which had goat-bells behind it, and went in. The place was empty, except for a ghostly string quartet playing Mozart, a large cat asleep on a pile of Indian cotton shirts, and an astoundingly pretty girl with red hair sitting behind the till. As soon as Malcolm walked through the door, she looked up from the poem she was writing in a spiral-bound notebook with a stylised cat on the cover and smiled at him.

Malcolm had always been of the opinion that pretty girls should not be allowed to smile at people unless they meant something by it, for it gives them an unfair advantage. He now felt under an obligation to buy something. That presumably was why the owner had installed a pretty girl in the shop in the first place, and Malcolm did not approve. It was exploitation of the worst sort.

'Feel free to look around,' said the girl.

Malcolm walked briskly to the back of the shop and tried to appear profoundly interested in beeswax candles. Although he had his back to her, he felt sure that the girl was still looking at him, and he remembered that he was the most handsome man in the world, which might account for it. A smirk tried to get onto his face, but he sent it away. He was, he assured himself, only imagining it, and even if he wasn't, there was bound to be a catch in it all somewhere. This was Taunton, not Hollywood.

For her part, Wellgunde was rather dismayed. Either her smile had gone wrong since she checked it that morning, or else this young man was immune to smiles, which would

91

be a pity. She had gone to the trouble of materialising this shop and all its contents just in order to be able to have somewhere to smile at the Ring-Bearer. A shop, the Rhinedaughters had decided, made an ideal trap for ensnaring unwary Ring-Bearers. Perhaps they had under-estimated him, Wellgunde thought. Certainly it had seemed a very straightforward project when they discussed it that morning. From all they had learnt about him, Ingolf's Bane was a foolish, sentimental and susceptible young man who would as instinctively fall in love with a pretty girl who smiled at him as a trout snaps at a fly. The only point at issue in their planning session had been which one of them should have the dubious privilege of being the fly. They had tried drawing lots, but Woglinde would insist on cheating. They had tried tossing for it, but Flosshilde had winked at the coin, and it kept coming down in her favour. So finally they had decided to make a game of it: whoever captivated the Ring-Bearer first would have to see the job through, but the others would buy her lunch at Maxim's.

To make it a fair contest, they had materialised three shops in the centre of Taunton. It was a reasonable bet that no-one would notice three shops suddenly appearing out of nowhere in the centre of town, for Taunton is like that, and it would be up to the Ring-Bearer to decide which one he went into first, and so who should have the first go.

Wellgunde frowned. She was going to have to make an effort.

'Are you looking for anything in particular?' she said sweetly.

There was another potential customer outside, looking through the window at a selection of herbal teas. She turned quickly and smiled at the door. The card obligingly flipped round to read 'Closed'. Things generally did what she wanted them to when she smiled at them.

'A present for my mother,' Malcolm replied, amazing himself with his own inventiveness.

'Does she like cats?' Wellgunde suggested. 'Most mothers do.'

'Yes, she does.'

'Then how about a spaghetti-jar with a cat on the front, or a tea-cosy in the shape of a cat, or a little china cat you can keep paperclips in, or a cat-shaped candle, or a Cotswold cat breadboard? We haven't got any framed cat woodcuts at the moment, but we're expecting a delivery this afternoon if you're not in a hurry.'

'That's a lot of cats,' said Malcolm startled.

'Cats and Cotswolds,' said the Rhinedaughter, brightly. 'You can sell anything with a cat or a Cotswold on it, although some people prefer rabbits.'

She smiled again, so brightly that Malcolm could feel the skin on his face turning brown. He began to feel distinctly uncomfortable.

'I'd better have one of those oven-gloves,' he mumbled.

'With a cat on it?'

'Yes, please.'

The girl seemed rather hurt as she took Malcolm's money, and he wondered what he had said.

'If she doesn't like it, I can change it for you,' said the girl. 'No trouble, really.'

'I'm sure she'll like it. She's very fond of cats. And cooking.'

'Goodbye, then.'

'Goodbye.'

Wellgunde watched him go, and frowned. 'Oh well,' she said to herself, 'bother him, then.'

She smiled at the shop, and just to please her it vanished into thin air. Then she walked down to the banks of the Tone and dived gracefully into its khaki waters.

'Well,' said one old lady to another as a chain of silver bubbles rose to the surface, 'you don't see so much of that sort of thing nowadays.'

Confused, Malcolm turned up Hammet Street. It was not surprising, he said to himself, that a girl, even a pretty one, should want to smile at someone looking exactly like Siegfried the Dragon-Slayer. And it was Siegfried's appearance, not his, that she had been smiling at, so really the smile was nothing to do with him. Besides, it was probably just a smile designed to sell cat-icons, in which it had succeeded admirably. He felt in his pocket for the oven-glove, but it didn't seem to be there any more. He must have dropped it. What a pity, never mind.

At the junction of Hammet Street and Magdalene Street, there was a health-food shop which had not been there yesterday. Of that Malcolm was absolutely certain, because he had parked his car beside the kerb on which the shop was now standing. He stood very still and frowned.

'Did I do that?' he said aloud. 'And if so, how?'

He knew the song about the girl who left trees and flowers lying about wherever she had gone; but trees and flowers are one thing, health-food shops are another. Either it had been built very, very quickly (after his recent experiences with builders at the Hall, Malcolm doubted this) or else it had appeared out of nowhere, or else he was hallucinating. He crossed the road and went in.

'Hello there,' said the bewilderingly pretty girl behind the counter. 'Can I help you?'

It was probably the dazzling smile that made Malcolm

realise what was going on. 'Hang on a moment, please,' he said, and walked out again. Next door was a furniture shop with a big plate-glass window. Fortunately, the street was deserted, and Malcolm was able to turn himself into the three Rhinedaughters without being observed. He found that he recognised two of them immediately. As an experiment, he smiled a Rhinedaughter smile at a chest of drawers in the shop window. It seemed to glow for a moment, and then its polyurethane finish was changed into a deep French polish shine.

'That explains it,' he said to himself, and did not allow himself to think that although that explained the smiles he had been getting, it did not explain the shops that had appeared from nowhere. Take care of the smiles, after all, and the shops will take care of themselves. He understood that the Rhinedaughters, the original owners of the gold from which the Ring was made, were after him, and their smiles were baits to draw him to his doom. Not that there weren't worse dooms, he reflected, but he had the world to consider.

Instead of walking away, however, he turned and went back into the health-food shop. Now that he knew that the smiles were only another aspect of this rather horrible game that Life was playing with him, and not genuine expressions of interest by pretty girls, he felt that he could deal with the situation, for he had a supreme advantage over the previous owners of the Nibelung's Ring. He had no vanity, no high opinion of himself which these creatures could use as the basis for their attack. All that remained was for him to deal with them before they did anything more troublesome than smiling.

'Hello again,' said Woglinde.

'Which one are you, then?' he replied, smiling back.

Woglinde looked at him for a moment, and then burst into tears, burying her face in her small pink hands. Instinctively, Malcolm was horrified; then he remembered Hagen, Alberich's son, whom the three Rhinedaughters had drowned in the flood, singing sweetly all the while.

'Thought so,' he said, trying to sound unpleasant (but he had lost the knack). 'So which one are you?'

'Woglinde,' sobbed the girl. 'And now you're all cross.'

The Rhinedaughter sniffed, looked up angrily, and smiled like a searchlight. A carnation appeared in Malcolm's buttonhole, but his resolve was unaffected.

'You can cut that out,' he said.

'Oh, well,' said Woglinde, and Malcolm could see no tears in her deep blue eyes. He could see many other things, but no tears, and the other things were rather hazardous, so he ignored them.

'Where did the shop come from?' he asked.

'Shan't tell you,' said Woglinde, coyly frowning. 'You're beastly and I hate you.'

'Girls don't talk like that any more,' said Malcolm. 'A thousand years ago perhaps, but not in the nineteen-eighties.'

'This girl does,' replied Woglinde. 'It's part of her charm. You've been looking for a nice old-fashioned girl all your life and now you've found one.'

Put like that, the proposition (accompanied by the brightest smile yet) was somewhat startling, and Malcolm turned away and looked at a display of organic pulses.

'You've been to a lot of trouble,' he said.

'I spent ages making it all nice for you,' said Woglinde.

'I don't like health food. Especially organic rice.'

'Oh, I'm *sorry*,' said Woglinde, petulantly. 'If I'd known, I'd have built you a chip-shop instead.' She checked herself;

she was letting her temper interfere with business. 'I still can, if you'd rather.'

'I wouldn't bother, if I were you,' said Malcolm. 'I expect you're sick of the sight of fish.'

'If you asked me to I would.'

'Forget it, please. I know what you want, and you can't have it.'

'Usually that's our line,' said the Rhinedaughter casually. Malcolm blushed. 'Oh go on,' she continued, 'it's our Ring, really.'

Perhaps the smiles had a cumulative effect. Malcolm suddenly felt a terrible urge to give her the Ring. He had already taken it off his finger before he knew what he was doing, and it was only when he caught sight of her face, like a kitten watching a beetle it intends to eat, that he felt the sense of danger. He thrust the Ring back on, so fiercely that he cut the skin between his fingers.

'I can't,' he said, sadly. 'I'd love to, but I can't. You wouldn't want it, really.'

Woglinde suddenly laughed, and Malcolm felt as if he was being smothered in gossamer, like a fly trapped by a spider. 'Don't be silly,' she cooed, 'I'd like it more than anything in the whole wide world. I think you're *mean.*'

Again there was a hideous temptation to give in, so strong that the Ring seemed to burn his skin. Malcolm could stand it no longer, and tried to command the Tarnhelm to take him away. But his mind could not issue the order; the smiles had got into it, as light gets into photographic film, and blurred all the edges. 'Stop that!' he shouted, and Woglinde winced as if he had slapped her. He tightened his hand round the Ring, and her face seemed to collapse. Suddenly, she was not pretty at all; she looked like a thousand-year-old teenager who wanted something she knew she couldn't have.

97

Then, just as suddenly, she was lovelier than ever, and Malcolm knew that she had given up.

'Sorry,' he said, 'but there it is.'

He turned and walked out of the shop, trying not to look back, but the urge was too strong. When he did look back, however, the shop was gone. He had won this bout, then; but was that all? It would probably be unwise to go swimming for a week or so . . .

After the fight, Malcolm needed a drink. He walked swiftly up Canon Street, heading for his favourite pub. But it wasn't there any more; instead, there was one of those very chic little wine-bars that come like shadows and so depart all over England. He had a horrible idea that he knew where this one had come from.

The wine-bar ('Le Cochonnet') was empty except for a quite unutterably pretty girl behind the bar, tenderly polishing a glass.

'You can put it all back exactly as it was,' said Malcolm, sternly.

The girl stared at him in amazement, and for a moment Malcolm wondered if he had made a mistake. But he looked at the girl again, and recognised the third Rhinedaughter. There couldn't be two girls like that in the world, unless he was very lucky.

'So which are you,' he said, 'Wellgunde or Flosshilde?'

'Flosshilde,' said the girl, carelessly. 'You've met the other two?'

'That's right.' He held up his right hand, letting the light play on the ring, 'And I'm not going to give it to you, either. It's not a toy, you know.'

Flosshilde studied the glass in her hand for a moment. 'All right,' she said. 'If you insist. Would you like a drink?'

★

Flosshilde had been rather proud of her wine-bar, and it was with great reluctance that she had agreed to change it back into the French Horn. But she did so with a smile.

'Won't the landlord and the customers be a bit disorientated?' Malcolm asked.

'Not really,' said Flosshilde. 'All I did was change them into chairs and tables, and they won't have felt anything. For some reason, when I smile at people and change them, they don't seem to mind.'

'I can understand that,' said Malcolm. 'Let me buy you a drink.'

'I'll have a Babycham,' said Flosshilde. 'No ice.'

When he returned with the drinks, Flosshilde leaned forward and whispered, 'Your Liz is over there in the corner with her boyfriend. The one you threw in the water.'

'So what?' said Malcolm coldly. 'She's not my Liz.'

'I could turn him into a frog for you, if you like,' whispered Flosshilde. 'Or I could smile at him without turning him into a frog. Your Liz wouldn't like that at all.'

'I'd rather you didn't,' said Malcolm. 'I'm not allowed to be malicious any more.'

'That sounds awful.' Flosshilde seemed genuinely sorry for him. 'Would it count if I did it?'

'Probably. But it's kind of you to offer.'

'Any time. I might just do it anyway. I don't like him, he's stuffy. I don't like stuffy people.'

'I'd better be careful, then,' said Malcolm. 'I've become very stuffy since . . .'

'That's not your fault,' said the Rhinedaughter.

'I shouldn't be doing this,' said Malcolm. 'Fraternising with the enemy.'

'I'm not really the enemy, am I?' Flosshilde smiled, but it wasn't a serious smile, just a movement of the lips intended to convey friendliness. Malcolm was intrigued.

'I mean, you're not going to give me the Ring, and why should you? That doesn't mean I hate you.'

'Doesn't it?'

'Course not.'

'Woglinde burst out crying.'

'She does that,' said Flosshilde. 'She's very bad-tempered. I'll tell her to leave you alone.'

'Would you?' Malcolm felt a strange sensation at the back of his head, a sort of numbness. He hadn't chatted like this to anyone for a long time.

'Are you staying in England long?' he asked, trying to sound uninterested.

Flosshilde grinned. 'If you like. It's the same for us, you know. We're all in the same boat. Of course, I've got the other two for company, but you know what it's like with sisters. They get on your nerves.'

'I know, I've got a sister.'

'Then we'll be company for each other,' Flosshilde said. 'I mean, we can go for drives in the country, or maybe take a boat up the river.'

Malcolm remembered Hagen, and said he didn't like boats.

'Won't your sisters mind?' he added nervously.

'Oh bother them,' said Flosshilde. 'Besides, I can tell them I'm working on you.'

'Will you be?'

'You'll have to wait and see,' said Flosshilde, carefully not smiling. 'Now, why don't you buy me lunch? I'm starving.'

Malcolm drove back to Combe Hall in a rather bewildered frame of mind, and nearly rammed a flock of sheep outside

Bagborough. Over lunch, Flosshilde hadn't mentioned the Ring once, except in passing (she knew some very funny stories about the Gods, especially Wotan) and seemed to be making no effort at all to lead him to his doom. That, of course, might simply mean that she was being subtle; but Malcolm had taken the precaution of reading her thoughts, and although he knew that one shouldn't believe everything you read in people's minds, he had been rather taken aback by what he had found. Of course, it was possible that she had deliberately planted those thoughts there for him to read, but somehow he didn't think so.

It seemed that Flosshilde had reconciled herself to the fact that the Ring wasn't going to be given to her, and she didn't really mind. Instead, she rather liked the Ring-Bearer. Nothing more than that, but never mind. Nor was it simply his assumed shape that she liked; she had seen that shape before when it had had the original Siegfried inside it, and besides, she didn't judge by appearances. That, it seemed, was not the way these curious other-worldly types went about things, for in the world they inhabited, so many people could change shape as easily as human beings changed clothes, and so you could never be sure whether a person was really handsome or simply smartly dressed. Flosshilde, however, thought that she and the Ring-Bearer might have something in common, and she wanted someone nice to talk to and go out with. There had been more than this, but Malcolm hadn't read it. He was saving it up, to read over lunch tomorrow . . .

'Well?' said Woglinde. 'And where have you been?'

'Having lunch,' said Flosshilde, 'at Carey's.'

'But you haven't got it?' said Wellgunde abruptly.

101

'True.' Flosshilde lay back on the bed of the Tone and blew bubbles. 'But who cares?'

Wellgunde stared at her sister, who closed her eyes and let out a rather exaggerated sigh. 'I think I'm in love,' said Flosshilde.

'Don't be ridiculous,' snapped Wellgunde. 'You can't be. You aren't allowed to be.'

'Oh, all right then, I'm not. But the next best thing. Or the next best thing to that. He's nice, in a quiet sort of way.'

'You should be ashamed of yourself,' said Woglinde, fiercely; but Wellgunde smiled, confusing a shoal of minnows who happened to get in the way. 'If it makes it easier for you to get the Ring,' she said softly, 'then you go ahead.'

'I'm not interested in the silly old Ring,' yawned Flosshilde. 'It's supremely unimportant.'

Wellgunde nodded. 'Of course. But it *would* be nicer to have it than not to have it, now wouldn't it?'

'I suppose so.'

'And there's no point in your liking him if he doesn't like you.'

Flosshilde made a vague grab at a passing roach, which scuttled away. 'I don't know. Is there?'

'And if he likes you, he'll be pleased to give you the Ring, now won't he?'

'I don't know and I don't care,' replied Flosshilde. 'We're just good friends.'

'You've only met him once,' said Woglinde. 'There's no need to get soppy.'

'There's every need to get soppy. I like being soppy. What's for dinner?'

'Trout with almonds,' said Wellgunde.

'Not fish *again*.'

Wellgunde perched on the edge of a broken wardrobe,

one of many that furnished the riverbed. 'Nobody says you shouldn't make friends,' she said gently. 'But what about us? We want our Ring back.'

'Once you've got it back, you can be friends with who you like,' said Woglinde, inspecting her toenails, 'though personally . . . They need doing again,' she added. 'There's something nasty in this river that dissolves coral pink.'

'Oh, be quiet, both of you,' said Flosshilde angrily. 'I'm sorry I told you now.'

There was silence at the bottom of the Tone for a while with both Flosshilde and Woglinde sulking. Finally Woglinde requested Wellgunde to ask her sister Flosshilde if she could borrow her coral pink nail varnish, and Flosshilde asked Wellgunde to tell her sister Woglinde that she couldn't.

'Be like that,' said Woglinde. 'See if I care.'

Flosshilde jumped up and floated to the surface.

'Now look what you've done,' hissed Wellgunde. 'You've offended her.'

'She isn't really in love, is she?' asked Woglinde nervously. 'That would be terrible.'

'I don't think so. She's just in one of her moods.'

'What'll we do?'

'Don't worry,' said Wellgunde calmly. 'Leave her to me.'

CHAPTER EIGHT

'Oh, for crying out loud,' said Wotan, putting down his fork with a bang, 'what do you want now?'

'Sorry,' panted Loge, breathless and sopping wet. 'I didn't realise you were still having breakfast.'

Wotan smiled wanly. 'Raining outside, is it?'

'Yes,' said Loge. 'Very heavily.'

'So what was so important it couldn't wait?'

'I think I'm on to something,' said Loge, sinking into a chair. The dining-room of Valhalla, the castle built by Fasolt and Fafner for the King of the Gods, was furnished in spartan but functional style. It had that air of grim and relentless spotlessness that is described as a woman's touch.

The Lord of Tempests looked at him suspiciously. 'If this turns out to be another wild goose chase,' he said, 'I'll turn you into a reservoir and stock you with rainbow trout.'

Loge shuddered. 'I'm sure there's something in this,' he managed to say. 'The ravens have sighted Alberich, and . . .'

'Aren't you going to offer your guest a cup of coffee?' Schwertleite the Valkyrie had come in with a crumb-brush and was ostentatiously brushing the table. 'I do wish you wouldn't bring work home with you.'

Wotan turned and glowered at his daughter, who took no notice. 'And ask him not to put his briefcase on the table.'

The Valkyrie swept out, and Wotan turned the full force of his glare on Loge. 'Now look what you've done,' he said. 'You've started her off.'

'But the ravens have seen Alberich and the Rhinedaughters, and they're in this village in England called . . .'

Schwertleite came back into the room with a bundle of newspapers in her arms. 'Ask your friend to sit on these,' she said sharply. 'I've just had those covers cleaned, although why I bother, I don't know.'

'Now you see what I have to put up with,' whispered Wotan. 'What's this about Alberich and the Rhinedaughters?'

Loge, perched uncomfortably on a pile of back numbers of *Die Zeit*, started to explain, but before he could get very far, the Valkyrie Grimgerde stalked into the room with a pot of coffee. She had resented making it and it would just be left to get cold, but she had made it all the same. 'I'm doing you some scrambled eggs,' she said accusingly to Loge.

'Please, don't bother.'

'I've started now,' replied Grimgerde impatiently.

Loge was about to say thank you, but the Valkyrie had gone back into the kitchen. Almost at once, Schwertleite reappeared, with her arms folded.

'There are footmarks all over the kitchen floor,' she said icily. 'Have you been tracking in and out?'

Before Wotan could reply, she too had gone. Wotan's daughters had a habit of asking leading questions and disappearing before anyone could answer them. They had been doing it for over a thousand years, but it was still profoundly irritating.

'. . . in a little village called Combe,' said Loge, 'which is in Somerset. Now why else . . . ?'

'What did you say?' Wotan hadn't been listening.

Loge took a deep breath, but could get no further. The Valkyrie Waltraute had come in with a plate of scrambled eggs. 'As if I didn't have enough to do,' she said, slamming the plate down. 'And mind the tablecloth.'

'Sorry,' said Loge.

'I wouldn't eat that if I were you,' Wotan muttered when she had gone. 'None of my daughters can cook, although God knows it doesn't stop them. I can cook but I'm not allowed in the kitchen.'

Desperately, Loge wondered what to do so as to offend neither the Thunderer nor his daughters. He picked some scrambled egg up on his fork, but did not put it in his mouth.

'I've been putting up with this for eleven centuries,' continued Wotan. 'Much more of it and I shall go quite mad.'

'The ravens,' said Loge for the fourth time, 'have found Alberich and the Rhinedaughters, hanging around in a little village in . . .'

'It all started when their mother left me,' continued Wotan, 'and was I glad to see the back of her. But my dear daughters, all nine of them, decided that I needed looking after. They didn't want to, of course. They all wanted to have careers and lives of their own. I wanted them to have careers and lives of their own, preferably in another hemisphere.'

As if to prove his point, the Valkyrie Waltraute came storming in. 'You've been eating the bread again, haven't you?' she said bitterly.

'That's what it's there for.'

'You've started a new loaf when there was half a loaf left in the breadbin. Now I suppose I'll have to throw it out for the ravens.'

'Half a loaf is better than no bread,' Wotan roared after her as she stalked out again. A futile gesture. The Father of Battles banged his fist on the table, upsetting a coffee cup. A deep brown patch appeared on the tablecloth and Wotan turned white.

'You did that,' he said to Loge. 'If they ask, you did that. I've got to live in this house.'

Loge, whose titles include the Father of Lies, was not too keen on this particular falsehood, but the alternative was probably metamorphosis into a disused canal. He nodded meekly.

'So we've all been stuck in this wretched great barn of a place, miles from anywhere, driving each other mad for a thousand years,' said the King of the Gods. 'They hate it as much as I do, but they'll never move.'

'At least there are only eight of them now,' said Loge. 'It must have been far worse when Brunnhilde was . . .'

Loge fell silent, terrified lest his lack of tact should arouse Wotan's anger. But Wotan only laughed. 'You must be joking,' he said. Imagine my delight when I'd finally managed to get one of them off my hands – and no question, Brunnhilde was the worst – and I thought that perhaps they'd all go away and at last I'd be allowed to wear my comfortable shoes in the dining-room. I fixed that miserable child up with Siegfried the Dragon-Slayer, the most marvellous man who ever lived. And look what she did to him.'

Loge nodded sympathetically; tact was all that stood between him and a future in fish-farming.

'Mind you,' said Wotan, 'he was lucky. Imagine what it

107

would have been like being married to her. Give me a spear in the small of the back any day.' The Lord of the Ravens shook his head sadly. 'They blame me, of course. They blame me for everything. The only people in the world who aren't entitled to.'

'About the Rhinedaughters,' suggested Loge.

'Ask them to do anything useful, of course, and you get bad temper all day long. No, my family is a great trial to me, and I am a great trial to my family. If I had my time over again . . .'

'The Hoover's broken,' said Waltraute, appearing in the doorway. 'I suppose I'll have to do the stairs with a dustpan and brush.'

'Yes, I suppose you will.' Wotan stood up, his one eye flashing. 'You'll enjoy doing that.'

He strode through the long corridors of Valhalla with Loge trotting at his heels like a terrified whippet, while all around him there came the calls of the Valkyries, informing him of further domestic disasters, until the vaulted ceiling that the Giants had built re-echoed with the sound.

'England, did you say?' whispered Wotan.

'Yes.'

'Oh, good,' said Wotan. 'Let's go there straight away.'

'Mind you,' said Wotan, 'I don't quite know how we're going to tackle this one.'

'Couldn't we just rush him?' Loge suggested. 'I'll hold his arms while you get the Ring off him.'

They stood and looked up at the electrically-operated gates of the Hall. A gardener in a smart new boiler suit walked up to them, holding a rake.

'You can't park there,' he said.

The long, sleek Mercedes limousine was blocking the

driveway. Wotan stared at the gardener, who took no notice.

'Move it, or I'll call the police,' said the gardener. 'I've told you once.'

'Certainly, right away,' muttered Loge. There was no point in causing unnecessary trouble. 'Sorry.'

'That's bad,' said Wotan, as they walked up from the village green, where they had parked the car. 'I tried closing up his lungs to make it hard for him to breathe, but it didn't work. We're too near the Ring-Bearer's seat of power to be able to achieve anything by force. I imagine that idiot was under his protection.'

Wotan stopped and studied the gates.

'There's no way through there by violence,' he said. 'We must be clever.'

For some reason or other, Loge had a horrible feeling that by We, Wotan meant him. 'What do you have in mind?' he asked.

'There are many things in the world that mortal men fear more than the Gods,' said Wotan, airily. 'I think it's about time that the Ring-Bearer was brought down to earth. He's a human being, not a God, and he's a citizen of a twentieth-century democracy.' Wotan chuckled. 'The poor bastard.'

Malcolm was feeling happier than he had for some considerable time. He had just had lunch with a remarkably pretty girl, he was going to have lunch with her tomorrow, and, best of all, his secretary had just told him that she was going to take her annual holiday in a week's time. She was, needless to say, going to the Cotswolds. Malcolm thought that they would probably make her an honorary member.

So, when the English Rose came knocking on his door at

109

four o'clock, he expected nothing worse than a recital of her holiday plans. He draped a smile over his face and asked her what he could do for her.

'There's a man downstairs,' she said, 'from the Government.'

Given what he had been doing since he acquired the Ring, it was understandable that Malcolm misunderstood this statement. He expected to find a humble messenger imploring him to take over the reins of State, or at least to accept a peerage. What he found was a sharp-faced individual in a dark grey suit with a briefcase.

'Herr Finger,' said the intruder, 'I'm from Customs and Excise. We're making inquiries about illicit gold dealing.'

For a moment, Malcolm forgot who he had become, and his blood froze. Like all respectable people, he knew that he was guilty of something, although what it was he could not say; and the arrival of a representative of the Main Cop only confirmed his suspicions.

'I don't know what you mean,' he stammered.

'About a month ago, a considerable sum of money in used currency notes was removed from the vaults of the Bank of England. Similar – withdrawals, shall we say? – were made from state banks all over the world. At the same time, large quantities of gold made an inexplicable appearance in the same vaults. Have you any comment, Herr Finger?'

Malcolm was too frightened to speak, and simply shook his head.

'On close examination, the gold was found to be part of a consignment supplied by a certain . . .' the man paused, as if choosing the right word '. . . a certain underground movement,' he continued, 'to a subversive organisation, based in this country but with international links. This

110

organisation has been secretly undermining the fabric of society for some time, Herr Finger.'

'Has it?' Malcolm's throat was dry.

'It most certainly has. And our investigations have led us to the conclusion . . .'

Malcolm, who for the last twenty-five years had done little in the evenings except watch the television, knew what was coming next. There was no point in running. Faceless men in lounge suits were probably aiming rifles at him at this very moment.

'. . . that you have some connection with this – this subversive ring.'

The word Ring exploded in Malcolm's mind like a bomb. He focused on the intruder's mind, and did not have to read very far.

'Now do you have any comment to make, Herr Finger? Or should I say Malcolm Fisher?'

Malcolm leaned back in his chair and smiled serenely.

'If only my mother could see me,' he said, and the serene smile became a grin. 'Chatting like this with a real God.'

'I beg your pardon? Mr Fisher, this is not a laughing matter.'

'You're Loge, aren't you? It's odd. I was frightened of you when I thought you were the taxman, but now you turn out to be a God, I'm not frightened at all.'

'Oh, well,' said Loge, 'I should have known better, I suppose. But Wotan thought it was worth a try.'

'It was,' said Malcolm. 'You had me worried, like I said. What were you going to do?'

'He'll murder me if I go back without it,' said Loge. 'He's got a horrid temper.'

'What can he do to you? You're immortal.'

'That's the trouble.' Loge was trembling. 'If you're

111

mortal, all they can do to you is kill you. But if you're going to live forever, they can really get you.'

'Surely not?'

'Don't you believe it. He'll turn me into an aquarium, I know he will.'

'I'll get the housekeeper to bring us some tea,' said Malcolm soothingly.

Loge calmed down slightly with some tea inside him, but the cup rattled in the saucer as he held it.

'I was meant to put the frighteners on you,' he said. 'First, I was to be a Customs man, then the VAT inspector, then the Fraud Squad, then MI5. If that didn't work, then I was to be the man from the IPU.'

'What's the IPU?'

'Inexplicable Phenomena Unit. Wotan was sure you'd believe in it. It would be something like all those science fiction films about flying saucers invading the earth, and there's always a secret Government agency that knows all about them but keeps them secret so as not to alarm people. They're the ones who come and zap the Martians in the last reel. And I was going to be them, threatening to zap you. Sometimes I think he lives in a world of his own.'

'He must be a difficult person to work for,' said Malcolm.

'Difficult!' Loge cast his eyes up to the ceiling. 'He's impossible.'

'But I thought you were the clever one,' said Malcolm.

'I used to be, back in the old days when life was much simpler. But progress has left me behind, I'm afraid, and Wotan has got more devious. And he's never forgiven me for the mistake I made in drawing up the contract for Valhalla.'

'Mistake?'

Loge nodded glumly. 'Oh, yes, it was a mistake all right, and I've never been allowed to forget it. A slip of the pen and now look at me.'

'What sort of a mistake?' asked Malcolm, purely from curiosity.

Loge sighed. 'I might as well tell you. You'll find out sooner or later. The contract with the Giants was that they built us the castle in return for trading concessions in Middle Earth, and the German for "free port" is *freihafen*. But the trouble was,' Loge said, and even after a thousand years he blushed, 'well, my handwriting has never been marvellous, and what I'd written looked more like *Freia zu haben*, which would mean that they would have the Goddess Freia as their reward for that bloody castle. I don't know what you're laughing at. It was a mistake anyone could have made.'

Malcolm, despite his ill-concealed mirth, could sympathise, for his own handwriting was none too good. 'But couldn't you explain the mistake?' he said.

'I did, God knows. But they wouldn't listen, and Wotan had just had a quarrel with Freia and was only too glad to get rid of her. He's always quarrelling with his relatives.'

Again, Malcolm could sympathise. 'Well,' he said, 'at least it explains how that bargain came to be made. I couldn't understand it, the way it is in the books.'

'Now you know.' Loge was depressed again. 'It was only because I suggested this Ring business that he didn't change me into something wet and nasty there and then. And that backfired too – well, you know all about that – and I've been one jump away from metamorphosis ever since.'

Malcolm felt a curious sense of authority, and his tone to Loge was pleasantly patronising. 'Don't worry,' he said, 'I won't let him turn you into anything.'

'And how exactly will you stop him?'

'I don't know,' Malcolm confessed. 'But he can't go throwing his weight about like that any more. He'll just have to face facts, he's had his time.'

Loge raised an eyebrow. 'Don't take this the wrong way,' he said, 'but for someone who was terrified of the Customs inspector a few minutes ago, you're remarkably confident.'

'I know. But that was real life. This is . . . well, it's real life too, but different somehow.' Malcolm was silent for a while, as he tried to work something out in his mind. 'You know how some people are good at some things and bad at others,' he said. 'For instance, some people are marvellous at business or the Stock Exchange or whatever, but they can't change a plug or iron a shirt. Maybe I'm like that. Maybe I'm hopeless at everything except being the master of the Ring, but I'm very good at that. I know how to do it, more or less, and only I can do it, and I'm happy doing it.'

'Are you?'

'Well, no. But I'm no more miserable doing it than doing anything else, plus I can do it well, and I can't do anything else. It's like some people are naturally good singers or snooker players or they can compose music, and they've never tried it so they don't know. And then they do try it, just by accident or for fun, never expecting they'll be any good at it, and there they are. I don't know,' he said despairingly, 'maybe I'm imagining it. Maybe it's so easy any fool can do it. But I'm not afraid any more – not of your lot, anyway.'

Loge stared at him in amazement. 'You've been drinking,' he said at last.

Malcolm shook his head. 'No, I mean it. I may be no good at all at real life, but this sort of thing – you can tell your boss to do his worst and see if I care. I've already seen off Alberich and the Rhinedaughters, and I'll deal with him too, if he makes a nuisance of himself. I mean, what can he do to me? I can understand all languages and read people's thoughts, so I'll always know what's really going on. I can change my shape, so anything he tries to attack me with I can either beat or run away from. And I don't think that's all, either. I don't think he's got any power against the Ring. If he wants to do something and I won't let him, then he can't do it. Stands to reason.'

'How's that?'

'Simple. Unless I do something wrong or think nasty thoughts, nothing unpleasant can happen in the world. So nothing unpleasant can happen to *me*, can it? I'm just as much a citizen of the world as anyone else, so I'm under my own protection.' Malcolm was quite carried away by this train of thought. 'What's that bit in the Bible about He saved others, He couldn't save Himself? You won't catch me falling for that one. And that's why I met that girl,' he went on, more to himself than to Loge. 'Nice things are happening to everyone else, so they're happening to me too.' He laughed for pure joy, and Loge tapped the side of his head.

'You're as bad as he is,' he said. 'Don't say I didn't warn you.'

'Don't worry about a thing,' said Malcolm, grandly. 'Everything will be fine, you'll see.'

Loge rose to his feet. 'I hope you're right,' he said. 'If not, come and feed the ducks on me on Sunday afternoons.'

Wotan leaned back in the driver's seat of the Mercedes, turning over Loge's story in his cavernous mind.

'He's right, up to a point,' said the King of the Gods. 'Like I thought, force and violence are no good, and besides, I'm not sure how far I could take them. I still

115

don't think I could actually take the Ring from him against his will without getting into serious trouble.'

'Who with?'

'Me, in my role as the God of Justice. If I did take it and I found that I wasn't allowed to, I would have to cease to exist. Damn.'

The Sky-God thought hard for a moment, then smiled. He had thought of something. Loge waited impatiently to hear what it was.

'It worked before,' said Wotan quietly. 'So why shouldn't it work again?'

Loge was mystified. 'What?' he asked.

'The Brunnhilde option,' said Wotan. 'Why not?'

'But it didn't work the first time,' Loge said. 'It failed miserably.'

'Because of the Hagen factor and the Siegfried aspect. And, if we're going to be honest about it, the Brunnhilde aspect, too. But now we're dealing with a different kettle of fish.'

The metaphor made Loge squirm. 'It's a terrible gamble,' he said. 'Don't blame me if . . .'

'As if I would. No, I think I've cracked it. He's just the sort of idiot who'd fall for it.'

'That's true.' Loge began to feel cautiously optimistic. 'Why shouldn't he be his own worst enemy, just like everyone else?'

Malcolm watched the black limousine driving away, and poured himself a small whisky. He was rather worried about what he had said; it was the first time he had ever talked to a God, and perhaps he should have shown more respect. He strolled into the garden, and a blackbird fluttered down and perched in a rose bush beside him.

116

'Have you seen a white moth with pale blue spots on its wings?' asked the bird.

'No,' replied Malcolm, 'but I've got some peanuts if you're hungry.'

'You can have enough of peanuts,' said the bird. 'Anyway, I wanted that particular moth. We've got people coming round for dinner tomorrow.'

'Good hunting, then,' said Malcolm. 'Try round by the buddleias.'

The bird cocked its head on one side. 'Thanks,' it said. 'Good idea. Oh, and by the way.'

'Yes?'

'Don't underestimate Wotan, whatever you do. There are more ways of killing a cat, you know.'

'What do you mean?'

The bird fluttered its wings. 'Don't ask me, I'm only a bird. Besides, it's my favourite proverb.'

'Hope you find your moth,' said Malcolm.

'So do I,' said the blackbird. 'Good night.'

CHAPTER NINE

Flosshilde was always beautifully dressed. She had been following fashion since the dawn of time, and her wardrobe occupied the space on the bed of the Rhine between Andernach and Koblenz. Not only did she follow fashion, she led it; she had been wearing figure-of-eight brooches when the Iron Age was still in its infancy, and it was her pioneering work that had given the ladies of sixteenth-century Europe the surcingle. In comparison, she thought, the twentieth century was drab, to say the least. Nevertheless, she had looked out a rather clever lemon-coloured pullover and a pair of black and white striped trousers which had, oddly enough, been in vogue at the height of the Hallstadt Culture. If you keep things long enough, she had learnt by experience, they eventually come back into fashion.

To add the finishing touches, she decorated her ears with Snoopy earrings and slipped over her slim wrist a bracelet of amber which had been given to her by the first King of the Langobards and which looked reasonably like tortoiseshell plastic. She would, she concluded, do.

'Sorry I'm late,' she said, as she sat down beside Malcolm in Carey's.

'You're not,' he replied. 'You're exactly on time.'

'Am I?' Flosshilde looked most surprised. She had always made a habit of being at least five minutes late for everything, especially dates and assignations. If she had subconsciously decided to be punctual, there was cause for concern . . .

'I had a visit from Loge yesterday,' Malcolm said.

'Loge?' Flosshilde's blue eyes opened wide. 'What happened?'

'He tried to frighten me, but I soon got rid of him,' Malcolm replied smugly. 'He's not too bad when you get to know him.'

Flosshilde was going to say something about this, but she somehow decided against it. Instead, she smiled.

'I know a funny story about him,' she said.

'Is it the one about the Valhalla contract?'

'Yes,' said Flosshilde, slightly annoyed.

'Tell me anyway,' Malcolm said and, to her surprise, Flosshilde found that she wasn't annoyed any more. She told him the story, and he laughed.

'You tell it better than he does,' he said.

'Of course I do,' said Flosshilde. 'I'm very good at telling stories. Have you heard the one about Hagen and the Steer-Horn?'

The name Hagen made Malcolm feel uncomfortable, and he wondered why she had mentioned it. Perhaps it was a sort of warning. Instinctively, he covered his right hand with his left, so as to hide the Ring.

'Go on,' he said nervously.

As she told the story (which was very funny), Malcolm found himself looking at her rather carefully. He had done this before, of course, for she was well worth looking at, and once Malcolm had accepted that there was a future in looking at her it had become one of his favourite occupations.

119

But he was looking for something else now. She was, after all, one of Them, and he would do well not to forget that. To reassure himself, he flicked through her subconscious mind and was delighted to find that there had been developments. It irritated him that he could not read his own inner thoughts, but he had a fair idea of what they were, on this subject at least. In his life to date, he had met very few girls, and most of those had been friends of his sister Bridget. As a result, he had tended to fall in love with all the rest, just to be on the safe side. Since there had been no risk of the love being returned, this was strictly his own business and nothing to do with anyone else. Only since he had met Flosshilde had he become aware that this was a rather foolish thing to do, and he had been relieved to find that the Rhinedaughter had not inspired the usual romantic daze in him that he knew so well. Instead, once he had got over the shock of seeing what was in her mind and wondering if she could really mean him and not some other Malcolm Fisher, he had carefully considered whether or not he liked her. He did, of course, but that was because she was nice, not just simply because she was there.

Tentatively, he lifted his left hand and used it to pick up his fork. The Ring was visible again, but she did not even look at it. Suddenly, a terrible thought struck Malcolm. Bearing in mind the conclusions he had just come to, what was he supposed to do next?

Flosshilde had seemed rather put out when he had told her that he would be busy for the rest of the day, but the statement had been partially true. There had been a letter from a certain L. Walker, of Lime Place, Bristol, that morning, and it seemed that L. Walker was coming to Combe Hall to catalogue the library.

The library, which was huge and contained no funny books, had come with the Hall when Malcolm bought it, and he had left it alone. Books, the estate agent had told him, provide excellent insulation, and since the heating bills would be very considerable in any event, he might as well leave them there even if he had no intention of ever reading them. Ever since he had moved in, however, the English Rose had been nagging him to have the library professionally catalogued, so that Malcolm would be able to know at a glance what he was missing. He had strenuously resisted these attempts, but he supposed that his secretary had booked L. Walker before she left for her holiday and deliberately not told him.

He drove back to Combe and went into the house. The housekeeper had been lying in wait for him, and he was tempted to make himself invisible before she could persuade him to buy a new vacuum cleaner – she had been demanding one for weeks, although Malcolm knew perfectly well there were at least four in the house already. Perhaps she was starting a collection. But lately he had felt guilty about avoiding people who were, after all, his employees and only doing their jobs, so he stood his ground, like Leonidas at Thermopylae.

'There's someone to see you,' said the housekeeper.

'Who is it?'

'About the library,' she said. 'From Bristol.'

She made it sound as if Bristol was somewhere between Saturn and Pluto. But to Malcolm, who had been dealing with strangers from Valhalla and Nibelheim for what seemed like years now, Bristol sounded delightfully homely.

'That'll be L. Walker,' he said. 'Where did you put her?'

The housekeeper said the lady was in the drawing-room,

and Malcolm had walked away before he thought to ask which one. Eventually, he found the stranger in the Blue drawing-room.

L. Walker was about five feet four, roughly twenty-three years old, with long, dark hair and the face of an angel. Malcolm, who knew exactly what an angel looks like, having turned himself into one during an idle moment, felt a very curious sensation, almost like not being able to breathe properly.

'Herr Finger?' said the girl. 'I'm Linda Walker. I've come to catalogue the library. Ms Weinburger . . .'

'Yes, of course.' Malcolm did not want to hear about the English Rose. He wanted to know why his knees had gone weak, as if he had just been running. There was a long silence while Malcolm tried to regain the use of his mind.

'Could I see the library, perhaps?' said the girl.

'Yes,' Malcolm replied. 'It's through here somewhere.'

He found it eventually, which was good work on his part considering that he had just been struck by lightning or something remarkably similar. He opened the door and pointed at the rows of books.

'That's it in there,' he said.

'Well,' said the girl, 'I think I'll start work now, if you don't mind. The sooner I start, the sooner I'll be out from under your feet.'

'There's no rush, honestly,' said Malcolm quickly. 'Please take as long as you like.'

The girl looked at him and smiled. Malcolm had come to believe that he was fairly well equipped to deal with smiles, but this was a new sort; not a happy, optimistic smile but a sad, wistful smile. It didn't say, 'Wouldn't it be nice if . . .' like the stock delivery of a Rhinemaiden, but, 'It would have been nice if . . .' which is quite different.

'Thank you,' said the girl, 'but I'd better get on.'

Malcolm began to feel that something he wanted was slipping through his fingers. 'Where are you staying?' he asked.

'At the George and Dragon,' said the girl. 'I hope that's all right. Ms Weinburger booked me in there.'

'You could stay here, if you like. There's masses of room.' As soon as he spoke the words, Malcolm wished he hadn't. There was something about this girl that made him feel like a predator, even though such thoughts had not crossed the threshold of his mind. The girl looked at him for about three-quarters of a second (although it seemed much longer). Then she smiled again, an 'It's hopeless and we both know that, but . . .' sort of a smile.

'I'd like that very much,' she said. 'If you're sure it'd be all right.'

As far as Malcolm was concerned, it could go in the Oxford Dictionary as a definition of all right. 'I'll get the housekeeper to get a room ready,' he said. 'How long will it take you, do you think?'

'About a week,' said the girl, 'if I start today.'

'But aren't you very tired, after your journey? How did you get here, by the way?'

'I got the train to Taunton and the bus to Combe,' said the girl.

Malcolm was shocked to think of a girl like this having to travel by bus and train. He wanted to offer to buy her a car, but she would probably take it the wrong way.

'Did that take long?' A stupid question, and none of his business. Why should he care how long it took? Oddly enough, the girl didn't say that. Instead, she answered the question.

'Oh, about three hours. I missed the connection at Taunton, I'm afraid.'

Try as he might, Malcolm could think of no way of prolonging the conversation. He had no idea what he should say or do next, which was a pity, since he could imagine nothing in the world more important.

'Well,' he said, 'I'd better let you get on, then. See you later.'

He left the library and walked slowly back to the drawing-room, bumping into several pieces of furniture on the way. This was awful, and he could see that plainly enough. Real life had caught up with him at last; not in the form of a Customs man or the Inexplicable Phenomena Unit, which he could probably have dealt with, but the juvenile delinquent with the golden arrows who had been making a dartboard of his heart since his voice had broken. This was no Rhinedaughter out of the world of his own in which he had been living and where he was master, but a fellow human being, a person, a potential source of great unhappiness.

'Oh God,' he moaned. 'Not again.'

He sat down on the stairs and looked across at the library door. If he went away, he might miss her coming out, and that would never do. Then it occurred to him that he could make himself invisible and go and watch her cataloguing books, which must surely be the most wonderful sight in the world. He closed his eyes and was lost to sight.

Beside the unsalubrious waters of the Tone, Flosshilde stood and watched a seagull trying unsuccessfully to catch and eat an abandoned tyre. She knew how it felt, in a way, and out of pure sympathy she smiled at the tyre, which turned itself helpfully into a fish. The seagull, who had known all along that persistence overcomes all obstacles, devoured it thankfully, which was hard luck on the fish but nice for the seagull. You can't please everybody all the time, Flosshilde reflected, and the relevance of this observation to her own case made her thoughtful.

Not that she had any logical reason to be anything but happy; but in matters of happiness, logic plays but a small part. First, it was annoying that Malcolm had preferred to spend the day with a stuffy old librarian than a gorgeous Rhinedaughter. Second, it was annoying that she should be annoyed. In fact, it was the latter irritation that was the worse, or so she hoped. The first unpleasant thing was merely a matter of her vanity (she told herself). The second unpleasant thing might have serious consequences for her career. An enamoured Rhinedaughter, like a blind chauffeur, is unlikely to progress far in her chosen profession. Try as she might, however, she was unable to feel greatly concerned about the prospect, and that was worse still . . .

'Bother,' she said.

Wellgunde, who had been circling slowly under the surface, jumped up onto the bank. 'Get you,' she said. 'All dressed up and nowhere to go.'

Flosshilde put her tongue out, but Wellgunde ignored her. 'I thought you'd have been out with your friend,' she said, shaking the water out of her hair.

'Well, I'm not,' replied Flosshilde.

'Playing hard to get, are you?'

At that particular moment, Flosshilde would have liked to be able to turn her sister into a narrowboat. 'Haven't you got anything better to do?' she said wearily.

'I'm keeping you company,' replied Wellgunde. 'You look as though you could do with cheering up.'

'I'm perfectly cheerful, thank you,' said Flosshilde coldly.

'It must be wonderful to be in love,' cooed Wellgunde. 'I'm terribly jealous.'

'I'm not in any such thing,' snapped her sister. 'But I can understand you being jealous.'

Wellgunde took out a mirror and examined herself lovingly. 'You're only young once, I suppose,' she said. 'You go ahead and enjoy yourself. Don't you worry about us.'

Flosshilde frowned. Sisters can be very annoying at times.

'Don't let it worry you that if you go off with this Ring-Bearer of yours, we'll never get our Ring back ever. Don't let it cross your mind that the Ring is all we've got, since we haven't got dashing boyfriends who have to disguise themselves as other people if they ever want to get anywhere.'

'Don't worry, I won't.'

'We're your sisters, after all. We don't want to stand in your way for a second. And if you think it's worth it, you go ahead. Well, since you're not going to be busy this afternoon, you might put a duster round the riverbed. It was your turn yesterday, but you were out.'

'Oh, go away,' said Flosshilde rudely.

'I'm going,' said Wellgunde placidly. 'I only popped up to tell you that while you've been moping about, we've been working.'

'I thought you said you were going to leave him alone.'

'We haven't been persecuting your precious darling, if that's what you mean. We've been chatting with Thought and Memory.'

'How fascinating.'

'Yes, it was rather. Apparently, they've been watching Combe Hall all day, and your friend was having ever such a long chat with an extremely nice-looking girl.'

Any doubts Flosshilde might have had about her feelings for Malcolm were dispelled by this news. She went as white as a sheet.

'Of course, they can't read his thoughts because he's the Ring-Bearer, so they can't be sure, but to listen to those two you don't have to be able to read thoughts to see what your friend thinks of his new friend. Written all over his silly face, they said.'

'That's nice for him,' Flosshilde said, very quietly.

'Well,' said Wellgunde, 'it's not so nice for us, is it? What if he gives her the Ring? Where would we all be then?'

Flosshilde said something extremely disrespectful about the Ring and dived into the Tone, leaving Wellgunde looking very pleased with herself. Perhaps, mused the eldest of the Rhinedaughters, she hadn't told her sister the whole truth, but then, she had gone off in a huff without giving her a chance. Her conscience was clear . . .

After spending the whole afternoon lugging heavy books about, Malcolm imagined, she would be sure to want a rest and possibly a drink. He wished he could have helped her, but that would have looked pointed, since one does not buy a dog and bark oneself. Besides, if he had materialised out of thin air and said 'Can I carry that for you?' she would probably have had a fit; another of the problems associated with dealing with a real person.

She was certainly conscientious, and Malcolm admired that, but she had carried on with her work for a very long time. When finally she seemed to be about to call it a day, Malcolm transported himself back to the stairs and wondered what on earth he was to do next. It seemed like hours before the library door opened, and still he hadn't thought of anything. He stood up quickly, and tried to look as if he was just passing.

'Finished for the day?' he asked.

'Yes, thanks,' she said, and smiled again. This smile, a

sort of 'If only . . . but no' smile, wiped Malcolm's mind clean of thoughts and words, and he stood gawping at her as if she was the one who had suddenly appeared out of thin air.

'Are you sure it's no trouble for me to stay here?' she said.

'No, of course not. I told the housekeeper to phone the George and Dragon.'

'Thank you, then,' she said.

'I took your suitcase up to your room,' he went on, as if this act had been comparable to saving her from drowning. 'And I've told the cook you'll be having dinner . . . If that's all right, I mean.'

That was not how he had meant to suggest that she should have dinner with him. He had wanted to suggest it casually. He had wanted many things in his life, and got very few of them. But the girl did not seem to mind. She said, 'Are you sure that's all right?' and Malcolm felt a tiny flicker of impatience within his raging heart, but it passed very quickly.

'It must be nice having a cook,' she said.

Malcolm felt the need to defend himself against a charge of hedonism. 'I'm afraid I'm a dreadful cook,' he said. 'And she sort of came with the place.'

The girl said nothing, and Malcolm forced some more words into his mouth, grabbing the first ones that came to hand.

'You know how it is,' he burbled, 'these great big houses.'

Utter drivel of course, but she seemed not to notice. 'Yes,' she said, 'we used to live in a huge old house. It was dreadfully difficult to keep it clean and warm.'

She seemed unwilling to expand on this point, and they

walked on in silence. Malcolm had no idea where they were going, but that did not seem to matter very much.

'Was it as big as this? Your house, I mean.' Any more of this, Malcolm thought, and I shall bite my tongue off.

'Yes,' said the girl. 'It kept me and my sisters very busy.'

'You've got sisters, then?' he went on, as if that were the most remarkable thing that he had ever heard.

'Eight,' said the girl. 'It's a large family. Are you *sure* it's all right me staying to dinner? I mean, you haven't got people coming or anything?'

'No,' Malcolm said, 'really. Shall we go and sit in the drawing-room?'

The girl was silent, as if thinking this over very carefully. 'Yes,' she said at last.

It was at this point that it occurred to Malcolm that he hadn't read her thoughts, to see if by any chance they resembled his, no matter how remotely. But he found that he didn't want to. It seemed somehow indecent, for she was not a God or a Rhinedaughter, but a human being. Besides, if she wasn't thinking along the same lines as he was, he really didn't want to know.

'You speak English very well,' she said, as Malcolm eventually found the drawing-room.

'Thank you,' Malcolm said, deeply touched, and only just managed to stop himself from returning the compliment. 'I went to school in England,' he said, truthfully. 'Can I get you a drink?'

'No, thank you,' said the girl, looking down at her feet.

'Are you sure?'

'Well, if you're sure . . .'

Malcolm was sure, but he felt it would be superfluous to say so. 'What can I get you?' he asked.

'A small sherry, please.'

Malcolm poured out a small sherry – very small, as it turned out, for he did not want her to think he was trying to get her drunk. 'Is that enough?' he asked.

'That's fine.' Another smile, this time a 'We can't go on like this, you know' smile.

'So how long have you been cataloguing?'

'About two years,' said the girl. That seemed to put the seal on that particular subject.

'I suppose it's like being a librarian,' Malcolm went on, and he reckoned that digging peat was probably easier work than making conversation under these circumstances. The girl agreed that it was very like being a librarian.

'How long have you lived here?' she asked, and Malcolm found that he could not remember. He had to think hard before he replied. Afterwards, there was a long silence, during which the girl drank a quarter of her small sherry. The temptation to read her thoughts was very strong, but Malcolm resisted it. It wouldn't be fair.

'So how do you set about cataloguing a library?' he asked. The girl told him, and that took up at least three minutes, during which time Malcolm was able to collect what remained of his thoughts. Summoning up all his powers of imagination, he compiled a list of questions and topics which might, with a great deal of luck, get them through dinner.

In the event, they nearly did, although Malcolm had to use a great deal of ingenuity. Why did he find it so easy to talk to Flosshilde, who was only a friend, and so difficult to keep a conversation going with the most wonderful person in the world? There was only one topic that he couldn't mention; on the other hand, it was the one topic he did want to discuss with her. Instead, they mostly seemed to talk about libraries, a subject that Malcolm had never given much consideration to in the past. At about half-past nine, even this theme collapsed into silence, and Malcolm resigned himself to yet another disappointment. The girl was obviously nervous and ill at ease; scarcely to be wondered at. She had come here to do a straightforward job of work, the job she had trained to do and at which she was no doubt highly competent, and instead of being allowed to go to a comfortable hotel where she could take her shoes off and read a good book, she had been compelled to listen to his inane ramblings. She must think he was mad. Certainly, she wouldn't be there in the morning. At first light, she would unlock her door and make a run for it, or climb out of the window down a rope of sheets. It was all unbearably sad, and as a human being he was a complete and utter failure. He had made the mistake of treating a normal, grown-up woman from the twentieth century as if she was something out of a romantic story, and he deserved all the heartbreak he was undoubtedly going to get.

'I expect you're very tired,' he said abruptly, 'after the journey and a hard day's work. I'll show you to your room.'

They tracked up the stairs in silence. It was still light outside, but she could read a book or something until it was time to go to sleep. At least he wasn't sending her to bed without any supper.

'Good night, then,' she said, and she smiled at him for the last time that day. It was a smile you could take a photograph by, and it said, 'I like you very much and it's a pity you think I'm so boring, but there we go.' The door closed in front of the embers of it, and Malcolm stood in the hall opening and shutting his eyes. To hell with being fair. He located her thoughts and read them. Then he read them again, just to be sure. Then he read them again, because he liked them so much.

131

'Well I'm damned,' he said slowly to himself. 'Well I never.'

Then he went to bed.

The two ravens floated down and perched on the roof of the Mercedes. Wotan put his head out of the window and said 'Well?'

'They've gone to bed,' said Thought.

'Separately,' said Memory.

'But not to worry,' said Thought. 'She's doing all right.'

Wotan frowned. 'But he can read her thoughts,' said Wotan. 'He'll just look into her mind and then it'll be all over. He'll chuck her out so fast she'll bounce all the way down the drive.'

Memory chuckled. 'I wouldn't worry on that score,' he croaked. 'He's dead meat. Head over heels.'

'And even if he does,' said his partner, 'he'll only make things worse for himself. I had a quick look myself.'

'Oh.' Wotan was baffled. 'You can't mean she fancies him?'

'Something rotten,' said Thought. 'You wouldn't read about it.'

'Oh, that's *marvellous*,' Wotan said, disgusted. 'Now I'll never get the perishing thing back.'

'Relax,' said Memory. 'You know her. Duty must come first, even if it means betraying the man she truly loves.'

'Especially if it means betraying the man she loves,' said Thought. 'She's a real chip off the old block, that girl.'

Wotan was forced to agree. Of all his eight surviving daughters, the Valkyrie Ortlinde most resembled her father in her capacity for self-torture. She would revel in it. Most of all, she would enjoy blaming him afterwards.

'We've cracked it,' said Wotan.

CHAPTER TEN

Alberich loathed travelling by air. This was partly the natural prejudice of one who had lived most of his life underground, partly because the food that they serve you on little plastic trays with hollow mouldings to hold the ketchup gave him violent indigestion. But he was a businessman, and businessmen have to travel on aircraft. Since there seemed to be no prospect of progress in his quest for the Ring, he had thought it would be as well if he went back to Germany for a week to see what sort of a mess his partners were making of his mining consultancy. He had no interest in the work itself, but it provided his bread and butter; if it did not exactly keep the wolf from the door, it had enabled him to have a wolf-flap fitted so that the beast could come in and out without disturbing people.

As luck would have it, he had been given a seat by the window, and he looked aimlessly out over the world that by rights should have been his. If he had had any say in its running, there would have been fewer cities and more forests. He let his attention wander for a moment.

Something was tapping on the window. He looked round, and saw a slightly bedraggled raven pecking at the thick Perspex with its beak. A second raven was beating the air furiously with its wings, trying to hover and fly at the speed of sound at the same time.

'What do you want?' he mouthed through the window.

The raven pecked away vigorously, and Alberich felt slightly nervous. If the stupid bird contrived to break the window, he would be sucked out into space. 'Go away,' he mouthed, and made shooing gestures with his fingers.

'Forget it,' Memory shrieked through the rushing wind. 'He can't hear a word you're saying.'

But Thought was nothing if not persistent. With his beak, he pecked a series of little marks onto the Perspex. When he was finished, Alberich was able to make out the words, 'Wotan says stay out of England,' written back to front on the pane. He nodded to the ravens to acknowledge the message, and they wheeled away exhausted. Alberich pondered this warning for a moment, then looked at his watch. They were due to land in Frankfurt in half an hour.

At Frankfurt Airport, he telephoned his partner.

'Dietrich?' he said. 'It's Hans. Look, I'm at Frankfurt now, but I've got to go back to England right away. There's a flight in three hours. Can you bring me some clean shirts and the papers on the Nigerian project?'

'What have you got to go back for?'

'What's that? Oh, would you believe I left my briefcase behind? With all the things I need for the Trade Fair?'

'Can't they send it on?'

'It'd take too long. I'm going back.'

'Fancy forgetting your briefcase.'

'I'm only human,' Alberich lied. 'Don't forget the shirts.'

To his surprise, Malcolm had managed to get some sleep, but he was awake by six. He went through the events of the previous day in his mind, trying to reassure himself that it had all happened. Something inside him told him that this strange happiness was bound to end in tears, but he put that down to his natural pessimism. Besides, there was one sure way of knowing whether things were all right or not.

He tuned his mind in to the early morning news and was reassured. No disasters had afflicted the world during the last day, although there had been one strange occurrence. A farmer from the small village of Combe in Somerset had been out shooting rabbits at a quarter to ten last night, and had seen his ten-acre field of wheat change before his eyes into ten acres of roses, peonies, narcissi, daffodils and tulips. The farmer, a Mr William Ayres of Combe Hill Farm, attributed this extraordinary mutation to a leak from the nearby Hinckley Point nuclear power station, although no such leak had as yet been confirmed by the CEGB . . .

Malcolm blinked, and for a moment was concerned. But Mr Ayres was bound to be insured, and even if he wasn't, he could pick the flowers and use them to decorate the church for his daughter's wedding. Malcolm laughed. He bore the Ayres family, both its present and prospective members, no ill will at all, and that was surely a good thing for the world.

It occurred to him that he had forgotten to tell the girl when breakfast would be ready. He jumped out of bed, thought up a light blue shirt and a pair of cream corduroy trousers, and transported himself across the house. As he passed the library, he heard cataloguing noises. Although it was only half-past six, the girl was working already. He listened carefully for her thoughts, and a tender smile hitched up the ends of his mouth. She was throwing herself into her work to take her mind off the sad feelings of longing in her heart. A soppy girl, Malcolm could not help thinking, but none the worse for that. He opened the library door and went in.

'You're up early,' he said.

'I hope I didn't disturb you,' said the girl anxiously.

'Not at all,' Malcolm replied. 'I'm usually awake by this time. Would you like some breakfast?'

After the inevitable 'If you're sure' ritual, she agreed to have a cup of coffee and a slice of toast, and Malcolm hurried down to the kitchen. The coffee machine seemed to take for ever, as did the toaster, but eventually he got what he wanted out of both of them and carried the tray up to the library. In his mind he tried to rehearse some way of bringing the conversation round to the issues he wanted to raise, but he had to give up the attempt. He would think of something when the time came, and he did not want to rush something as important as this, even if the result was a foregone conclusion.

Let other pens dwell on joy and happiness. It is enough to record that Malcolm hijacked a discussion on card-indexes and used it to convey his message. Although he could read the girl's thoughts and so avoid all misunderstandings, he still found it heavy going, and heard himself using words and phrases that would have seemed excessively sentimental in *True Love* magazine; but everyone has a right to make fools of themselves once in their lives. The main thing was that everything was going to be all right now, and he had managed to persuade her of this. She had seemed rather diffident at first, but he had got so used to her saying, 'Are you sure you don't mind?' and, 'If you're sure it's no trouble,' that he took no notice of her words and simply watched her thoughts going round, like the figures on a petrol pump. When the appropriate reading came up, he took her hand and squeezed it gently. Through the

136

snowstorm of emotions that raged around him, he heard a tinkling sound, like a coin dropping on the floor. Suddenly this seemed very important, and he looked down. On the polished wooden floor he saw the Ring, which had somehow slipped off his finger. He felt a sudden urge to give it to her; for what better gift could there be than the whole world? She was still holding his hand, tightly and trustingly, so that it would be incredibly churlish of him to do anything except sit absolutely still and be loved. There was also a particularly fine smile going on, and he let the Ring lie there until it was over. Just to be sure, however, he covered the Ring with his foot. Everything that needed saying had now been said, and it was obviously the time for action: a kiss, or something of that sort. But Malcolm could not bring himself to initiate such a move, although he could not imagine why. 'One thing at a time,' whispered a voice in his brain. 'Let's not get carried away.' So he contented himself with putting his arm tenderly round her shoulders, and suggesting that they go for a walk in the garden. For once, the girl did not ask him if he was sure that would be no bother, and they stood up, still entwined.

'Just a moment,' Malcolm said. 'Don't go away.'

He stooped down swiftly and picked up the Ring. After a moment's hesitation, he pushed it back onto his finger. It felt loose and uncomfortable.

'So how did you get her to agree to it?' Loge said. 'It must have been difficult.'

'Not really,' said Wotan. 'There was one of those grim silences we know so well in our family, then she said "If you insist," and there we were. I was amazed, as you can imagine. I'd thought up all sorts of arguments – you always said you wanted to work in the family business, it'll get you out of the house, a change is as good as a rest, that sort of thing – and I didn't have to use any of them. Women are strange creatures.'

'Are you sure she's up to it?'

'Positive. You've only seen her in the domestic mode, nagging and persecuting.'

'Which one was it again?'

'Ortlinde. She's the best-looking, and the droopiest. Mind you, with eight of them, I tend to get them mixed up. Maybe I should get them wearing numbers on their backs like footballers. I think Ortlinde's the second from youngest. Fancy another?'

'No, thanks, I'm driving.'

'So am I, but who cares? This is something to celebrate.' Wotan pulled open the drinks cabinet behind the front seat and took out a bottle of schnapps. 'Here's to two birds with one stone. I get control of the Ring and shot of a dopey daughter at the same time.'

'I hate to say this . . .' said Loge.

'I know, I know, it didn't work before and all the rest of it. But that was different.'

'Not so different.' Loge knew he was pushing his luck, but it had to be said. Besides, if it all went wrong, Wotan would be so furious that he would be lucky to get away with being turned into a trout hatchery. 'After all, Siegfried was roughly the same sort of proposition. He'd never had a girl before, either.'

'Siegfried wasn't a drip,' said Wotan crisply. 'This one is. So's she. She's so wet you could grow cress on her.'

'She didn't strike me as wet the other morning.'

'Ah,' said Wotan, 'that's different. That's her complicated little psyche belting away, that is. You see, my daughters are all the same. The way they see it, I've ruined their lives for them by making them stay at home in that bloody great house, stunting their emotional growth and all the rest of it, when they should have gone out into the world and had a good time. And you can see their point, I suppose. That house is a liability.' Wotan scowled at the very thought of it, and the first drops of rain started to fall. 'It's difficult to explain my family to a normal, sane person, but I think it goes something like this. They've been cooped up in Valhalla ever since their mother left, with nothing to do but be resentful and tell themselves how inadequate and unlovable they are, and how nobody could ever be interested in them because of their stunted personalities (stunted by me, it goes without saying). And they take all this out on their poor old dad by making his life almost as miserable as their own, in the tried and tested way you saw the other day.'

Loge had been nodding his head and making sympathetic noises until he felt quite dizzy. He didn't want to hear any of this, but Wotan seemed determined to tell him. A combination of schnapps and relief was making him unwind, although whether he would be any safer to be employed by unwound than tensed up remained to be seen. Rattlesnakes, Loge remembered, usually unwind just before they bite.

'So at home they really let fly. Not that we have long, earnest conversations about the state of our tortured personalities, thank God. No, they've decided that they can't talk to me, I'm delighted to say, and so what they do is they sublimate it all – I think that's the right word, isn't it? – into endless domestic trivia, like who had the Sellotape last and how can you expect me to find things if you will insist on moving them. But put them down in the outside world, and they turn into fluffy little bunnies, wouldn't say boo to a goose, you know the sort of thing. I don't know which is worse, actually. At least they keep the place clean. Anyway, no self-confidence is the root of it all, so if our Ring-Bearer can convince Ortlinde that he's serious about her and that somebody really loves her in spite of everything, he'll need a crowbar to get her off him. Serve the idiot right, that would.'

'But if she hates you so much, what makes you think she'll get the Ring for you? Won't she just go off with her Redeemer and leave you to get on with it?'

'That was worrying me, I must admit, but when I thought it over, I saw just how clever I'd been,' said Wotan smugly. 'The fact that she really does love him in her own, unique, screwed-up way means she can't fail. You see, the last thing my daughter wants is to be happy. She'd hate it. No, what she wants is to be finally, definitively *un*happy, and for it all to be my fault. It'd finally confirm all her dearest illusions about how her life has been ruined. People like that would far rather be right than happy. No, she'll get that Ring if it kills her.'

Loge wiped his forehead with his hand, and wished that he could go away and do something less stressful for a change, such as drive the chariot of the Sun or make the crops grow. But that was out of the question.

'The only thing that could go wrong is if he finds out who she really is,' Wotan said, pouring himself another drink. 'But my guess is that he won't want to find out, so unless somebody tells him, he won't work it out for himself. I think he's just as bad as she is. In fact, they're perfectly suited to each other. Who knows, they may even stick together after she's got the Ring off him, and I'll never have to see her ever again. Wouldn't that be perfect? Then there would only be seven of them, one for every day of the week. But it's unlikely,' he added sadly. 'Like I said, she'd go mad if she were happy.'

The rain had stopped, and Loge deduced that Wotan was in a good mood for once. That removed the immediate threat of transformation, but he still felt uneasy. Over the last few thousand years, Loge had found that Wotan's good moods always tended to come before periods of universal misery.

'So what do we do now?' he asked.

'Leave her to it,' said Wotan, leaning back in his seat. 'I always knew she'd come in useful one day.'

Love, the songwriter says, is the sweetest thing, and too many sweet things can make you feel slightly sick. But Malcolm had got through the endearments and sweet nothings stage quite safely, and had finally got the girl to tell him all about herself. She had not wanted to, and as he listened to the story that eventually came pouring out, he could quite understand why. Not that he was bored; but an overdose of tragedy can cause roughly the same symptoms as boredom, such as a strong desire to change the subject. That, however, would not be tactful. He only hoped that he would not be called upon to give an equally full account of himself, which might call for more inventiveness than he felt himself capable of.

'You see,' said the girl, 'none of us could ever really *talk* to my father, and my father could never really *talk* to us, so that in the end I found I couldn't even talk to my sisters. We all just bottled it all up inside ourselves, really, until we wanted to hit out at each other. But we couldn't, because of not being able to talk. Do you see what I'm getting at?'

'Sort of.'

'And it was obvious that my father was absolutely heart-

141

broken when my mother left him. He tried to put a brave face on it, of course, but we all knew that she had let him down as well as letting us down, and that somehow we had let him down as well. And, of course, he feels that he's let us down, and so now we can't communicate at all.'

'That's dreadful,' Malcolm said, wishing he hadn't raised the subject in the first place. It was obviously very painful for her to talk about her problems like this, and he hoped that she would stop and not upset herself further. But no such luck.

'And we could all see how much of a disappointment we were to him. He wanted us to have careers and achieve something in the world, but we knew we couldn't leave him like that after my mother had left him, because he would feel left out and that would be awful.'

'But you've got a career,' said Malcolm, brightly.

The girl looked startled, as if she had made a mistake. 'Well, sort of,' she said. 'But it's not a proper one.'

'But you don't live in the family house any more, do you?'

'Yes. No. Well, sort of. I share this flat, but I go home a lot too.'

The girl stopped talking and stared at her shoes. They were sensible shoes and had seen many seasons, like her sensible tweed skirt and her honest cream pullover. Her mother had probably bought them for her, Malcolm thought, just before she left.

'Well,' he said, trying to sound cheerful, 'you've got me to look after you now.'

They sat down on a bench and looked out over the park. It was a beautiful morning, although there had been one brief shower, and as soon as all the tragic stories had been got over with, it would all be perfect.

'What do you like doing?' Malcolm asked.

'Oh, I don't know really.' She thought about it for a long time. 'Walking, I suppose. And I quite like my work. Well, no, 1 don't really, but it's better than nothing.'

'Let's go for a stroll by the river,' Malcolm said firmly.

They walked in silence for a while, and stopped to admire the view of Farmer Ayres' prodigious crop of assorted flowers. In the distance, a BBC camera crew were unrolling miles of flex, so it would probably all be on the 9 O'Clock News that evening. Malcolm wanted to tell her that he had laid the flowers on for her benefit, to show how much he loved her, but he could not think of a way of explaining it all.

'Who's that girl on the river bank waving at you?'

Malcolm followed her finger and recognised Flosshilde. His heart fell. 'That's just a friend of mine,' he said. 'No-one important.'

'I think she wants to say something to you . . . Oh.'

Malcolm could have sworn that she had recognised Flosshilde, but that was obviously impossible, so he did not even bother to check her thoughts. He wanted to walk away and pretend he hadn't seen the Rhinedaughter, for he could not be bothered with her just now. After all, she was a very pretty girl, and Linda might jump to quite the wrong conclusions. Unfortunately, it was too late now. He put his arm around Linda's shoulders rather as a Roman legionary might have raised his shield before facing an enemy, as Flosshilde ran across to join them.

'Hello,' said the Rhinedaughter, and there was something very strange about her manner. 'Hope you don't mind, but I've been for a swim in your river.'

Nervously, Malcolm introduced her to the girl. Flosshilde looked at Malcolm for a moment, then turned and smiled radiantly at the girl, so that for an instant Malcolm was convinced that something terrible was going to happen. But nothing did, and Malcolm reassured himself that he must have been imagining it. For her part, Flosshilde looked very slightly disappointed, although Malcolm could not think why.

'Don't I know you from somewhere?' Flosshilde asked. 'Your face is very familiar.'

'I don't think so,' said the girl, nervously. She was obviously very shy.

'Must be my imagination, then. Well, I must be going. Oh, and I won't be able to make lunch tomorrow. Sorry.'

'Some other time, then,' said Malcolm. 'See you.'

'I expect so,' said the Rhinedaughter. 'Have fun.'

She ran lightly down to the river and dived in. For some reason, the girl did not seem surprised by this, and Malcolm was relieved that he would not have to try and find some explanation. He dismissed Flosshilde from his mind.

The Rhinedaughter circled for a few minutes under the surface, then slowly paddled upstream to a deep pool where she knew she could not be seen. It had been pointless trying to turn the woman into a frog, the daughters of Wotan are not so lightly transformed. At least she had given the Valkyrie notice that she had a fight on her hands.

It was all very well saying that, but Flosshilde had no stomach for a fight. It was inconceivable that Malcolm didn't know who she was or what she was likely to be after, and if he was so much in love that he was prepared to take the risk . . . After all, he had apparently been prepared to take a similar risk with her before the Valkyrie showed up, and obviously he had not been in love then, just lonely.

And any fool could see that Ortlinde was completely smitten, so it seemed likely that she too had given up hope of getting the Ring. After all, Malcolm was in a unique position to know what was going on inside her head. So he could take care of himself.

Vanity, said Flosshilde to herself, and wounded pride, that was all it was. That anyone could prefer a stuffy old Valkyrie to her was naturally hard for her to believe, but Malcolm obviously did, and that was all there was to it.

From the cover of a small boulder, she peered out. The Young Couple were kissing each other rather awkwardly under the shade of an oak tree. Flosshilde shrugged her shoulders and slid back into the water, as graceful as an otter. Beside her, she was aware of her sisters, swimming lazily in the gentle current.

'Told you so,' said Wellgunde.

'I couldn't care less,' said Flosshilde. 'And if you say one word about the Ring, I'll break your silly neck.'

'Wouldn't dream of it, would we?' replied Wellgunde smugly.

'I'm bored with England,' said Flosshilde suddenly, as they reached the head of the Tone. 'Why don't we go back home?'

'What a good idea,' said Woglinde. 'Let's do that.'

CHAPTER ELEVEN

At Valhalla the Wednesday afternoon General Meeting of the Aesir, or Company of Gods, is presided over by Wotan himself. At these meetings, the lesser divinities-thunderspirits, river-spirits, cloud-shepherds, Valkyries, Norns, nixies, powers, thrones, ettins and fetches – have an opportunity to bring to Wotan's attention any matters which they feel require action on his part, and receive their instructions for the next seven days. There is also a general discussion on future strategy and a long-range weather forecast.

Loge, as secretary to the Company, had the unenviable task of keeping the minutes of each meeting and presenting the agenda. At the meeting that immediately followed the Ring-Bearer's entrapment by the Valkyrie Ortlinde, he found himself having to reorganise the entire programme to give enough time for a thorough discussion, only to find that the discussion that followed was over much sooner than he had anticipated. There were votes of thanks from the Company to Ortlinde and Wotan, which were duly entered in the records, and Waltraute inquired how long Ortlinde was likely to be away and who was supposed to do her share of the housework while she was absent. Loge was then compelled to proceed to Any Other Business with well over an hour of the scheduled time still to go.

'I would like to bring to the Chairman's attention the fact that the light-bulb on the third-floor landing of the main staircase of Valhalla has gone again, and I would request him to replace it immediately,' said Schwertleite, 'before someone trips over and breaks their neck.'

'That's not nearly as dangerous as the carpet on the back stairs,' said Grimgerde. 'I've asked you hundreds of times to nail it down properly, but nobody ever listens to a word I say.'

Loge was writing furiously. All the minutes of meetings had to be made in runes, which cannot be written quickly.

'May I suggest,' said Wotan, grimly attempting to make himself heard, 'that this is neither the time nor the place . . .'

'Next time you stub your toe in the dark because you couldn't be bothered to replace a light-bulb . . .'

Wotan put his hands in front of his one eye and groaned audibly. 'We were discussing the Ring,' he muttered.

'And please don't put your elbows on the table,' interrupted the Valkyrie Helmwige. 'I spent the whole morning trying to get it looking respectable after you spilt coffee all over it.'

Wotan made a vague snarling noise at the back of his throat. 'This is a meeting of the Aesir,' he growled, 'and I would ask you to behave in an appropriate manner.'

'While we're on the subject,' retorted his daughter, the Driver of the Spoil, 'you might try dressing in an appropriate manner. Why you insist on wearing the same shirt three days in a row . . . How am I expected to get the collars clean?'

147

'Any other business,' Wotan said, but his growl was more like a whimper.

'You've got whole drawers full of shirts you never wear,' said Grimgerde, with a world of reproach in the deep pools of her blue eyes. She hadn't had a new shirt, or a new anything, for four hundred and twenty years, but she didn't complain. She never went anywhere anyway.

'I shall wear what the hell I like when I like,' said Wotan, and what had intended to be authority when the words passed his vocal cords was definitely petulance when the sounds emerged through the gate of his teeth. 'Now, can we please . . .'

A general baying of Valkyries drowned out the voice of the Sky-God, and Loge stopped trying to keep the minutes of the meeting. Over the centuries, he had evolved his own shorthand for the inevitable collapse into chaos that rounded off each Wednesday afternoon in the Great Hall. He sketched in a succession of squiggles under the last intelligible remark he had been able to record and began drawing sea-serpents.

The discussion had moved on to the topic of leaving the tops off jars when a rock-troll, who had been thoroughly enjoying the conflicts of his betters, noticed something out of the corner of one of his eyes. He nudged the middle-aged Norn with mouse-blond hair who was knitting beside him, and they turned and stared at the doorway of the Hall. One by one, the minor deities, then the Vanir, then the High Gods themselves abandoned the debate and gazed in astonishment at the three rather pretty girls who had wandered in through the Gates of Gylfi.

It was at least a thousand years since the Rhinedaughters, who were responsible for the noblest river in Europe, had attended a Wednesday afternoon meeting. No-one except

Wotan and Loge could remember exactly why they had stopped coming. Some said that they had been expelled for flirting with the cloud-shepherds at the time of the Great Flood. Others put it down to the girls' natural frivolity and apathy. Wotan and Loge knew that the river-spirits had walked out in tears after the stormy debate that followed the theft of the Ring from Alberich and had not been back since, although both Gods correctly attributed this continued absence to forgetfulness rather than actual principle.

'Well I never!' whispered the Norn to the rock-troll. 'Look who it is!'

The rock-troll nodded his head. Since he had been created out of solid granite at the dawn of time, this manoeuvre required considerable effort on his part, but he felt it was worth it. 'It's the Girls,' he hissed through his adamantine teeth.

It was Wotan himself who broke the silence. 'What the hell do you want?' he snapped.

'We just thought we'd pop our heads round and say hello,' said Wellgunde sweetly. 'It's been simply ages.'

The silence gave way to a hubbub of voices, as each immortal greeted the long-lost members of their Company. Most vociferous were a group of cloud-shepherds who, several centuries before, had arranged to meet the Rhinedaughters for a picnic at the place which has since become Manchester, and who had been waiting there ever since. Only the Valkyries and their father seemed less than delighted to see the Rhinedaughters back again. Wotan suspected that he knew the reason for their visit, while his daughters felt sure that the river-spirits hadn't wiped their feet before coming into the Hall.

'So,' said Wotan, when the noise had subsided, 'what have you been doing all these years?'

149

'Sunbathing, mostly,' said Woglinde truthfully. 'Doesn't time fly when you're having fun?'

'It's all right for some,' whispered the Norn to the troll. But the troll seemed uneasy. 'Something's going to happen,' he said, and he sniffed loudly, as if trying to identify some unfamiliar smell.

'Is that all?' laughed Wotan, nervously jovial. 'Or have you been doing any work?'

'Depends on what you call work,' replied Wellgunde. 'The river sort of runs itself really. But we have been looking at other rivers to see if we can pick up any hints.'

'Sort of an exchange visit,' said Woglinde, helpfully.

'For example,' continued Wellgunde, 'we visited a river called the Tone in England. Not very helpful, I'm afraid.'

'But guess who we bumped into while we were over there,' cooed Woglinde. 'Go on, guess.'

'I hate guessing,' said Wotan irritably, and he picked up a document and began to study it diligently. Since he was to all intents and purposes omnipotent, it was not surprising that he could read a sheet of paper that was palpably the wrong way up.

'Ortlinde, that's who,' said Flosshilde, who had not spoken before. Wotan made no reply, being obviously engrossed in his document. Suddenly, Flosshilde smiled at the papers in his hand, which turned into a small dragon. Wotan dropped it with a start, and it crawled away under the table. 'Now what on earth was she doing there?'

The Norn had covered her eyes. She was fond of the Rhinedaughters, with whom she had spent many hours exchanging gossip, and Flosshilde's conjuring trick, performed in front of so many witnesses, was as clear a case of treasonable assault on the King of the Gods as one could hope to find. The penalty for this offence was instant metamorphosis, usually into a bush of some kind, and it was common knowledge that Wotan had been desperate for some pretext for getting rid of the Rhinedaughters ever since they had first emerged from the waters of their native river. Slowly, the Norn lowered her hands. The Girls were still there, still in human shape.

'I'll tell you, shall I?' continued Flosshilde. 'She was there trying to get the Ring-Bearer to give her our Ring, which you should have given back to us a thousand years ago. So will you please tell her to stop it and go away?'

The Norn covered her eyes again, but she need not have bothered. Wotan simply looked away and threw a piece of cheese to the small dragon, which had curled up on his lap.

'If you don't,' said Flosshilde, clear without being shrill, 'we'll tell him who she is. Are you listening?'

There was a terrible silence. Never before had anyone, mortal or immortal, dared to threaten the Lord of Tempests in the Hall of his stronghold. Even the rock-troll held his breath, and the beating of his basalt heart was the only audible sound in the whole assembly. Wotan sat motionless for a moment, then rose sharply to his feet, sending the small dragon scampering for the safety of a coffee-table. He looked the Rhinedaughter in the eye, and the Norn held her breath. Then Wotan shook his head in disbelief, and marched out of the Hall.

'*Not* across the floor I've spent all morning polishing,' wailed the Valkyrie Gerhilde, but her father took no notice. The meeting broke up in disorder, and the troll and the Norn hurried off to the Mortals' Bar for a much-needed drink.

'I dunno,' said the rock-troll. 'I've never seen the like.'

'He just sat there,' said the Norn.

'Who did?'

'Wotan. When Flossie turned that paper into a dragon. It's Kew Gardens for her, I thought, but he just sat there. Didn't do a thing.'

'I didn't mean that,' said the rock-troll. 'I meant the other thing.'

The Norn wasn't listening. 'What I want to know is,' she continued, 'who is bluffing who? Is it the Girls bluffing Wotan, or Wotan bluffing the Girls, or are they all at it?'

The troll frowned and scratched his head, producing a sound like two millstones. 'What are you on about?' he asked.

'You *are* a slowcoach, aren't you? If the Girls wanted to stop Ortlinde from nobbling the Ring-Bearer, why didn't they just tell him who she was, instead of coming here and making threats to Wotan?'

The troll thought about this for a moment, then nodded his head. He was not so grey as he was granite-looking, and he could see that there was indeed an inconsistency.

'What I think,' said the Norn excitedly, 'is that the Ring-Bearer already knows who Ortlinde is, and he couldn't care less. They've tried telling him, and he doesn't want to know.'

'How do you make that out?' asked the troll.

'Simple,' said the Norn, smugly. 'They've tried telling him, like I said, and he isn't interested. But they know that Wotan doesn't know that the Ring-Bearer knows who Ortlinde really is. So they threaten to tell the Ring-Bearer, hoping that the threat will make Wotan tell Ortlinde to chuck it and come home.'

The troll stared at the bottom of his glass, trying to unravel the Norn's sentence. The Norn took this silence to mean that the troll was not yet convinced, and elaborated her point.

152

'You see, if Wotan doesn't know that the Ring-Bearer knows, then he'll be afraid in case the Girls tell the Ring-Bearer, and the Girls will try and get him to make some sort of a deal. The Girls can't make the Ring-Bearer chuck Ortlinde, because the Ring-Bearer presumably knows already – I mean he must know, mustn't he? But they can get Wotan to tell Ortlinde to chuck it if they can make him think that the Ring-Bearer doesn't know. Do you see what I mean?'

'Did you think all that up for yourself?' said the troll, full of admiration. The Norn blushed.

'That's very clever, that is,' said the troll. 'But what about the other thing?'

'What other thing?'

'You know.' The troll made a vague gesture with his huge paw. 'The other thing. I smelt it when the Girls walked in.'

It was the Norn's turn to look puzzled. The troll made a great effort and thought hard.

'Why was it,' he said at last, 'that old Wotan didn't turn the Girls into something when they gave him all that lip? You answer me that.'

'He tried to,' said the Norn. 'Just before he stomped off.'

'Exactly,' said the troll. 'He tried to, but he couldn't. There was something stopping him.'

'What?' cried the Norn, enthralled.

'I dunno, do I? But they brought it in with them. I smelt it. There was something looking after them, or at least it was looking after Miss Flosshilde. Didn't you smell it too?'

'I'm no good at smells,' confessed the Norn, who lived on a bleak, wet fell and had a permanent cold as a result. 'Was it some sort of Power, do you think?'

The troll had done enough thinking for one day. His mind was made of sandstone and, besides, he had other things on it. He looked at the Norn for a moment and for the first time in his life attempted a smile.

'You're very clever, you are,' he said. 'Do you come here often?'

The Norn blushed prettily. She noticed that the troll had very nice eyes, and if one of them happened to be in the middle of his forehead, who cared? The conversation veered away from the Ring-Bearer and the strange-smelling Power, which was ironic in a way; for the change of subject and the emotions that had prompted it were largely due to their influence.

The Norn had been right up to a point. Malcolm had discovered who the girl he loved really was, but not from the Rhinedaughters, or even Alberich, who had rushed back from Germany to tell him. He had heard and finally believed the news only when a sparrow had perched on his shoulder in Bond Street and chirped the information into his ear. By that time, of course, Malcolm was engaged to the girl, which made things all the more difficult . . .

It had only taken thirty-six hours for Malcolm and the girl who had come to catalogue his library to become engaged to be married. Malcolm was not quite sure why he had felt such an urgent need to get official recognition for this strange and unexpected outbreak of love in Middle Somerset. But it seemed the right thing to do, like getting a contract or a receipt. To his utter astonishment, his proposal had been accepted. The girl had simply looked at her shoes for a moment, smiled at him sadly, and said, 'If you're sure . . .' Malcolm had said that he was sure, and the girl had said something along the lines of Yes.

One is meant to do something wildly demonstrative on such occasions, but Malcolm felt too drained to waste energy in running about or shouting. In fact, he realised, he felt rather depressed, although he could not imagine why. For her part, the girl was even more taciturn than usual. The pretty scene had taken place beside the river in the grounds of the Hall, and they had sat in total silence for a while before getting to their feet and walking back to the house. At the door, the girl turned and looked at him for a moment, then muttered something about getting on with the catalogue.

'Catalogue?' Was she thinking about wedding presents already? 'What catalogue?'

'Of the library.'

'You don't want to bother with that, surely? I mean . . .'

'Oh, but I must.' The girl looked at him again, not as one would expect a girl to look at her future husband. Nor was it an 'Oh God what have I gone and done' look; just a look, that was all. Then she went up to the library.

Malcolm sat down on the stairs and put his hands over his ears. He felt confused, and no thoughts would come into his mind. With a tremendous effort, he called up the aspects of the situation that required his immediate attention, and tried to review them in the detail that they seemed to warrant.

Unlikely as it seemed, he had just succeeded in getting himself organised for perhaps the first time in his life. He had fallen in love, and for a change the girl at the other end felt the same way. Instead of letting this chance slip through his fingers, he had got everything sorted out, and that was all there was to it. There was no earthly reason why he shouldn't get married; he had a house and money, which was what a married man was supposed to need, along with a wife. If there had been anything wrong with the idea, then the girl wouldn't have said Yes. She was obviously happy with the arrangement, and it went without saying that it was what he wanted most of all in the whole wide world. Was it? Yes, he concluded, it probably was. Mind you, it did seem a terribly grown-up thing to be doing, but then again, it would be, wouldn't it? So far as he could see, he was Happy. He lacked nothing, and had all sorts of nice things to look forward to.

Malcolm leaned forward, resting his elbows on his knees. It occurred to him that he had only known this girl for about a day and a half, and that he was being a bit hasty. He dismissed this thought, which was simply cowardice. The trouble was, he reckoned, he was probably afraid of being happy, of having what he really wanted. For some reason or other, which he could not be bothered to work out.

He got to his feet and walked slowly to the library. The girl was sitting at a table with a pile of books on it, writing something in what looked like a ledger. She did not hear him come in, and he stood looking at her for a moment. Life, he realised, was a fragile thing, and time and opportunity should not be wasted.

'Blow that,' he said, and the girl started. 'Let's go and buy a ring.'

His words had broken a deep silence, and silence followed them, so that Malcolm had the feeling that he was talking to himself. This would never do.

'Come on,' he pleaded. 'You don't have to do that now. Everything's going to be all right now.'

Oddly enough, the girl seemed to understand what he meant by that, which was more than he did himself. She smiled (why did she always smile and never laugh?) and said Yes, she would like that. So they went downstairs and Malcolm walked out to the garage to get the car.

Alberich was sitting on the bonnet, eating a ham roll.

'This is my lunch, you realise,' said the Nibelung. 'About the worst thing I could possibly have, barring lobster.'

'What are you doing here?' Malcolm asked.

'I came straight back from Germany,' continued Alberich. 'I saw the two of you together just now, and I knew in a minute what had happened.'

'Thank you.'

You know who she is, don't you?'

Malcolm stared at him. 'Of course I do,' he said. 'Do you?'

'Well, of course.'

Malcolm frowned. How in God's name did Alberich know who she was? Did he have a library too? Malcolm suddenly felt that he didn't want to know.

'I know all about her,' he said. 'And we've just got engaged. We're going to London to buy a ring.'

'*Buy* a ring?' said Alberich, genuinely surprised. 'I'd have thought that was unnecessary.'

Malcolm did not understand this remark, so he assumed it must be a joke. Perhaps in the back of his mind he had an idea that Alberich was trying to tell him something very important, but if that was the case he managed to ignore it. He squeezed a polite laugh out of his lungs, and unlocked the car.

'Hang on, though,' said Alberich.

'Sorry, I haven't got time,' said Malcolm. 'I think we should get it in Bond Street. That's where all the jewellers' shops are, aren't they?'

'Why not Amsterdam? Or Johannesburg?' asked Alberich quietly.

'She wouldn't understand about the Tarnhelm,' Malcolm said. 'It might frighten her.'

'Most unlikely. Are you sure you know . . .?'

Malcolm started the engine and pressed the accelerator hard. Perhaps Alberich was saying something tremendously important; if he was, he couldn't hear a word of it. The Prince of the Nibelungs hopped off the bonnet and banged on the window. Malcolm wound it down and shouted, 'I'll see you when we get back. The housekeeper will make you a cup of tea, I expect.' Then he let in the clutch and drove furiously out of the garage.

Alberich stood for a moment and scratched his head. Then it occurred to him that he had been wasting his time. He picked up a spanner which was lying on the floor of the garage and hurled it at the wall.

Malcolm deliberately parked on a double yellow line in the middle of Bond Street. It was that sort of a day. If a traffic warden came and wrote him a ticket, he could tell her that he was engaged to be married to the most wonderful girl in the world. He wanted to tell people that, if only to hear himself say it. Anyway, he was feeling much better now, if a trifle hysterical.

The girl seemed to have cheered up, too. Almost for the first time since he had known her, she had laughed properly, and that was a wonderful sound to be anywhere near. In fact, Malcolm was at a loss to know what had got into her, for she behaved very childishly in all the jeweller's shops they went into. She insisted on trying on all the rings they saw, taking them to the window to see what they looked like in the light, and then saying that they wouldn't do. The stones were the wrong colour, or too small, or too big, or the settings were the wrong shape. It almost seemed as if she wasn't taking this business seriously.

They had tried six shops, and it was nearly half-past five.

'It's no good,' said the girl. 'I don't like any of the ones we've seen. And I'm the one who's going to be wearing it; For ever and ever,' she added, tenderly. For some reason, this remark struck Malcolm as being rather out of character, but he put it down to excitement.

'We can try that one over there, if we're quick,' he suggested.

'No,' said the girl, 'I know the ring I want.' And she told him. As she did so, it began to rain.

The two sparrows that had been eating crumbs outside the largest of the jeweller's shops looked at each other.

'Did you hear that?' said the first sparrow.

'Don't speak with your beak full,' said the other.

'But, Mum,' replied the first sparrow, 'it's him. And he's going to give her the Big Ring.'

'It's none of our business. And you'll catch your death if you don't get under cover this instant.'

'But, Mum,' insisted the first sparrow, 'if he gives her the Big Ring it'd be terrible, wouldn't it?'

'How many times must I tell you not to listen to what other people are saying? It's rude.' The second sparrow flapped her wings nervously. It was indeed terrible, and she didn't want to get involved.

'But do you think he knows how terrible it would be? Do you?'

'Quiet! People are staring.'

'It's rude to stare,' replied the first sparrow, who had been told this many times. 'If he doesn't know, shouldn't we tell him? Because if we don't . . .'

Two ravens had appeared in the sky, wheeling slowly and noiselessly above the street. Nobody noticed them; they had come to see, not to be seen.

'It isn't him at all,' said the second sparrow nervously,

'it's just your imagination. If you don't come in this minute, I'll tell your father.'

Malcolm was standing very still. The girl was smiling at him, saying nothing. He wanted to give her the Ring. He could see no reason why he should not. Almost from the first moment he had met her, he had wanted to give her the Ring, and now he was going to do it. It was the right thing to do. It was the only thing to do.

The young sparrow hopped morosely under a parked van. His mother was scolding him, but he wasn't listening. Surely it couldn't be right that the Ring-Bearer should give the Ring to Wotan's daughter. His mother stopped chirping at him for a moment, and stooped down to peck at a bottle-top. Now was his chance.

'Please,' said the girl. 'I'd like it very much.'

Malcolm took the Ring between the first and third fingers of his left hand and started to pull it off. He was afraid that it might not come away easily, but it slid off effortlessly, and he held it for a moment. The girl was still smiling, not holding out her hand, not making a movement of any sort. He tried to read her thoughts, but he could not. He could feel the rain running through his hair, but he did not know what it was. It was right that the girl should have the Ring. It would be very easy to give it to her. Nothing at all could be easier, and then they would be properly engaged.

The sparrow forced itself through the air like a bullet and landed awkwardly on Malcolm's shoulder. He did not seem to notice. He had other things on his mind.

'Don't do it,' shrieked the bird. 'She's Wotan's *daughter*!'

For a moment, Malcolm did not know where the voice was coming from. Then he felt feathers brushing the side of his face, which made him jump. As he started, he dropped the Ring, which rolled into the gutter.

'She's Wotan's daughter. She's Wotan's daughter, she's his daughter!' screamed the sparrow. Malcolm swung his left hand furiously through the air and clapped the palm of it onto his right shoulder. He felt something fragile snapping under the fingers, and the voice stopped suddenly. The dead bird rolled down his arm and fell onto the pavement. It looked like a child's toy or a hockey-puck, and it had landed in a puddle.

Then the girl stooped down to pick up the Ring. Without knowing what he was doing, Malcolm covered it with his foot. It was all he was able to do, but apparently it was enough. The girl stepped backwards, and she had a look on her face that Malcolm did not like very much.

'I really do love you,' she said.

Without even wanting to, Malcolm found himself reading her thoughts.

'I love you too,' he said, and he bent down and picked up the Ring. 'If I offered this to you, would you take it?'

'Yes,' said the girl.

'And you'd give it to your father?'

'Yes.'

Malcolm closed his fist round the Ring. 'It's raining,' he said, 'you'll catch cold.'

The girl looked at her shoes and said nothing. He slowly put the Ring back on his finger. He wanted her to have it more than ever, but it felt terribly tight now, and he doubted whether he would be able to get it off again without soap and water. There was some quotation about there being a providence in the fall of a sparrow, but he had never really understood what that meant.

He opened the car door for her. 'Are we still engaged, then?' he asked.

'I don't know,' she said. 'Are we? I mean, is there any point?'

'But we love each other, don't we? Yes, we do,' he added, for he knew how indecisive she could be at times. 'And there's all the point in the world.'

'Everything I told you about my family is true,' she said, fastening her seat-belt. 'So I don't think there is any point, really, is there?'

Malcolm could not quite follow that one, but he wasn't bothered about it. He could read her thoughts. This was all *so silly*.

When they were on the motorway, Malcolm broke the silence that had lasted since they had left London.

'Obviously you know who I am,' he said. 'So you know I can read thoughts. I can read exactly what you're really thinking.'

The girl said nothing.

'Which is probably just as well,' said Malcolm irritably, 'since you never say anything. But I can see what you're thinking, so it's no use pretending. For crying out loud, you love me more than I love you.'

'That's for you to say.'

'Then be quiet and listen. You don't have to give him the Ring.'

'You don't have to keep it.'

Malcolm wanted to grab hold of her and shake her, but he was being overtaken by a lorry and needed both hands for the wheel. 'Don't you understand anything?' he shouted. The girl stared at the floor and said nothing.

'If I was feeling as bloody miserable as you are, I'd burst into tears,' he said savagely. 'But you won't let yourself do that, will you?'

He pulled over onto the hard shoulder and stopped the

car. Two ravens were circling overhead. Malcolm said a lot of things, some of them very loudly, some of them very quietly, and after a while he started to cry. But the girl said nothing, and there was no point saying any more.

'All right, then,' he whispered, 'you can have it. But not yet. Not yet.'

'I dunno,' said Thought, as he watched the car draw up at Combe Hall. 'Humans.'

The doors opened, and Malcolm and the Valkyrie Ortlinde climbed out.

'Now what?' whispered Memory.

Malcolm put his arm around the Valkyrie, and she rested her head against his face. The sharp eyes of the ravens could easily pick out the Ring, glittering on his finger. Neither the mortal nor the Valkyrie said a word as they went into the house, but the air was full of thoughts, and the ravens felt very frustrated that they could only read Ortlinde's half of them.

The door of the house closed and the two ravens sat thoughtfully for a while, listening to the wind sighing in the pine trees that surrounded the Hall. They had seen many things in their time. They had seen Alberich screaming with rage and pain when Loge tore the Ring from his chained hands. They had seen Hagen drive his spear between Siegfried's shoulders, and Hagen himself struggling for the last time in the floodwaters of the Rhine. Nothing surprised them any more.

'Thick as two short planks, both of them,' said Memory at last.

CHAPTER TWELVE

The girl – Malcolm could not bring himself to think of her as Ortlinde – was up at the crack of dawn cataloguing away like a small tornado. She at least had her work to occupy her mind; not that it was her proper work, of course.

Malcolm's own work was not going so well. According to the BBC, a rail disaster in Essex had been narrowly averted, and a nuclear reactor in Kent had been shut down in the nick of time, just before it had a chance to make the English Channel a little bit wider. Needless to say, these unhappy incidents had all taken place at the same time as he had been struggling to keep control of the Ring. It was an added complication, but no more. It wasn't that he couldn't care less; he cared desperately, but what could he do? He was the master of the world, but not of himself.

Alberich had been waiting for him when he returned from London. In fact, he had been pacing up and down in front of the garage all day, which had scarcely helped his digestion, with the result that he lost his temper when he caught sight of Ortlinde and called her some rather crude and unpleasant things. Malcolm had been on the point of hitting him again, but the dwarf had realised the danger he was in and apologised to the Valkyrie, blaming his bad manners on a cucumber sandwich he had been rash enough to eat while he was waiting. Now he had come back, and was sitting in the drawing-room, drinking milk.

'I know what you're going to say,' Malcolm said.

'Yes,' replied Alberich, 'you probably do. Whether you understand it or not is another matter. Giant's blood may have made you perceptive, but it hasn't stopped you being plain stupid.'

'Thank you,' replied Malcolm sullenly, 'but I can do without personal abuse.'

'Listen,' said the Nibelung. 'I told you before that you were too nice to be a proper Ring-Bearer. Ring-Bearers can't be like that. Sure, it worked well enough to start off with, but then it went all wrong. Well, didn't it? A nice but enamoured Ring-Bearer is capable of doing more damage in forty-eight hours than Ingolf managed in a thousand years. You're human; you can't help it. But you aren't qualified to hold the ring if you're human. Don't you see?'

'No.'

Alberich frowned. It was as if someone had said that they could not understand why rain makes you wet. It would take some explaining.

'Take my case,' he said. 'I'm not human, I'm delighted to say, but even so, the first thing I had to do before I was able to make the Ring in the first place was to forswear Love and all its tedious works. Whoever thought up that particular requirement knew what he was about, believe you me. Not that I was ever romantically inclined myself; my heart has often been burnt but never broken. Anyway, this made me immune from the one single greatest cause of idiocy in the world. Since I took the pledge, I have been

165

smiled at by Rhinedaughters, yearned at by Valkyries, and generally assaulted by beautiful people of every species, all to no effect. And I don't even have the miserable thing any more. I'm just a peripheral character, especially now that you appear to have dismantled the curse I so cleverly put on the Ring. Or perhaps you haven't.' Alberich was thoughtful for a while. 'Perhaps this Ortlinde nonsense is the curse catching up with you as well. If it is, I'm sorry. Oddly enough, I don't feel any real animosity towards you, even if you are as stupid as they come. Curse or no curse, though, you've fallen head over heels into the oldest trap in the book. You really aren't fit to be allowed out on your own, let alone be the master of the universe.'

'I never asked for the job,' said Malcolm wretchedly.

'That's true, you didn't. But who cares? Shall I tell you about Love?'

'Must you?'

'Yes. The human race – we'll confine our attention to your mob to start with, although what I say is applicable to virtually all mammals – the human race has achieved so much more than any other species in the time it's been on this earth – a couple of million years, which is no time at all; about as long as it takes a sulphur-dwarf to learn to walk – that the imagination is unable to cope with all the things that the human being has done. The human race *created* Things. They built wonderful buildings, invented wonderful machines, brought into being poetry, music and art. To beguile their eighty-odd years they have every conceivable diversion, from the symphonies of Beethoven to the Rubik's Cube. They can rush round in sports cars, they can shoot elephants, they can travel around the world in days, or even hours. In virtually every respect, they have made themselves the equals of the Gods. Most of all, they

166

have all the Things in the world at their disposal to use and entertain themselves with. And what do they like doing best of all? They like taking off all their clothes – clothes over which they have expended so much effort and ingenuity – and doing biologically necessary but profoundly undignified things to other human beings. Any pig or spider can do that, it's the easiest thing in the world. But you bloody humans, who can do so much that no other species could ever do, you can't do *that* efficiently. You agonise over it. You make an incredible fuss over it. You get it all wrong, you make each others' lives miserable, you write dreary letters and take overdoses. You even invent a medicine that deliberately makes the whole process futile. My God, what a species!'

The dwarf fell silent and drank some milk. Malcolm could think of no answer to the case as Alberich had presented it, although he felt sure that there was a flaw in it somewhere. Alberich wiped his moustache and continued.

'And so you give this irregularity in your minds a name of its own. You call it Love, which is meant to make everything all right. Rather than try and sort it out or find a vaccine, you go out of your way to glorify it. I mentioned your art and your poetry just now. What are your favourite themes? Love and War. The two things that any species can do, and which most species do so much more sensibly than you lot – screwing and killing – are the things you humans single out to make a song and dance about. Literally,' said Alberich, who above all else detested musicals. 'Now be fair,' he continued, 'can you honestly say that a member of a species with this ancestral fallibility should be allowed to rule the universe?'

'But isn't everybody the same? Don't the Gods and Goddesses ever fall in love? And didn't you once try and chat up the Rhinedaughters?'

Alberich winced. 'It is true that the High Gods do occasionally fall in love. You have, as a matter of fact, singled out the one race nuttier than your own. We Elementals have a far better record. The spirits of wood and stone have been known to make idiots of themselves, and I myself did go through a bad patch, I will confess. The spirits of wind and water – the Rhinedaughters, to take an excellent example – have so far proved entirely bulletproof. But even when we do go haywire, we get over it very quickly and very easily. We see how stupid it is, and we pull ourselves together. Look at me. And your lesser Gods, your phenomena and abstractions and so on, have no trouble at all. Seriously, I should consider giving it best and handing the Ring on to a more suitable keeper.'

'Such as?'

'Modesty forbids.'

Malcolm shook his head sadly. 'It's not that I don't accept what you've told me,' he said. 'You've got a point, I'm sure. But I can't give you the Ring, much as I'd like to. I've promised to give it to her.'

'But surely . . .' Alberich rose to his feet, and then sat down again, a hand pressed to his abdomen. 'Don't say I'm getting an ulcer,' he moaned, 'not on top of everything else.'

'You see,' Malcolm went on, 'the Ring isn't about all that any more. It's the only way I can prove to her that I really do love her. Don't you see how important that makes it?'

At times, Alberich said to himself, there are worse things even than dyspepsia. 'You haven't been listening,' he said.

'Yes, I have. But she's the most important thing in the world.'

'If you weren't bigger than me,' said Alberich, 'I'd break your silly neck. Make yourself shorter and say that again.'

Malcolm wanted to explain, but that would clearly be

pointless. The Nibelung, he could see, had no soul. He offered his guest another glass of milk, but the offer was curtly refused, and Alberich left in a huff.

Having filled himself with the conviction that what he was doing was right, Malcolm went down to the library to seek confirmation.

'Hello,' said the girl.

'Hello, Ortlinde,' he replied. 'Funny, isn't it, the way all the people I talk to nowadays have German names?'

'You've got a German name.'

'No,' he said. 'My name's Malcolm.'

'They didn't tell me that,' said the girl. 'I think it's a nice name.'

'So is Ortlinde.'

'Thank you. It means Place of the Lime Tree.'

'I know.'

Malcolm remained standing where he was, feeling rather uncomfortable. The girl hadn't moved either, and Malcolm was put in mind of a boxing match he had once seen where both fighters had refused to leave their corners at the start of the first round.

'Are you really cataloguing the library?' he asked.

'Yes,' replied the girl, who sounded rather offended.

'Sorry. Did you really train as a librarian, then?'

'No,' said the girl, 'I never had an opportunity to have a career. But we've got millions of books at home, and my father never puts them back where he got them from. He's very untidy.'

'How old are you?' Malcolm asked suddenly.

'One thousand, two hundred and thirty-six.'

'I'm twenty-five,' said Malcolm, and he made some sort of a joke about having always preferred older women. Ortlinde smiled wanly.

169

'There's no point, is there?' she said.

'No point in what?'

'In going on like this,' she said. 'It's not your fault, really. It's my fault.'

She was looking down at her sensible shoes again; Malcolm wished that she might learn some sense from them. 'I lied to you,' she continued, 'I was sent to do something and I haven't even managed to do that. It's just that nobody's ever loved me before, and I haven't loved anyone before. But you'll be all right, I know you will. You'll meet someone else, and . . .'

'I don't want to meet anyone else,' Malcolm shouted. 'Ever again. I'm going to give you the Ring as soon as . . . as I've sorted everything out,' he finished lamely.

'But you can't. If you did, you would know I've let you down, and I would know that too, and you wouldn't be able to communicate with me and I wouldn't be able to communicate with you and this terrible resentment would build up and neither of us would be able to talk to each other . . .'

She talked, Malcolm thought, in the same way as a rabbit runs; terribly fast for a short burst, then a long, long pause, then another breathless sprint; and every few words, a little nervous smile that made him feel as if someone were crushing his heart like a cider-apple. Unless he found some way of cheering her up, life with her would be intolerable. On the other hand, life without her would be equally intolerable or even worse, so what could he do?

'Of course we'll be able to talk to each other,' he said firmly. 'All I have to do is give you the Ring, and I'll give it to you because I want to, because it'll show you that I love you more than anyone else or anything else in the whole world.'

'No, you don't. You can't. You mustn't.'

Malcolm felt as if someone had asked him his name and then contradicted him when he answered. 'Why not?' he asked.

'Because I'm not a nice person at all,' replied the girl, gazing tragically at her shoelaces. 'I'm nasty, really.'

'No, you're not.'

'Yes, I am.'

'No, you're not.'

She's probably never been to a pantomine, Malcolm reflected, so she wouldn't know. 'Really, you're a wonderful person, and I love you, and you love me, and it's all so bloody simple that any bloody fool could get it right. Don't you understand?'

Malcolm was shouting now, and the girl had gone all brittle, like a rose dipped in liquid oxygen. 'Come on,' he said, lowering his voice with an effort, 'we had it all sorted out a few hours ago. Don't you want to be happy?'

There was a long silence; not a pause for thought, but an unwillingness to communicate. It was like trying to argue with a small child.

'Well, don't you? Look at me when I'm shouting at you.'

'I don't know,' said the girl, looking even further away.

'Then . . .' Malcolm did not know what to say. Words were bouncing off her like bullets off a tank. 'Then you'll just have to trust me,' he said. He had no idea what that remark was supposed to mean, but it sounded marvellous. He put his arm nervously round her shoulder; there was no resistance, but it felt like touching a corpse, which was strange. Up to now, she had been the warmest person he had ever known.

He left the library and wandered out into the drive. A small white Citroën was drawing up; it was the English

171

Rose, back from her holiday. Malcolm groaned, and felt a totally unreasonable surge of resentment towards her. He knew that it had not really been his secretary who had invited the girl down to catalogue the library and so messed up his life. But on another level it had been, and that level suited Malcolm perfectly. He had found someone to blame for all his troubles.

'That bloody librarian you hired,' he started.

'Pardon me?' said the Rose. 'I engaged no librarian.'

'Yes, you bloody did. Linda Walker, Lime Place, Bristol.'

The Rose looked mystified. 'To catalogue the library? But Herr Finger, you refused categorically to permit me to arrange for any such operation to be performed. I obeyed your instructions on that point to the letter. The person you referred to is unknown to me.'

'Oh,' said Malcolm. 'Then I'm sorry.'

The Rose looked at him curiously through her spectacles.

'Is there a person of that name – Linda Walker of Lime Place – currently engaged in the work you described?' she asked.

'Yes.' Malcolm suddenly realised that he couldn't explain. 'Well, now she's here she'd better get on with it, I suppose.'

But the Rose seemed intrigued. 'Would she by any chance be a young person?'

'Yes, I think so.' One thousand, two hundred and thirty-six. Well, you're as young as you feel.

'Excuse me one moment.'

Before he could stop her, the Rose scuttled into the house. Malcolm followed, but his secretary proved surprisingly fleet of foot. She had reached the library door before Malcolm caught up with her, and she threw it open.

'For Chrissakes, Lindsy,' she wailed, 'what are you doing here?'

'Hello, Mother,' said the girl.

'Believe me,' said the Rose, 'it was none of my doing. I came here specifically to prevent any such occurrence.'

The three of them were assembled in the drawing-room: Malcolm slumped in an armchair, which threatened to swallow him whole, the Rose perched on the arm of the sofa, and the Valkyrie Ortlinde, the Chooser of the Slain, sitting on a straight-backed chair staring rigidly at a spot on the carpet. The English Rose had sent for tea; it had arrived, and was going cold.

'Who exactly are you, then?' Malcolm forced himself to ask.

'I am Erda,' said the Rose, 'also known as Mother Earth.'

'But you're American.'

'That is so; but only by adoption, so to speak. I went to the United States – long before there were any States, united or otherwise – to be as far away as possible from my ex-husband, the God Wotan. Since he refused to allow me access to my daughters, I could see no point in remaining in Europe.'

'You're Mother Earth,' Malcolm said dumbly. He wanted to argue this point. For a start, she was much too thin to be Mother Earth, but that line of argument would probably cause offence. He could see no reason to disbelieve the claim. Its very improbability made it plausible enough.

'And this,' continued the Goddess with a sigh, 'is my daughter Ortlinde. I need not ask what she is doing here.'

The girl said nothing, which was entirely as Malcolm

173

had expected. 'Will someone please explain all this to me?' he asked pitifully. 'I'm only human, after all.'

'Certainly,' said Mother Earth. 'When I perceived that you had obtained the so-called Nibelung's Ring, I took it upon myself . . .'

'How did you find out?'

'I heard it from a nightingale who was present at the scene of the incident. I took it upon myself to place myself in a position where I could take an observer's role, and so masqueraded as your secretary.'

'But they said you'd been here for years.'

'I am not without influence with the local minor deities,' said the Rose loftily. 'I am afraid you were misled.'

'You mean the auctioneer and the estate agent and all those people were gods of some sort?'

'Certainly not. Only the previous owner, Colonel Booth. He is the spirit of the small trout-stream that runs through the grounds of the house. It was through his co-operation that I was able to secure the use of this house, which I knew you had always wanted to live in.'

'And he's a god?'

'Only a very minor one. Many people are, you know; about one person in two thousand is a god or a spirit of some sort. Of course, most of these are mortal and wholly oblivious of their divine status. We prefer to keep it that way. It's like your English system of appointing laymen as Justices of the Peace.'

'And where's Colonel Booth living now?' Malcolm asked, expecting the man to appear from the stream at the bottom of the garden.

'I obtained a transfer for him to a tributary of the Indus. His family had served in India for generations, and he was most keen to keep up the tradition.'

Malcolm rubbed his forehead with the heel of his hand, but it did no good. The Rose continued.

'I assumed this watching brief with the express intention of making sure that my ex-husband did not try the so-called Brunnhilde option on you. In the past, as you are no doubt aware, it met with some degree of success in the case of your predecessor Siegfried, and I felt sure that if other options failed him Wotan would not hesitate to use it again. I had thought, however, that he had given up for the time being, and so took my annual holiday in Stroud.'

'Why Stroud?'

'I am very fond of Stroud. Apparently, as soon as my back was turned, Wotan implemented this strategy.' The Rose paused, and looked sternly at her daughter. 'Perhaps you would care to leave us, Lindsy.' The girl got up and wandered sadly away.

'I must state,' continued the Rose, 'that I have only the best interests of the world at heart, and so my daughter's personal feelings must not influence my actions at all. Nor must they influence yours.'

'You're fired.'

'Mr Fisher, you do not seem to appreciate the gravity of the situation in which you find yourself. The situation as of now is extremely serious, and global security is at stake. To date, you have acted in a highly responsible manner towards the inhabitants of the world, and I felt confident that you could continue with this work without any undue interference from me.'

'Hold it,' said Malcolm. 'You arranged that damned gymkhana thing, didn't you?'

'Correct.'

'You must have known I'd have wanted to get my own

175

back on Philip Wilcox. There was nearly an air disaster because of that.'

'It was a risk I had to take. Had you continued to remain enamoured of Elizabeth Ayres, serious repercussions would have ensued on an international scale. I had to ensure that such an occurrence would not take place. Similarly it is of the utmost importance that I dissuade you from continuing in a state of love with regard to my daughter Ortlinde. The love syndrome is a condition which no Ring-Bearer should be in for any prolonged period of time.'

'I know, I know,' Malcolm muttered. 'I've heard all that.'

'Then,' continued the Goddess, 'you will be aware that the termination of this unfortunate situation must be expedited. It is as simple as that, Mr Fisher.'

Malcolm laughed loudly for rather longer than the remark justified.

'Your natural reaction, I know, is to protest that the matter is not in your control,' said the Rose. 'This is self-deception on your part.'

'Is it really?' Malcolm turned away and counted to ten. 'Why is it,' he said at last, 'that everyone I meet these days turns out to be a Goddess? You're a Goddess, she's a Goddess, the housekeeper is probably a Goddess.'

'Incorrect,' said the Rose.

'Oh, good. Look, I don't care, I just want to be left alone.'

The Rose continued with the same measured intonation, rather like the Speaking Clock. 'Correct me if I am mistaken, but you were primarily attracted to my daughter simply because you believed that she was not a Goddess but a normal, ordinary mortal. A somewhat counter-intuitive reaction for a human being, if I may say so; it seems to be a

176

commonplace of human love that the lover believes his beloved to be in some way divine.'

This, Malcolm realised with a shudder, was the Rose's idea of a joke. After a pause for laughter, which was not rewarded by the expected reaction, she continued.

'Now that it transpires that she is not a mortal but merely a Goddess, your affection for her should logically cease. You may argue that she loves you . . .'

'You noticed that, did you?'

'Indeed. But her feelings towards you are simply the result of unclear thinking and underlying emotional problems, which I fear have now reached a point where the most competent analyst would be unable to help her. By extending reciprocal affection towards her, you will only cause her emotional situation to deteriorate; so, Mr Fisher, if I may be counter-factual for a moment, if you care about my daughter, you must stop loving her. It would likewise be in your own interest to desist, since you are doing considerable harm to your own emotional state which, I hardly need tell you, is by no means satisfactory.'

For the first time, Malcolm felt pity for Wotan. This sort of thing all day long would try the patience of any God.

'My husband was a similarly unbalanced person,' continued the Rose. 'His case should provide you with a most graphic illustration of the dangers of embarking on a serious relationship when the balance of the mind is, so to speak, disturbed. In short, Mr Fisher, it is imperative that you abandon your intention of giving the Ring to my daughter. You must set your personal feelings on one side entirely.'

'Get knotted,' said Malcolm violently. It was no way to talk to a Goddess, but he was past caring.

'Should you fail to do so, I regret to have to inform you

that you may well be directly responsible for global cata-
clysm. If my ex-husband were to resume control of the
Ring, the consequences for the future of humanity would
be at the very least severe, and quite probably grave. You
yourself would undoubtedly fail to find the happiness you
misguidedly believe would result from a relationship with
my daughter; added to which, you would certainly be
involved along with the rest of humanity in any potential
Armageddon-type scenario that might arise as a result of
my ex-husband's ownership of the Ring. In short . . .'

'Wrong,' said Malcolm. 'Wrong on every point.'

'Pardon me?'

'Where you go wrong is, you think that she'll give the
Ring to her father. She won't. Never in a million years. You
see, it'll be a present from me, the best present I could possibly give her. She'd never give it to Wotan or anyone else.
She loves me, you see. In fact,' Malcolm said dreamily,
'she'll probably give it straight back again, and then everything will be all right.'

'I perceive,' said the Rose, rising to her feet, 'that I have
been wasting my time with you, Mr Fisher. You have failed
to grasp the significance of anything I have said to you. I
can only implore you to reconsider your decision with the
utmost diligence.'

'What do you actually do?' said Malcolm. 'What's your
job?'

'Mostly,' said Mother Earth, 'I sleep. My sleep is dreaming, my dreaming is thinking, my thinking is
understanding. Consequently, my normal role is consulta-
tive, not executive. Only in exceptional circumstances,
such as a threat of universal oblivion, do I undertake any
active part in the day-to-day running of the world.'

'Yes, but what do you actually *do*?'

'I advise people,' said Mother Earth.

'Like the United Nations does, you mean?'

'There is, I suppose, a degree of similarity.'

'You're still fired. Now get out of my house.'

'Mr Fisher,' said the Rose, sitting down again, 'before I go and attempt to reason with my daughter, on the unlikely chance that she might listen to sense, let me explain to you the nature of what you call love. It is a purely functional system in the human operational matrix. With the lower animals, the urge to reproduce is a purely instinctive thing. The human race, being rational, requires a distinct motivation to reproduce. It has therefore been programmed to process the reproductive urge in a unique way.'

'Just out of interest,' said Malcolm, 'did you design the human race?'

'Correct. As I was saying . . .'

'Ten out of ten for the Ears and the Eyes,' said Malcolm, 'the Feet and the waste disposal system not so hot. Friday afternoon job, I always thought.'

'You are thinking of the hardware, Mr Fisher, which is the result of the evolutionary process, and for which I claim no credit or otherwise. My work was entirely concerned with the software, what you would call the feelings and the emotions. As I was saying, the human race needs a reason for everything it does, a reason it can understand within its own terms of reference. Love, companionship, sympathy, affection and understanding are simply the rewards that human beings must receive if they are to be motivated to do something that creatures of their intelligence and sophistication would normally regard as below their dignity. There are so many better things they could be doing. How long does a human being live, Mr Fisher? Between seventy and ninety years, given optimum conditions. Without some powerful motivating factor, they could not be expected to devote a major proportion of their extremely short lives to the creation and education of other human beings. Therefore, it was necessary to provide them with an incentive, one which they are programmed to accept as worthwhile. Love is nothing, Mr Fisher. You would do well to ignore it completely.'

With that, the English Rose departed, leaving Malcolm alone. His only reaction to these revelations, straight from the horse's mouth, was that it was a dirty trick to play on anybody. But the fact remained that he was human, and he was in love, and that nothing else mattered. If that made him a fool, then so be it; blame the person who invented the state in the first place. But he knew all about love; it was as real as anything else in the world and he could not deny its existence. He resolved to find Ortlinde and give her the Ring at once.

But she wasn't in the library, or anywhere in the house. Perhaps she had gone away. Perhaps her mother had sent her away, or taken her away by force. In his confusion, Malcolm did not use the Tarnhelm to take him to where she was; instead, he ran through the house and grounds calling out her name at the top of his voice. At last he saw someone sitting on the riverbank and ran across. The figure turned and, to his despair, Malcolm saw that it was only Flosshilde.

'Have you seen her?' he panted.

Flosshilde could not read people's thoughts like Malcolm could, but she could guess who he was asking after. 'Yes,' she said, 'I saw her just now down by the little wood, where you get that nice view over the valley. Not that she's looking at the view, she's sitting there looking at her feet again. Size six, at a guess. Mine are size four.'

'Thank you.' Malcolm turned to go, but the Rhinedaughter called after him.

'Well?' he said. 'What is it? I'm in a hurry.'

'I know,' said Flosshilde sadly. 'I've just got back from Valhalla. I was trying to get Wotan to send her away.'

'Not you as well.'

'It's for your own good.' Malcolm scowled at her, and she felt suddenly angry. 'Well, it is. But I failed. Wotan tried to turn me into a hedgehog and it was all for your sake.'

'A hedgehog? Why a hedgehog, particularly?'

'Fleas and things. But he didn't manage to do it for . . . for some reason or other.' Flosshilde had been wondering what had prevented Wotan from making that transformation. The one plausible theory she had come up with was what had given her hope.

'I'm sorry he failed,' Malcolm said, and started to walk away. Flosshilde waited till his back was turned, then deliberately pushed him into the river.

As he hit the water, Malcolm's mind was filled with images of the fate of Hagen, whom the Rhinedaughters drowned, and he instinctively turned himself into a rowing-boat. But the water was only two feet deep at that point, and after a moment he turned himself back again. For all her grief, Flosshilde could not help laughing.

'Shut up,' Malcolm snapped.

'I didn't mean it unkindly,' giggled Flosshilde. 'That was very resourceful of you.'

Malcolm had got his shoes and socks wet. He applied to the Tarnhelm for replacements. 'You just watch it in future,' he said sternly.

'You watch it,' said the Rhinedaughter. 'And look at me when I'm talking to you.'

181

It was true that Malcolm was looking at his shoes, but only to see what the Tarnhelm had provided him with. 'Have you been listening to us?' he said furiously. 'When we were talking just now?'

Flosshilde sat down on the bank and combed her long hair with an ivory comb that Eric Bloodaxe had given her many years ago. 'No,' she said, 'I've got better things to do with my time than listen to that sort of rubbish.'

Malcolm sat down beside her. 'Go on, then,' he said. 'I'm listening.'

'I went to see Wotan,' she said, putting the comb away. 'I tried to get him to call Ortlinde off. But he said he couldn't. I don't know if he was telling the truth or not, actually. Because if you go off with her, you'll be terribly unhappy, honestly you will. Even if it does work out, and you give her the Ring and she accepts it and all that . . .'

'How come everyone knows about that?' Malcolm said bitterly. 'You must have been listening.'

'It's the most important thing in the world right now,' said Flosshilde gravely. 'What do you expect? Like it or not, you're dealing with the Gods now. I know you don't like us very much, but we're important people. But never mind about the world and things like that. I couldn't care less about the silly old world, or the Ring, or anything. If you go off with her, you'll be utterly wretched. She'll make you miserable, I know she will.'

Flosshilde tried to open her mind to make it easier for him to read her thoughts, but apparently he wasn't interested.

'How the hell could you know?'

'Because you're not like that. You think you're in love with her, but you're not. You think that because she's in love with you, you've got to be in love with her. It doesn't work like that.'

'You're talking nonsense. It's not like that at all.'

'Shut up and listen, will you? You don't understand the meaning of the word Love. It's not that great big romantic thunderbolt you think it is. You saw her, you fell for her, your heart went mushy inside you. That's all totally silly; it doesn't happen that way. You don't know the first thing about her. How could you, you've hardly got two sentences out of her since you met. What are the two of you going to do for the rest of Time, sit around staring at your shoes, trying to make conversation? You both think you're in love, but you're deceiving yourselves. She thinks she's in love because she's always been treated like a piece of old cheese, and then you come along, looking like Siegfried himself, the most important man in the world, and start adoring her. And you fell in love with her because she's there and you thought she was a human being and so she counted. There's me, you thought; a real live girl, not a Goddess or a water-nymph, is actually in love with me. Whoopee, I'm not a failure or inadequate or as boring as hell, let's get married.'

'Have you finished?'

'No. You're stupid and silly and romantic, and you deserve to be miserable all your life. What sort of a world do you think you're living in? You're only fit to mix with Gods and fairies. You don't stand a chance in the real world.'

'Now have you finished?'

'You think you're strong and marvellous, don't you? But you're as blind as a bat and they're leading you by the nose. It's them, don't you see? It's Wotan's grand design, and you've fallen straight into the trap. I thought there was more to you than that, but I was wrong.'

Malcolm did not even bother to unravel this skein of

metaphor. He stood up and walked away. When he was safely out of earshot, Flosshilde began to cry. As she sat weeping, her sisters put their heads above the water.

'You're just as bad as he is,' said Wellgunde.

'What sort of a world do you think you're living in?' sneered Woglinde. 'You're stupid and silly and romantic, and you deserve to be miserable all your life. Very well put, I thought.'

They laughed unkindly and swam away.

'Hello,' said Ortlinde.

'Hello,' said Malcolm. 'What are you doing here?'

'I wanted to be on my own,' she replied.

'I love you,' said Malcolm. He had grown used to saying that, and he no longer felt any embarrassment as the words passed his lips.

'You mustn't,' said the girl. 'Really, I'm not a nice person.'

'You said that before,' said Malcolm angrily. 'Don't try to be clever with me. I drank Giant's blood, remember? I can read what you're really feeling.'

'I've got no feelings, really. No emotions, no anything. Don't you see? I'm a Valkyrie, I'm Wotan's daughter. I can't be anything else, however hard I try. And if you try and make me be something I never can be, you'll only hurt yourself. I can't be hurt any more, I was born hurt. But I don't want to hurt you. So please leave me alone.'

Malcolm could not understand, but that was all right. He didn't want to understand and he didn't need to. He knew that she loved him, and this knowledge was like a gun in his pocket. So long as he was armed with it, no-one could touch him.

'If I give you the Ring, you'll take it?'

'Yes.'

'And you love me?'

'Yes.'

'What is so bloody fascinating about your bloody shoes? You love me?'

'Yes.'

'Oh, *good*. That's settled, then.' Malcolm shut his eyes and sat down, exhausted.

'No, it's not.' The tone of her voice had not altered, and she was still looking away. Malcolm could only feel frustration and anger, and he wanted to break something. The clouds grew dark, and there was a growl of distant thunder.

'You see?' said Ortlinde, sadly. 'That's why it wouldn't be any good.'

Malcolm could not understand this at first; then he understood. The storm was gathering fast, and rain was beginning to fall.

'Wotan never did it better himself,' she said.

'But I'm not like Wotan. He's a God and he's mad.'

If only you'd seen my mother when she was younger,' went on Ortlinde. 'But they tell me I'm just like she was at my age.'

'One thousand two hundred and thirty-six?'

'More or less. That was before she left my father and went to America, of course. And my father was a nice person then, everyone said so. Do you know what he did to convince her that he loved her? My mother, I mean? You see, there was some sort of difficulty about them, just as there is about us. Anyway, to prove he really loved her, my father deliberately put out his left eye.'

'How could that possibly have helped?'

'I don't know, he never told me. We never talk about things like that. Besides, everything was different then, so it probably had some special significance. Anyway, that's how he got like he is now, that and marrying my mother. That's what love does to people like you and me and him, if we let it take over. The best thing to do with all feelings like that is to wait until they go away. They don't mean anything, you know. They hurt, but they're only feelings. They don't draw blood or make it difficult for you to breathe. They're all in the mind. Life is about eating and drinking and sleeping and breathing and working, and not being more unhappy than you absolutely have to.'

'For crying out loud,' said Malcolm. 'It's not like that.'

'What's it like, then?'

'I don't know, really.' Malcolm was unable to think for a moment. 'But isn't it just two people who love each other, and they get married and live happily ever after. I mean, so long as we love each other, what the hell else matters?'

Ortlinde made no reply. It was raining hard, but she didn't seem to mind. She was very, very beautiful, and Malcolm wanted to hold her in his arms, but on reflection he realised that that would not be a good idea. He called upon the Tarnhelm to provide him with a hat and a raincoat, and when they materialised he gave them to her, for he did not want her to catch cold. Then he walked away.

A pair of ducks had settled on the surface of the river, and as Malcolm walked back to the house they called out to him.

'Thanks for the weather,' they said.

'I'm sorry?'

'Nice weather for ducks,' explained one of them. 'Get it?'

'Very funny,' said Malcolm. He stopped and looked at the two birds, male and female. 'Excuse me,' he said.

'Yes?'

'Excuse me asking, but are you two married?'

'Well, we nest together,' said the female duck, 'and I lay his eggs. What about it?'

'Are you happy?' Malcolm asked.

'I dunno,' said the female duck. 'Are we?'

'I suppose so,' said the male duck. 'I never thought about it much.'

'Really?' said the female duck. 'I'll remember you said that.'

'You know what I mean,' said the male duck, pecking at its wing feathers. 'You don't go around saying "Am I happy?" all the time, unless you're human, of course. If you're a duck, you can be perfectly happy without asking yourself questions all the time. I think that's what makes us different from the humans, actually. We just get on with things.'

'But you do love each other?' Malcolm asked.

'Of course we do,' said the male duck. 'Don't we, pet?'

'Then how in God's name do you manage that? It's so difficult.'

'Difficult?' said the female duck, mystified. 'What's difficult about it?'

'So you love him, and he loves you, and you both just get on with it?'

'Do you mind?' said the male duck. 'That's a highly personal question.'

'I didn't mean *that*,' said Malcolm, 'I meant that because you love each other, it's all right. That's enough to make it all work out.'

'What's so unusual about that?'

'Everything,' said Malcolm. 'That's the way it seems, anyway.'

'Humans!' laughed the male duck. 'And it's the likes of

you run the world. No wonder the rivers are full of cadmium.'

At the door of the house, Malcolm stopped. He did not want to go in there, and there was no reason why he should. After all, he had the Tarnhelm, so he could go where he liked. He also had the Ring, so he could do what he liked. This was not his home; it was only a tiny part of it. He owned the world, and everything in it, and it was high time he looked the place over. He closed his eyes and vanished from sight.

CHAPTER THIRTEEN

When sufficiently drunk, Loge will tell you the story of the first theft of the Ring by himself and Wotan from Alberich. According to him, when he realised that the Giants Fasolt and Fafner were determined to exploit his clerical error to the full and claim the Goddess Freia as their reward for building the castle of Valhalla, he decided that the only conceivable way out of his difficulties would be to find an alternative reward which the Giants would prefer.

Finding an alternative to freehold possession of the most definitively beautiful person in the universe, the Goddess of Beauty herself, was no easy matter, and Loge searched the world in vain for anyone or anything who could think of one, starting with human beings, going on to the lower animals, and finally, in desperation, trying the trees and the rocks. The only creature, animate or inanimate, who could think of anything remotely preferable to Freia was the Nibelung Alberich, and when Loge asked him to explain, Alberich rather foolishly told him about the Ring, which first gave him the idea of stealing it.

Malcolm had heard this story from Flosshilde, who did

an excellent impression of Loge when drunk, and it was at the back of his mind when he began his world tour. He hoped very much that things had changed since the Dark Ages. Certainly, some things were very different now; Freia, for example, had long since fallen in love with a wood-elf, with whom she later discovered that she had nothing in common. Centuries of quiet desperation and comfort eating had taken their toll, and Freia was no longer the most beautiful person in the world. In addition, attitudes have altered significantly since the Dark Ages, with the discovery of such concepts as enlightenment, feminism and electricity; Malcolm hoped he would quickly find that he was in a minority in regarding Love as being the Sweetest Thing. A quick survey of the thoughts of the human race would, he felt, help put his troubles in perspective.

With magical speed he crossed the continents, and the further he went the more profoundly depressed he became. Admittedly, the concept of love took on some strange forms (especially in California), but by and large the human race was horribly consistent in its belief in its value.

No matter how confused, oppressed, famished or embattled they were, the inhabitants of the planet tended to regard it as being the most important thing they could think of, and even the most cynical of mortals preferred it to a visit to the dentist. Not that they were all equally prepared to admit it; but Malcolm was able to read thoughts, and could see what was often hidden from the bearers of those thoughts themselves. Furthermore, with very few exceptions, the human race seemed to find its favourite obsession infuriatingly and inexplicably difficult, and considered it to be the greatest single source of misery in existence.

Not that that was an unreasonable view these days. Human beings, as is well known, cannot be really happy unless they are thoroughly miserable, and as a result of Malcolm's work as Ring-Bearer, there was little else for them to be miserable about. Wherever he went, Malcolm saw ordered prosperity, fertility and abundance. Just the right amount of rain was falling at just the right time in exactly the right places, and at precisely the best moment armies of combine harvesters, supplied free to the less developed nations by their guiltily prosperous industrial brothers, rolled through wheat-fields and paddy-fields to scoop up the bounty of the black earth. Even the major armament manufacturers had given up their lawsuits against the United Nations (they had been suing that worthy institution in the American courts for restraint of trade, arguing that World Peace was a conspiracy to send them all out of business) and turned over their entire capacity to the production of agricultural machinery. The whole planet was happily, stupidly content and, in order to rectify this situation, mankind had fallen back on the one source of unhappiness that even the Ring could do very little about.

Despite this lemming-like rush into love, there was a curious sense of elation and optimism which Malcolm could not at first identify. He was sure that he had come across it somewhere before, many years ago, but he could not isolate it until he happened to pass a school breaking up for the holidays. He remembered the feeling of release and freedom, the knowledge that for the foreseeable future – three whole weeks, at least – all one's time would be one's own, with no homework to do and no teachers to hate and fear. It was as if the whole world had broken up for an indefinite summer, and everyone was going to Jersey this year, where there are donkeys you can ride along the beach. All this, Malcolm realised, was his doing, the fruit of his own innocuous nature. He remembered that when he was a child, a princess had chosen to get married on a Wednesday, and all the schools in the country had been emancipated for the day. It had been on Wednesdays that his scanty knowledge of mathematics came under severe scrutiny from a bald man with a filthy temper, and he would gladly have given his life for the marvellous lady who had spared him that ordeal for a whole week, allowing him to spend his least favourite day making a model of a jet bomber instead. Malcolm understood that he was now the author of the world's joy, just as the princess had been in his youth.

Actually seeing the results of his work made Malcolm feel unsteady, and at first he did not know what to make of it all. The world was happy, safe and in love, all except a certain M. Fisher who controlled the whole thing, and a small number of supernatural entities, who were out to stop him. There seemed to be an indefinable connection between everyone else's happiness and his own misery, and he began to feel distinctly resentful. This resentment was foolish and wrong, but he could not help it. He had never wanted to take away the sins of the world. Once again, the old pattern was being fulfilled. Everyone else but him was having a thoroughly good time, and he wasn't allowed to join in. His subjects didn't deserve to be happy; what had they done, compared to him, to earn this golden age? Before he realised it, he was muttering something to himself about wiping the silly grins off their faces, and the clouds around the globe began to gather.

The first drop of rain hit the back of his hand as he sat in Central Park, watching the ludicrously happy New Yorkers

192

gambolling by moonlight in what had recently been declared the Safest Place in the USA. A group of street musicians, dressed in frock-coats with their faces painted in black and white squares, were playing the Brandenburg concertos to an appreciative audience of young couples and unarmed policemen, and Malcolm began to feel that enough was enough. He wanted to see these idiots getting rained on, and his wish was granted. As the musicians dived for cover among the trees and rocky outcrops, a tiny Japanese gentleman saw that Malcolm was getting wet and ran across to him with an umbrella. Smiling, he pressed it into Malcolm's hand, said 'Present', and hurried away. Malcolm threw the umbrella from him in disgust.

He sat where he was for many hours, the rain running down his face, and tried to think, but he appeared to have lost the knack. For most of the time he was alone, and the only interruptions to his reverie came from the scores of ex-pushers who had moved out of cocaine into bagels when the bottom fell out of drugs. Just before dawn, however, a pigeon floated down out of a tree and sat beside him.

'Don't I know you from somewhere?' Malcolm asked the pigeon.

'Unlikely,' replied his companion. 'You were never in these parts before, right?'

'Right,' Malcolm said. 'Sorry.'

'That's okay. Have a nice day, now.'

The pigeon busied itself with bagel-crumbs, and Malcolm rubbed his eyes with his fingertips.

'The way I see it,' said the pigeon, 'you care about people, right? That's good. That's a very positive thing.'

'But where's the point?' Malcolm said, and reflected as he said it that he was starting to sound like the bloody girl now. 'I mean, look at me. I've never been so wretched in my whole life.'

'That's bad,' said the pigeon, sympathetically. 'By the way, are you British, by any chance?'

'Yes,' said Malcolm.

'They had a British week over at Bloomingdales. Scottish shortbread. You get some excellent crumbs off those things.'

Already the first joggers were pounding their way across the park, like ghosts caught up in some eternal recurrence of flight and pursuit. Two policemen, who had been discussing the relative merits of their personal diet programmes, paused and watched Malcolm as he chatted with the pigeon.

'There's a guy over there talking to the birds,' said one.

'So he's talking to the birds,' said the other. 'That's cool. I do it all the time.'

Malcolm looked round slowly. Only he knew how fragile all this was. The pigeon looked up from its crumbs.

'You seem depressed about something,' it said.

'I've got every right to be bloody depressed,' replied Malcolm petulantly. 'Everyone's happy except me.'

'My, we *are* flaky this morning,' said the pigeon. 'You should see someone about that, before it turns into a complex.'

'Oh, go away.'

'You're being very hostile,' said the pigeon. 'Hostility is a terrible thing. You should try and control it.'

'Yes, I suppose I should. Do you know who I am?'

The pigeon looked at him and then returned to his crumbs. 'Everybody is somebody,' it said. 'Don't feel bad about it.'

'I thought you birds knew everything,' Malcolm said.

'You can get out of touch very quickly,' said the pigeon. 'Have you been on TV or something?'

'How come,' asked Malcolm patiently, 'I can understand what you're saying?'

The pigeon acknowledged this. 'This makes you something special, I agree. But I'm terribly bad at names.'

'It doesn't matter, really.'

'I know who you are,' said the pigeon, suddenly. 'You're that Malcolm Fisher, aren't you? Pleased to meet you. Can you do something about this rain?'

Malcolm did something about the rain. It worked.

'And could you maybe make the evenings a tad longer?' continued the pigeon. 'This time of year, the people like to come out and sit by the lake and eat in the evenings, and this is good for crumbs. So if you put say an extra hour, hour and a half on the evenings, there wouldn't be that scramble about half-seven, with all the pigeons coming over from the east. It's getting so that you have to be very assertive to get any crumbs at all, and I don't think being assertive suits me.'

Malcolm promised to look into it. 'Anything else I can do?' he asked.

'No,' said the pigeon, 'that's fine. Well, be seeing you.'

It fluttered away, and Malcolm shut his eyes. He felt very tired and very lonely, and even the birds were no help any more.

At Combe Hall a small group had gathered in the drawing-room. It was many centuries since they had met like this, and they were very uncomfortable in each other's company, like estranged relatives who have met at a funeral.

Alberich broke the silence first. 'He has no right to go off like this,' he said. 'It's downright irresponsible.'

'Why shouldn't he go off if he chooses to?' replied Flosshilde angrily. 'He's been under a lot of pressure lately, poor man. And we all know whose fault that is.' She looked pointedly at the mother and daughter who were sitting on the sofa.

'Let's not get emotional here,' said Mother Earth. 'Unfortunately, we are all in his hands, and we can do nothing but wait until he sees fit to return.'

'I wasn't talking to you,' said Flosshilde. 'I was talking to her.'

Ortlinde said nothing, but simply sat and stared at the floor. Flosshilde seemed to find this profoundly irritating, and finally jumped up and put a cube of sugar down the Valkyrie's neck. Ortlinde hardly seemed to notice.

'That will do,' said Mother Earth firmly. 'Lindsy, perhaps it would be best if you went into the library.'

'Oh no you don't,' said Flosshilde. 'I want her here where I can see what she's doing.'

'This is what comes of involving a civilian,' said Alberich impatiently. 'Whose idea was it, anyway?'

'It certainly wasn't mine,' said Mother Earth. 'The first I knew about it was when I heard the reports.'

'That's what I can't understand,' said Alberich. 'Who is this Malcolm Fisher, anyway? Anyone less suited to being a Ring-Bearer . . .'

'But he's doing wonderfully,' said Flosshilde. 'Everything is absolutely marvellous, or at least it was until *she* showed up.'

'I'm not denying that,' said Alberich. 'But the fact remains that he's just not like any other Ring-Bearer there's ever been. Perhaps that's a good thing, I don't know. But if you girls had your way, he could easily turn out to be the worst Ring-Bearer in history.'

'Don't look at me,' said Flosshilde. 'I'm on his side.'

'Who chose him in the first place, that's what I want to know,' Alberich continued. 'That sort of thing doesn't just happen. I mean, look at the facts. He accidentally runs over a badger, who happens to be Ingolf. It doesn't make sense.'

'I confess to sharing your perplexity,' said Mother Earth. 'This is by no means what I had intended . . .' She stopped, conscious of having disclosed too much.

'Go on, then,' said Alberich. 'What was meant to happen?'

'I am not at liberty . . .'

'Since it didn't happen,' said Alberich, 'it can't be important.'

Mother Earth shrugged her bony shoulders. 'Very well, then,' she said. 'The Ring was supposed to pass to the last of the Volsungs.'

'There aren't any more Volsungs,' said Flosshilde.

'Incorrect. Siegfried and Gutrune did in fact produce a child, a daughter called Sieghilde.'

'I never knew that,' said Alberich.

'Nobody knew. I saw to that. Sieghilde was brought up at the court of King Etzel of Hungary, where she married a man called Unferth. A most unsuitable match, I may say, of which I did not approve. Unfortunately, I was too late to be able to prevent it.'

'And then what happened?'

'I have no idea. Unferth was an itinerant bard by profession, and I lost track of him in his wanderings. By birth he was a Jute, but he never returned to his native Jutland. I can only presume . . .'

Flosshilde ran out of the room

'What's she up to now?' muttered Alberich. 'Why can't people sit still?'

197

'Anyway,' continued Mother Earth, 'given the quite remarkable fecundity of the Volsung race, I have little doubt that the family is still extant, and I have spent a great deal of time and effort in trying to trace the survivors of the line. Who could possibly make a better Ring-Bearer than the descendant of Siegfried the Dragon-Slayer? But to date my inquiries have been fruitless.'

'So you think there's a Volsung or two wandering about out there just waiting for a chance to snap up the Ring?' said Alberich. 'That's all we need.'

'On the contrary,' said Mother Earth, 'I still regard the Volsung option as being the best possible solution. The Fisher episode is surely nothing but a strange and unplanned complication which will undoubtedly resolve itself in time. As soon as the missing Volsung is traced and apprised of his destiny, we can all get back to normal.'

'That's not exactly fair on our young friend Malcolm Fisher,' said Alberich. 'He deserves more consideration than that. I presume that your Volsung would get hold of the Ring in the same way that his ancestor Siegfried obtained it from Fafner.'

'That ought not to be necessary,' said Mother Earth hurriedly. 'No, he has had his part to play as caretaker of the Ring, and to date I must grant you he has played it very creditably. Only this present difficulty has marred an unexpectedly satisfactory period in the Ring's history. Recent events, however, have highlighted the underlying weakness in his emotional composition which makes it obvious that he is not to be trusted with the Ring on a long-term basis. Unfortunately, as we have recently been made to realise, there is very little that any of us can actually do, when the chips are, so to speak, down, to influence matters. Thanks to Wotan, and of course to my daughter here, all may yet be lost.'

At this moment, Flosshilde came back into the room, carrying a volume of an Encyclopedia.

'Say what you like about old Misery-guts there,' she said, 'she's made a good job of that library. Here we are.'

She laid the book down on the table. 'The Jutes,' she said, 'were part of the Anglo-Saxon alliance that colonised Britain after the Romans went home.'

'I seem to remember hearing something about it at the time,' said Alberich, 'now that you mention it. Go on.'

'If your Unferth was a Jute, perhaps he came over to Britain with the rest of them. Have you tried looking here?'

Mother Earth raised an eyebrow. 'I must confess that this is a line of inquiry that has not previously occurred to me. These islands have always been so unremarkable, heroically and theologically speaking, that I never for one moment imagined that the Volsung line might be found here. It is of course possible.'

Flosshilde seemed excited about something. 'Where would the records be?' she asked. 'This is worth following up.'

'The main archive is at Mimir's Well,' replied Mother Earth. 'I think it would be in order to check this new lead.'

'So what are we waiting for?'

'My dear young woman,' said Mother Earth, 'you don't expect me to abandon this highly delicate situation at this crucial juncture simply to go chasing through the files. It can certainly wait until Mr Fisher returns from his holiday and this present difficulty has been satisfactorily resolved.'

'Why are you so interested in tracking down this Volsung, anyway?' said Alberich suspiciously. 'I thought you were on Fisher's side.'

'Don't you see?' said Flosshilde. 'If we find the person who ought to have the Ring, Malcolm won't be able to give it to *her*, because it won't be his to give away to anyone. He's got wonderful principles, he'll see at once that he has to give it to this Volsung person, and then everything will be all right.'

Alberich shook his head. 'You overestimate him,' he said. 'Besides, what guarantee do we have that this Volsung will be any more suitable than Malcolm Fisher?'

'I can reassure you on that point,' said Mother Earth. 'I am, after all, the ancestress of the Volsung race. Admittedly, Wotan is their male ancestor, but that cannot be helped now.'

'You mean this Volsung would be her cousin?' Flosshilde asked, pointing rather rudely at Ortlinde.

'In strict form, yes.'

'Even so,' said Flosshilde, 'it's worth a try.'

'The Volsung race,' continued Mother Earth, 'was specifically designed from the outset to be Ring-Bearers. They have built into their software all the heroic qualities required to carry out that office in a satisfactory manner. Even after centuries of dilution, the fundamental ingredients ought still to be present. I have no doubts at all in my mind that if a Volsung or Volsungs can be found, our problems will be at an end. But first, it is essential that Mr Fisher's ridiculous idea of giving the Ring to my daughter . . .'

'Now there I agree with you,' said Flosshilde. 'Here, you. Haven't you got anything to say?'

'No,' mumbled Ortlinde.

For a moment, Flosshilde felt very sorry for the Valkyrie. Although she would have liked everything to have been Ortlinde's fault, it palpably wasn't, and the girl herself was probably having a rather horrid time. But Flosshilde hardened her heart.

'Why don't you do something useful for a change?' she said. 'You nip across to Mimir's Well and look up the records, if you're so good with libraries.'

Ortlinde shrugged her shoulders and started to get to her feet.

'Stay where you are,' commanded her mother. 'I'm not letting you out of my sight until this has been cleared up.'

Ortlinde sat down again.

'Well, someone's got to go,' said Flosshilde.

'You go, then,' said Alberich. 'You're only getting under our feet here, anyway.'

Flosshilde made a face at him. Mother Earth raised her hand for order.

'I shall telephone the Elder Norn,' she said. 'She is a most competent woman, and I'm sure Mr Fisher will not begrudge us the cost of the call.'

To telephone Valhalla from the Taunton area one has to go through the operator, and the process can take a long time. While Mother Earth was thus engaged, Alberich took Flosshilde on one side.

'You're up to something,' he said.

'No, I'm not.'

'Yes, you are. You're going to try and nobble this Volsung, aren't you? You failed to nobble Malcolm Fisher, so you want a chance at someone a bit more vulnerable, or at least with better taste.'

The Rhinedaughter shook her head sadly. 'My nobbling days are over,' she said. 'I've been nobbled myself.'

'Go on!' said Alberich incredulously. 'I thought it was all an act.'

'I wish it was,' sighed Flosshilde. 'But it isn't.'

'But what on earth do you see in him?'

'I don't know,' said Flosshilde. 'I suppose he's just different. He's sweet. I really have no idea. But I want to get him out of all this before they do something horrid to him.'

Alberich smiled. 'This is unusual for you, Flosshilde,' he

said. 'I always thought you were the hardest of the three. Woglinde dries her face with emery paper and Wellgunde cleans her teeth with metal polish, but you were always the really tough cookie. And now look at you.'

'All good things must come to an end,' said Flosshilde, 'and I don't suppose he'll ever be interested in me even if he does get rid of her. Which is funny, really,' she said bitterly. 'After all, he's nothing special and I am, Heaven knows. But there you are.'

'There you are indeed,' said Alberich. 'Good luck, anyway.'

Mother Earth put down the receiver.

'Would you believe,' she said, 'the Elder Norn is away on her honeymoon. Apparently, she has married a rock-troll she met only recently at a Company meeting. But the Middle Norn has agreed to do the necessary work in the archives, so we can expect results shortly.'

'Well, that's something, anyway,' said Flosshilde, sitting down and putting her feet up. 'Now what shall we do?'

At that moment the door opened and Malcolm walked in. His hair was wet, although it had not been raining in Somerset.

'They told me you were all in here,' he said.

'If you've got nothing better to do,' said the Valkyrie Grimgerde, 'you could fix that dripping tap in the kitchen.'

'I'm busy,' Wotan said angrily, but the Valkyrie had gone. He leaned back in his chair and poured himself another large schnapps. Despite the schnapps he was profoundly worried; it had been a long time since he had heard anything from Somerset, and surely his daughter should have succeeded in her mission by now. She was not, he was fully prepared to admit, an outstandingly

202

intelligent girl, but intelligence was not really required, only beauty and a certain soppiness. Both of these qualities she had in abundance.

'Must you sit in here?' asked the Valkyrie Siegrune. 'I want to hoover this room.'

'Go and hoover somewhere else!' thundered the God of Battles. The Valkyrie swept out without a word, leaving Wotan to his thoughts and his schnapps. He bore the human no ill-will, he decided. His handling of the world, he was forced to admit, had been largely adequate. But this state of affairs could not be allowed to continue indefinitely, and if Operation Ortlinde failed, he could not see what else he could reasonably do.

'If that child messes this up,' he growled into his glass, 'I'll turn her into a bullfrog.' He closed his eye, and tried to get some sleep.

When he woke up, he saw that he was surrounded on all sides by daughters. Even allowing for his blurred senses, there seemed to be an awful lot of them. To be precise, eight . . .

'So you're back at last, are you?' he said. 'Well, where is it?'

All the Valkyries were silent, staring sullenly at their shoes, which were identical. When you have eight daughters, you can save a lot by buying in bulk.

'Where is it?' Wotan repeated. 'Come on, give it here.'

'I haven't got it,' Ortlinde said softly. 'He doesn't want me.'

'You stupid . . . what do you mean?'

He had spilt schnapps all over the covers of the chair, but none of his daughters said a word. This could only mean that Ortlinde had failed him, and they were all feeling terribly guilty.

'He wouldn't give it to me,' said Ortlinde sadly. 'He said

that he loved me, but he couldn't give it to me. I knew it would happen, sooner or later. So I came home.'

'But why not?' screamed Wotan. 'You had the sucker in the palm of your hand and you let him get away.'

'I know,' said the girl. 'I've let you down again. I'm sorry.'

'Get out of my sight!' Wotan shouted. The girl bowed her head and wandered wretchedly away to clean the bathroom.

After a short battle with his temper, Wotan managed to control himself, and surveyed his seven other daughters with his one good eye.

'Right, then,' he said briskly, 'who's going to be next?'

There was a long silence. Nobody moved.

'Very well, then,' Wotan said. 'Grimgerde, go and do something useful for the first time in your life.'

Grimgerde shook her head. 'There's no point,' she said. 'He knows all about us.'

'He's been talking to Mother,' said Waltraute.

'He'd recognise me as soon as I walked through the door,' Grimgerde continued. 'It wouldn't work. I'm sorry.'

For a moment, Wotan was stunned. Then, with a roar like thunder, he leapt to his feet and ran out of the room. All the lights had gone out all over the house.

'We've let him down again,' said Grimgerde sadly.

'If only we could *talk* to him,' said Waltraute.

'Where's the point?' said Rossweise. 'We wouldn't be able to communicate with him.'

They went to fetch the Hoover.

CHAPTER FOURTEEN

Malcolm did not know where the others were, nor did he care much. He only knew that Ortlinde had gone. She had packed her suitcase, said goodbye, and walked down the drive, and for all Malcolm knew he would never see her again. Of course, he could not accept this; it seemed incredible that it could all be over, and at the back of his mind he felt sure that it was only a meaningless interruption to an inevitable happy ending. The girl loved him. He loved her. Surely that ought to be enough to be going on with. But she had gone away, and the part of his mind that still dealt with reality told him that it was for ever.

The room in which he had chosen to sit had not been used for many years; there were dust sheets over several pieces of furniture, and he tried to imagine what they looked like under their protective covers. There was half a tune he had heard in New York drumming away in his head; it was not a tune with any emotional or nostalgic significance, but it was there, like a fly trapped behind a windscreen, and he sat and listened to its endless repetitions for a while. In front of him were ten or fifteen sheets of paper on which he had started to write many drafts of the letter that would set everything straight. But the right words somehow eluded him, like a cat that refuses to come in when called. He could concentrate on nothing, and his eyes focused of their own accord on the walls and corners of the room.

'There you are,' said a girl's voice behind him. 'I've been looking for you everywhere.'

He knew even before he looked round that it was only Flosshilde. He said nothing. He did not resent her intrusion; nothing could matter less. He imagined that she would say something or other and then go away again.

Flosshilde sat in the window-seat and put her feet up on a chair. 'You don't mind me being here, do you?' she said.

'No,' he replied.

'I wanted to get away from the others. They were being awfully stuffy about something.'

Malcolm said nothing. He did not believe in the existence of anything outside this room, except of course for Ortlinde, and he wasn't allowed to think about her any more.

'Do you want to talk about it?' Flosshilde asked.

'No,' said Malcolm.

'I didn't think you would. She was rather beautiful, wasn't she?'

'She isn't dead, you know,' said Malcolm irritably. 'She still is rather beautiful for all I know.'

'What made you change your mind?'

'I had to do something. That seemed better than the other thing. I don't know. I did what I thought was for the best.'

'I think you were right, if that's any help. No, of course it isn't, I'm sorry. I'll be quiet now.'

'You can talk if you like,' Malcolm said. 'It wasn't bothering me.'

'Can you play pontoon?'

'No.'

'I'll teach you if you like.'

'No, thanks.'

'I know a game where you take a piece of writing – anything will do – and each letter has a number – A is one, B is two and so on – and you play odds against evens. Each sentence is a new game, and the side that wins gets five points for each sentence. Odds usually win, for some reason. That's what I do when I'm feeling unhappy. It takes your mind off things.'

Malcolm wasn't listening, and Flosshilde felt like a castaway on a desert island who sees a ship sailing by without taking any notice of his signals. Perhaps it would be better, she thought, if she went away. But she stayed where she was.

'Shall I tell you the story about the time when the Giants stole Donner's hammer and he had to dress up in drag to get it back?'

'If you like.'

She told the story, doing all the voices and putting in some new bits she hadn't thought of before. It was a very funny story, but Malcolm simply sat and looked out of the window. Flosshilde wanted to cry, or at the very least hit him, but she simply sat there too.

'I want your advice,' she said.

'I don't think it would be worth much.'

'Never mind. One of my sisters is dotty about a man, and he's dotty about a girl, and she doesn't fancy him at all. What should she do?'

'Are you being funny?' Malcolm asked bitterly.

'No, really. What do you think she should do about it?'

'Grow up and get on with something useful.'

'I see. Aren't you sorry for her?'

'I suppose so. But I'm not really in the mood just now.' He turned away and looked at the wall.

'I'm sorry,' said Flosshilde. 'I'll shut up now.'

She studied her fingernails, which were the best in the world. King Arthur had often complimented her on her fingernails.

'Would you like me to go and talk to her?' Flosshilde said after a long silence.

'Who?'

'Ortlinde, silly. Perhaps there's something I could say . . .'

'I thought you couldn't stand her. Why is that, by the way?'

'Oh, I don't know,' lied Flosshilde. 'We quarrelled about something a long time ago.'

'Tell me about her. You probably know her a lot better than I do.'

'Not really,' Flosshilde said. 'I've known her on and off for years, of course, but only very generally. I find it pretty hard to tell those sisters apart, to be honest.'

'Are they all like her? Her sisters, I mean.'

'Very. Ortlinde's probably the nicest-looking, now that Brunnhilde's . . . And Grimgerde's quite pretty too, in a rather horrid sort of way. Big round eyes, like a cow.'

'I'm not really interested in her sisters. She said that the rest of them were all much nicer than she was, but I don't believe her. What did you quarrel about?'

'I honestly can't remember. It can't have been anything important. Is there anything at all I can do?'

'No,' said Malcolm. 'Perhaps you'd better go. I'm not in a very good mood, I'm afraid.'

Flosshilde took her feet daintily off the chair and walked out of the room. Once she had closed the door safely behind her, she shut her eyes and closed her hands tightly. It didn't help at all, and if she screamed somebody would hear her. She went downstairs.

From the landing, she could hear an excited buzz of voices in the drawing-room: Alberich and Erda and someone else, whose voice was vaguely familiar. The newcomer turned out to be the Middle Norn, a round, fair-haired woman in a smart brown tweed suit. She had brought a huge briefcase with her, and the floor was covered with photocopies of ancient parchments. Erda and the Norn were down on their knees going over them with magnifying-glasses, while Alberich was at the desk taking notes.

'. . . And she married Sintolt the Hegeling,' the Norn was saying, 'and *their* son was Eormanric . . .'

'What's going on?' Flosshilde asked.

'There has been a rather singular development,' said Erda, looking up from the papers on the floor. She had fluff from the carpet all over her jacket. 'We have succeeded in tracing the last of the Volsungs.'

'Really?' said Flosshilde. She wasn't in the least fascinated, for it scarcely seemed to matter now. Still, it would be something to do, and if she got bored she could play her word-game.

'I think you will be surprised when you hear it,' continued Mother Earth. 'Let me just go through the stemma for you.'

'Don't bother on my account,' said Flosshilde. 'I'll take your word for it.' She sat down and picked up a magazine. 'Just tell me the name.'

'There are three living descendants in the direct line,' said the Norn, taking off her spectacles. 'Mrs Eileen Fisher, of Sydney, Australia; her daughter Bridget, also of Sydney; and her son Malcolm, of Combe Hall, Somerset.'

209

In an instant, Flosshilde was kneeling beside them. She bullied the Norn into going over every link in the complex genealogical chain, which spanned over a thousand years. The descent was indeed direct, from Siegfried the Volsung, Fafner's Bane, to Bridget and Malcolm Fisher.

'I hurried over as soon as I found out,' said the Norn. 'Of course, you know what this means.'

'No,' admitted Flosshilde, breathlessly. 'Go on.'

'Well,' said the Norn, putting back her spectacles. 'Siegfried was, at least in theory, a subject of the Gibichung crown when he married Gutrune. Certainly, Sieghilde was a Gibichung subject, and so the Ring, if we accept that it was Siegfried's legitimate property, is subject to Gibichung law in matters of inheritance. Gibichung law is of course very complicated, and on the subject of testament it verges on the arcane, but it so happens that I have made a special study of the subject.' The Norn paused, as if expecting some words of praise. None were forthcoming. 'Anyway, hereditary as opposed to acquired property cannot, under Gibichung law, pass to the female heirs but is only transmitted through them to the next male heir. That is to say, to the female it is inalienable and she has no right to assign or dispose of it. She can only keep it in trust until the next male heir comes of age at fourteen years.'

'What are you going on about?' said Flosshilde.

'Although his mother is still alive and his sister is older than him, Malcolm Fisher is, according to Gibichung law, the rightful heir to the Nibelung's Ring.'

'Which ring?'

'My bloody ring,' said Alberich impatiently. 'Your ring. *The* Ring. Look, if we're going to be all legal about this . . .'

'Human law,' said Mother Earth loftily, 'has no bearing

on property that is or has been owned or held by a God. Since the Volsung race is descended from Gods and is therefore semi-divine, and since the Ring was, if only for the space of a few hours, once held by the Gods Wotan and Loge, the Ring is subject only to divine law.'

'Oh,' said the Norn, clearly disappointed. 'Never mind, then.'

'Under divine law,' said Mother Earth, 'property descends by primogeniture alone. Mrs Eileen Fisher, Mr Fisher's mother – and the eldest surviving Volsung, is therefore the legitimate legal heir to the Nibelung's Ring.'

'What about me?' shouted Alberich.

'And me,' added Flosshilde. 'It was ours to begin with, remember.'

'The gold was,' said Alberich. 'But I *made* the bloody thing.'

'I was about to say,' said Mother Earth, severely, 'that under divine law, right of inheritance is subordinate to right of conquest.'

'What?' Flosshilde was now utterly confused.

'It means,' said Alberich bitterly, 'that if I take something away from you it becomes mine, and if they take something away from me it becomes theirs. That's divine law. Marvellous, isn't it?'

'In other words,' said the Norn triumphantly, 'it amounts to the same thing as Gibichung law. It belongs to Mr Fisher.'

There was a baffled silence as the four immortals pondered the significance of all this.

'Be that as it may,' said Mother Earth at last, 'the fact remains that Malcolm Fisher, if not *the* last of the Volsungs, is one of the last of the Volsungs – certainly, he is the most recent of the Volsungs, which is roughly the same

211

thing – and as such is by birth and genetic programming one of the three most suitable people in the world to be the Ring-Bearer. Goddammit,' she added.

Flosshilde could hardly contain her excitement. 'Just wait till I tell him,' she said. 'He'll be thrilled.'

'I hardly think it would be suitable at this juncture . . .'

Flosshilde made a rude face and left the room.

'That child is scarcely helping matters,' said Mother Earth.

'Guess what,' said Flosshilde, bursting into the room. 'You're a Volsung.'

'I'm sorry?' Malcolm said.

Flosshilde told him everything, putting in explanations where she felt they would be necessary. 'So you see,' she said, 'you're not really human at all. You're one of us. And *she is* your cousin.'

Malcolm laughed. 'What a coincidence,' he said sardonically.

'But don't you care?' said Flosshilde. 'You're virtually a God. You're descended from the world's greatest hero. Aren't you pleased?'

'No,' said Malcolm truthfully. 'I couldn't care less, to be honest with you. Of course, I always knew there was something wrong with me, but now that I know what it is, I don't see that it's going to make a great deal of difference.' He continued to stare out of the window.

'Oh, for pity's sake!' Flosshilde was angry now. She had so wanted him to be pleased and excited, and he wasn't. 'You're hopeless.'

'Very probably. And besides, from what you said, Bridget is the real Volsung, or the eldest, or whatever. That doesn't surprise me in the least. Judging by what I've heard about Siegfried lately, it sounds like she takes after him a whole lot.'

Flosshilde knelt down beside him and put her hands on his elbows. 'But she hasn't done what you've done. She hasn't made the world a wonderful place or defeated Wotan. You have, all on your own. You're the real hero, much more than Siegfried was, even.'

'Really?' Malcolm shook his head. 'I don't think so. I've stopped living in a make-believe world, you see. Just finding out that I'm a make-believe person doesn't make any difference. It's not going to change anything.'

'But you don't understand . . .'

'That's the one thing I have got right,' he said, looking straight at her. 'I *do* understand, and that's the only good thing that's come out of this whole rotten mess. I've been living in a world of my own and . . .'

'But the world *is* your own,' Flosshilde almost shouted. Suddenly Malcolm began to laugh, and Flosshilde lost all patience with him. As long as she lived, she told herself as she walked furiously out of the room, she would never understand humans.

On the landing she met the Norn, who seemed agitated. 'Call him,' she said. 'Something terrible is happening.'

Across the Glittering Plains, which stretch as far as the eye can see from the steep rock on which the castle of Valhalla is built, Wotan had mustered the Army of the Storm. In their squadrons and regiments were assembled the Light and Dark Elves, the spirits of the unquiet dead, the hosts of Hela. At the head of each regiment rode a Valkyrie, dressed in her terrifying armour, the very sight of which is enough to turn the wits of the most fearless of heroes. Around his shoulders, Wotan cast the Mantle of Terror, and on his head he fastened the helmet that the dwarves had made him from the fingernails of dead champions in the gloomy caverns of Nibelheim. He nodded his head, and Loge brought him the great spear Gungnir, the symbol and the source of all his power. When he had first come to rule the earth, he had cut its shaft from the branches of Yggdrasil, the great ash tree that stands between the worlds, causing the tree to wither and die and making inevitable the final downfall of the Gods. Onto this spearshaft, Loge had marked the runes of the Great Covenant between the God and his subjects.

Wotan raised his right hand, and the Valkyrie Waltraute, who closes the eyes of men slain in battle, led forward his eight-legged horse, the cloud-trampling Sleipnir. Above his head hovered two black ravens.

'If you get mud on that saddle,' said Waltraute, 'you can clean it off yourself.'

Without a word, Wotan vaulted onto the back of his charger. As the first bolt of lightning ripped the black clouds he brandished the great spear as a sign to his army, the *Wutende Heer*.

It was over a thousand years since the hosts of Valhalla had ridden to war on the wings of the storm, and the world had forgotten how to be afraid. Like a vast cloud of locusts or a shower of arrows they flew, blotting out the light from the earth. At the head of the wild procession galloped Wotan; behind him Donner, Tyr, Froh, Heimdall, Njord and Loge, who carried the banner of darkness. Close on their heels came the eight Valkyries: Grimgerde, Waltraute, Siegrune, Helmwige, Ortlinde, Schwertleite, Gerhilde and Rossweise, baying like wolves to spur on the grim company that followed them, the terrible spirits of fear and discord. Each of the eight companies bore its own hideous banner –

Hunger, War, Disease, Intolerance, Ignorance, Greed, Hatred and Despair; these were the badges of Wotan's army. Behind the army like a pack of hounds intoxicated by the chase followed the wind and the rain, lashing indiscriminately at friend and foe. Below them, forests were flattened, towns and villages were swept away, even the mountains seemed to tremble and cower at the fury of their passing. With a rush, they swept over the Norn Fells and past the dead branches of the World Ash. As they passed it, lightning fell among its withered leaves, setting it alight. Soon the whole fell was burning, and the flames hissed and swayed at the foot of Valhalla Rock. As the army of the God of Battles passed between the worlds, the castle itself caught fire and began to burn furiously, lighting up the whole world with a bright red glow.

The army passed high over the frozen desert of the Arctic, convulsing the ice-covered waters with the shock of their motion, and flitted over Scandinavia like an enormous bird of prey, whose very shadow paralyses the helpless victim. As they wheeled and banked over Germany, the Rhine rose up as if to meet them, bursting its banks and flooding the flat plains between Essen and Nijmegen. Wotan, his whole form framed with the lightning, laughed when he saw it, and his laughter brought towers and cathedrals crashing to the ground. And as the army followed its dreadful course, black clouds of squeaking, gibbering spirits leapt up to swell its numbers, as all the dark, tormented forces of the earth were drawn as if by capillary action into the fold of the Lord of Tempests. The very noise of their wings was deafening, and when they swept low the earth split open, as if shrinking back in horror. But however vast and awesome this great force might seem, most terrible of all was Wotan, like a burning arrow at its head. As he flew headlong over the North Sea, the heat of his anger turned the waters to steam, and soon the forests of Scotland were blazing as brightly as Valhalla itself. As the army neared its goal, it seemed to concentrate into a cloud of tangible darkness, forcing its way through the air as it bore down like a meteor on one little village in the West of England.

'What's going on?' shouted Malcolm. The noise was unbearable, and through the splintered windows of the house a gale was blowing that nearly lifted him off his feet.

'It's Wotan,' yelled Alberich, his face white with fear. 'He's coming with all his army.'

'Is he indeed?' Malcolm replied. 'I want a word with him.'

All the lights had gone out, but the brilliance of the ball of fire that grew ever larger in the northern sky dazzled and stunned the watchers, so that even Mother Earth had to turn away. But Malcolm walked calmly out of the shattered door and stood in the drive. His hair was unruffled and his eyes were unblinking, and on his finger the Ring felt easy and comfortable. Out of the immeasurable darkness that surrounded it the awful light grew ever more fierce, until the very ground seemed to be about to melt. Like a falling sun, it hurtled towards the ruined house, straight at the Ring-Bearer, like a diving falcon.

'All right,' said Malcolm sternly. 'That will do.'

The light went out, and the world was plunged into utter darkness. A hideous scream cut through the air like a spearblade through flesh, and was held for an instant in the hollow of the surrounding hills. Then it died away, and the cloud slowly began to fall apart. Like a swarm of angry bees suddenly confounded by a puff of smoke, Wotan's army sank out of the air and disintegrated. The black vapours dissolved, and the gentle light of the sun fell upon the surfaces of the wrecked and mangled planet.

'And before you go,' said Malcolm, 'you can clear up all this mess.'

Like a film being wound back, the world began to reassemble itself. Smoke was dragged out of the air back into the stumps of charred trees. Bricks and stones slipped back into place and once more were houses. Glass reformed itself smoothly into panes, and the cracks faded away. The flooded rivers slid shamefacedly back between their banks, taking their silt with them, and the earth silently closed up its fissures. While this remarkable act of healing was taking place, a pale mist formed and hung in the still air above the surface of the world, and the light of the sun was caught and refracted by it into all the colours of the spectrum. Malcolm had never seen anything so beautiful in his entire life.

'What is it?' he asked a passing dove. The bird looked puzzled for a moment.

'Oh, *that*,' it said at last. 'That's just the Test Card.'

Malcolm shrugged his shoulders and walked back into the house.

The drawing-room seemed to be deserted, and Malcolm had come to the conclusion that everyone must have got bored and gone away when he heard a voice from under the table.

'What happened?' said the voice.

'Nothing,' said Malcolm. 'It's over now.'

Looking rather ashamed of herself, Mother Earth crawled out from her hiding-place. 'I dropped my god-damned glasses,' she mumbled. 'I was just looking for them, and . . .'

'Are you sure they're not in your pocket?' asked Malcolm sympathetically. Mother Earth made a dumb show of looking in her pocket and, not surprisingly, there they were. 'Thank you,' she said humbly.

'You're welcome,' said Malcolm.

Alberich and the Middle Norn emerged from behind the sofa. To his amusement, Malcolm saw that Alberich was holding the Norn's hand in a comforting manner.

'There now,' said the dwarf, 'I told you it would be all right, didn't I?'

The Norn beamed at him, her round face illuminated by some warm emotion. 'I don't know what came over me,' she said.

'That was very clever,' Alberich said to Malcolm, forgetting to let go of the Norn's hand even though the danger was past. 'How did you manage it?'

'What, that?' said Malcolm diffidently. 'Oh, it was nothing, really.'

Alberich and his new friend walked to the window. In the sky there was a deep red glow, which could have been the sunset were it not for the fact that it was due North. Alberich looked at it for a long time.

'I never did like them,' he said at last.

'Who?' Malcolm asked.

'The Gods,' said Alberich. Then he turned to the Norn. 'You look like you could do with some fresh air,' he said. 'Do you fancy a stroll in the garden?'

It seemed very probable that she did, and they walked away arm in arm. Malcolm shook his head sadly.

'Who was that, by the way?' he asked Mother Earth, who was busily brushing the fluff off her jacket.

'The Middle Norn,' said Mother Earth.

'Doesn't she have a name?'

'I don't know. Probably.'

'What's that light in the sky? I thought I'd put everything right.'

'That is the castle of Valhalla in flames,' replied Mother Earth quietly. 'The High Gods have all gone down. They no longer exist.'

Malcolm stared at her for a moment. 'All of them?'

'All of them. Wotan, Donner, Tyr, Froh . . .'

'*All* of them?'

'They went against the power of the Ring,' said Mother Earth with a shrug, 'and were proved to be weaker.'

'And what about the Valkyries?' Malcolm's throat was suddenly dry.

'They were only manifestations of Wotan's mind,' said Mother Earth. 'Figments of his imagination, I suppose you could say.'

'But they were your daughters.'

'In a sense.' Mother Earth polished her spectacles and put them precisely on her nose. 'But what the hell, I never really got on with them. Not as *people*. They were too like their father, I guess, and boy, am I glad to see the back of him.'

'And they're all dead?'

'Not dead,' said Mother Earth firmly. 'They just don't exist any more. I wouldn't upset yourself over it. In fact, you should be pretty pleased with yourself. By the way, did Flosshilde tell you about . . .?'

'Yes,' said Malcolm, 'yes, she did.' He was trying to remember what Ortlinde had looked like, but strangely enough he couldn't. He felt as if he had been woken up in the middle of a strange and wonderful dream, and that all the immensely real images that had filled his mind only a moment ago were slipping away from him, like water that you try and hold in your hand.

'Let me assure you,' said Mother Earth, 'that you have in no sense *killed* anybody.'

'I don't believe I have,' said Malcolm slowly, 'I think I'm beginning to understand all this business after all. By the way, what happens now?'

Mother Earth came as close as she had ever done to a smile. 'You tell me,' she said. 'You're in charge now.'

Malcolm looked at the Ring on his finger. 'Right,' he said, 'let's get this show on the road.'

Mother Earth yawned. 'I'm feeling awful sleepy,' she said. 'I guess I'll go to bed now, if you don't mind. If I don't get my thousand years every age I'm no use to anybody.'

'Go ahead,' said Malcolm. 'And thanks for all your help.'

'You're welcome,' said Mother Earth. She was beginning to glow with a pale blue light. 'I didn't do anything, really. It was all your work.'

Malcolm smiled, and nodded.

'Remember,' she said, 'whatever you feel like doing is probably right.' She was indistinct now, and Malcolm could see a coffee-table through her.

'Sorry?' he asked, but she had melted away, leaving only a few sparkles behind her in the air. Malcolm shrugged his shoulders.

'Never mind,' he said aloud. 'She's probably on the phone.'

Two very bedraggled ravens floated down out of the evening sky and pecked at the window-pane. Their feathers were slightly singed. Malcolm opened the window and they hopped painfully into the room.

'Hello,' said Malcolm. 'What can I do for you?'

The first raven nudged his companion, who nudged him back.

'We were thinking,' said the first raven. 'You might be wanting a messenger service.'

'Now you've taken over,' said the second raven.

'You see,' said the first raven, 'we used to work for the old management, and now they've been wound up . . .'

'What do you do, exactly?' Malcolm asked.

'We fly around the world and see what's going on,' said the raven, 'and then we come and tell you.'

'That sounds fine,' said Malcolm. 'You're on.'

The second raven dipped its beak gratefully. 'I was thinking of packing it in,' he said. 'But now the old boss has gone . . .'

'What are you called?' Malcolm asked.

'I'm Thought,' said the first raven, 'and this is Memory.'

'When can you start?'

Thought seemed to hesitate, but Memory said, 'Straight away.' When Malcolm wasn't looking, Thought pecked his colleague hard on the shoulder.

'Fine,' said Malcolm. 'First, go and make sure that all the damage has been put right. Then check to see if any of the old Gods are still left over.'

The two ravens nodded and fluttered away. When they were (as they thought) out of earshot, Thought turned to Memory and said, 'What did you tell him that for?'

'What?' said Memory.

'About us starting straight away. I wanted a holiday.'

'Don't you ever think?' replied Memory. 'This is the twentieth century. They've got telephones, they've got computers, they've got Fax machines. They don't need birds any more. Nobody's indispensable, chum. You've got to show you're willing to work.'

'Oh, well,' said Thought. 'Here we go again, then.'

After a while, it occurred to Malcolm that he hadn't seen Flosshilde since the storm had died away. At the back of his mind something told him that now that Ortlinde no longer existed, it was time to move on to the next available option, but he recognised that instinct and deliberately cut it out of his mind. It was the old Malcolm Fisher instinct, the one that made him fall in love and be unhappy. He was finished with all that now. He knew of course that there was such a thing as love, and that if you happen to come across it, as most people seem to do, it is not a thing that you can avoid, or that you should want to avoid. But you cannot go out and find it, because it is not that sort of creature. The phrase 'to fall in love', he realised, is a singularly apt one; it is something you blunder into, like a pothole. Very like a pothole. In his case, however, he had had the fortune, good or bad, to blunder into a badger, not love, and since he was not accident-prone, that was probably all the accidental good fortune he was likely to get. As for Flosshilde – well, since the passing of the Valkyries, she was officially one of the three prettiest girls in the universe, but only superficial people judge by appearances. Malcolm himself could be a prettier girl than Flosshilde just by giving an order to the Tarnhelm, although it was unlikely that he should ever want to do that. The fact that she was a water-spirit was neither here nor there; he himself was a hero, descended from Mother Earth and a now non-existent God, but he doubted whether that had any influence on his character or behaviour. He suddenly realised that Wotan and Erda and all the rest of them had been his relatives. That at least explained why he had been frightened of them and why he had found them so difficult to cope with.

He smiled at this thought. Family is family, after all,

and he had just blotted most of his out. But now he was on his own, which, bearing in mind the case of his unhappy predecessor, was probably no bad thing. It would be foolish to go looking for a consort now that the world depended on him and him alone. A trouble shared, after all, is a trouble doubled.

Nevertheless, he wondered where Flosshilde had got to. Everyone seemed to have drifted away, and for a moment he felt a slight panic. He sat down on the stairs and tried to think calmly. To his relief, he found this perfectly possible to do.

Wotan, he reflected, had gone to one extreme, but Ingolf had gone to the other. One had been caught up in a noisy and infuriating household which had driven him quietly mad. The other had curled up in a hole and allowed his dark subconscious to permit the world to drift into the twentieth century, with all its unpleasant consequences. He sought a happy medium between these two extremes and in particular considered carefully all that Mother Earth had told him. Then he got up and whistled loudly. To his surprise, nothing happened. Then he realised his mistake and went through to the drawing-room. There were the two ravens, huddled upon the window-sill.

'Everything's fine,' said Thought, as soon as Malcolm had let them in. 'All the Gods have cleared off.'

'Except Loge,' said Memory. 'He offered us all the dead sheep we could eat if we didn't tell you he was still around, but we thought . . .'

'I've got nothing against Loge,' said Malcolm. 'But how come he didn't go down with all the others?'

'He was a bit puzzled by that,' said Memory. 'Apparently, there he was, surrounded by Gods one minute, all on his own feeling a right prat the next. He thinks it's down to him being a fire-spirit and not a real God.'

'Tell him he can have his old job back if he wants it,' said Malcolm.

'I'll tell him,' said Thought, 'but I think he's got other plans. He was talking about going into the wet fish business. Muttered something about he might as well do it himself before somebody did it to him. Gloomy bloke, I always thought.'

'Anyway,' said Malcolm, 'did either of you see Flosshilde?'

'Flosshilde,' said Memory thoughtfully. 'Can't say I did. In fact, I haven't seen any of the girls since before the Big Bang.'

Malcolm suddenly felt very ill. 'But they weren't High Gods, were they?' he said. 'I mean, they couldn't have . . .'

'Wouldn't have thought so,' said Memory, 'but you never know with those three. Very deep they were, though you wouldn't think it to look at them. But they were always mixed up with some pretty heavy things, like the Rhinegold and the Ring. Could be that they had to go along with the rest.'

Malcolm sat down heavily, appalled at the thought. He couldn't understand why he was so horrified, but the idea of never seeing Flosshilde again suddenly seemed very terrible. Not that he was in love with her; but he knew now that he needed her very urgently.

'Find her,' he snapped. 'Go on, move. If you're not back by dawn, I'll turn you both into clay pigeons.'

The ravens flapped hurriedly away into the night, and Malcolm closed his eyes and groaned. He had just bumped into something, and it felt horribly disconcerting.

'Oh, God,' he said aloud. 'Now look what I've done.'

*

Alberich and the Middle Norn looked in to say goodbye, and found Malcolm in a strange mood. He seemed upset about something but would not say what it was, and his manner seemed cold and hostile. The Norn felt sorry for him, but Alberich seemed in a hurry to get away.

'I don't like it,' he said. 'Something's gone wrong.'

'What could possibly go wrong now?' said the Norn coyly.

'I don't know,' said Alberich, 'but when it does, I want to be safely underground, where it won't matter so much.'

They walked in silence for a while, as the Norn nerved herself to ask the question that had been worrying her.

'Alberich,' she said.

'Yes?'

'Don't take this the wrong way, but weren't you supposed to have foresworn Love?'

'Yes,' said Alberich, 'but I'm allowed to change my mind, aren't I?'

'But I didn't think you could. Not once you'd sworn.'

'That was conditional on my still wanting the Ring. And now that I couldn't care less about it . . .'

'Couldn't you?'

'No.' He felt rather foolish, but for some reason that was all that seemed to be wrong with him. An unwonted harmony seemed to have overtaken his digestive system.

'To celebrate,' he said daringly, 'let's go and treat ourselves to the best lunch money can buy in this godforsaken country. I've heard about this place where you can get very palatable lobster.'

The Norn stared at him. 'Are you sure?' she said.

Alberich smiled at her fondly. 'Don't you start,' he said.

It was nearly dawn by the time the ravens came back. They perched on the window-sill exhausted, for they had been

225

flying hard all night. Through the open window, they could see the new Lord of Tempests sitting where he had been when they had left him several hours before. He was staring at the ground, and he looked distinctly irritable.

'He's not going to like it,' whispered Memory.

'You tell him,' replied Thought. 'You're the one with the words.'

'Why's it always got to be me?' said Memory angrily. 'You're the eldest, you tell him.'

'How do you make that out?'

'Stands to reason, dunnit? You can't have memory before thought, or you wouldn't have anything to remember. Well, would you?'

Memory clearly had right on his side, and so it was Thought who tapped gingerly on the pane and hopped into the room first. Malcolm looked up, and there was something in his eyes that both ravens recognised.

'Well?'

'Nothing, boss,' said Thought. 'We did all the rivers oceans, seas, lakes, lochs, lagoons, burns and wadis in the world. Even did the reservoirs and the sewers. Nothing. Looks like they've just . . .'

Malcolm let out a long, low moan, and Thought stepped back nervously, expecting every moment to be turned into a small flat disc made of pitch, earmarked for certain destruction. But Malcolm simply nodded, and the two birds flew thankfully away.

'Now look what you've gone and done,' said Thought bitterly as they collapsed onto a fallen tree beside the troutstream. 'You've gone and got us saddled with another bloody nutter. The last one was bad enough . . .'

'How was I to know he'd go off his rocker?' said Memory. 'He looked all right to me.'

'You never learn, do you?' continued Thought. 'We could be well away by now, but no, you've got to go and *volunteer* us. If we ever get out of this in one piece . . .'

In view of the threat recently uttered by the new Lord of the Ravens, that seemed improbable. Dawn was breaking in the East, and Thought regarded it sourly.

'Look at that,' he said. 'No imagination, this new bloke.'

'Come on,' said Memory. 'We might as well have another go.'

They lifted themselves wearily into a thermal and floated away.

CHAPTER FIFTEEN

For about a week after the going-down of the old Gods, Malcolm was kept rather busy. Minor spirits and divine functionaries called at all hours of the day and night with papers for him to read and documents to sign, most of which were concerned with trivial matters. The remaining Gods had been stripped of the last few vestiges of authority by the destruction of Wotan and, try as they might, they could not persuade the Ring-Bearer to transfer any of his duties or powers to them. In the end the majority of them accepted the new order of things, and the few recalcitrant deities who continued to protest found themselves posted to remote and uninhabited regions where their ineffectual energies could be expended without causing any real disturbance.

In an effort to appear positive, Malcolm created a new class of tutelary deities. The rivers and oceans had long had their own guardian spirits, originally installed when shipping was the main form of transport in the world. In the last few centuries, however, this role had diminished, whereas the roads and railways had gone without any form of heavenly representation. Malcolm therefore assigned most of the redundant spirits to the railway networks and motorways, a system which seemed to satisfy most requirements. He commissioned the Norns to set up a system of appointments: all gods wishing to be assigned a road or a railway had to take a written exam, and were posted according to the results they obtained. Since their duties were strictly honorary, it made little difference to the world at large, but it seemed to please the divine community. It gave them a purpose in life, and when one is dealing with immortals, that is no mean achievement.

There were also vacancies in existing posts to be filled, for many river-spirits and cloud-shepherds had perished with their master in the attack on Combe Hall. Again, the Norns were given the task of drawing up a list of unfilled posts with a parallel list of suitable candidates. Malcolm, who was unfamiliar with divine prosopography, had to rely heavily on the judgement of his advisers, but for some reason virtually all the supernatural beings he met were patently terrified of him, and this terror, combined with his ability to read thoughts, made corruption or favouritism seem unlikely.

He found the terror he inspired in his subordinates extremely hard to understand. Admittedly, his patience was sorely tried at times, for all the gods and spirits took themselves extremely seriously even though their power was non-existent; and he had to admit that he did sometimes lose his temper with them, causing the occasional shower of unplanned rain. But the world continued to thrive and prosper, with only the epidemic of love and romance spoiling an otherwise perfect situation. One thing did worry him, however: the Tarnhelm seemed to have developed a slight fault. Occasionally, after a particularly trying meeting or a long night of paperwork, he found to his disgust that he had changed his shape without wanting to, and for some reason the shape the Tarnhelm selected for him was invariably that of Wotan. This and a curious craving for schnapps gave Malcolm pause for thought, but he dismissed his fears as paranoia, and carried on with the work of reorganisation.

But he was not happy. Although he could not remember what she had looked like, he knew that Ortlinde was very much on his mind, and he could not help feeling horribly guilty about having caused her to cease to exist. He closed up the library at Combe Hall, but the house itself seemed to be haunted by her, and eventually he decided that the time had come to leave it for good. He sent for Colonel Booth (whose real name, he discovered, was Guttorm), thanked him for the loan of his house, and started to look for a new place to live. Somehow, he felt no enthusiasm for the task, and although the Norns, whom he found invaluable, continually sent him details of highly attractive properties all over the world, he found it difficult to summon up the energy to go and view them. Then one day the Younger Norn remarked that there was always Valhalla itself . . .

'But I thought it had been burnt down,' Malcolm said.

'Burnt, yes,' said the Norn. 'Down, no. The shell is still intact. I've had the architects out there, and they say it could easily be made habitable again. Of course, the best builders in the world were the Giants, and they're all dead now, but they were always expensive and difficult to work with . . .'

That, Malcolm felt, was something of an understatement. Nevertheless, the idea seemed curiously attractive, and he went out with the Younger Norn to look at the place.

'You could have tennis-courts here, and maybe a swimming-pool,' said the Norn, pointing with her umbrella to what had once been the Crack of Doom. 'Or if you don't like the idea of that, how about a rock garden? Or an ornamental lake? With real gnomes,' she said dreamily.

'I think I'd rather just have a lawn,' Malcolm replied. 'And some rosebeds.'

The Norn shrugged, and they moved on to inspect the Steps of Unknowing. 'How about a maze?' suggested the Norn. 'Appropriate, really.'

'No,' said Malcolm. 'I think a garage might be rather more use.'

'Please yourself. Anyway, you like the place?'

'Well, it's quiet, and the neighbours aren't too bad. I lived most of my life in Derby,' Malcolm said. 'It's certainly different from there. But it's rather a long way from the shops.'

'I wouldn't have thought that would have worried you, having the Tarnhelm and so on.'

'True,' said Malcolm, 'but sometimes I like to walk or drive, just for a change.'

'No problem,' said the Norn, 'we'll build you a replica of your favourite city. Valhalla New Town, we could call it.'

The thought of a heavenly version of Milton Keynes was almost enough to put Malcolm off the whole idea, but he asked the Norn to get some plans drawn up and hire an architect. The work would be done by the Nibelungs, who would do a perfectly good job without making unreasonable demands, as the Giants had done.

On the way back, they passed the charred stump of a tree, which had once been the World Ash. To their amazement, they saw a couple of green shoots emerging from the dead and blackened wood.

'That tree's been dead ever since Wotan first came on the scene,' said the Norn. 'It represents the Life Force, apparently.'

'Get someone to put one of those little wire cages round it,' said Malcolm. 'We don't want the squirrels getting at it.'

Malcolm returned from his trip to Valhalla feeling rather tired, not by the journey but by the company of the Younger Norn. He sat down in the drawing-room and took his shoes off; he wanted a quick glass of schnapps and ten minutes with the paper before going to bed. He was getting middle-aged, he realised; but such considerations did not really worry him. Youth, he had decided, was not such a big deal after all.

He looked out over the trout-stream and suddenly found himself in tears. For a moment he could not understand why; but then he realised what had caused what was, generally speaking, an unusual display of emotion. The trout-stream had reminded him of Flosshilde, whom he missed even more than the shoe-inspecting Valkyrie. He had treated Flosshilde very badly . . . No, it wasn't guilt that was making him cry. He had shut it out of his mind for so long that he imagined that it had gone away, but now he knew what his real problem was.

He had heard a story about a man who had gone through life thinking that the word Lunch meant the sun, and it occurred to him that he had been in roughly the same situation himself. Until very recently, he had not known what the word Love really meant; he had thought it referred to the self-deceptive and futile emotion that had plagued him since he first had enough hair on his chin to justify buying a razor of his own. On the night of the confrontation with Wotan, he had suddenly realised his mistake; he had loved Flosshilde then, just at the very moment when she had ceased to exist. So horrible had that thought been that he had excluded it from his brain; but now it had come back and taken him by surprise, and he could see no way of ever getting rid of it. The sorrow he had felt for Ortlinde was little more than sympathy, but he needed the Rhinedaughter. The thought of going to live in Valhalla or being the ruler of the Universe without having her there was unbearable; the thought of being alive without having her there was bad enough.

He shook his head and poured out some more schnapps. Many momentous and terrible things had happened and the Gods had all gone down, just to teach Malcolm Fisher the meaning of the word Love. Had he paid more attention to his English teacher at school, he reflected, the whole world might have been saved a great deal of trouble. He picked up the local paper, and saw a photograph of a tall girl and a man with large ears standing outside a church. Liz Ayres had married Philip Wilcox. He smiled, for this fact meant nothing to him at all. The sooner he got out of this house, the better.

Someone had left the french windows open. He got up and closed them, for the night was cold; summer had passed, and it would be unethical of him to extend it for his own convenience. It had been a strange season, he reflected, and it was just as well that it was over now. The world could cool down again, and he could allow it to rain with a clear conscience.

'Why am I doing all this?' he said aloud.

Now at last he understood. It was blindingly obvious but because he was so stupid he hadn't seen it before. The world, now God-free and generally purified, was no longer his to hold on to. He must give the Ring to his sister

233

Bridget. She, after all, was older than him, and much cleverer, and generally better equipped to handle difficult problems. He was only the intermediary. Everything fell into place, and he felt as if a great burden had fallen from his shoulders. If only he had done it before, Flosshilde would not have gone down and he might even have had a happy ending of his own; but he had been foolish and wilful, just as his mother would have expected. He had suffered his punishment, and now there was no time to lose. As he had said himself, Bridget was the member of the Fisher family who most resembled the glorious Siegfried. It explained why Ingolf had been so surprised when he had heard his name; he had been expecting *Bridget* Fisher on that fateful night.

He looked at his watch, trying to calculate what time it would be in Sydney. Hadn't Mother Earth herself said something about the Ring rightfully being Bridget's property, because she was the eldest? It would, of course, be difficult to explain it all, for his word carried little credibility with his immediate family; if he said something, they naturally assumed the reverse to be true. But Bridget was wise and would immediately understand, even if his mother didn't. With luck, they would let him keep the Tarnhelm, but if Bridget needed it of course she must have it. He swallowed the rest of his drink and called for an overcoat.

He looked quickly in the mirror to make sure that his hair was neat and tidy (his mother was most particular about such things) and saw to his astonishment that he didn't look like Malcolm Fisher at all. Then he remembered that he was still wearing the Tarnhelm. He would need that to get to Australia, but he might as well stop pretending to be somebody he wasn't.

'Right,' he commanded, 'back to normal.'

The image in the mirror didn't change. It was still the Siegfried face he had been wearing for so long.

'Back to Malcolm Fisher,' he said irritably. 'Come on, jump to it.'

No change. Angrily, he felt for the little buckle under his chin, which he hadn't even noticed for so long now. It came away easily, and he pulled the chainmail cap off and tossed it onto the sofa.

No change. The face that stared stupidly at him out of the mirror was the face of Fafner's Bane, Siegfried the Volsung. He groaned, and knelt down on the floor. Once again, his mother had been proved right. He had stuck like it. From now until the day he died, he was going to have to go around with the evidence of his deceit literally written all over his face.

Worse, he could not even remember what he really looked like. If he knew that, he might be able to get some sort of clever mask made. But the picture had completely vanished from his mind. He picked up the Tarnhelm and gazed at it hopelessly, feeling as he had done when, as a child, he had broken a window or scratched the paint. He had done something awful which he could not put right, and it was all his fault.

The next morning was bright and cold, and Malcolm woke early with a headache, which he prosaically blamed on the schnapps. To clear his head, he strolled down by the trout-stream and stood for a while kicking stones into the water.

'Do you mind?' said a girl's voice.

He knew that voice. He tried hard not to recognise it, because the girl it had belonged to had gone up in a cloud of theology, along with the rest of the High Gods. He had sent his two ravens out looking for the owner of that voice, and they had searched the earth for many days without finding her. She no longer existed, except in the memories of a few unusual people. So what was she doing in his trout-stream?

'Is that you?' he said stupidly.

'Of course it's me,' said the voice irritably. 'Who do you think it was, the *Bismarck*?'

He scrambled down the bank, slipped, and fell in the water. As he did so, it occurred to him that he couldn't swim, and he had forgotten that the trout-stream was only two feet deep. In his panic, he also forgot about the Tarnhelm, and had already resigned himself to the prospect of death by drowning when Flosshilde fished him out.

'Sorry,' she said. 'Did I startle you?'

That was one hell of a leading question, and rather than try and phrase an answer that might not be held against him in future, he replied by throwing his arms around her and kissing her, clumsily but effectively. It had not entered his mind that she might object to this; luckily, she seemed to like it.

'Where the hell have you been?' he said at last.

Flosshilde grinned. 'Did you miss me?' she asked superfluously.

'I thought you'd been zapped,' he said.

'Oh. So you have missed me.'

'Of course I've bloody missed you. Where have you been?'

'On holiday.'

'On *holiday*.'

'Yes,' said Flosshilde, and she could not understand why Malcolm found this so strange. 'We'd planned to go to the

Nile Delta again this year, but then that Ortlinde business blew up and by the time it was all over everywhere was full. So we went and stayed with our cousins on the seabed. It was rather boring actually. They're terribly stuffy people, and they've got a pipeline running right through the middle of their sitting-room.'

'So that's why Thought and Memory couldn't find you.'

'Were they looking?'

'They've been doing little else since you vanished. You might have let me know.'

Flosshilde grinned again. 'I didn't know you cared. Honestly, I didn't. I only came back to look for a comb I'd left behind.'

That was not strictly true, except for the bit about the comb, but she hoped he wouldn't notice. It had been no fun at all on the seabed and she hadn't been able to get him out of her mind. His reaction to her last remark was therefore likely to be rather important.

'Well, I do care. I care a whole lot.'

'Yes,' said Flosshilde, remembering the scramble down the bank and the kiss, 'I think you probably do. Snap. By the way, you're all wet.'

'Am I?'

'Yes. Perhaps it would be a good idea if we got out of the water.'

Malcolm could see no reason for this, for he was happier standing in two feet of water with the girl he loved and needed than he had ever been on dry land. But if she thought it would be a good idea, he was willing to give it a try. They climbed out and sat down under a tree. It so happened that it was the same tree that Ortlinde had been standing under when he had first kissed her, but he couldn't be expected to remember everything.

'Let's not talk about it,' Flosshilde said. 'You know what that leads to. Let's just have a nice time for the rest of our lives.'

Put like that, it seemed perfectly simple. Malcolm leaned back against the oak tree and thought about it for a moment. Whatever he felt like doing was probably right. He had that on the very best authority.

'Fair enough,' he said. 'But first I must give the Ring to my sister Bridget.'

'Don't be silly.'

'But I've got to. You see . . .'

'Don't be *silly*.'

'All right, then,' Malcolm said. 'I'll give it to you.'

He took off the Ring, looked at it for a moment, tossed it up in the air, caught it again, and slipped it onto the fourth finger of her left hand. Then he waited for a second. Nothing happened. Flosshilde stared at him with her mouth wide open.

'It suits you,' he said.

'What did you do that for?'

'First,' said Malcolm, 'because it was originally yours. Second, because you're much older and cleverer than I am. Third, because I love you. Fourth, because it's worth it just to see the look on your face.'

Flosshilde could think of nothing to say, and Malcolm savoured the moment. It was probably the last moment of silence he could expect from her for many, many years.

'Are you sure?' said Flosshilde.

Malcolm started to laugh, for it had been Ortlinde's favourite phrase, and soon Flosshilde was giggling too. 'No, but honestly,' she said, 'it's the Ring. Be serious for a moment.'

'Serious?' Malcolm grabbed her arm and pulled her

close. 'Don't you see? That's the last thing in the world I can afford to be. Ever since you went away, something terrible has been happening to me. I couldn't think what it was, even though everyone was trying to tell me. Even the Tarnhelm. I was turning into Wotan. I was starting to become just like him.'

'Never,' said Flosshilde. 'You couldn't be. For a start, he was taller than you.'

'I could, and I nearly did. When I realised it, my first reaction was to give the Ring to my sister Bridget, because everyone always said she was so much more responsible than me. But you were right, that would have been the worst possible thing I could have done. Then you came back, and I suddenly understood. The only person in the world that that thing is safe with is you.'

'Me? But that's impossible. I'm not a nice person at all.'

'Not you as well.'

'No, I mean it. I'm probably not cruel or malicious, but I'm thoughtless and frivolous. I wouldn't take the job seriously, and the world would get into an awful mess. I'd forget to make it rain at the right time, because I'd always want it to be fine for sunbathing, and if I was bored with it being January, I'd make it July again, and then everything would get out of gear. I'd be hopeless at it, really.'

'That's what I thought when I started. And it hasn't turned out too badly, has it?'

Flosshilde frowned and bit her lip, a manoeuvre she had often practised in front of the mirror. 'Oh, go on, then,' she said, 'just to please you I will.'

'That,' said Malcolm triumphantly, 'is the best possible reason. You've passed. Congratulations.'

'I still think,' said Flosshilde, holding up the Ring to the light to admire it, 'that you're being a bit hasty . . .' She tailed off. 'You're right,' she said. 'It does suit me. It'll go very nicely with that gold evening dress I got in Strasbourg.'

She took one more look at the Ring and promptly dismissed it from her mind, for she had more important things to think about. 'Why the sudden change of heart?' she asked. 'I mean, when I left for the seabed, you were still madly in love with that stuffy old Valkyrie with the interesting shoes. You aren't going to change your mind about me, are you?'

'I hope not,' said Malcolm. 'We'll have to see, won't we?'

'Did I ever tell you the story . . .?'

'Later.'

'It's a very funny story.'

'Did I ever tell *you* the story of the idiot who ran over a badger?'

'I know that one.'

'But I tell it very well, and it's the only really funny story I know.'

'Go on, then.'

He told her the story and she laughed, although she knew that she could have told it rather better herself. In fact, she could have done his voice rather better than he could. But it didn't matter. This was happiness, she realised, even more than sunbathing or the parties they used to have at Camelot. She was slightly disappointed with herself for being made happy so easily, for she had always thought of herself as a rather glamorous, sophisticated person. Nevertheless, it would do very nicely to be going on with.

Malcolm listened to her laughter, and for the first time in his life he knew that everything was going to be all right.

Niceness, he realised, was not enough, and Love was only part of the rest. You had to have laughter, too. Laughter would make everything come out right in the end, or if it didn't nobody would notice. He started to tell her about his plans for the new Valhalla. She liked the idea, and started making suggestions about how the place should be redecorated. These mostly seemed to consist of swimming-pools, flumes and ornamental lakes, and he realised that sooner or later he was going to have to learn how to swim. The thought made him shudder, but he put it on one side.

'By the way,' he said. 'I suppose you're immortal.'

'I think so. Why?'

'Isn't that going to make it rather difficult for me? You see, I'm not.'

Flosshilde shook her head. 'I solved that one some time ago,' she said.

'Did you now? That was thoughtful of you.'

Flosshilde blushed, spontaneously for once, and realised that she hadn't quite timed it right, which was unusual for her, since she was unquestionably one of the three best blushers in the world. But Malcolm didn't seem to have noticed, and it was nice to be with somebody who didn't criticise when you got things wrong.

'I looked it up in all the books,' she went on, 'and there's no problem. Every time you feel yourself getting old, you just turn yourself into someone younger.'

Malcolm shook his head. 'I don't think the Tarnhelm works any more,' he said sadly, and he told her about his attempts to go back to being Malcolm Fisher. She laughed, and told him not to be so silly.

'Haven't you learnt anything?' she said. 'You tried to turn yourself into Malcolm Fisher. You *are* Malcolm Fisher. Of course it didn't work.'

Malcolm didn't quite follow that, but he was reassured. There didn't seem to be anything else to worry about now, so he suggested that they went in and had some breakfast instead.

'Just a moment,' said Flosshilde.

She looked hard at the Ring, held her breath and pointed at the sky. A small pink cloud appeared out of nowhere, rushing across the sky until it was directly overhead. There was a blinding flash of pink lightning, and the cloud had vanished. The air was filled with pink rose petals, and a flight of flamingos climbed gracefully into the air.

'No,' said Flosshilde, 'maybe not. It seemed like a good idea at the time.'

'It's the thought that counts,' Malcolm said. 'Come on, I'm hungry.'

They walked into the house, and the two ravens who had been eavesdropping from the branches of the oak tree looked at each other.

'I think that's nice,' said Memory.

'Idiot,' said Thought. 'Is that a dead rabbit I can see over there?'

'Where?'

'Just by that patch of nettles.'

'Now you're talking,' said Memory.

They glided down and started to peck. It was a good, meaty rabbit, and they were both hungry. When he had finished, Memory wiped his beak neatly on his leg and stood thoughtfully for a while.

'Did you ever see that film?' he said.

'What film?'

'Can't remember. Anyway, it reminds me a bit of that. Happy ending and all.'

Thought shook his head. 'Don't like happy endings,' he said. 'They're a cop-out. Life's not like that.'

'I dunno,' said Memory. 'Sometimes it is.'

'You're soft, you are,' said Thought scornfully. 'Come on, time we were on our way.'

They sailed up into the sky, and began their day's patrol. Wherever life was stirring and brains were working they flew, their bright round eyes missing nothing, their ears constantly alert. But today was going to be another quiet day in the best of all possible worlds. After a while they grew bored, and turned back. As they flew over the little village of Ralegh's Cross, they saw three workmen with pickaxes trying to break up a strange outcrop of rock which had appeared in the middle of the road some months earlier. But their tools would not bite on the hard stone, and they had given it up for a while.

'What I want to know is,' said one of the men, 'how did it get there in the first place?'

Memory dived down and perched on the rock which had once been the Giant Ingolf. 'It's a long story,' he said.

But the man wasn't listening.

YE GODS!

For Kim,
who, for once,
liked one of my books

CHAPTER ONE

'**Y**ou mean God,' said the insurance man dubiously, 'singular.'

'That's not what the woman told me,' said the voice at the other end of the line. 'Gods, she said, plural. Quite definite about it. Even spelt it – G-O-D-S. Me, I just believe what I'm told. Anyway, does it make any difference?'

'Well . . .' The insurance man hesitated. No reason why it should, in layman's terms, but when it comes to policies of insurance, one has to be careful. Insurance contracts, as any lawyer will tell you, are contracts of the utmost good faith, which probably explains the references to acts of God. God singular; not plural. If it was an act of gods, plural, would he need to send the claimant more than one claim form?

'You still there?' said the voice.

'Yes, still here,' said the insurance man, and he noticed that he had bitten halfway through the stem of his pencil. 'Could we just run this through one more time?'

The voice sighed. 'All right.'

'Your two pet rattlesnakes,' said the insurance man, 'somehow got out of their tank—'

'Which conforms,' emphasised the voice, 'to the strictest Ministry regulations. I've got receipts.'

'Yes, I'm sure. They somehow got out, anyway, crossed the main road, and crawled up the drainpipe of Number Seventeen, where they entered the bedroom of Mrs. Derry's six-month-old baby. Who strangled them.'

'That's it, yes.'

'Mrs. Derry then told you about the incident, and claimed that it was an act of the gods.'

'Gods, yes.'

'I see.' The insurance man choked suddenly; he had swallowed the severed end of his pencil, rubber and all. 'Right, fine, well, I'll get a claim form off to you in tonight's post and we'll take it from there, shall we? Thank you so much.'

He put the phone down, and blinked about four times. Gods? Snakes? He hadn't heard such a load of old cod since the last lot of heavy storms . . .

Inside his head, a sweet, extremely feminine but distinctly authoritative voice told him that he'd better believe it all the same.

The insurance man looked over his shoulder, but there was nobody there. He got up and opened the door; the next-door office was empty. In the end he even looked in the desk drawers and the waste-paper basket. Nothing. Inside his head the voice asked him what he thought he was doing. Then it giggled.

Two months later, Mrs. Derry's snake-fancying neighbour opened his post, looked at the cheque, whistled, and immediately phoned a pet shop to enquire about their special deal on anacondas.

In the back garden of his house, Mr. Derry was digging a

very large hole. Every now and then he stopped and looked nervously over his shoulder. His wife stood by and said nothing.

'I mean,' said Mr. Derry, leaning on his spade and sighing, 'where did he *get* it from, that's what I want to know.'

Mrs. Derry mumbled something under her breath, and looked at the dead bear. Her best duvet cover concealed the upper parts, the massive head and enormous chest, but it wasn't big enough to reach down to the feet.

'And it's not,' said Mr. Derry, 'as if it's the first time.'

Mrs. Derry nodded uncomfortably. All over their small garden were the irregular shapes of small burial mounds; wolves, tigers, wild boar, and that very peculiar lizard thing. Soon there wouldn't be a single geranium left.

'Quite soon,' Mr. Derry said, wiping his forehead with a handkerchief, 'someone is going to notice something. Like, some zoo keeper somewhere is going to see all the empty cages.'

Mrs. Derry made a little whimpering noise. 'I've told him, Doug,' she said, 'I've said, it's naughty, don't do it. But he just doesn't listen. He's only three, for heaven's sake; he don't know right from wrong yet.'

'Don't give me that,' Mr. Derry replied. 'When I was his age I didn't go around thumping dangerous animals. If I so much as laid a finger on the cat, it was straight up to bed and no tea. Panthers . . .'

Mrs. Derry bit her lip. Perhaps she should have told him right at the start, with the snakes. Or before that, even.

'Right,' said Mr. Derry, 'that should be deep enough. Now, you just get round that side and push.'

As he bent down, he became aware of something and stood up quickly. A small child was scampering happily down the path. In one hand it held a two-foot length of scaffolding pipe; in the other, the tip of the tail of an enormous crocodile.

'Oh for crying out loud,' said Mr. Derry. 'Not another one.' He looked around him wearily and sighed.

'Well,' he said, 'bang goes the rockery.'

It wasn't going terribly well, decided the games teacher.

Well, it never was the most brilliant of occasions; school sports days never were. But that was usually because all the contestants would far rather be at home watching the snooker, not because . . .

He ducked. A javelin, travelling like a small cannon-shell, passed about an inch over his head, embedded itself in the pavilion door and quivered resentfully. At the other end of the field, a small seven-year-old was looking rather sheepish.

It had been the same, the games teacher remembered, with the discus and the shot-put. As for the egg-and-spoon race, that was best forgotten about. He passed his tongue across his dry lips and looked quickly at the programme. Four-hundred-and-forty-yard race. What could possibly go wrong with that?

The contestants were lined up, and the games teacher lifted his little flag.

'ON YOUR MARKS,' he said, 'GET SET, G . . .'

Something very fast started moving round the track. A few seconds later, it had completed four circuits and had wandered off into the bushes at the edge of the field, from which it emerged a little later trailing a large dead fox. Bigger than a fox, really, almost wolf-sized.

'Jason,' said the games teacher, 'put that down just a moment, would you?'

'Yes, sir.'

'Jason,' said the games teacher, 'do you know what . . . sportsmanship means?'

'Yes, sir.'

The games teacher swallowed hard. The boy was looking up at him with innocent, trusting eyes. Unfortunately, a large number of parents were also looking at him, and their body language was rather less appealing. He was going to have to ask the youngster to throw the next race.

'It means,' said the games teacher, 'sometimes letting somebody else win. Do you understand?'

'Yes, sir.'

'I know,' the games teacher went on, 'I know it's not really fair, but sometimes in this life, Jason, we have to cheat in order to be fair. Do you see what I'm . . .?'

'I know, sir,' said the boy. 'And I did try.'

The games teacher swallowed. 'What?'

'I keep trying, sir,' said the boy. 'But somehow . . .' looked down at his feet and blushed.

He was discovering that sometimes it isn't easy, being a Hero.

Mr. Derry parked the car, same as usual, got out and went to open the garage doors. He opened them. He stared.

After a few seconds, he rubbed his eyes. It was still there.

'That does it,' he said. 'It's got to stop.'

He closed the doors, pushing the tip of an outstretched trunk out of the way with his toe, and went into the house. There was a dead gorilla on the coatrack, so he put his anorak on the chair instead.

'Phyllis,' he called, 'there's a dead elephant in the garage. It's got to stop, do you hear me?'

The lounge door opened and a strange figure appeared in the doorway. Blue light burned around his shoulders,

251

and his eyes burned deep scars on Mr. Derry's retinas. In his hand he held a slice of walnut cake.

'Doug,' said Mrs. Derry's voice from behind the apparition's shoulder, 'here's an old friend of mine I'd like you to meet.'

'Yes,' said Mr. Derry, 'I understand all that—' He closed his eyes, eased his brain carefully into first gear and opened them again. 'I think,' he went on. 'But why all the bears and wolves and tigers and . . . ?'

Outside, the garden was a blaze of colour, as the first marigolds turned their golden faces to the sun. In between them, the white tips of innumerable rib cages poked out through the earth.

'Well.'

The stranger took a deep breath. This wasn't going to be easy.

'You see, Mr. Derry,' he said. 'Douglas,' he added.

'Young Jason isn't like other boys his age.' Mr. Derry nodded vigorously. 'He has this sort of – well, you might say it's in the blood. You might say he – well, takes after his . . .'

Mr. Derry was about to protest, but then he remembered what he'd just heard. He wished, somehow, that he could feel angry about it, but that was apparently a luxury he wasn't to be allowed.

'You do a lot of that?' he asked. 'Clobbering wild beasts and so on?'

'No, no, not at all,' said the stranger, 'that's not what I'm trying to get at. It's more a sort of instinct, really, among Us.'

'You?'

'Us,' said the stranger, 'yes. Really, it's what we're here

252

for.' He remembered something. '*Were* here for, that is. Were there for,' he experimented. 'Anyway, it's just a phase We all go through.'

'You mean he'll grow out of it?'

'Probably.'

'And how long will that take, do you think?'

The stranger wished he hadn't asked. Sure, all his other children *had* grown out of it, eventually, but it had taken rather a long time, if you were using a mortal timescale. And what with the erosion of the rain forests and the disappearance of natural habitats, it looked like the supply of large feral cats was going to run out long before young Jason had tired of braining them.

'Look at it another way,' said the stranger.

'Yes?'

Oh hell, thought the stranger, what's the point? You try being nice to them and where does it get you? 'Do you know who I am?' he said.

'Well,' Mr. Derry said, 'you told me just now you were Jason's real . . .'

'Yes,' said the stranger, 'but as well as that?'

'As well as that?' Mr. Derry said. 'No.'

The stranger told him. He didn't say anything; it would be impossible to communicate this particular piece of information verbally. Instead, he just relaxed his grip on his disguise very, very slightly.

Mr. Derry fell on his knees and started to bang his head on the carpet. He didn't know why; it just seemed the right thing to do. All around him, beams of blue and gold light leaped and sparkled. The air crackled with static electricity. In the kitchen, the silver plate started to peel off the canteen of cutlery that had belonged to Mr. Derry's grandmother's cousin. Just then, the back door opened, and Jason came in backwards. Behind him, he was towing the carcass of an enormous lion.

'Hi, Dad,' he said absently.

'Hi, son,' said the stranger.

Jason dumped the lion, kicked it scornfully, and put his school satchel on the table. He looked at the stranger.

'Is it all right if I go to the football with Stuart and Terry on Saturday?' he asked. 'Terry's dad said he'd take us.'

The stranger considered for a moment. 'I suppose so,' he said, 'so long as you get your homework done first. And mind you come straight back,' he added. 'You know how your mother worries.'

'Okay, Dad,' said Jason, and went upstairs.

The stranger grinned, and tiny flashes of lightning played round the light fittings. 'It's a shame they have to grow up, isn't it?' he said.

Mr. Derry looked up, his face a curious mix of fear, reverence and jealousy. 'You've met, then?' he said.

'Oh yes,' said the stranger, 'who do you think picks him up from school every day?'

Mr. Derry turned and glowered at his wife, who shrugged.

'Anyway,' said the stranger, 'if all the er . . . animals and things are bothering you, just say the word and I'll send someone, all right? Mercury or . . . well, someone,' he concluded. The thought of asking Mercury to go traipsing across the solar system with a huge dust-pan and brush every evening to sweep up his younger brother's mess wasn't exactly appealing. 'Don't give it another thought,' he added. He turned to Mrs. Derry. 'Nice seeing you again,' he said, shuddering slightly. 'We mustn't leave it so long next time, must we?'

He smiled weakly, snapped his fingers, and stepped into

the great golden chariot which had suddenly materialised on the carpet. There was a peal of thunder and he was gone.

On his way back to the Palace of the Sun, Jupiter found himself feeling strangely guilty. Perhaps it was seeing how old and flabby the female mortal had become. It had only been – what, ten years? Twelve at the most, and already she was starting to look like a dried apricot. He shook his head sadly, whipped up the horses, and galloped through the fiery gases of the Sun's outer rays, hoping that his wife hadn't noticed he'd been out.

She had.

Apollo, sheltering under the rim of a huge bronze shield, looked at his watch.

'How long've they been at it now?' asked a voice from the corner of the ceiling.

'Six hours,' Apollo replied. 'And if you knew how silly you looked up there, you'd come down at once.'

The spider twitched nervously, slid quickly down its thread, and joined Apollo under the shield, where it changed back into Minerva, ex-Goddess of Wisdom.

'Push off,' Apollo said, 'there isn't enough room for two.'

A thunderbolt whizzed past his ear and crashed into the billows of burning helium that made up the conservatory floor. There was a shower of brilliant blue sparks, one of which landed on Minerva's nose.

'Ouch,' said Minerva. 'Move over, Pol, for pity's sake. It's not safe out there.'

Apollo shrugged. 'It's not exactly marvellous back here, either,' he said, and Minerva noticed that his eyebrows were singed. 'Just makes me feel better, that's all.'

255

Out in the blackness beyond the crystal windows, a comet suddenly appeared, blazed fervently for a few moments and burned itself out. Apollo relaxed slightly.

'I'll say this for Auntie Ju,' he said, 'her aim always was terrible.'

'You remember when Vulcan was born,' Minerva whispered, 'and He chucked him off the edge?'

'Vividly,' Apollo replied. 'Who do you think it was had to explain to the people of Lemnos why they suddenly had an extra valley where the mountains used to be?'

'I forgot.'

'Wasn't easy, Min,' Apollo went on. 'There's such a thing as prestige, you know. Can't go telling mortals their island's just been flattened by a falling God. There'd be grumbling. You know, why don't you look where you're putting your bloody great feet, that sort of thing. You can lose a lot of respect that way.'

Minerva nodded. 'Good job we don't have to worry about that any more,' she said. 'And it's always *Him*, isn't it?' she added in a whisper.

Apollo looked over his shoulder carefully, then nodded. 'It's just not fair,' he said. 'And it was always us got the blame. I suppose that was why we had to leave.'

Minerva sighed. 'You miss the old place, then?'

'Sometimes,' Apollo admitted. 'I mean, this is all very nice in its way, but . . .'

They both ducked instinctively as a mass of burning magma whistled overhead and exploded. Far off, a voice like a female earthquake was saying that it wished it had listened to its mother.

'What I want to know is,' said Minerva, 'if they do split up, who'll get custody of the Fates?'

Suddenly, there was quiet. Dead silence.

'Come to that,' said a dreadful voice, 'who is it leaves her toenail clippings lying around the bedroom carpet every time she has a . . .?'

There was a blinding flash of red light, a dull thump that set the moons of Pluto wobbling on their axes, and a terrific hissing noise.

'She's thrown the kettle at him,' said Minerva.

'And missed,' Apollo added. 'Come on, let's make a run for it while we can.'

They jumped up and ran, crouching, towards the stables.

'We'll take mine,' Apollo said. 'It's faster.'

Minerva nodded. Her chariot was drawn by four silver owls; this was only proper for the ex-Goddess of Wisdom, but it didn't make for a smooth getaway.

It was only when they had passed the moons of Venus that they dared look back. Even from this distance, they could hear a voice like a shrill avalanche pointing out that at least she didn't leave wet footmarks all over the bathroom floor whenever she had a bath. Minerva winced.

'And people wonder,' she said, 'why I never married.'

Picture if you can (don't be ashamed if you can't) the highest point of the Caucasus mountains. Imagine the bare crags, the dizzying ravines, the blinding whiteness of the snow.

On the very highest peak, there is a human figure. The shape is human, but the scale is somehow wrong; this figure is huge. It covers the mountainside like a man-shaped town.

It is sprawled, face down, like a body that has just fallen from a high window. Its wrists and ankles are bound with adamantine chains (adamant is not the first choice of

257

experienced chain-makers, but since what's keeping the prisoner there is the wrath of God, that is largely academic) to the surrounding peaks. Around the prisoner's body circles a great, red-beaked eagle. You are looking at Prometheus.*

You guessed? Well done.

The eagle lifts itself towards the eye of the Sun, banks and swoops down, extending its meat hook talons; it pitches on the prisoner's back and drives its beak into the half-healed flesh. Then, as it has done twice a day since the creation of the World, it starts to gorge itself on the prisoner's liver.

'Huh,' it says, again. 'No onions.'

Prometheus lifts his shaggy head from the rock. His teeth are clenched, his eyes screwed shut, his lips parted in a scowl of effort. He is trying not to giggle.

Thousands of millions of years ago, when the gods first created Man, Prometheus took pity on the wretched, naked mortals and stole fire (and something else) from heaven. He carried the fire down to Earth in a hollow stalk of fennel and gave it to Mankind, so that they would have warmth in winter, light in darkness, and something to boil the kettle over. The gods, as a matter of fact, didn't mind too much about the fire. It was the other thing that aggravated them.

'Morning,' said the eagle.

'Morning,' replied the good giant.

The eagle hesitated for a moment and stared at the clouds through its cruel, lidless eyes. 'Weather's on the turn again,' it said.

'Oh yes?' replied the giant politely.

*It's a *myth* that Prometheus was rescued by Hercules. That's what they want you to believe . . .

258

'More snow,' said the eagle. 'Heavy frost, I shouldn't wonder. Anything I can do for you?'

'You could turn my page if you like,' said the giant.

'Hold on,' said the eagle, wiping its beak on its wing-feathers. Then it hopped over to the giant's head, flipped over the leaf of the huge book spread out under the giant's nose, and weighted the pages down with small stones to stop them blowing over in the biting wind.

'Good, is it?' asked the eagle.

'It's okay,' said the giant. 'Not as good as his last one, though.'

'You can't win 'em all,' said the eagle.

Prometheus wiggled his ears – it was the only gesture he could make, what with the chains and everything – and sighed. 'A bit self-indulgent in places,' he continued. 'Slightly over the top, you know. Still, it'll do.'

'You got much more to read?' asked the eagle.

Prometheus considered. 'No, not really,' he replied. 'Could you just switch on the dictating machine before you go?'

'Sure,' said the eagle, scratching its ear with a meat hook talon. 'Oh, and by the way.'

'Yes?'

'Faldo was one up on the thirteenth,' said the eagle, 'with Ballesteros trailing by three and Langer nowhere. I thought you'd like to know.'

'That's right,' groaned Prometheus, 'cheer me up.'

The eagle shrugged its wings. 'I could bring you a radio,' it said. 'No trouble.'

Prometheus smiled. 'That's very kind of you,' he said, 'but how could I switch it off when it started playing music again? It's not exactly fun and games up here as it is without Vivaldi banging away at you as well.'

'Well, if you're sure . . .'

The eagle spread its wings, pressed the record button on the dictating machine perched beside the giant's nose, thanked him for lunch and soared away. Soon it was nothing but a tiny speck among the distant peaks.

No, what really got up the noses of the immortal gods wasn't fire. Give human beings fire, they reasoned, and sooner or later they will use it to burn each other's houses down, which scores four any day of the week and six when the moon is in Scorpio. It was the other thing they could never forgive. Remembering, Prometheus chuckled. Then he lifted his head and started to roar with laughter.

'What time is it?' asked Apollo as they raced across the firmament towards the Earth.

'April,' Minerva replied. 'If we get a move on, we'll be there in time for Easter.'

They looked at each other for a moment. Then they started to snigger.

Among the gods, there is a dispute as to which one of them originally thought of Christianity; or, as they call it, the Great Leg Pull. Apollo has the best claim, but a sizeable minority support Pluto, ex-God of the Dead, on the grounds that he has a really sick sense of humour.

How would it be, suggested the unidentified god, if first we tell them all to love their neighbour, pack in the killing and thieving, and be nice to each other. Then we let them start burning heretics.

It is therefore scarcely surprising that the Olympians find it hard to keep a straight face when they think of the religion that has effectively replaced them all over the world (except, of course, for parts of California). What they think

260

of as the world, at any rate; the Olympians were always a touch on the xenophobic side and preferred to ignore the existence of the world beyond the frontiers of the Roman empire, probably because the inhabitants couldn't speak Greek or Latin and the gods could speak nothing else. They tried, of course; they tried speaking very loudly and slowly, but the mortals didn't understand, taking the peculiar noise for thunder.

The chariot of the Sun soared down over the Iberian peninsula, causing a flurry of frantic arguments amongst half the air traffic controllers in Europe, and landed on a hillside outside Delphi.

'Why are we stopping here?' Minerva asked.

'I just want to see if there are any messages,' replied Apollo. He hopped out of the chariot, transformed himself into a small, elderly German with a video-camera, and made his way down towards the ruins of his temple.

Over the lintel of the door of the Treasury of the Athenians is an inscription. Time has ground it almost smooth, but that still doesn't excuse the generations of distinguished classical archaeologists who translated it as

KNOW THYSELF

when it actually says

WHILE YOU WERE OUT

and certainly doesn't explain why none of them has ever gone on to read the rest of it. This would, of course, be difficult, as the text of the inscription changes subtly every few years.

The German tourist paused and looked up at the faint

261

lettering. As he did so, he became aware of a small, dumpy female figure beside him.

'Betty,' he said, 'I do believe your writing is getting worse.'

'Sorry,' said the female. 'It's my arthritis,' she explained.

'Ah.' Apollo made a mental note to do something about it. 'Anything important, was there?'

Betty-Lou Fisichelli, the eight-thousand-and-sixth Sibyl of Delphi, took a notebook from her bag and started to leaf through it. 'Napoleon called,' she said, 'please call back . . . Bit late for that now, I suppose. A guy from Chicago wants to know how the Bears are going to do this season. There was a party of British guys with portable telephones who asked – I may have got this down wrong – they asked if it was the right time to sell Guilt.'

'Gilts,' corrected Apollo. Then he grinned wickedly. 'If they come back,' he said, 'tell them yes. Anything else?'

'No, I don't think so,' said the Sibyl. 'Oh yes, there was a woman asking about her kid. Seems he's been playing her up or something. Sounded like hyperactivity to me: you know, too much chocolate. Phyllis somebody.'

Apollo turned round and stared at her. 'Phyllis Derry?' he demanded.

'That's right,' said the Sybil. 'Was it important?'

Apollo ignored her. 'When was this?' he asked.

'About . . .' The Sibyl looked at her watch. It had two concentric dials: one for human and one for Divine time. 'About January,' she said. 'Sorry,' she added, 'you didn't say you were expecting . . .'

'That's all right,' said Apollo quietly, 'I wasn't. Look did she leave a number?'

'I think so,' said the Sibyl, leafing through her book. 'Hold on a moment . . . No, that's the Delphi Pizza Express. Now, let me just . . .'

262

Apollo frowned. Something scuttled about nervously under the Earth's crust. Several large olive trees wilted on the hillside opposite. The Sibyl swallowed hard and found the right page. 'Got it,' she said. 'It's . . . Look, is that a five or a three?'

'I don't know, do I?' replied the god, and for a moment the EC olive oil lake seemed likely to dry up for a year or so.

'I think it's a five,' said the Sibyl nervously. She wrote the number out again, tore out the page and handed it to the god, who smiled grimly and thanked her. 'If she calls again,' he added, 'just let me know immediately, will you?'

The Sibyl trembled slightly. 'How?' she asked.

Apollo looked blank for a moment, and then snapped, 'Use your bloody imagination.' Then he turned himself into a swarm of bees and buzzed off.

'Have a nice day,' the Sybil whispered, and made a note in her book: If *Phyllis Derry calls back, tell A. at once*. Then she turned round and walked away slowly, reflecting (not for the first time) that she hadn't wanted the lousy job in the first place. Partly it was the industrial relations – women through the ages who had offended Apollo suddenly found themselves transformed into flowering shrubs, and Ms. Fisichelli, who came from New York, where they don't hold with such things, shuddered at the very thought. She had a cousin called Myrtle, from Wisconsin, and that was bad enough. Mainly, though, it was the feeling that she hadn't spent ten years of her life at a selection of universities getting her Doctorate in Classical Philology just to be a glorified receptionist. Many was the time, she reminded herself, that she'd been on the point of giving in her notice and telling him what he could do with his gods-damned job. Then she would catch sight of a clematis or a wisteria

263

and decide to put it off till tomorrow. But the worst part of it, if she was going to be honest, was the job description. For, of course, the senior priestess of the Delphi Oracle isn't called the Sibyl at all. The correct term is the Pythoness, and Ms. Fisichelli, who was only human – well, mostly human – could only take so much.

A small American lady tapped her gently on the arm, mistaking her for the tour guide. The Sibyl turned and glowered at her.

'Excuse me,' said the lady, 'do you think it's going to rain?'

Ms. Fisichelli grinned. The god had given her the gift of prophecy, but so what?

'No,' she said.

CHAPTER TWO

In the beginning was the Word. Nobody knows what it actually was, although it would be nice to think it was 'Sorry.'

After a while, the Word began to feel bored. It checked its spelling, but that was all right. It tried rhyming with itself, but it had an idea that that made you go blind. It put itself into italics, but they hurt. There was nothing for it but to create some other words and see what happened.

To begin with, the Words just bounced about, like a lot of random particles; and when they bumped into each other, small bits and corners were chipped off, fell through space, acquired momentum and became Matter. Then, most of the original Words decided to form a gang, dress up in white sheets and beat the pulp out of the Adjectives, who they felt were getting above themselves, and so engrossed did they become in this that they failed to notice that a rival group of sentient beings had materialised out of nowhere. By the time they realised they were not alone, the Words had been scooped up, parsed senseless and imprisoned in the first ever word processor.

The newcomers were the gods. According to the oldest

265

versions of the story, there were three of them: Cronus, Rhea and Thing.

Cronus created order out of chaos. Rhea separated darkness from light and wallpapered the firmament with stars. Then they coated the Words with molecules, until each one had become the thing it stood for, and set them to work colonising the firmament. In all the excitement they forgot about Thing, who was no good at carpentry and tended to trip over the paste-bucket. When the work of creation was finished, the gods stepped back and looked at it, and saw that it was good; or, at least, that it could have been worse. They knocked off for the week-end.

When he was quite sure that they'd all gone, Thing crept out of the supernova in which he'd been hiding, brushed stardust off his trousers and scowled.

He'd show them.

Softly but persuasively, he announced himself to the Words as they clanked about awkwardly in their new shells. You don't like the gods, he said, I don't like them; let's teach those mothers a lesson they'll never forget.

The Words didn't say anything; they just nodded. Then Thing took a deep breath and dematerialised, turning his body into billions of tiny particles. The Words shrieked, as well they might – each one felt like an oyster who's just had a full-sized pearl inserted into it.

It was some time before the gods found out about this, and by then it was too late. All they could do was hope and pray (as it were) that none of the little bits of Thing ever got into the hands of the newly-created human race; because if they did, there'd be trouble. And, thanks to Prometheus, trouble there was . . .

★

Jupiter put down the asteroid he had been about to throw and blushed.

'I'm sorry, too,' he said. 'And yes, you're still my fluffy little wifekin.' He transformed the asteroid into a huge bunch of flowers and handed it to Juno, who simpered slightly.

Far overhead, a comet with a large, jagged sliver of solidified helium sticking right through it expressed the wish that the great Sky-King could have found it in him to say that a few minutes earlier. He had been knocked some way off his trajectory, and if there's one thing that really upsets comets, it's being late. Messes things up for the princes, they say. Makes the beggars get uppity.

'I didn't mean to get so cross, Jo,' said Juno pacifically. 'I don't know what came over me.'

'That's all right.'

'But you did promise . . .'

'I know,' said Jupiter. 'And I'm sorry.'

'It's not that I mind you . . . well, turning into things. You're like that, and that's fine. It's just . . .'

'What?'

'Jo,' said Juno, as winsomely as a great Sky-Queen can (which is not very), 'why do the little bastards always have to be Heroes?'

'I don't know,' Jupiter confessed. 'They just do, that's all.'

'They upset things, you see,' Juno continued. 'They get difficult. They go about righting wrongs and protecting the mortals.'

'I know,' Jupiter sighed. 'I don't like it either.'

'They rescue princesses,' Juno continued. 'They kill dragons. They retrieve golden fleeces. They bring back the Secret of Truth. You can't put something down for five minutes without some hero or other scuttling off with it.

267

And you can't just tread on them or give them scarlet fever, that's the worst thing. They're all woven into the Skein of Destiny, and you know what that's like. Ladders as soon as look at it.'

'Yes,' said Jupiter, smiling like a doorknocker. 'I had noticed. Look . . .'

'And now,' said Juno remorselessly, 'it looks like you've gone and sired another one of the little terrors. What's it called, by the way?'

'Jason.'

'Jason,' Juno repeated. 'Scarcely original.'

'True,' Jupiter replied, 'but inconspicuous. Look, it'll be different this time, promise. We aren't *involved* any more, remember. So what if the little toerag does succeed in banishing Discord from the Earth . . .'

'If he does,' snapped Juno, 'she's not coming back here. Last time we had her to stay, she left grubby marks on all the towels.'

'Whatever,' said Jupiter firmly. 'Fulfilling his destiny, then. Even if he does succeed in fulfilling his destiny, who gives a toss anyway? Nobody believes in us any more, so what possible difference could it make? It'll just make the Game that bit more interesting,' he added, wickedly.

Juno gave him one of her looks. 'You are going to tell them?' she said.

'Eventually,' Jupiter replied.

'Eventually?'

'Yes,' said the Father of Gods and Men with a chuckle. 'Just as soon as I've had a chance to put a few side-bets on.'

Meanwhile, on another part of the sun, it was Mars's go.

Mars, ex-God of War, can easily be distinguished from his fellow gods by his twitch. Most things bring it on – the

268

ticking of a clock, the sound of a speck of dust settling on a distant asteroid, even (especially) dead silence. Years of living with it had got on the nerves of the other eleven Olympians. That just made it worse.

The place of Mars, Feeder of Vultures, has traditionally been in the forefront of battle. This was originally no problem; in the good old days when the nastiest thing Mankind had thought up by way of settling disputes between neighbours was a poisoned arrow, golden armour, no worries. However, things had changed rather, what with armour-piercing ammunition, high explosives, napalm, chemical weapons, Exocets and Cruise missiles; in fact, the only thing that hasn't kept up with the times is Mars's defensive capability, which still consists of about three millimetres of gilded, low-tech bronze.

Theology is at best an imprecise science. The best definition of an immortal is someone who hasn't died yet.

Hence the fact, not perhaps widely enough known, that on his shield Mars has painted probably the biggest CND symbol in the entire galaxy. Next time you go to one of those big demonstrations, look out for a tall, thin, gaunt chap with a serious nervous tic. That'll be Mars.

Sitting opposite him in the observation dome of the sun was his three-quarter-sister-once removed (divine relationships are rather complex), the ex-Goddess of the Moon, Diana. Unlike Mars, nobody ever shoots at her and therefore she tends to be a trifle scornful of Mars's new-found pacifism. To her, as to the rest of Olympus, the way to a man's heart is through his ribcage.

'Seven,' said Diana. 'Hold on, here we go. One-two-three-four-five-six-seven and here we are. Now then.'

She took a golden tile from the neat stack that hovered in the air beside the bejewelled abacus and read it.

'You are assessed for street repairs,' she recited disgustedly. 'Pay one billion drachmas for each city . . .'

She peered down at the surface of the planet and counted. Then she reached for her trusty bow and arrow, drew careful aim and skewered a dense bank of cloud hovering over a major Western city. At once the cloud burst, sending furious torrents of water rushing through the streets. Mars turned his head away, hoping she wouldn't notice.

'There,' she said happily, 'that's saved me a few bob.'

Roofs floated by on their way to the sea. Mars opened his eyes and decided, for only the seventh time that day, that this was a truly horrid game.

'I'm not sure,' he said, in a high, strained voice, 'that you're allowed to do that.'

'You reckon?'

Mars's head twitched sharply a couple of times. Diana was giving him one of her looks.

'On the other hand,' he said, 'who cares? My turn, isn't it?'

He picked up the dice-shaker, threw hard and prayed. This is an unusual thing for a god to do, but he'd got into the habit during the Cuban missile crisis and it was hard to stop. The dice wobbled for a moment and landed.

'Lucky you,' Diana said. 'Double four.'

Another reason why Mars hadn't kicked the habit was that it seemed to work. Funny, that; when human beings used to pray to him, it had always been a complete washout.

'Let me see,' Mars said. 'That's nice, peace negotiations under way in Geneva, strategic arms limitation talks resumed, cease-fire in the Middle East conflict . . .'

Diana shook her head. She threw.

'Twelve,' she said. 'Go to . . . Oh, *nuts*!'

Thank you, said Mars under his breath, whoever you are. Three whole throws and not a shot fired in anger. Not even a shot fired in a spirit of reckless jollity, which can sometimes be a great deal worse. The Driver of the Spoil crossed his fingers, shook the dice-box gently, and spilt the dice.

Nine.

Mars twitched like a fisherman's float with a whale on the end of the line and turned towards the Earth. The wail of sirens was dimly audible across the emptiness of the solar system.

'Fire alarm?' he asked hopefully.

No chance. Pausing only for his head to stop moving long enough for him to put his helmet on it, Mars shouldered his shield and spear, whistled for his chariot, and trudged off to war.

Three small lumps of rock in the middle of a frozen sea.

The nearest land: the Argentine coast, approximately two hundred miles away. Natural resources: rock, ice and snow (in season). Strategic value: nil. Population: four.

Until recently, of course. Now, the population is fluctuating around the twelve thousand mark, as huge numbers of men hop out of big green aeroplanes on the ends of pieces of string tied to sheets. Down below, someone is staging an impromptu fireworks display.

In the middle of it all stands Mars, Destroyer of Men, holding a golden spear with the spearhead shot off and feeling a complete nana. Fortunately, he is invisible and his body, being composed of ichor and ambrosia, doesn't give off enough heat to attract the attention of the large number of heat-seeking missiles nosing about in the air like psychotic dolphins. Cautiously, his head bobbing up and down like one of those nodding dogs you see in the backs of cars, Mars starts to unwrap his sandwiches.

Cheese and gherkin, notes the Father of Battles with disgust. Cheese and gherkin, as if I didn't have enough to put up with as it is.

From the hill with the machine-gun on it came a succession of peculiar noises, which set Mars's head going like a beam-engine. First there was a terrible yelling noise, then a smart crackle of rifle-fire and some loud, deep thumps, then another yell and some screams of pure panic. Then loud cheering. Then silence.

Mars peered cautiously over the rim of the wrecked armoured personnel carrier, behind which he had taken prudent if inglorious shelter. The shooting appeared to have stopped. The only noise was the distant song of birds and the sound of the cheekpiece of Mars's helmet tapping against the mangled turret. What, asked the Widow-Maker, the hell is going on?

Gingerly, he took off his helmet, balanced it on the tip of his spear, and lifted it into the air. No bullet-holes or shrapnel-gashes appeared in it. Nobody seemed interested. It was probably some sort of diabolical trap.

On the other hand, Mars said to himself, maybe it isn't, and what the hell, you can only die once, if that. He rose unsteadily to his feet, put the helmet on, and whistled for his chariot. Odd, he reflected as he climbed up behind his four coal-black, red-eyed coursers, the way nothing ever seems to hit the bloody chariot. Sometimes I think they must do it on purpose. He gripped the reins, picked an unexploded mortar-shell out of the fold of his cloak, and shouted 'Giddyap!' in a voice like the crash of colliding battalions.

The battle was over. Even Mars, who had learned the hard way not to judge by appearances, was convinced of that. It was the way the soldiers were leaning thoughtfully on their rifles and looking out over the stricken field while the senior staff officers gave interviews to the *News at Ten* that convinced him. Mars tethered the chariot to a crashed helicopter, alighted, and crept over to where a slightly dishevelled man in a blue anorak was talking loudly to a television camera. Beside him, two technicians in leather jackets were operating a large portable electric fan, to give his hair the authentic wind-blown look.

'The Battle of Mallard Esplanade,' shouted the man above the whirr of the fan, 'is over. Shortly before three o'clock this afternoon, the entire enemy land forces surrendered to a man, it seems as the result of an unprecedented act of gallantry by a young private in the Catering Corps, Private Jason Derry, who apparently charged them single-handedly. This is Danny Bennett, *News at Ten*, Mallard Esplanade; George, you're standing on my holdall.'

Mars rubbed his eyes with the heel of his hand, took off his shield and threw it in the back of the chariot. Great, he thought, marvellous; now let's get out of here quick before these lunatics change their minds. And a big thank you to Private Jason Derry, whoever the hell he is . . .

Jason Derry?

Mars twitched so violently that the chariot drew up suddenly in mid-air, executed a remarkable banking manoeuvre, and force-landed on a strip of wind-blasted grass in the valley below. Being stuffed full of land-mines, it blew up.

After a while, the tip of a charred and frantically nodding plume appeared above the lip of the crater, and Mars slowly drew himself up by his fingertips. Having ostentatiously dusted himself off and thrown a collection of mangled sheets of metal and the ragged remains of a Cloak of Invisibility into a nearby ditch, he whistled for a rather badly dented chariot, swore at the horses, and departed sunwards, just as a camera crew looked up in the hope of filming incoming Harriers.

'Hey,' said the chief cameraman, pointing a trembling finger at the sky. 'Hey just look at that, will you?'

The reporter looked up, nodded and shrugged.

'If you ignore them,' he said, 'they just go away. Anyone got a pen?'

CHAPTER THREE

Jason got up, looked around him, and wondered where he was. It didn't take him long.

He was lost.

Pity, but never mind. When you're a Hero, being lost isn't exactly the end of the world, just a passing inconvenience between adventures. It happens to all of them, and they know how to deal with it.

For example; round about the end of the second reel, the Hero has usually been kidnapped and whisked away by helicopter to a secret location miles from anywhere where the villain tries to do away with him by some entertaining but hopelessly over-involved means. The Hero gets out of that, natch, and sprints out of the secret location just in time to clamber onto the wing of the villain's light aircraft, which is just taking off. Then there's a spectacular fight, the villain comes to a bad end, and the Hero has just enough time to leap out of the plane before it collides with the side of a mountain. We are, you realise, miles from anywhere by this point. No trains. No public transport of any kind.

Five seconds later, the Hero is strolling into the bar of

the Casino, wearing a dinner-jacket, all ready for the final car/lorry/armoured personnel carrier chase sequence, which will end in a cloud of rolling flames out in the middle of the desert somewhere. Have you ever stopped to look at what these Heroes wear on their feet? No? Well, it certainly isn't walking shoes.

There is a perfectly simple explanation for all this. Behind every Hero travels a small semi-divine functionary driving something not unlike one of those motorised golf buggies. In the trunk there's three changes of clothes, assorted lethal weapons, a first aid kit and usually a thermos of hot soup. It's strange that so few people know about this handy and convenient service; perhaps it's something to do with Heroes being basically insecure. Or perhaps they all take it so much for granted that they forget to mention it.

Jason looked round, whistled irritably and tapped his foot. A moment later, the old familiar wheezing noise reached his ears as the buggy – a sort of deluxe version of the obese golfer's friend – bumped over the rocks towards him.

'What kept you?' he said.

'Sorry, boss,' said the driver, 'the power pack went flat just outside Kabul. You try getting two torch batteries in a fundamentalist Moslem country, you'll soon see whether you've got what it takes.'

'Where are we?' Jason asked, brushing a little dust off his immaculately-tailored battledress.

'Caucasus mountains,' said the driver. 'I think. Let's have a shufti at the map.' He pushed forward the passenger seat of the buggy to reveal a useful luggage area, which was crammed with the sort of old rubbish you and I keep in glove compartments, plus a few stun grenades and a copy of *War and Peace*. Heroes' drivers have to do a lot of waiting about.

'Here we are,' said the driver at last, and emerged with a well-thumbed atlas. 'Now, let the dog see the rabbit, if that's Tbilisi down over there . . .'

Jason made an impatient noise. 'And anyway,' he said, 'what am I here for?'

The driver shrugged. 'Funny you should ask that,' he said, 'the other day I was reading this book by Descartes, and he says . . .'

'No, no,' said the Hero, irritably, 'what I mean is, why have I ended up here, when I thought I was going back to Aldershot?'

The driver wriggled uneasily in his seat. 'Now, boss,' he said, 'you know I'm not allowed to tell you things like that. Signed the Celestial Secrets Act, haven't I? It's not fair, asking me things like . . .'

'All right, all right,' said Jason, 'just so long as this is where I'm meant to be, you know, right now.'

'Don't worry about that,' said the driver. 'Bang on.'

'Well,' confessed the Hero, 'sometimes I wonder, you know? I haven't really got the hang of all this, somehow. I mean, Daddy did say . . .'

'What?'

'He said,' replied Jason, 'that I should do what I was told and keep my mouth shut. Fair enough, I suppose, but . . .'

Heroes have these short intervals of what can only be described as Doubts, and the driver had heard it all before. Take Arjun, for example. Many was the time he'd had to give him a good talking-to on the eve of a big battle. 'Don't you worry about all that,' he said. 'The big fellas know what they're doing; you just carry on and enjoy yourself.'

Jason nodded, reassured. Ever since Daddy had told him, a few months ago now, just before his eighteenth birthday party, that he was a Hero and it was high time he stopped daydreaming about a career in hotel management and went out in search of his Destiny, he had done his best not to look back. And it had been fun, so far, hitting people, charging machine-gun nests, pulling the barrels off tanks with his bare hands, all that sort of stuff. Most of the boys he'd been to school with still thought smashing up space invader machines was a wild time.

'Anyway,' said the driver, 'far be it for me to drop any heavy hints, but I think your destiny lies over there.' He pointed at a nearby hillside.

'What, the one with the trees?'

'No,' said the driver patiently, 'the one with the goats and the small shack. I think you'll find there's someone over there waiting for you.'

'Ah,' said Jason, 'right, then. In the shack?'

'Very probably,' sighed the driver. 'Why don't you go and find out?'

Overhead, a huge eagle hugged a thermal and scanned the surface below. When he saw the human figure plodding grimly up the hillside he let out a squawk you could have heard in Azerbaijan. Then he swooped suddenly to recover the copy of *Time* he'd been carrying in his beak, looped a swift loop, and sped away.

In the shack, Jason found an old woman. She was sitting by a fire stirring a big pot. A pair of black ravens perched on her shoulders, making her look like an old-fashioned bedstead.

'Hiya,' said Jason. 'Where to?'

The old woman scowled at him. This was her one big scene, and she wanted to make the most of it.

'Sit down, boy,' she said, and pointed with a gnarled finger at a low stool on the other side of the pot.

'No offence,' Jason said, 'but can we skip all that? I've

278

had a hard day, what with having to parachute out of the Hercules when the rockets hit it, then landing in the tree, then getting the motorbike started and being chased for thirty miles over rocky terrain with helicopters shooting at me. Then,' he added, 'getting the flat tyre. So if we could just . . .'

'You'll sit still,' said the old woman, 'and like it.'

'Bloody hell,' Jason whined rebelliously, but the old woman gave him a look which put the helicopter gunships firmly in context. He sat.

'Whither away, stranger?' said the old woman, after a gratuitously long pause. 'It is seldom we see strangers in these lonely parts,' she ad-libbed.

'I go to seek my Destiny,' said Jason woodenly. He'd say it, but he was damned if he was going to ham it up.

'Your Destiny?' said the old woman. She managed the capital D rather better than he did. 'And where will that lead you?' She cackled. Cackling is a dying art, so they say.

'Over . . . Look, have I got to say all this shit?'

'Yes.'

'Oh, come on,' Jason pleaded. It made him feel so self-conscious. 'I mean,' he said, 'if we skip it no one'll ever know.'

'I will,' said the old woman. 'Say it.'

'No.'

'Very well, then,' she said grimly, and reached for her knitting.

About five minutes later, Jason cleared his throat and said, very quickly;

'I-go-in-search-of-the-source-of-the-mystic-Power-the-Power-of-the-Sun, all right?'

The old woman nodded. 'Know,' she said, 'that I am not what I seem.' She put down her knitting and grinned. Jason looked at her.

'Well?'

'Well what?'

'Get on with it,' Jason said.

'You're supposed,' said the old woman, 'to register surprise.'

Jason indicated that he would shortly be registering extreme annoyance, and the old woman put down her knitting quickly. 'Know,' she said, 'that I am none other than Hecate, Witch-Mother of the Mountains, and I shall grant you one wish . . .'

'*One* wish?'

'You never heard of the cutbacks? *One* wish, to help you to achieve your heart's desire. But choose carefully; the gifts of the gods are very . . .'

'Tell me,' said Jason firmly, 'what I'm supposed to do next. Or,' he added, 'I'll thump you one, okay?'

The old woman glowered at him. 'Over there,' she said, 'turn left at the second thorn bush, follow your nose till you come to a pillar of fire, left then left again through the Clashing Rocks, then straight on, you can't miss it.'

'Miss what?'

'It,' said the old woman. 'Now push off.'

Jason got up and headed for the door. 'Hang on,' he said, 'you've forgotten something.'

'Have I?'

'Yes.'

'Oh.' The old woman tutted loudly. 'That's what comes of rushing things,' she said. 'You lose your place.'

From under her chair she pulled out a long cloth bag. 'See,' she said, 'this is the Sword of . . . Oh sod the thing, the cover's got caught on the pommel somewhere. Look, you hold this end and when I say "Pull" . . .'

There was a tearing sound; then a metallic clang.

'Anyway,' said the old woman, leaning forward, 'this is the Sword of Glycerion, which may only be tamed by the pure in heart. To all others it brings Death. Wield it well, my son, for . . . hey, didn't anyone ever tell you it's rude to snatch?'

'Right,' said Jason, looking at the Sword with mild disgust, 'about bloody time too.' He got up and strode towards the door.

'May the Power be with you,' the old woman called out after him.

'Oh, drop dead,' Jason replied. Then he clumped out to seek his Destiny.

'Your throw.'

'Right.'

Rattle rattle rattle. Clonk.

'Four and five, that's eight.'

'Actually, Pol, that's nine.'

'All right, it's bloody nine, then. One two three four five six seven eight oh, that's charming, that is.'

'Go back three spaces.'

'Yes, thank you, Vul, I can read, you know.'

Riffle riffle.

'GET OUT OF TROUBLE FREE. Oh well, that's worth having, isn't it? Your turn.'

Rattle rattle rattle rattle. Clunk.

Onetwothreefourfivesixseven *eight*.'

Pause.

'Oh.'

'Hello,' called Jason. 'Anyone at home?'

He leaned against the doorway of the curious stone building, rested the Sword of Thingummy against a pillar, and tied his shoelace. Heroism was all very well, he reckoned, but if he'd wanted to do a lot of walking he'd have become a postman.

Nothing happened. Jason put his newly-secured foot back on the ground and tapped it.

'Hello,' he repeated. 'Anybody there? I haven't got all day, you know.'

From somewhere inside the ruined temple there was the sound of someone dropping something, and the something breaking. 'All right,' said a sweet, enchanting female voice testily. 'Just wait a minute, will you?'

Then two women appeared in the doorway. Let us take the time to describe them.

First things first: they are a pair of absolute honeys. No mistake about that. You expect to see the title of a glossy fashion magazine floating above their heads in big block capitals.

One of them is tall, noble, austere. She is dressed in a simple, demure white robe, and on her head is a plain band of yellow gold. In the crook of one arm she carries what you instinctively know is a golden palm-branch symbolising something you can't quite remember. Her hair is the same colour as the band and the branch and her eyes are a sort of refrigerated blue. She doesn't happen to be wearing a sash right now, but if she was you could bet your life savings and next month's pay check that it would have VIRTUE embroidered on it.

The other one is dark, smouldering and has more curves than Le Mans and Indianapolis put together. In the crook of her arm she carries what used to be called a cornucopia – a sort of metallic cream horn with fruit in it – and what she's wearing is largely academic. She does, however, have a sash, but instead of LUXURY it has 'Miss Personality North-West Area 1992' on it, presumably in the vain hope of leaving something about the wearer's appearance to the imagination. In her mouth she has a couple of hairpins, and she doesn't look too pleased.

'Ready?' said Luxury, through the hairpins.

'Sorry?' Jason said.

'Oh come on,' said Luxury. 'I've got a lemon soufflé on the gas; let's not muck about.'

'Oh,' said Jason, blushing slightly, 'yes, right. I've got to choose, have I?'

'That's it,' said Luxury, 'and if you could see your way to getting a move on, we'd both be most terribly grateful, all right?'

'Er,' said Jason.

'Look,' said Luxury, 'if you're worried about hurting our feelings, don't be, okay? Just get on and choose, and then we can all carry on with what we're supposed to be doing.'

'I'm sorry,' said Jason, 'but shouldn't there be roads?'

The girls frowned and looked at each other. 'You what?' they said.

'A crossroads,' Jason explained. 'One road leading straight, narrow and uphill, towards a distant prospect of the battlements of the Shining City; the other winding broad and downhill, leading to, you know, thing.'

The girls looked at him.

'Well,' said Virtue, 'yes, now you come to mention it, strictly speaking. But since you seem to know all that already, do you think we could possibly . . .?'

'Ah,' said Jason. 'Yes, of course. Well . . .'

Thirty seconds passed. Luxury looked at her watch. Considering where it was pinned, this was no mean achievement.

'I'm sorry,' said Jason, 'and I hate to be difficult, but I'm going to have to insist on the roads.'

283

There was a deep sigh. 'Please yourself, then,' said Luxury. 'Look, will you just hold on a minute while I turn down the gas? Vir, do the roads for me, there's a love.'

Virtue nodded.

Jason stared. There, in front of him, lay two roads, just as he'd imagined them. Except that the road of Luxury was paved with violets, not primroses, and the road of Virtue had a big sign saying NO SERVICES FOR 200 MILES beside the verge.

'Will that do?' said Virtue.

'Well . . .' Jason replied. This should be easy, of course, but . . .

Just then Luxury came back, removing a pinny with *The World's Best Cook* on it. 'Got it working, Vir?' she asked.

'Just about,' Virtue replied. 'Better get someone in to look at it tomorrow though, otherwise we won't . . .'

The words dried on her lips. From out of the blue a large yellow placard had appeared and plonked itself down at a point just before the two roads diverged. On it was traced, in letters of synthesized fire, the word

DIVERSION

and a big white arrow pointing due west.

'Ah,' said Jason happily, and followed the arrow.

'Clever,' said Vulcan with grudging admiration. 'Lermontov's gambit on a double fluke score. Neat.'

Apollo gave him a worried look, such as William Tell might have given Isaac Newton. 'Actually . . .'

CHAPTER FOUR

He had been walking along the Diversion for about twenty minutes, whistling tunelessly and eating an apple he'd found in the pocket of his battledress, when Jason met the Erymanthian Hydra.

Since we took time out to describe Virtue and Luxury, let us also paint a verbal picture of the Erymanthian Hydra. You'll like this.*

Picture to yourself a bull, just an ordinary bull. Now paint it gold. Now remove the head – this is one we prepared before the programme – and add the head of a lion. Using a pair of long tweezers, tease out the hairs of the lion's mane and replace them with six-foot-long hissing vipers. If you have any vipers left over, nip out the bull's tail and pop them in there. Now remove the feet (do not discard; these can be used to make a nourishing stock) and substitute for them the talons of a gryphon. If you have no gryphon, a hippocamp will do just as well. Garnish with the wings of a dragon. Run away, terribly fast.

*So to speak. If you do find yourself enjoying what follows, we recommend that you seek professional help.

The Erymanthian Hydra is a confounded nuisance. It eats people. And cars. And railway shunting yards. It makes disconcerting howling noises in the middle of the night and has been known to tear open dustbin bags with its chalcedony talons.

As it saw Jason approaching, the Erymanthian Hydra sniggered softly, lifted up its ghastly head, ran a comb through its vipers, and sprang out from behind its rock.

'Hello,' it said. 'I'm the Erymanthian *ouch*!'

Jason sheathed his sword, lifted the monster's severed head by its still-hissing locks, and looked around for a rubbish-bin.

Demeter, ex-Goddess of the Earth, sat down on the cushion recently vacated by Vulcan, blew her nose, and looked at the Earth.

'How's he doing?' she asked.

Apollo looked round, refused the offer of a freshly-baked upside-down cake and frowned.

'It's hard to say,' he replied, 'on account of, I don't know what he's supposed to be doing yet.'

Demeter raised an exquisitely plucked eyebrow and reached for the score-card. 'Easy,' she said. 'Visit to Kingdom of Colchis,' she read out, 'passing through Caucasus mountains. Meets Witch (2), gives Judgment of Jason (6), slays Erymanthian Hydra (10) . . .'

'Yes, yes, all right,' said Apollo, 'but what's he do in the end?'

'I'm getting to that,' replied Demeter, running her finger down the envelope. 'Thessalian Centaurs . . . Recovers Golden Fleece (2,000; replay). Where's he got to now?'

'That's just it,' Apollo said. 'You see, he's going the wrong way.'

286

'You what?' Demeter looked up sharply.

'He's going the wrong way,' Apollo repeated. 'Look.'

'He can't be.'

'He is,' Apollo assured her. 'There, see for yourself.'

The two gods focused their eyes and zoomed in on a rocky outcrop in the Caucasus. On a low crag stood a group of well-armed Thessalian Centaurs. Most of them had their arms folded. Some were tapping their hooves. Their leader had given up looking at his watch and was shaking it to see if it had stopped.

'He's late?' Demeter guessed. The intellectual requirements for making corn grow are not stringent.

'More than that,' Apollo replied. 'He's missed them out completely.'

The two deities looked at each other.

'Perhaps,' Demeter ventured, 'he's just chicken.'

Apollo looked down at the spot on the hillside where the blood of the Erymanthian Hydra had just burnt a crater in the living rock. 'No,' he said, 'I don't think it can be that. It's more as if he's . . . well, going somewhere else.'

Demeter raised both eyebrows this time. 'But that's impossible,' she said.

'Well,' Apollo replied, 'it's very unprofessional.'

Demeter scratched her nose thoughtfully and, from sheer force of habit, produced half a million bushels of barley from behind her ear. 'Never heard of such a thing,' she said. 'Next thing, he'll be having a mind of his own. Can't have that.'

'What, he can't?'

'No, we can't.'

'Oh, I see.'

Apollo leaned forward and twiddled with a free-floating knob. The Earth seemed to grow larger.

287

'So where exactly is he headed?' Demeter asked.

'Good question,' Apollo replied. 'Now, let's see . . .'

Apollo produced a pair of field glasses. 'We might know that,' he said, 'when we've worked out where he's going.'

'Clever,' Demeter said, impressed. 'Whose turn is it, by the way?'

Apollo looked up. 'Do you know,' he said, 'I'd completely forgotten about the Game. Let's see, now; my go's over, and so it's you and . . .'

He fell silent, and his lips were pursed. 'I see,' he said. 'Or at least it's possible. I suppose.'

'Who is it?'

'Guess.'

Demeter's forehead wrinkled like a thrice-ploughed field. 'You know I'm no good at guessing,' she said. 'You'll have to tell me.'

Apollo said nothing, and handed her the Celestial Envelope.

'Oh,' said Demeter. 'Oh gosh!'

So what exactly was it, you are no doubt asking, that Prometheus stole from the gods and brought down to Earth, presumably not hidden in the hollow stalk of a piece of fennel?*

It is a dark night on the slopes of Mount Olympus. The Thirteen Olympians are sitting round the flickering light of Apollo's tripod, on the rim of which a number of tiny three-dimensional figures made out of coloured light are scurrying about in some sort of frantic dance. From the interior of the tripod comes the faint sound of music. The gods are watching *Life Wish III*.

*Otherwise it'd have got burnt.

288

Jupiter leans back in his chair and pulls the ring on a can of nectar. Demeter emerges from the kitchen with a tray of stars in batter and advises her fellow gods to eat them while they're hot. All is for the best in the best of all possible worlds.

Down below, however, on the surface of the Earth, things are not quite so jolly. Far from it. In their dark caves, our earliest forefathers huddle goose-pimpled in the smelly skins of mammoths and nibble listlessly at drumsticks of raw mouse. There is silence, except for occasional choking noises or the elder of the tribe saying how thoroughly unpleasant all this is. Then more silence, eventually broken by another elder saying that it is true that this is unpleasant, but that being eaten by the sabre-toothed tiger is probably worse.

Back to Olympus. The thirteenth Olympian quietly gets up from his place on the sofa, puts his slippers on and creeps away into the kitchen. From the vegetable rack he selects a suitable fennel stalk, lights a match and pops it in. He waits for a moment, until he is satisfied that the small glow of fire is thoroughly concealed. Then he tiptoes off the edge of the mountain and sprints away towards Earth.

He stops outside a large cave and knocks on the rock. After a while, a man in an ill-fitting goatskin comes to the mouth of the cave and peers at the stranger.

'Oh,' he says. 'It's you again, is it?'

Prometheus peers anxiously at the sky. 'Yes,' he whispers. 'Look . . .'

'Piss off,' says the mortal and makes a gesture with his arm. What he is trying to do is slam the door in the Titan's face; since there is no door, however, he has to rely on mime.

'Look . . .' Prometheus hisses urgently.

'No,' says the mortal, 'you look. We've had enough of you, got it? After last time.'

'Ah.'

'Yeah,' snarls the mortal. 'Dunno how you've got the nerve to come back here after that.'

Prometheus winces slightly. 'I told her,' he said. 'Don't open it, I said.'

The mortal makes a contemptuous noise. 'You told her,' he repeated. 'Don't you know *anything* about women?'

Prometheus shakes his head. 'I did warn her,' he repeated. 'Pandora, I said, just leave it alone and . . .'

'And you expected her not to open it?' said the mortal.

'Yes.'

'When it had *Open With Care, Free Gift Inside* written on it?'

'Well . . .' Prometheus flushed slightly. 'All right,' he conceded, 'so that was a bit of an error of judgment on my part. This time, though, I promise you, I'll make it up to you. Here.' He thrust the fennel-stalk into the mortal's hand. 'What d'you make of that, then?' he said eagerly.

'Fennel salad,' said the mortal. 'Thanks a lot.'

'No,' said Prometheus, 'just look inside it, will you?'

The mortal peered inside, then reared back, clutching his eyebrows. 'Ouch!' he explained.

'It's fire,' said Prometheus, proudly.

'So that's what you call it,' growled the mortal, rubbing the tip of his nose. 'And you know what you can do with that, my fine friend.'

'Wait a minute,' Prometheus said. He explained about fire.

He explained that with fire, you could see in the dark ('I thought that was carrots,' the mortal interrupted). How you could cook food. How you could smelt metal. How

290

you could boil water, killing the germs, producing steam that could turn a turbine. How you could . . .

The mortal wasn't listening. He was looking across the darkened valley to where a neighbouring tribe were tentatively building the first log cabin, and grinning mischievously.

'Right,' said the mortal, 'thanks, much obliged, don't let me keep you.' He turned to go back in the cave.

'Hold on,' said Prometheus, 'I haven't finished yet.'

The mortal stiffened. 'Oh yes?' he said warily. With his left hand he groped for the heavy flint axe he kept behind the door for just such occasions.

'Fire,' said Prometheus, 'is all very well in its way, but I've got something that's really going to change your lives.'

'Change?' enquired the mortal. 'Or just shorten?'

'Change,' Prometheus assured him, 'out of all recognition. From being wretched creatures of a day, dragging out a pointless existence in semi-bestial squalor . . .'

'Here,' said the mortal's wife from inside the cave, 'I heard that.'

'Instead,' Prometheus said urgently, 'you will be the sons and daughters of light, peers of the blessed gods, basking in the glow of the Golden Age of the world. Promise,' he added.

'Oh yes?' said the mortal, his fingers tightening on the handle of his axe. 'That good, is it?'

'Yes,' Prometheus replied. 'Listen to this.'

He cleared his throat, drew himself up to his full height and said, 'When is a door not a door?'

The mortal frowned, puzzled. 'What's a door?' he asked.

Prometheus asked himself to give him strength. 'No,' he said, 'listen. When is a door not a door?'

The mortal shook his head. 'Dunno,' he replied. 'Maybe if I knew what a door was in the . . .'

'When,' Prometheus howled desperately, 'it's *ajar*!'

The mortal was about to wield the axe when something strange, something that had never happened before, started to take place inside him. It was, he remembered later, a bit like a cough, except it seemed to start in the pit of the stomach, float up into your brain, slosh around for a moment and then come out of your mouth.

For the first time in the history of the human race, a mortal laughed.

Prometheus sagged exhausted against the wall of the cave while the mortal staggered about, his sides heaving with laughter. The rest of the tribe came sprinting up and stood staring at him in disbelief.

'That's a good one, that is,' said the mortal, wiping the tears from his eyes with the back of his hand. 'When it's a jar,' he repeated, and dissolved into a fresh torrent of hysterical laughter.

'Well,' said Prometheus, 'it's not *that* good. There's this other one about a chicken . . .'

The mortal ignored him and turned to the rest of the tribe. 'Here,' he spluttered, 'you lot, listen to this. When is a *door* not a *door*?'

The tribe looked at each other. 'What's a . . .?' one of them started to say.

'When it's a JAR!' roared the mortal, and quickly stuffed his hand in his mouth. There was a deadly silence.

'You've been chewing those funny leaves again,' said the mortal's wife at last. 'I told you, didn't I, they give you those turns . . .' Then, simultaneously, something clicked in the tribal consciousness. They all started to laugh. No studio audience ever found anything quite so funny.

'Well,' said Prometheus, backing away, 'I can see you've all got the hang of that quite nicely, so I'd better be getting back. Don't bother to see me out . . .' And that, of course, is why Prometheus was stripped of his divinity, hounded off Olympus, chained to a rock and condemned to everlasting punishment by his fellow gods, for the one crime that they could never forgive. But by then it was too late; the harm had been done. Even the Great Flood was powerless to eradicate the effects of Prometheus's treachery from the Earth; for when the waters finally rolled back, a small pun was found clinging to the side of Mount Ararat, and eventually became the ancestor of all the Polish jokes in the history of the world. At last, after aeons of enslavement and repression, Mankind had found a weapon with which to fight the gods. A mere thousand or so years later, in fact, the gods gave the whole thing up as a bad job, as we have already heard, and retreated to the sun; where the few indigenous life-forms, if asked what's black and white and red all over, will simply look at you and ask if you're feeling all right.

Actually, as you will have guessed, this triumph of Man over the gods was inevitable, ever since the Third Primordial, Thing, had made up his mind to get his own back on his uppity nephews. You will have worked out, without any assistance from the narrative staff, exactly what Thing was the God of and what it was that he inserted into each of the Words when Jupiter, Neptune and Pluto weren't looking.

What you may not have realised, however, is that deep down inside them, the gods still haven't given up the fight. Oh no. Not quite. Not yet.

CHAPTER FIVE

Jason scrambled up the last few feet, regained his balance, and looked about him.

He wasn't certain whether or not he was enjoying this.

Up to a point, he said to himself, yes, fine. The belting large predators, charging machine-guns, beheading fabulous monsters, OK. The thinking, no. Nature had, after all, designed him as a superb natural fighting machine equipping him with shoulders like boulders, arms like tree-trunks, sinews like ships' cables and thews (whatever they might be) of a similar high quality. He could lift articulated lorries, leap over crevasses, climb skyscrapers and shoot the eyebrows off a gnat at five hundred yards with anything from an assault rifle to a bow and arrow improvised from a TV aerial and a rubber band.

These accomplishments tended to give him a rather straightforward, positive view of life; any lip off you, he said to the world, and you'd better watch out. Or rather he didn't. You'd expect him to, of course; his father (the shiny one with the thunderbolts, not the one who grew dahlias) undoubtedly did. He didn't. He tended to see the world as a rather endearing mistake that someone would be bound to put right sooner or later. It fascinated him. He rather liked it. The urge to kick seven kinds of shit out of it on the rare occasions when it offered him any hesitant resistance didn't come easily to him.

He liked flowers, too.

Large predators, machine-guns and fabulous monsters had better look out when he was anywhere in the neighbourhood because he didn't hold with them; that was simple enough. They were big enough to look after themselves, they annoyed people and they had it coming. And insofar as Heroism consisted of putting that sort of thing in its place, he was definitely in favour of it, particularly as against, say, accountancy, as a vocation.

The problems were rather more subtle, but Jason wasn't one of those Heroes who define subtlety as not walking off the edges of high buildings. What worried him most of all was the feeling that somehow or other he wasn't in control. Not that he had any particular wish to control anything that wasn't organically attached to him; if someone were to offer him a throne, he would probably decline on the grounds that they didn't agree with him. But he did feel that it would be rather nice to be in control of his own body, actions and – above all – thoughts. And he had this nasty feeling that he wasn't.

Someone, somewhere, somehow was taking advantage of him to get things done which ought not to be done; and if only he were in full possession of the facts, he wouldn't have any part of it. It was as if there was this little voice in the back of his head which sometimes asked him, as he was washing off the blood or scoring another notch on the gunstock, whether that had really felt *right*. If it did, said the voice, that's just great, I'm very happy for you. If not . . .

The voice had this really aggravating habit of rounding

off its remarks with three dots, and Jason was inclined to regard that as something of a cop-out. To which the voice replied that if that was how he felt, that was fine, really it was, but . . . Sometimes, Jason considered, the little voice got right up his nose. However . . .

Jason's brow furrowed, and he looked around for the Centaurs. No Centaurs. Funny. The Dream had implied that good, thoroughbred Centaurs were getting a bit scarce these days, and anybody who had any pretensions to being constellation material would be a fool to turn down the chance of kicking the shit out of the ten hand-picked guaranteed genuine specimens who would just happen to be passing through the Caucasus later on this afternoon. Chance of a lifetime. Go for it.

Perhaps, Jason said to himself, they saw me coming and ran for it. That, he knew, would be the sensible course, and the mortal part of him told him that if he was a Thessalian Centaur and got word that a semi-divine headbanger was in the area and would be along as soon as he'd finished lopping the head off an Erymanthian Hydra, he'd be off out of it as fast as his hooves could carry him. But Centaurs, of course, aren't like that. Probably explains why they're getting so rare.

Unless . . .

Not you again, said Jason to the back of his head. Look, either finish the bloody sentence or shut up, will you? Not for the first time, he felt that the back of his head was becoming a pain in the neck.

Perhaps, Jason said to himself, I'm lost. But if I were lost, there'd be George with the golf buggy; and George was nowhere to be seen. So I can't be lost; therefore I must be here. Funny.

Jason looked round once more, but he could see nothing

except mountains, and from what he could remember of his Theory lessons, there weren't any merit points to be gained by getting heavy with the geography. He scratched his head, sat down on a rock and waited for something to happen.

He was hungry.

It had been a long time since he'd had that apple, and there was nothing more edible than a small oak-tree for as far as he could see. That puzzled him, too. Food, like transport, is generally laid on for Heroes by the Management – when was the last time you saw a Hero breaking off in mid-pursuit for a quarter-pounder and a chocolate shake? – and Jason had come to take it for granted. Actually, the food was pretty terrible but Jason's mother had been one of those women who think boiled potatoes are the staff of life and so he didn't know any better. Army catering had come as a pleasant surprise to him.

Time passed. The sun – when Apollo called it a day the contract for solar services had been put out to tender, and a consortium of Australian entrepreneurs had made the winning bid – rolled slowly across the sky. A mild breeze ruffled Jason's hair, reminding him that he'd left his hat behind when he'd parachuted out of the doomed Hercules. He was still hungry. If anything, hungrier.

He stood up, filled his lungs with air, and shouted.

'George!' he called. 'Where's my dinner?'

Nothing. Not so much as a fruit pastille. Jason's monumental jaw set in a firm line, and he gripped the Sword of Whatever-it-was with grim determination. Then he remembered something and drew a small, crumpled card from the top pocket of his battledress.

PIZZA TO GO, it read. WE DELIVER – ANYTIME, ANYWHERE.

That solved that, then. All he needed now was a callbox.

*

Jason stopped, swore and threw the Sword of Thingy on the ground. He had had enough. It was just as well for the Thessalian Centaurs that they were nowhere in sight, or they'd have been lunch.

After four hours of searching, Jason had failed to find a single phone booth in the Caucasus mountains. Well, there had been one; but it only took Phonecards.

Nor had he found any food. The few stringy tufts of grass that clung to the rock were inedible, the leather of his boots was stale and the stones were off. He was starving.

Pretty soon, he thought, I'm going to start seeing things. My brain will start playing tricks on me, and I'll have visions of huge cheeseburgers.

I said, he repeated to himself, I'll have visions of huge cheeseburgers.

Cheeseburgers . . . ?

Ah, so you're still there, are you? Yes, cheeseburgers with a large fries, banana shake and an apple fritter. Chop chop. Now.

Jason listened hard, but all he could hear was the distant sound of three dots laughing. He gave up, retrieved the sword, and plodded on towards the far summit of the mountain.

Then, from nowhere, a huge eagle appeared. It hung in the air just long enough for Jason to see the paper bag and styrofoam cup clutched in its talons, then launched itself into a thermal and whirled away before he had time to pick up a stone and let fly. He stood motionless and watched it recede, until it was barely discernible among the rocky crags.

Then it started to grow larger. It was circling. It was coming back.

Jason muttered under his breath, grabbed an aerodynamic stone and started to run. The force of windpressure had probably turned the chips stone cold by now, but that didn't seem to matter.

The eagle seemed to sense that it was almost in range, for it wheeled sharply, lifted and soared away. A single chip spilled out of the bag and floated, sycamore-seed like and mocking, down to the ground. Jason ate it. Then he sprinted away after the eagle.

Just when he'd given up all hope, the eagle turned a third time. This time, it dived. It came at Jason like a Rapier missile, low and exceedingly fast. He raised the stone and let fly, but his senses were weak from hunger and he missed, albeit by a fraction of an inch. As the eagle swept past him, Jason fancied that it gave him a filthy look. He ignored it and stooped for another stone, but too late. The eagle had gone again, this time for good.

'Hell!' Jason said. Then he licked his thumb, just in case there had been some vinegar on the chip.

And then it was back again; this time, hanging absolutely still in the air, just out of range, watching him coldly from round yellow eyes. It's waiting for me to give up, Jason thought. Bugger that. He lurched to his feet, wavered for a moment as his weary knees protested, and launched himself at the eagle.

The eagle waited for a moment, then changed position ever so slightly. A chip wafted down, and Jason sprang on it like a tiger.

Then the eagle moved again. Another chip descended. Then another movement, and another chip. Jason realised that he was being led, step by step, chip by agonisingly weary chip, towards the summit of the tallest mountain.

He didn't care. He didn't care that his body was no longer his own, that he was being manipulated by a large bird, just so long as there was salt and vinegar on the manipulations. The eagle seemed to sense its triumph, for a small slice of tomato and a sliver of lettuce drifted out of the sky and settled on the grey stone.

Jason did a quick calculation and worked out that at this rate he'd be in Istanbul before he got a square meal. But that didn't matter. All that mattered was the next chip. He gave in.

Then the eagle fluttered down, pitched beside him and dropped the paper bag and the milk shake onto the ground.

'Have a nice day,' said the eagle.

The explanation is as follows.

Every choice, every seemingly irrevocable act – the white shirt rather than the blue one, Jane rather than Paula, dying and so on – is not an end but a beginning. The alternative is not sealed off; instead, reality is bifurcated and forks off at that particular point. At the critical moment, what was formerly one world becomes two, one a carbon copy of the other. In the one world, marmalade is spread on the slice of toast; in the other, honey.

Thus, although there is only one planet Earth, and it is the only one in the galaxy capable of sustaining life, there are innumerable Earths each with its own subtle variations. The variations are not, of course, infinite, as there have been a finite number of event horizons calling a new Earth into existence. There are, however, an awful lot of them, and to a greater or lesser extent, depending on how things work out, each Earth has all of us on it. Thus there is somewhere – or was, at any rate – an Earth on which there are still dinosaurs, an Earth on which Napoleon captured Moscow, an Earth where all the videos are Betamax.

There are, however, such things as the Laws of

Possibility; and it is also universally acknowledged that everything in the world has an effect, direct or indirect, on everything else. On what we might call the Betamax worlds, therefore, the lesser or incorrect choice generally sets in motion a chain of causalities which eventually results in the Laws being infringed and the entire world slowly fading away into a tiny point of light, which then goes out.

Only one of the Betamax worlds has yet to fade away completely, and this is because some extremely powerful forces are being exerted to keep it in existence. This is the world on which Prometheus, on that fateful night, tried telling the caveman the one about the Englishman, the Pole and the Corcyraean, thereby completely failing to communicate the divine spark of humour to the human race.

Of course, the gods aren't consciously keeping it going, because they know that this would be impossible. Any interference by the gods in the alternative-world process is strictly forbidden by the Laws – in particular, Section 45 (a) (ii) of the Possibility Act and Schedule 8, Article 57 of the Monkeying About With Time (Prohibition) Act, as amended – and the only thing the gods can truly be said to be afraid of is the Possibility Police; who, it is well known, have an innate bias against anyone who regularly flies without wings and walks on water, and have been waiting for a chance to catch the gods out of line ever since the Primeval Dawn. Subconsciously, however, the gods find it impossible to sever the final link between themselves and their counterparts in what they cannot help feeling were the Good Old Days; and some of them, who understand about such things, have recently taken to messing about with the thin dividing line between the conscious and the subconscious. They realise that, as things stand, it can only be a matter of time before affairs on the Betamax world get so completely out of synch that they will have to let go, and therefore if there is ever to be a chance of going back, undoing Prometheus's betrayal and snatching the Joke back from the human race, something will have to be done fairly quickly.

The eagle dropped the last chip, wheeled in a dizzying spiral, and dived. As Jason lunged forward and caught the descending chip, he saw that the eagle had pitched on something, folded its wings and was sitting there, looking at him sideways.

The thing looked remarkably like a telephone booth.

Forgetting that he'd just had a quarter-pounder with cheese, large fries and a banana shake (albeit by instalments) Jason summed up his last remaining dregs of strength, hauled open the door and fell inside.

He lifted the receiver to his ear. Against all his expectations, he heard the familiar bored-cat noise and searched in his pocket for some change. He had some. It fitted in the slot. He dialled the number on the crumpled card, and waited.

'Hello,' said a voice, 'this is Pizza To Go. Sorry there's no-one here to take your call right now, but if you'd like to leave a message after the tone . . .'

Jason got no further than 'thoughtless, stupid bastards' before the pips went, taking with them his last coin. He slumped against the booth wall and replaced the receiver feebly.

Then the phone rang.

Odd, the way one can never resist the summons of a telephone ringing. There is, in fact, a reason for this. Purely by chance, the telephone engineers have chosen for

302

the dialling tone the exact notes of the Last Summons, by which the Judges of the Dead will call up the souls of the departed to the final tribunal. Of course, the Last Summons will be considerably louder, since the dead are notoriously hard of hearing. However, some ghosts are sharper-eared than others, and the ringing of the telephone occasionally attracts them from the Asphodel Plains. This accounts for the phenomenon known to students of the paranormal as the Crossed Line.

Anyway, Jason picked up the receiver.

'Yes?' he said. 'What?'

There was a silence at the other end of the line, as if whoever it was wasn't used to being talked to like that. Jason, however, was past caring.

'Well?' he said.

'Well what?' It was an elderly, rather querulous voice, high and dry. That, at any rate, was all Jason could deduce from the small sample he had been given – not, frankly, that he was all that bothered.

'Well yourself,' he said. 'Who is this, anyway?'

Another thing about telephones is that every unknown voice on the end of a telephone line always wants to talk to Carol. Is Carol there, they ask. Could I speak to Carol, please? There is either some enormous conspiracy going on, or else Carol is getting a hell of a lot of calls from people wanting to leave an order with the Chinese Takeaway.

'Am I speaking to' – the voice hesitated, as if it was reading something off a piece of paper – 'to Jason Derry?'

'Yes,' said Jason.

'Then please replace the receiver – not yet, of course – and walk five hundred yards due west, turn through seventy-five degrees and walk a further two hundred yards

303

due north. Then turn through ninety degrees. Please replace the receiver *now*.'

The line went dead, and Jason shrugged. Being a Hero he didn't know the meaning of fear, just as the average person doesn't know the meaning of the word *foumart*.* The fact that there had been a voice giving him directions might well mean that if he followed the directions he would meet the owner of the voice. The owner of the voice might have some food. If the worst came to the worst, he could always eat him.

Jason sighed and opened the door of the phone booth. As he did so, the eagle spread its wings and soared away. Jason checked with his compass; the eagle was going due west.

He paced out five hundred yards – difficult, since the terrain was uneven – made a guess at seventy-five degrees and turned. The eagle banked and set off in the direction he had just decided on. Pretty shrewd guess, huh?

Hundred and ninety-seven, hundred and ninety-eight, hundredanninetinine, and *turn* . . .

Jason opened his eyes and blinked.

He was looking up at a hillside, far away in the distance. Chained – yes, they were chains – to the rocks was the body of a huge man, lying face downwards. There was a raw scab roughly the size of a steel works, on the small of his back, over which the eagle was standing. The eagle had got bigger too. Very much bigger. There was blood all over its beak, and its eyes were huge yellow globes. Jason may still not have known the meaning of fear, but he would have been prepared to hazard a guess.

*polecat

'Punctuality,' said the giant, in a voice like the sea, 'is the politeness of princes. But not, apparently, Heroes. If you look under the small rock by your left foot, you will find a packet of sandwiches.'

Jason looked.

'Where?' he said.

'Under the small rock by your . . .'

'What small rock?'

'The small rock by your . . . Just a moment, please.'

The giant made an expressive gesture with his left ear, and the eagle hopped over and stood by his head. They whispered together for a moment.

'Did I say two hundred paces north?' said the giant. 'I'm sorry. Try going ten paces further.'

Jason uprooted his legs and advanced.

'Right,' he said, 'got the small rock. No sandwiches, though.'

'Ah.' The giant wiggled his ear again. The eagle hopped forward.

'Is it a squarish brown rock?' asked the giant.

'I don't know,' Jason replied. 'It's hard to say with rocks. They all look the . . .'

'Try going back a bit.'

'Ah,' said Jason, 'got that. Small, squarish brown rock. Sandwiches. Yes.'

'Oh *good*,' said the giant. 'Now perhaps we can get down to business.'

'Fire away,' Jason said, with his mouth full.

'Allow me to introduce myself,' said the giant. 'My name is . . .'

'There wouldn't be any mustard, would there?'

'No,' said the giant.

'Pity.'

'My name,' said the giant, 'is . . .'

'Pickle?'

There was a long silence. Jason guessed that there probably wasn't any pickle.

'My name,' said the giant, and then paused, as if waiting for a further interruption. 'There is,' he said, 'no piccalilli. And my name is Prometheus.'

'Prometheus?'

'Prometheus, yes. Nor is there any salt.'

Jason chewed thoughtfully. 'I've heard of you,' he said. 'I think.'

'Have you really?' said the giant. 'I'm *so* thrilled. Now . . .'

'My dad,' Jason said, 'says you're a traitor to your class and you sold us all down the river. My dad says . . .'

'No doubt he does,' said the giant. 'That's just the sort of thing I would expect your father to say. What of it?'

'Nothing,' Jason replied. 'Which river?'

'I expect he was speaking metaphorically,' said the giant. 'I think he was simply trying to express his disapproval of me. You should be able to gather from what you can see that your father disapproves of me.'

'The chains and the eagle and everything?'

'Well,' said the giant, 'it could be that I'm sunbathing and the chains are here to prevent me getting blown away by a freak gust of wind, but that wouldn't really explain away the eagle, now would it? Yes, your father has a pretty low opinion of me, all things considered. And I,' added the giant proudly, 'have an even lower opinion of him. And what do you think of that?'

'How do you mean?' Jason said, chewing.

'Let me put it another way,' said the giant. 'On the one hand, you owe your father filial respect, love and obedi-

306

ence. On the other hand, I happen to know the where-abouts of a packet of chocolate biscuits and a can of diet Pepsi. The decision, of course, must rest with you. Only you can . . .'

'Where?' said Jason quickly.

'Hidden,' replied the giant. 'Now, if you will do me a little favour, I'm sure the eagle will be happy to . . .'

'Yes,' said Jason. 'Hurry up, will you, I'm starving.'

The giant raised his head petulantly. 'Not so fast, young man,' he said. 'First, you will have to listen to a certain amount of tedious explanation.'

'All right,' Jason said, 'but make it quick, because . . .'

'In the beginning,' said the giant slowly, 'was the Word . . .'

'What do you mean,' said Diana angrily, 'you've lost him?'

'Just that,' Apollo replied. 'One minute he was there, standing about looking hungry, the next minute he was gone.'

Diana made an exasperated noise and turned to Demeter.

'Dee,' she said, 'you tell me. It's no use trying to get any sense out of Pol when he's in one of his moods. What's been happening?'

Demeter shrugged. 'He's absolutely right,' she said. 'He just sort of walked out of sight. Bing,' she added.

Diana frowned and turned to Minerva, who was leaning on her spear-shaft looking sage. Pure habit.

'But that's impossible,' she said. 'Heroes can't just dis-appear. Perhaps he's gone down a hole or something.'

'I thought of that,' said Apollo, ignoring the fact that he was apparently too idiotic to be audible. 'So I tried the infra-red scanner. Nothing. Look.'

He flicked a free-floating switch and the Earth suddenly looked as if it was bathed in blood.

'Satisfied?' said Apollo. 'Nothing. Nor has he borrowed a Cloak of Invisibility, wandered into another dimension or disguised himself in a false beard and a raincoat. He's just gone. Phut!'

Diana set her lips in a thin line. Bing she could just about handle, but phut! was something else. 'Don't be so feeble, Pol,' she said. 'Send a messenger or something.'

Apollo grinned at her. 'I did,' he said. 'I've had Sleep, Death, Thought, Time and Indigestion flying backwards and forwards over the Caucasus for the last twenty minutes. Nothing. Except,' he added, 'a bloody great big chit for mileage allowance, which *someone* isn't going to be too pleased about . . .'

Diana sagged slightly. 'Perhaps they didn't look *properly*,' she ventured. Minerva gave her a look.

'All right,' said Minerva, 'but he must be somewhere. Everyone always is. Have you spoken to his driver?'

'George,' said Apollo, 'is at this very moment trying to convince thirty-two very irritable Thessalian Centaurs that his master has just had to pop back for a pair of winged sandals and will be along in a minute. He's as baffled as the rest of us.'

Minerva bit her lip. On her right shoulder, her owl shifted from leg to leg nervously.

'Well,' she said, 'obviously he's out there somewhere, but . . .'

'Look,' said Apollo, 'didn't I just . . .?'

'Let me finish, will you? But,' Minerva went on, 'all reasonable and diligent enquiries . . .'

'Thank you.'

'. . . have failed to reveal exactly where,' Minerva said.

'We are gods, and nothing can be hidden from us. Except,' she went on, 'by other gods.'

There was a short pause.

'Oh,' Demeter said, 'I see what you're driving at. You think one of us . . .'

Minerva breathed in in the manner she usually reserved for her male relatives. 'No, dear,' she said, 'Not one of us here now, because none of us, not even Pol, would be so very childish. One of us gods, on the other hand, as opposed to the mortals or the Tooth Fairy, yes. That, I would suggest, narrows the field down a bit, wouldn't you think?'

Demeter blinked. 'Does it?' she asked.

Minerva smiled terribly. 'Apollo, dear,' she said, 'why don't you take Demeter away and find her something to grow? I'm sure we needn't detain her further, and perhaps we'd all get on that bit faster if . . .'

'Oh do shut up, Min,' Demeter said. 'And get to the point, if you've got one.'

'Very well, then,' Minerva said. 'What I'm trying to suggest to you is this. A Hero has disappeared. He must be out there somewhere. Therefore a god must have hidden him. Now, don't you think that points rather at Someone in Particular?'

Even Demeter couldn't fail to catch her drift. The poet Homer describes Jupiter as He Whose Delight Is In Thunder, but poets have to be polite. His fellow gods prefer to describe him as He Whose Delight Is In Being Bloody Difficult.

'He wouldn't,' Diana said, 'would he? I mean, why?'

Minerva smiled. 'Bonus points,' she said.

'Bonus points?'

'Precisely,' Minerva replied. 'Typical underhand cheating.'

Gods, it should be explained, have no objection to overhand cheating, which they prefer to call Fate. Overhand cheating consists of wiping out whole cities with the plague or flattening your opponent's best Hero with a thunderbolt. Anything that is devious, however, or smacks of low cunning, they regard with great distaste, largely because it's usually too clever for them to follow.

'What he's done,' Minerva went on, 'is to magic this Jason away for three or four moves, and then he'll pop him back in when we least expect it. Then one of us'll be left with a headless dragon or a defeated army and absolutely nothing at all we can do about it. Well, I for one . . .'

'I'm not so sure,' said Apollo.

Minerva turned and looked at him. 'Well,' she said, 'if you have an alternative explanation, I'm sure we'd all be only too pleased . . .'

'No,' Apollo confessed, 'I haven't. I just don't think . . .'

'I know,' Minerva interrupted. 'You never have, either. Now then, I suggest that we send Mercury, with the Lamp of Truth and the Celestial Trufflehound. That ought to have him out of it in no time.'

Just then, a shining portal opened in the wall of the sun and all the gods rose instinctively to their feet. They always do. Partly this is because all gods, despite their incessant bickering and backbiting, have an innate respect for the Father of Gods and Men. The fact that He tends to throw those who don't off the battlements also has something to do with it.

'Right,' said Jupiter, taking his place on the golden throne that none but he ever dared sit in, 'who's the smartass?'

'Right,' said Jason, 'fine. Now, about those cakes . . .'

Prometheus sighed. 'And so,' he said, 'what do you think?'

310

'Think?'

'Yes,' said Prometheus. 'About the morality of it?'

'*Morality?*' Jason's brow furrowed, and he considered long and hard. 'Dunno,' he said at last.

'You don't know,' Prometheus repeated. 'I see. I must say that I find that tremendously encouraging.'

'It's not something I think about a lot,' said Jason, 'morality.'

'Really?'

'Not,' he went on, 'in my line of work. I'm more, you know, blue-collar. Mine not to reason why, that sort of thing.'

'You're more,' said the Titan slowly, 'a sort of hired thug?'

'Exactly,' Jason said. 'The way I see it is, somebody somewhere knows what's going on, so who am I to make difficulties?'

'Well now,' said Prometheus, 'I know what's going on, and I'm prepared to pay in hard confectionery. What about it?'

Jason frowned. 'What,' he said, 'me take orders from you instead of him?'

'Very neatly put. Yes.'

'I don't think he'd like it,' Jason said. 'And, well, you know what happens to people who . . .'

Prometheus laughed and rattled his chains until the mountains shook. 'Yes,' he said, 'I have a pretty shrewd idea. A pity. Well, I'm sorry to have troubled you. The biscuits are three paces east under the roots of a thornbush. The eagle will show you.'

Great, Jason said to himself as he tore open the packet and put tooth to chocolate. Great . . .

Not *you* again. Go away.

Sure . . .

I said go away, will you? I really don't need this right now.

Exactly . . .

All right then, out with it. What are you getting at?

Nothing . . .

Good, because if you haven't got anything to say, you can just push off and leave me in . . .

In . . .

Slowly, Jason got up, finished his mouthful, and turned to face the giant.

'Excuse me,' he said.

The giant turned his head – imagine Hounslow suddenly picking itself up and rolling over on one side and stared at Jason, who saw the two round blue eyes for the first time. He swallowed and choked on a crumb.

'Yes?' he said softly.

'Well,' Jason said, 'I don't suppose there's anything I could do without him actually knowing, is there?'

Prometheus laughed. 'As it happens,' he said, 'there is.'

CHAPTER SIX

Although it was now over five years since Sergeant Smith had had his funny experience, he still hadn't recovered from it, and his superiors at the Axe Cross police station had long since decided that being a desk sergeant was all he was fit for now. As they saw it, when batty old ladies came in claiming to have seen flying saucers, they would at least be sure of a sympathetic audience.

Anyone less likely than the sergeant to be a dreamer of dreams it is hard to imagine. A long, hard youth spent watching fights outside chip shops and arresting the more seriously injured participants should have cauterised his powers of imagination many years ago; but the fact remained that he claimed to have seen Something, and ever since he had been as unshakable in his story as an interviewing officer telling the court that during interrogation the defendant had repeatedly got up and banged his head violently against the leg of the table.

It had happened, Sergeant Smith insisted, on a Thursday, about a quarter past eleven at night, bang in the middle of Pool Street, just opposite the bus shelter. This guy had appeared out of nowhere, wearing a sort of bronze bodywarmer and a short skirt, screaming blue murder and carrying what the sergeant, a man of limited vocabulary, could only describe as a bloody great sword. Naturally, the sergeant had immediately taken up a position behind the bus shelter for the purposes of more efficient surveillance, and from there he had a clear view of the man running down Pool Street as far as the Co-op, stopping dead in his tracks and being confronted with some kind of very big reptile, which he proceeded to attack. During the course of the struggle, what the sergeant stubbornly maintained was a bloody great hand materialised out of thin air, grabbed the man and the strange beast, lifted them up in the air and deposited them both in the carpark of the Bunch of Grapes; whereupon the tarmac of the carpark turned bright pink and started to glow eerily. As the combatants touched down, big black letters appeared on the surface of the carpark, spelling out the legend TRIPLE DEED SCORE.

Then the man had cut off the reptile's head, and the sergeant fainted.

Subsequent investigation of the scene of the alleged incident revealed nothing but three sets of car keys and a half-eaten doner kebab, and the only other person who claimed to have seen anything unusual had been a regular customer of the Bunch of Grapes, who saw unusual things as a matter of course. The fact that when, a year or so later, a new landlord from up north somewhere took over the Grapes he changed the name of the place to the George and Dragon was dismissed as sheer coincidence.

It so happened that Sergeant Smith was for once not dwelling on this incident when a woman walked into the police station and asked to report a missing person.

'I wouldn't have troubled you,' she said, looking over her shoulder, 'but my, er, husband's a bit of a worrier.'

'Oh yes?' said the sergeant, and reached for the book. 'So who's gone missing, then?'

'My son,' said the woman.

'Name?'

The woman thought for a moment. 'Mine or his?' she asked.

'Let's start with yours, shall we?' said the sergeant.

'Derry,' said the woman. 'Phyllis Eva.'

'Right,' said a voice from the cloud of heat, 'let's all get our fingers out and clear up this mess, shall we?'

The other gods took his words as a sign that they could sit down now, and all began talking at once. Jupiter banged the altar in front of him with the butt end of his thunderbolt and cleared his throat with a sound like the Alps falling onto a drumskin.

'First,' – the word resounded in the utter silence 'first,' – said Jupiter, rather less loudly this time, 'let's find out who saw him last.'

Apollo stood up nervously, holding an envelope between shaking fingers. 'Well,' he said, 'I've been trying to reconstruct his movements, and so far as I can make out, his driver took him up to the Witch's hut. There he collected the Sword of . . . of . . .' Apollo looked down at his notes. 'Glycerion, used it to slay the Erymanthian, er, Hydra, and then went to make the Judgment of Jason.' He paused self-consciously.

'And?' said Jupiter. 'Presumably he then followed the Road of Virtue. What next?'

'Actually,' mumbled Apollo, 'he didn't.'

Jupiter frowned, his eyebrows like mating rain-forests. 'Didn't he?'

'Strictly speaking, no,' said Apollo. 'Not as such.'

315

'You mean he followed the Road of Luxury?' Jupiter enquired. The Old Fool was keeping his temper remarkably well in the circumstances, the other gods felt, but they couldn't help noticing that it had started raining quite heavily down below on the Earth. 'This is something to do with this new Free Will crap everyone's always on about, I suppose. Still . . .'

'Actually,' Apollo interrupted, 'he followed the Road Marked *Diversion* . . .'

'Sorry?'

'Diversion,' Apollo whispered.

There was a very long silence; so deep that the gods could hear the rain lashing down on Earth, millions of miles away. Good, Demeter said to herself, for the crops.

'Diversion,' said Jupiter quietly. 'I see.'

'It was my go, you see,' Apollo went on, 'and there was a ten-point Killer Scorpion left over from the Wanderings of Odysseus in a cave just round the corner, and I thought, since he was there it'd be no trouble if he just . . .'

'You diverted him?'

'More or less, yes, I suppose you could say that, really, though it was more a sort of short-cut, because it should have brought him out by the Thessalian Centaurs if only he'd followed the little yellow markers like he was supposed to, and the scorpion has been getting up the noses of the locals for ages now and it really did seem like a good idea at the . . .' Apollo's jaw gradually stopped moving and he swallowed hard, smiled and speculated as to where he would be likely to land.

'And that,' Jupiter said, 'was the last anyone saw of him?'

Apollo nodded, rather more times than was necessary. Uncharacteristically, Jupiter managed to keep his feelings under control, admittedly only by blowing the stars

316

known to astronomers as Orion's Belt into a million pieces.

'Ah well,' he growled, 'we all make mistakes, don't we? And it wasn't as if you did it on purpose, or could be expected to know what'd be likely to happen. I mean,' he added savagely, 'it's not as if you're bloody well omniscient, is it?'

'No, er . . .'

'The main thing,' Jupiter went on, 'is to keep calm, and not go doing anything silly' – and as he spoke, a jagged fork of lightning crashed into a nuclear power station in the Urals – 'which we all might regret later. It's all too easy, in circumstances like these' – a long-dormant volcano in the Andaman Islands let out a horrifying burp that was felt in Melbourne – 'to go all to pieces and make matters very much worse, but if we all try and keep absolutely . . . WHAT THE HELL DID YOU THINK YOU WERE PLAYING AT, YOU DICKHEAD?'

Out in the silence of deep space, the enormous masses of flaming matter released by the explosion in the constellation of Orion were suddenly drawn together as by an unseen hand to form new stars, thereby preserving the equilibrium of the cosmos and forming a new star-pattern known to future generations of astronomers as Orion's Braces. A junior nuclear technician was declared a Hero of the Soviet Union for having the foresight to nail an improvised lightning conductor to the side of his generator, and as the seismic ripples in the Indian Ocean subsided, the major powers issued simultaneous denials and postponed all nuclear tests for a week. It even stopped raining.

'OF ALL THE . . .' Jupiter checked himself, closed his eyes and counted up to forty million. 'Do you realise, you stupid little git, what you've done?'

317

Apollo shook his head.

'Then,' the Thunderer went on, 'perhaps it's time you had a little geography lesson. Starting,' he added, 'with a field trip.'

Observers at the new European Observatory in Switzerland later swore blind that a very large meteorite landed heavily in the Caucasus Mountains. However, it all happened so fast that nobody else saw it, and it was later put down to a bit of fluff getting on the lens of the telescope.

'Can you hear me down there?' Jupiter said.

Apollo picked himself up out of his crater, dusted himself off and said 'Yes.'

'You are now,' Jupiter went on, 'in the Caucasus Mountains, not far from the scene of the Choice of Jason. You have, in fact, been Diverted.' Jupiter chuckled. 'Anyway,' he went on, 'just over there' – forked lightning helpfully indicated the direction – 'is where a Certain Very Bad Person is chained to a rock. Now do you see what I'm getting at?'

Apollo nodded.

'Good,' said Jupiter. 'Now do you see what a silly billy you've been?'

The ex-God of the Sun said Yes, he saw perfectly and it went without saying that he'd never do anything so idiotic ever again and it was typical of Jupiter to take such a reasonable view of the whole episode and would it be too much trouble to send Aesculapius the Healer down when it was quite convenient because he thought that he'd clumsily managed to break his leg.

Jupiter sighed. 'That's all right, then,' he said. 'Go and fetch him, somebody. And fill in that hole,' he added, scowling at the crater. 'Mortals tend to notice things like that these days.'

Shortly afterwards, Apollo was restored to the Council of Heaven, smelling strongly of liniment but otherwise intact. Jupiter moved on to the next stage in the debate.

'Anyway,' he said, 'where were we? Oh yes, Jason. Well, we now know where he went, but we still don't know where he got to. Mercury!'

There was a sudden rush of air, and Mercury, messenger of the gods, was standing among them. On his feet were winged sandals, in his left hand the caduceus which is his badge of office, in his right hand three large, flat cardboard boxes.

'Right,' he said, 'a Deep-pan Seafood Special, extra tuna, a Pepperoni Feast with . . . Oh.'

There was an awkward silence, broken only by the tapping of Jupiter's jackhammer fingers on the arm of his throne.

'Now look, Merc,' he said, not unkindly, 'sure, times are hard, but moonlighting . . . no. Get rid of it, all right?'

Mercury nodded passively, and the boxes vanished. Oddly enough, the pizzas did get delivered in the end, but in a totally different dimension and without the garlic bread.

'Now,' said Jupiter. 'I want you to go to Earth, find Jason, come straight back. Do you think you can remember that, or shall I burn it onto the back of your brain for you?'

Mercury smiled thinly. 'Thanks,' he said, 'I'll manage.'

'You sure?' Jupiter asked. 'It'd be no trouble.'

'Sure,' said Mercury. Paranoia, perhaps; but he had this feeling that Jupiter had never quite forgiven him for trying to get the other gods to form a union. 'I'll be right back,' he said.

A few minutes later, he was sitting cross-legged on a mountaintop in the Caucasus.

319

'Here you are,' he said cheerfully. 'You did say hold the onions, didn't you?'

Prometheus, his mouth full, nodded. 'How's business?' he asked.

Mercury shrugged. 'Could be worse,' he said. 'It's not that there isn't a demand; it's the damned overheads. You seen a Hero about here lately?'

Prometheus frowned and spat out an olive-stone. 'Hero?'

'Yeah.' Mercury scratched his ear. 'Six nine, maybe six ten, serious muscles, chin like a snowplough, very bad attitude towards large carnivores. Ring any bells?'

Prometheus thought for a moment, then shook his head. 'Mind you,' he said, 'maybe I'm not the person to ask. Try the eagle.'

'Oh yes,' Mercury said, 'where is the eagle today? Last time I saw it, it was coming out of a Burger King. You not feeding it properly or something?'

'Something like that,' Prometheus said. 'We had a quarrel. I said to it, "Look, just get off my back, okay?" and it took offence.'

'Sensitive creatures, eagles.'

'Very. Still, we've made it up since. In fact, we're having lunch again soon. On me.'

'Glad to hear it. Look,' said Mercury, 'love to stay, got to go. if you see that hero, just give me a shout, right?'

'Will do.' Prometheus stirred a little. 'Oh, Merc, one last thing.'

'Yes?'

'Can I have my book back? Only I've just got to the bit where Perry Mason's noticed the missing cake-tin, and . . .'

Mercury, patron god of thieves, grinned apologetically. 'Sorry,' he said, 'force of habit. Cheers.'

Mercury departed, and Prometheus, having counted, lifted his head and whistled. From a cave in the nearest mountain, the eagle emerged.

'Sometimes,' it said, 'life can be a real bitch, can't it?'

Prometheus grinned. 'Forget it,' he said. 'I reckon it's a good sign. We've got them rattled.'

The eagle raised the area of its head-feathers most closely approximating to the human eyebrow. 'Trouble with rattling gods,' it remarked, 'they tend to get nasty. Might take it out on you. And I've got to watch my diet. The quack keeps saying, eat more green vegetables. Last thing I need is having to stuff myself with kidneys as well as . . .'

Prometheus wiggled his ears reassuringly. 'Don't worry,' he said. 'Quite soon they'll have other things on their minds, believe you me. Anyway, I suppose we'd better let them find him, or else they'll do something to someone else and we can't have that. What did you do with him, by the way?'

The eagle grinned. 'I left him at Baisbekian's Diner,' it replied, 'eating honey cakes. Shall I fetch him?'

'Better had,' said Prometheus. 'Oh, and Eagle . . .'

The eagle stopped in mid-launch and beat the air with its huge wings for a moment. 'Yes?' it said.

'Thanks.'

'Don't mention it,' said the Eagle, blushing under its feathers, and soared away.

Mercury, meanwhile, had completed a lightning-fast survey of the Caucasus and was starting to worry; so preoccupied was he, in fact, that he flew over the Kislovodsk People's Bank without lifting so much as a kopeck. If he returned to the sun without finding the mortal, he was going to be in trouble; and with his record, that might not be pleasant.

Just when he had almost given up hope, a blinding flash of blue light caught his eye. He looked down and saw the sunlight sparkling on the Sword of Damn It's On The Tip Of My Tongue, Begins With G. He dived.

Outside Baisbekian's Diner, Jason was pulling his seventh plate of honey cakes towards him and lifting his fork when he became aware of a very old woman leading a donkey across the town's dusty square. He noticed the glitter of gold* under the hem of her long black skirt, sighed, and put the spoon down. 'Over here,' he called.

Mercury tied the donkey to a tree and hobbled over. 'These look good,' he said, and ate one.

'I see,' Jason observed. 'You come all the way from the sun to help me eat my dinner. That's service.'

Mercury scowled. 'Leave it, all right?' he said through a mouthful of baklava. 'Things have been very tense round our way because of you, very tense indeed. Where have you been, anyway?'

Jason shrugged. 'Here,' he said, 'eating. You ask the waiter.'

'But why here?'

'I was hungry. I fancied eating Caucasian for a change. You can get bored with pizza.'

---

*Traditionally, when on Earth the gods adopt mortal guise. Because of the confusion this tends to cause, however, there is a convention that they leave one of their divine attributes visible to give at least some warning to reasonably perceptive mortals. Thus, if a large woman with an owl on her shoulder runs over your foot with her trolley in the supermarket, it is wise not to say anything you might later regret.

322

Mercury gave him a look. 'Fine,' he said. ' You're supposed to be out there mutilating centaurs, but instead you're having lunch. That's great, really.'

'Right,' Jason replied dangerously, 'glad you approve. Because today I've flown halfway across the world in a freezing cold Hercules air freighter with no buffet facilities, been shot down by surface-to-air missiles but not fed, chased by crack Soviet mountain troops who didn't offer me so much as a KitKat, told my destiny by a witch who had nothing in her larder except dried newts' tongues, attacked by an inedible giant lizard, and flirted with by two allegorical women on diets. I am now having breakfast. And lunch. And dinner. All right?'

Mercury shrugged. 'All that starch and carbohydrate is doing the most appalling things to your body, you realise. You keep it up, in five years you're going to have arteries like an underground railway.'

'Suits me.'

'Great.' Mercury shook his head sadly and liberated another slice of honey cake. 'Meanwhile,' he said, 'there's centaurs out there getting impatient.'

'Someone should try giving them something to eat,' Jason replied. 'Then perhaps they'd go away and stop bothering people. And give me back my magic sword before I brain you with it.'

Mercury sighed. 'Sorry,' he said. 'It's not as if it gives me any pleasure, either. I've got this lock-up garage, right, absolutely stuffed with non-stick frying pans, car radios, synthetic fur coats . . . You couldn't give half of it away.' He smiled. 'Anyway,' he said, 'I can see you're busy, so I'll leave you to it. I'll buzz your driver, OK? I expect he's wondering where you've got to.'

'What I need,' Jason said, 'is one of those bleeper things,

you know, radio pagers. When you see George, tell him to put some bread rolls in the toolbox.'

The old woman got up painfully, stretched her stiff back, surreptitiously pocketed a spoon and retrieved her donkey. A few seconds later, a small electric wagon rumbled into the empty village square and the hungry stranger got up, left some money on the table, and climbed into the cart. The village blacksmith paused, a glowing red horseshoe, gripped in his pincers, and turned to his apprentice.

'You saw that?' he said. 'That's tourism, that is.'

The apprentice grinned, and the smith chucked the horseshoe into a bucket of water, where it fizzed angrily. Soon afterwards, the smith had smelted some more ore and was beating out a wrought-iron magazine-rack with 'A Present From Bolshoy Kavkaz' worked into it in flowing Cyrillic characters. Thirty years later, he managed to sell it for two roubles to the manager of the local farmers' cooperative, who needed something to keep his delivery notes in.

'Jason,' Mrs. Derry said. Sergeant Smith looked up.

'Here,' he said, 'I know that name from somewhere, don't I?'

Mrs. Derry looked down at her shoes. 'If it's about the tiger,' she said, 'we told the man, we'll pay for a new one. That's no problem . . .'

Sergeant Smith gave her a startled look, and then thought better of it. 'Isn't he the one who's out in the Carwardine Islands?' he asked. 'You know, the war hero?'

'What?' said Mrs. Derry. 'Oh yes, that's right, that's Jason.'

'Charged a machine-gun nest or something, didn't he? Won the war and all that.'

'Yes,' sighed Mrs. Derry, 'that's our Jason.'

'Oh.' Sergeant Smith bit his lip, drawing blood from sheer force of habit. 'I see. Well, actually, Mrs. Derry . . .'

'Yes?' she said hopefully. 'He didn't write, you see. He always writes, and I was worried . . .'

The sergeant's face became grave. 'Actually, Mrs. Derry,' he said, and hesitated. 'Didn't you hear the radio this morning, then?'

'No. Was there something . . .?'

'Mrs. Derry,' said the sergeant, 'I have to tell you that the plane he was on, coming home like, it sort of strayed over Soviet air space and got – well, shot down. Sort of.'

Mrs. Derry said nothing. The sergeant swallowed. How do you tell people?

'There wasn't anybody killed,' he said, 'like, no bodies or anything. Except, you see, they couldn't find your Jason. I mean, it was definite he was on the 'plane but when the rescue party got there and they called the roll he, well, wasn't there. If you follow me.'

'Wasn't there?'

'That's right.'

'Oh,' said Mrs. Derry, 'that's all right then, I expect his Dad fetched him home. You had me going there for a moment, you really did.'

'His Dad . . .?'

'That's right,' she said. 'Maybe you should ring the Defence people,' she added, 'in case they're worried or anything. Well, thanks ever so much, sorry to have bothered you.' She smiled and turned to go.

'I . . .' Sergeant Smith started to say something. It would have been tremendously helpful; about how it's no good lying to yourself, you have to face the fact that he's not coming home, I know, I know it's bloody hard, Mrs. Derry, but sooner or later you'll just have to come to terms with it, we all do, believe me, but that's the only way you're going to be able to pick up the pieces and start again . . .

Mrs. Derry turned back and smiled. 'Was there something?' she said.

'Mind how you go,' said Sergeant Smith.

Megathoon, alias Crazy Horse, President of the Larissan Chapter of the Original Thessalian Centaurs, looked up and snarled.

'And what sort of time do you call ouch?' he said. Then he fell over.

The other Centaurs looked at each other for a moment then, very sheepishly, they started backing away, taking off their leather jackets and crash helmets as they did so.

'And where do you think you're going?' Jason said.

'Who, us?'

'Yes,' he replied, drawing the Sword of Sounds Like Mice Weary On Or Something and tapping the blade with his fingers. 'You.'

'We're just innocent bystanders,' said a Centaur, trying to cover his more equine parts with his helmet, 'who just happened to be passing. Nothing to do with us, honestly.'

'Oh yes?' said Jason. 'Then how come you've all got the bodies and legs of horses?'

'Have we?' asked the Centaur. It looked down and feigned amazement. 'Well,' it said at last, 'as soon as I get back to Thessaly I'm going to sue that bloody pharmaceuticals company.'

'Come off it,' Jason said. 'I know perfectly well you're bloodthirsty, subhuman cannibal mutants, the result of the morbid nuptials of Chaos and Darkness. So the sooner we get started, the sooner I can have something to eat. Ready?'

'Mutants, yes,' said the Centaur. 'Yes, I think we're all prepared to hold our hands up to that one, you've got us there. But the rest of it, bloodthirsty and cannibalistic, I think that's being a bit extreme, don't you, lads?'

The other Centaurs grunted – or whinnied – their agreement. Jason raised an eyebrow.

'In fact,' said the Centaur quickly, 'I would say even mutants is a bit of a misnomer, really. More like disabled, I'd say. Like, if you could see your way to regarding these as a sort of rather more convenient substitute for a wheelchair, perhaps we could all understand each other a lot better. You know, raise your consciousness a bit, abandon your deeply-ingrained cultural stereotypes, that sort of thing. In fact, I'd go so far as to say you're being a bit, well, horsist, wouldn't you?'

'Horsist?'

'Yes.'

'I thought,' said Jason, 'he was a Saxon king who invaded Kent.'

'Hengist,' the Centaur corrected him. 'And Horsa. A Horsist is someone who has this outmoded bias against horses.'

'Horses I like,' said Jason, 'Centaurs I beat into pulp. Who's next?'

The Centaur went white under its fur. 'Toss you for it?' he suggested.

'No,' Jason replied.

'Best of three?'

'No.'

'Would it help if I also pointed out that we are an ethnic minority?'

'No.'

The Centaur gulped. 'Look,' he said, 'perhaps if we just

talked it over, as between intelligent human . . . well, sub-human . . .'

'Nobody,' said Jason grimly, 'calls me prejudiced and gets away with it.'

The Centaur swore miserably, drew its sword and charged. The last thought that passed through its mind before it lost consciousness was that the real trouble with Heroes was that they always had to know best.

At approximately half-past eleven that night, a small electric cart whirred its way up Pool Street, past the Friendship House, past the George and Dragon, past the butcher's, and stopped at the Post Office. A tall man in a golden helmet and battledress jumped out and posted a letter. As he was about to get back in, a policeman came round the corner and stared at him.

'Bugger me,' said the policeman. 'You again!'

The man stopped and turned round slowly. His hand tightened on a canvas sack he was carrying, but since it was dark the policeman didn't see that. Instead he strode forward and stood between the tall man and the small electric cart, which he appeared not to have seen.

'I want a word with you,' said the policeman.

The tall man frowned. 'Can't it wait?' he said. 'My mum'll be worried and besides, my dinner'll be going cold.'

'Never mind about your bloody dinner, son,' said the policeman, 'what about my reputation in the force?'

'What about it?' said the tall man.

'Look,' said the policeman. 'I don't want none of your lip. You're coming straight down the station and you're going to tell me what you were doing outside the George and Dragon this time five years ago. And don't tell me you were . . .'

The policeman's words trailed away into a sort of gibbering murmur which three dots are really quite inadequate to express.

'You know what this is?' said the tall man.

'Erg,' replied the policeman.

'This,' said the tall man, 'is the Sword of . . . of . . . Anyway, if you don't take your hand off my sleeve in five seconds flat, I'll take it off for you. Got that?'

'Erg,' the policeman assured him.

'Thank you,' said the tall man. 'Now,' he said, 'for your information, five years ago I was still at school, and I didn't hang around pubs at half-eleven at night. Got that?'

'Erg.'

'Sure?'

'Erg.'

'Good.' He turned and put one foot in the golf cart. 'Oh,' he said, 'by the way.'

'Erg.'

'In case you were wondering, I'm a figment of your imagination. You've either been drinking or working too hard, and you didn't see me. Clear?'

'Erg.'

'Because,' the tall man said, 'I've had just about enough of everything today, with the definite exception of food, and I really can't be bothered with the likes of you, so I suggest you go home and sleep it off. Right?'

'Ouch!'

About five minutes later, a small group of youths who had just been thrown out of the George and Dragon for extremely antisocial behaviour happened to trip over a recumbent police sergeant in the middle of Pool Street. Having tripped over him a few more times (for luck) they assisted him to his feet and enquired as to his health. They also stole his radio and his handcuffs, but the labourer is worthy of his hire.

'Fine,' said the policeman, wiping the blood absently from his chin. 'I'm fine, really. Now you go on home before I . . .'

'Wassup, Smithy?' asked one of the youths. 'You been seeing things again or something?'

The police sergeant shook his head vigorously. 'I ain't seen nothing,' he said. 'I just walked into a lamppost, that's all.'

Jason Derry opened the front door, waved goodnight to his driver and walked in.

'Hiya, Mum, Dad,' he called, 'I'm home.'

'That you, Jason?' came his mother's voice from the kitchen.

'Yes,' Jason replied. 'Anything to eat? I'm starving.'

'There's some sandwiches,' Mrs. Derry replied. 'Jason.'

'Yes, Mum?'

'You haven't . . . well, got anything with you? Anything that needs burying, or . . .'

Jason quietly opened the door of the cupboard under the stairs and hid the Sword of Glycerion behind the ironing board. 'Course not,' he said.

The kitchen door opened. 'Your Dad's out,' she said. 'How was the war?'

'Oh,' said Jason, 'we won.'

'That's nice, dear.'

Jason remembered something. 'Sorry I forgot to write,' he said. 'You weren't worried, were you?'

'Of course not, dear,' said Mrs. Derry, looking away. 'Why should I be worried, when your dad . . . your other dad, I mean, said he'd keep an eye on you?'

'Him!' Jason said contemptuously.

'Jason!' replied his mother. 'How many times have I told you not to speak disrespectfully of your father? You really . . .'

Jason scowled. 'Sorry,' he said. 'Forget it, all right? I've had a hard day. What's in the sandwiches?'

His mother noticed a slight cut on the knuckles of his right hand. 'You've been fighting,' she said.

'That's right,' Jason replied. 'You remember, the war, all that stuff. Ham, is it?'

'Yes, dear,' said Mrs. Derry. 'You going to have a bath before you go to bed?'

'In the morning,' Jason said, yawning. 'Right now . . .'

Mrs. Derry gave him a meaningful look and said 'Sharon rang.'

Jason yawned again. 'Oh yes?' he replied and yawned again, this time artificially.

'Twice.'

'Wouldn't want her 'phone bill, then,' said Jason. 'Any Coke in the fridge?'

'Yes,' sighed Mrs. Derry. 'I think so. You could phone Sharon tomorrow. It's her day off.'

Jason winced. 'Look, Mum,' he said, 'that'd be really great, only I've got a lot on tomorrow. Maybe next week, all right?'

His mother sniffed and went up to bed. Jason stood in the hall for a few seconds longer, shrugged and went to look for the sandwiches.

It is the tradition, now well over three thousand years old, that the Sybil or Pythoness of Delphi trains her successor in her priestly duties. Betty-Lou Fisichelli, for example, had been trained by the Old Pythoness (confusingly named

331

Sybil), who in turn had been initiated into the Mysteries by her predecessor, the great Madam Arcati.

In her small but well-appointed flat in the suburbs of Delphi, Ms. Fisichelli was on the point of explaining the Great Primordial to her apprentice.

'Have you got all that?' she said, 'or would you like me to run through it one more time?'

'No,' said the apprentice, helping herself to a handful of olives, 'that's fine. So then what happened?'

'Well,' said Betty-Lou, 'after Prometheus had told the Joke to the caveman, of course all the gods were furious. They just sort of flipped.'

'Really,' said the apprentice, removing a stone from her mouth with more grace than the act properly required. 'And?'

'And so,' said the Pythoness, 'once they'd gotten control of themselves again . . .'

'Have an olive.'

Ms. Fisichelli hesitated. 'No thanks,' she said.

'They're good, really.'

'Well . . .'

A moment later, the Pythoness spat out a stone into the ashtray and continued, 'When they'd gotten control of themselves, they all decided to see if they couldn't do something about it. So first they grabbed Prometheus and chained him to this rock up in the Caucasus somewhere, and they got this eagle . . .'

'Go on,' said the apprentice, crossing the room to the drinks tray, 'I'm listening.'

'They got this eagle . . .'

'Can I get you something?'

'No, thanks,' said the Pythoness. There was no doubt about it, Mary was a natural Pythoness, virtually, well,

332

instinctive, but she sometimes wished she didn't find it all quite so easy. When she'd been doing basic training, she'd had to sit up nights learning this stuff by heart. 'They got this eagle,' she said, 'and every morning and every evening, it tears out Prometheus's liver with its beak.'

'Heavy!'

'And every afternoon,' Ms. Fisichelli went on, slightly shaken, 'and every night, the liver sort of, well, grows again. And that's how Prometheus was punished for his betrayal of the gods.'

Mary was sitting down again, cross-legged on the sofa, her mouth full of olives and retsina. 'Haven't you missed something?' she said.

'Have I?'

'About the Unbinding,' Mary said. 'You know, how one day . . .'

'Oh yes,' the Pythoness said, 'right. One day, it is prophesied, a Hero will come who will cut the chains, slay the eagle, and release the god . . .'

'You sure?'

The Pythoness frowned. 'About what?'

'About the eagle,' Mary said. 'That bit doesn't sound right.'

'Doesn't it?' Betty-Lou asked, puzzled. 'Why not?'

Mary shrugged and removed another olive-stone. 'Oh, I don't know,' she said. 'Don't mind me. Go on.'

Betty-Lou folded her hands in her lap. 'The next thing the gods did,' she continued, 'was try to devise a plan to remove Laughter from the world. Unfortunately, everything they did failed; whatever they inflicted on the mortals, the one thing they steadfastly refused to give up was Laughter. And so the Divine Plan has yet to be carried out, and Laughter lies hidden somewhere in the bowels of the earth, so deep that even winged Mercury, the messenger of the gods, cannot find him. One day, however, it is written that a young demi-god, son of Jupiter himself, will discover the hiding-place of the unseemly sprite and will carry him back to heaven where he belongs. Then the gods will return, mortals will once again respect them and know their place, and the new Golden Age will begin . . .'

The Pythoness broke off her narrative. Her apprentice was giving her one of those disconcerting looks of hers. 'Well?' she asked brusquely.

'A new Golden Age?'

'Yes,' said the Pythoness firmly, 'that's right.'

'Just like the first one, huh?'

'Yes,' said the Pythoness, firmly. Nobody could object to *that*, surely?

'That would be,' the apprentice went on, 'the time when we mortals lived in caves, dressed in skins and ate raw meat, couldn't read or write, died young of horrible diseases, got eaten by wild animals, were thoroughly scared of the dark, and couldn't even take our minds off it all by having a good laugh about something.'

'Yes,' said the Pythoness.

'And that was the Golden Age?'

'Yes.'

'Fine,' said the apprentice. 'I see. Sorry, you were saying?'

'Yes,' said Ms. Fisichelli, 'well, I think that's about enough for one evening, don't you? Anyhow, it's getting late, and I've got essays to mark and . . .'

'Okay,' Mary said, uncurling herself enchantingly from the sofa, 'thanks a lot. See you tomorrow at the seminar.'

'Yes, yes indeed,' said the Pythoness, absently. 'Early Classical epigraphy, isn't it?'

'The use of computers in modern archaeology,' Mary corrected her. 'Or is that Friday?' she added kindly.

'No,' said the Pythoness, 'you're quite right. What could I have been thinking of? See you then.'

'Goodnight, then.'

'Goodnight.'

The Pythoness listened for the soft click of the door closing, and then sat down to do some nice, comfy worrying. It was, she reminded herself, her duty to select a suitable successor from the archaeology students who attended her classes at the American School, and by and large she was convinced that she'd made the right choice. Such aptitude. Such intuition. Such ability to learn. Greek, even, on her mother's side, though her father was a nicely prosaic mining engineer from Pennsylvania. It was almost, Betty-Lou told herself, as if she knew it all already. And yet there was something not quite exactly right about Mary Stamnos.

'It's no good, dammit,' she said to herself as she poured out two saucers of milk (one for her cat and one for the Sacred Serpent). 'He'll have to be told.'

'Well?' Minerva demanded, 'so where was he?'

'Eating,' Apollo replied.

Minerva frowned. 'I don't seem to remember asking you what he was doing,' she said. 'Where was he?'

'At some sort of village café in the Caucasus,' Apollo said, trying his best to be very sweet to his sister, 'eating.'

'All the time?'

'Yes,' Apollo confirmed. 'Mercury interviewed the waiter specially. It all tallies perfectly. He was there from when they opened right through to closing time. The waiter remembers him very well because he left a tip big enough to enable the waiter to open his own tractor factory, and he says . . .'

Minerva gave him a look. 'No, you mark my words, something has been going on, and the only possible explanation is that You-Know-Who was involved.'

'I don't, actually.'

'What?'

'Know who.'

Minerva made an exasperated gesture and mimed someone laughing while carrying a stalk of fennel. 'Oh, *him*,' Apollo said quickly. 'No, apparently Merc questioned him very closely. And, of course, the Eagle. Nothing. Couldn't have been lying, he reckoned, or he'd have known. Very shrewd, Merc is, sometimes, and lying . . . well, it's a sort of hobby of his, so . . .'

He could tell from the way she was looking at him and the owl on her shoulder was sniggering into its wing-feathers that his big sister wasn't convinced. So what, Apollo thought, neither am I, particularly. I just want to get Min off my back so I can look into it myself.

'Anyway,' he went on, 'one thing's for sure – there's no harm done. Mission accomplished, ten Centaurs reduced to quick-fry steak and the Golden Fleece safely recovered and restored to the Sacred Grove at Blachernas,* so I guess the best thing is just to pretend it never happened, okay?'

'No it is not,' Minerva said. 'There's going to have to be an enquiry.'

Apollo nodded vigorously. 'Oh yes,' he said, 'there'll definitely have to be an *enquiry*, no doubt about that. In fact,

*Fortuitously now the Kavkad branch of the Standard Chartered Bank.

I'd say you'd better get it set up straight away. Sooner the better, really, don't you think?'

Minerva nodded and stalked away, and Apollo grinned. How Minerva had got to be Goddess of Wisdom, he said to himself, was another story entirely but nothing to do with her IQ.

Having satisfied himself that Minerva really had gone away and wasn't hiding behind a helium flare eavesdropping, Apollo put down the lyre he'd been pretending to restring and switched on the Commentary.

'And now we're going over to the ringside where Derek is just about to have a word with President George Jones, the American premier, whose team the Yankees have just succeeded in putting a manned space station into lunar orbit. Well, George, I bet you're over the moon about this one . . .'

A scowl flitted over Apollo's face and he clicked the switch off. There was more to all this, he felt, than met the All-Seeing Eye, even if the effects hadn't immediately made themselves noticeable. He went to find Mars.

He found the ex-God of War in the bar, pouring himself a large ambrosia and ginger ale with a shaking hand.

'Do you know,' Mars said, 'what those crazy bastards nearly did to me?'

'No,' Apollo said, 'Look . . .'

'I mean,' Mars went on, 'they wanted to run their own show, so it stands to reason, they don't need me to fight their battles for them any more. How I see it, I'm just in the way. In fact,' he added bitterly, 'that's it exactly, except that what I'm usually in the way of is something made of lead and travelling fast. Look, Pol, see what those jerks in the Middle East did to my armour?' He held up what at first sight looked like a collander, but which turned out to be a helmet with holes in it. 'Well,' he said, 'this time I've had enough. First thing, I'm going to go to him and I'm going to lay my cards on the table. JOM, I'm going to say, either you let me have some decent protective clothing or else you can stick your lousy job up where the sun shines out of; and if he wants to chuck me off the Edge, that's all right by me, because right now . . .'

Apollo gave him a soothing smile and the torrent of words subsided. Smiling was probably what Apollo was best at.

'While you were down there,' he said, 'you didn't happen to notice anything – well, *odd*, did you?'

Mars laughed miserably. 'Depends what you'd call odd, doesn't it?' he replied. 'I mean, if a whopping great SAM missile up the backside is odd, then yes, I did. Really, Pol, I ask you, I was just standing there minding my own business and wham! Be honest with me, chum, do I look like a bloody tank?'

'Possibly,' Apollo said. 'Maybe they were just nervous. Or bad shots. But apart from that, did you see anything which sort of caught your eye? Out of the ordinary, anything like that?'

Mars poured himself another drink, a lot of which ended up on the bar-top. 'Out of the ordinary?'

'That's it.'

'Let's see,' Mars said. 'The Sri Lankans beating up on the Tamils. The Ethiopians stomping on the Eritreans. The Chinese swapping missiles with the Vietnamese. The Irish shooting up the British. The British shooting up the Argentines. The Americans dropping bombs on the Libyans. The Libyans setting off bombs under everybody else. No, can't say that I did.'

'Right,' Apollo said, 'fine. Only while you were out, you see, we lost a Hero.'

Mars shook his head vigorously. 'Wasn't me,' he said. 'All the ones who copped it today were complete cowards, the lot of them.'

'No,' Apollo said, 'not lost in that sense. Mislaid. He sort of wandered off for a bit between choosing the Path of Virtue and duffing up some Centaurs.'

'I don't know, really,' said Mars, sloshing his drink round in his glass thoughtfully. 'Heroes, you know, they're a bloody funny lot, believe you me.'

'What are you getting at, exactly?' Apollo enquired patiently.

'Simple,' Mars said. 'It doesn't say this in any of the books, mind, but I've been watching the little creeps long enough to have twigged this one for myself. They don't belong in the human race. They aren't human. Mortal, maybe, but not human. Or not *exclusively* human. Do you see what I'm getting at?'

'No.'

'Ah.' Mars reached for the bottle again. 'Fancy one?'

'Not just now, thanks.'

'Suit yourself. Let me put it another way. You remember how there are all the different worlds, because of the bifurcation of thingy and all that stuff we had to learn when we were kids?'

'Some of it,' Apollo replied. 'Actually, I spent most of those lessons looking out of the window.'

'Me too,' Mars admitted, 'but I looked up my notes the other day. Now the way I think it works is that your Hero, being all sort of different, he can flip back and forward between the different possible worlds all at the same time. Like, suppose there's a choice . . .'

339

'As it might be,' said Apollo, 'between conspiring with Prometheus and sitting under a tree eating shish kebabs?'

'Exactly,' said Mars, 'very imaginative example, that. Suppose there's a choice between your two courses of action, right? Your ordinary mortal makes the choice, and he splits off into two different mortals on two different worlds. One does the conspiring; one has the kebabs. All clear so far?'

'Give or take a bit, yes.'

'Well,' said Mars, wiping a drip off the rim of his glass and licking his finger, 'where I think Heroes are different, because of some sort of basic intrinsic weirdness in their molecular structure or some such crap, is that they can come up against one of these choices, bifurc-whatsits, and there's a sort of third choice that suddenly opens up for them out of nowhere, just for them, specially. Means they can have their cake and eat it, if you like; no, that's not actually what I mean. What I mean is, if they've got to make a choice between having the cake and eating it, then sometimes, because they're Heroes and not ordinary, they get the option of having a doughnut instead. Do you see what I mean or have I lost you completely?'

'Vaguely,' said Apollo, thinking of the Road Marked Diversion. 'But that's impossible, surely.'

'Let's leave what's possible and what's not possible out of it, shall we?' said Mars. 'Walls have ears, and all that. What I'm saying is that Heroes are . . . well, I think "jammy bastards" puts it quite nicely, don't you?'

'Possibly,' Apollo replied. 'So what you're saying is, if a Hero had a choice between fighting some Centaurs and having lunch, he might find himself doing neither. He might sort of wander off into another dimension or . . .'

'Dimension's the wrong word,' Mars interrupted firmly.

'That's all strictly theology-fiction, not theology-fact. But I think – and you've got to bear in mind this is just me speaking after I've had a nasty shock from a rocket – I think what you've just described is entirely possible. Well, not possible, in fact completely impossible; but I'd be willing to bet it could happen, with a Hero.' He drained his glass, wiped his mouth on his sleeve and stood up. 'Who knows?' he said. 'Come to that, who really cares, anyway? Who needs to understand the perishers when you can outlive them, that's what I always say.'

Apollo laughed politely. 'Very true,' he said. 'Still, if you could keep your eyes open for me . . .'

'That depends,' said Mars, 'on what's visible through them at the time.'

CHAPTER SEVEN

At approximately half-past five the next morning, the door of Mr. and Mrs. Derry's house opened and Jason Derry came out. He was carrying a long canvas sack and a plastic carrier bag.

The sun rose in a confusion of pink seepage and presented the first commercial break of the day. Unfortunately for the consortium of Antipodean tycoons who manage it now, very few mortals have the necessary satellite dishes and decoding equipment to receive the signals it broadcasts, but Australians are nothing if not patient. Just as soon as the fossil fuels run out, they argue, and everyone starts taking solar energy seriously, then we'll have 'em.

By a curious accident probably connected with his unique genetic makeup, Jason Derry was a natural receiver of the sun's subliminal messages, albeit on a subconscious level only, and he had often wondered why looking directly into the sun made him want to change to low-fat margarine and take out unnecessary life assurance. He had eventually managed to come to terms with the problem by telling himself not to be so bloody stupid.

342

A small electric buggy whined up to the front gate and stopped.

'Morning, George,' Jason said.

'Morning, Boss,' the driver replied. 'Where to?'

Jason grinned. 'Glad you asked that, George,' he replied. 'Been a change of schedule.'

'Oh yes?' said George cautiously. 'Been rather a lot of those lately, haven't there?'

'Yes,' said Jason, undoing the top of the canvas sack, 'and there's going to be a lot more. You know what this is?'

George nodded. 'Sure,' he said. 'It's the Sword of Glycerion.'

'What was that last bit again?'

'Glycerion.'

'Oh,' Jason said, after a moment. 'That's what I thought the old bag said, but I reckoned I must have got it wrong. Anyway, the point is that it's very sharp, George, very sharp indeed.'

'I know,' George said. 'So?'

Jason frowned. 'Oh come on, George, don't be so damned thick. I'm threatening you.'

'Are you?' said George, mystified. 'Why?'

'Because I want to intimidate you into doing what I tell you,' Jason said irritably, 'that's why. Why else, for pity's sake?'

'But Boss,' George said, 'I always do what you tell me, don't I?'

'Yes, yes,' Jason said, 'but that's because I always tell you what I'm *supposed* to tell you. Look,' he went on, 'I'm not in the mood for deep metaphysical discussion so let's just get going, shall we, before anybody notices.'

George shrugged. 'Whatever you say, Boss. Next stop Thessaly.'

343

'No,' Jason said, 'Piccadilly Circus.'

'You sure?' said George. 'Look, it says here on the manifest: Larissa, ancient capital of Thessaly . . .'

'That's what I've been trying to tell you, George,' said Jason wearily. 'We aren't going to Thessaly, we're going to Piccadilly Circus. Instead,' he explained.

'Why?'

'Shut up and drive the bloody car, will you?'

The little electric buggies supplied to Heroes are manufactured by Vulcan, ex-God of Fire and Craftsmen, and being of divine manufacture they can burn off Porsches without going into second gear. They also come with a twenty-million-year warranty and centralised locking as standard. It therefore took George less than thirty seconds to get to Piccadilly Circus; which was just as well, since it then took an hour and a bit to find a parking space.

'Will here do you?' George asked.

'Here'll do fine,' Jason replied. 'I shouldn't be more than a couple of hours.'

'I hope you know what you're doing.'

'So do I.'

George shrugged. 'Please yourself,' he said. 'What's in the carrier bag?'

'Sandwiches,' Jason said, 'and a thermos. If anyone wants me, tell them I died of cholera, OK?'

Jason climbed out, tied up the canvas bag carefully, and descended the stairs to the Underground station, where he stood in front of the ticket barrier and waited. After a few minutes, a very tall, thin man with a flower in his buttonhole walked up to him and coughed.

'The worship of Mithras,' he said slowly, 'has all but died out in Saxmundham.'

'You what?'

344

'The worship of . . . Oh bugger, sorry,' said the tall man. 'Thursday is not a good day for peeling onions.'

'Friday,' Jason replied self-consciously, 'is even worse if you happen to be left-handed. So you're Virgil, are you?'

'Sh!' said the tall man, 'keep your ruddy voice down, will you? I'm not supposed to be here.'

'I know,' said Jason. 'Neither am I.'

'I told them at the office,' Virgil went on, ignoring him, 'I was going to a seminar on "Whither Hexameters Today?" at Spoleto, but I bet someone's going to phone through and find out I'm not there. I'm a fool to myself to be doing this.'

'You're dead,' Jason said; 'what's it to you?'

'Just because you're dead,' Virgil hissed darkly, 'doesn't mean they aren't still out to get you. Anyway, this is definitely the last time I get mixed up in anything like this.'

Jason tapped his foot ever so slightly. 'All right,' he said, 'you've made your point; now let's get on with it, shall we? And next time I need a guide to the Underground, I'll buy one of those little maps.'

Virgil gave him a poisonous look and produced a couple of tickets from his raincoat pocket. They weren't like ordinary subway tickets, being luminous and made of gold. 'Don't lose them,' he said. 'Right. Abandon Hope All Ye, and all that stuff. This way.'

They walked for a long time down gloomy winding passages which echoed with unearthly noises. All around them, Jason became aware of what looked suspiciously like souls in torment – murderers, parricides and people trying to find the westbound platforms. For all that he was a Hero, he shuddered slightly.

'It only goes to show,' Virgil was saying, 'the truth of the old saying that a friend in need is a pest. Just because I showed Dante the way through the Inferno when he got lost that time – you know, one poet helping another and all that stuff, though that's a myth if ever I heard one; you try asking a poet to help you mend a puncture in the rain and see how far you get – just because of that, they've got it into their heads I'm a sort of one-man package holiday company. Mind you,' he went on, 'I blame my agent, the damn fool. He encourages them. He's got me taking a party of schoolchildren round the Dutch bulb fields next month, which really isn't my idea of a good time. I'll never forget . . .'

'Virgil,' Jason said.

The Mantuan turned his head. 'Yes?' he asked. 'What?'

'Are we going the right way?'

Virgil sniggered unpleasantly. 'Down here,' he said, 'there isn't a right way. The right way is to go by bus. We go left here, I think.'

'But we've been walking for ages,' Jason said.

'True,' Virgil replied, helpfully.

'So which line are we taking?'

'Ah,' said Virgil, 'that'd be telling.'

They turned a corner and came across a busker. He had a hat with no bottom and a guitar with no strings, and when he opened his mouth, no sound came out. A mouth organ hovered round his head like a large chrome hornet, buzzing ominously and occasionally swooping in and biting his ear. Virgil stopped and felt in his pocket.

'Oh good,' he said, 'I thought I had some somewhere.' He took out two pesetas, a corroded pfennig and a fruit-machine token and dropped them into the hat. They vanished.

'A sad case,' said Virgil. 'In life he was a great conductor but one Christmas he agreed to appear on one of those television comedy-variety programmes and after that it was downhill all the way. First it was chat shows, then double-glazing commercials, and when he died, it was straight down here. Diabolical, what they come up with sometimes.'

Jason stared. 'You mean he's *dead*?' he asked.

'Of course,' Virgil replied. 'You're in the Underground now, you know.'

Around the next corner they came across a woman. She was crouched on the ground, hard up against the tiled wall of the corridor, with her hands clenched over her ears, in which were the earphones of a Sony walkman. Although the music was plainly audible to Virgil and Jason as they passed by, it was clear that the woman couldn't hear a note of it.

'That one,' Virgil commented with a shudder, 'speaks for itself.'

For someone who didn't know the meaning of Fear, Jason was beginning to feel decidedly edgy; but since Virgil seemed to be taking it all in his stride, he did his best to conceal it. Thus, when a haggard woman with staring eyes jumped out at them and demanded to know the way to Platform Seven, and Virgil told her, and she darted off in the opposite direction, Jason fought back the impulse to whip out the Sword of Sod It I've Forgotten Again and sweep her head off, and just stood back feeling embarrassed.

'Another hopeless case,' said the poet, as the woman's hysterical laughter died away in the distance. 'Her crime was forever to be nagging her husband to ask someone the way whenever they got lost. Serves her right, I suppose, but still . . .'

It had been getting darker and darker the further they went, so that now they could only make out the walls of the corridor in front of them by the glow of the burning

347

graffiti-artists conveniently nailed just above head height at regular intervals. The shadows in between contained strange, shuffling figures who made disturbing noises, which Jason did his best to ignore.

'Nearly there,' Virgil said. 'I'd better warn you, the next bit's not for the squeamish.'

'Oh *super,*' Jason murmured.

They turned yet another corner and came to a set of steps, which led down to a short passageway. Onto the walls of the passageway were glued a number of screaming, struggling people, on whose faces demoniac posters were drawing in moustaches. Then they came out onto a platform. It was empty.

'Here,' Jason said, 'this isn't too bad.'

'You wait,' Virgil chuckled grimly.

There was a clanking noise in the distance which gradually got closer, and a Tube train appeared. As it went past them, Jason could see it was filled with wan, spectral figures, all standing on one another's feet.

'Once a commuter,' said Virgil, 'always a commuter. Horrible, isn't it?'

The train slowed down and stopped, and the doors opened. Some of the people inside made a dash for it and tried to get out, but at once the doors slammed shut on them with sickening force. Jason noticed with a spurt of terror that the doors had teeth.

'Can't say they weren't warned,' Virgil said sadly. 'Do Not Obstruct The Doors, it says, plain as the nose on your face. Hang on, it'll stop soon.'

After what seemed to Jason a very long time, the doors finished chewing the people and a big red tongue appeared and drew them back inside. The doors closed, and when they opened again the carriages were empty. From somewhere near the driver's compartment came an unmistakable belch.

'Right,' said Virgil. 'I don't know about you, but I like having my back to the engine.'

Jason grabbed his sleeve. 'I'm not getting in *that*,' he said.

Virgil gave him a contemptuous look and got into the carriage. Behind him, Jason sensed that there were people coming down the steps onto the platform that he really didn't want to meet, and so he closed his eyes and stepped in. The doors closed.

When Jason opened his eyes, all he could see was a perfectly ordinary Underground carriage, and Virgil sitting on one of the seats, meditatively stirring a large pile of ash and charred bones. Jason winced.

'Let me guess,' he said, 'this is a No Smoking carriage.'

'On the contrary,' Virgil replied. 'Only here, the train smokes the people. Sit down and have a rest. It gets a bit hairy in a minute.'

'Not again!'

Apollo nodded.

'Honestly,' Minerva said. 'We're going to have to get him one of those collars with a little bell on it. Right, then, where did you see him last?'

'Piccadilly Circus,' Apollo said. Minerva raised both eyebrows.

'Really,' she said. 'Well, well, fancy that. No prizes for guessing where he's gone, then.'

'Let's not be too hasty about this,' Apollo said. 'Maybe he just wanted to catch a train or something.'

Minerva ignored him. 'You stay there,' she said. 'I'll go and see where Pluto's got to.'

After a long search she eventually found the ex-God of the Dead lying down, in a beautifully-tailored box, in the cupboard under the Stairs of the Dawn. She made an exasperated noise and tapped on the side of the box with her foot.

'Job for you,' she said. 'Up you get.'

'I've retired,' Pluto murmured sleepily. 'Go away.'

'If you're not up and dressed in five minutes,' warned Minerva, 'it's a wet sponge down the back of the neck for you, my lad. We'll be in the observation saloon.'

When she got back to the saloon, Apollo was studying the Earth through some kind of optical instrument, which he unsuccessfully tried to hide between his knees when he realised his sister was back in the room. Minerva made a familiar clicking noise with her tongue and held out her hand. Reluctantly, Apollo gave her the instrument.

'How does it work?' she asked.

'I'm not entirely sure,' Apollo replied. 'Apparently it sort of picks up waves of random particles activated by disturbances in the fabric of possibility.'

Minerva frowned. She was hopeless with gadgets but refused to admit it. 'Like a smoke detector, you mean?'

'Something like that, yes.'

'Got anything?'

Apollo shook his head. 'He left a trail of fused alternatives all the way down to somewhere under the Cafe Royal, but then the screen just went white and started bleeping at me, so I switched it off. My guess is that it means he's already entered, you know . . .'

'Yes,' said Minerva hurriedly. Gods do not like to mention the place directly beneath the cellars of Hamley's by name if they can help it. Bad vibes.

'Which means,' Apollo went on, 'he's effectively given us the slip, doesn't it?'

'Nonsense,' Minerva said, and as she spoke Pluto walked in. He was wearing a black dressing-gown and slippers, and he was yawning. He hadn't had a haircut or trimmed his fingernails for a very long time.

'Well?' he asked sleepily. 'What's going on?'

'We need someone to go out to, er, Regent Street for us,' Minerva said.

Pluto scowled. 'Oh come on, Min,' he said. 'You know that place gives me the willies.'

Minerva gave him a look. 'Don't be such a baby,' she said.

'All right,' said Pluto, 'you go.'

'It's your kingdom.'

'Was,' Pluto reminded her. 'I sold out to an Anglo-French consortium, remember? They were going to try and link it up with the Paris metro. Bloody silly idea if you ask me, but . . .'

'Yes,' Minerva interrupted, 'now, if you've quite finished, you can be getting along. We're looking for a Hero, tall, muscular, blond, the usual thing, answers to Jason Derry. I'll put him up on the screen for you.'

Minerva fiddled with the controls for a moment, and a thousand-mile-high hologram of General De Gaulle appeared in the night sky just below the Great Bear. 'Whoops,' said Minerva, 'sorry, wrong disc. Now, try that.'

General De Gaulle was sucked back into the heart of the Pole Star and was replaced by Jason Derry, standing with one foot on the severed head of a huge reptile and looking bored. 'That's him,' Minerva said. Jason vanished.

Pluto stood scowling at where the hologram had been for a few seconds and then tightened the cord of his dressing gown. 'Dangerous, is he?' he asked.

'Depends what you mean by dangerous,' Apollo said. 'In general terms, globally speaking, yes he very probably is. On the other hand, I don't imagine he'll try and bite you.'

'Sod it,' said Pluto, 'I think I'll take the dog.'

The train stopped.

Jason looked out of the window. There was nothing to see.

'Where are we?' he asked. Virgil looked at him gravely.

'You should know better than to ask questions like that, son of Jupiter,' he replied. 'Particularly here, of all places.'

'Why?' Jason asked. 'We haven't broken down or anything, have we?'

'No,' Virgil said, looking down at the floorboards, 'not exactly. This is where we were supposed to come to. It's what you told me you wanted to do.'

Jason nodded. 'So why aren't the doors opening?' he asked.

'They don't.'

'How do you mean?'

'This isn't a station,' Virgil told him. 'If anything, it's a state of mind. This is where the train stops, but you can't get out here.'

'Why not?'

'You're probably the first person in the history of Creation ever to ask that,' Virgil replied. 'The doors don't open here for pretty much the same reason as they don't open the windows on Concorde. The environment out there is somewhat hostile.'

'Is it?' Jason looked hard, but he couldn't see a trace of any sort of environment, hostile or not; there was just that sort of darkness that means that all you can see is your reflection in the window. He said as much to Virgil.

'That,' Virgil answered, 'is the whole point. There *is* nothing out there. It's probably the largest accumulation of nothing in the entire cosmos.'

'Oh,' Jason said. 'In that case,' he added, after a pause, 'someone's been pulling my leg.'

'Really?' Virgil studied his fingertips. 'And who might that have been?'

Jason felt a slight twitching under his scalp. 'Oh, just someone I met,' he said. 'And he told me that – well, something I was looking for was to be found at the Underground stop directly under Hamley's. And I said that as far as I knew there wasn't one, and he said I should ask you to take me there. So I did, and now you're telling me I can't get out here.'

'I said nothing of the kind,' Virgil replied. 'All I said was that if you're so incredibly fed up with life that you want to get out here, the doors aren't going to aid and abet you. That's all.'

Jason leaned back in his seat and sighed. That seemed to be that, he told himself. And yet . . .

'Virgil,' he said, 'can I ask you something?'

'Be my guest,' said the Mantuan.

'If you had a little voice in the back of your head,' said Jason, 'that kept telling you to . . . no, *suggesting* that you do things that you really don't want to do, because they're dangerous and you don't understand why they need doing anyway, how would you react?'

'I'd have a lobotomy,' Virgil replied unhesitatingly. 'Nothing worse than a chatty brain, I always say.'

'I see,' said Jason. 'Only I have this awful feeling that I ought to get off the train here and go and look for – well, the thing. It. I don't want to,' he added, 'not one little bit, but somehow I feel that I should. Do you understand?'

Virgil nodded. 'Indeed,' he replied sadly. 'I wouldn't worry about it, if I were you. Lots of people get that.'

'Oh,' said Jason, encouraged. 'Do they?'

'Yes, masses,' Virgil replied. 'Just before they get killed. A lot of people do get killed, you see, and . . .'

'Will I get killed if I get out of this carriage?' Jason asked. 'For certain, I mean; no possibility of survival.'

'I wouldn't say that,' said Virgil.

'What are my chances, then?'

'I really couldn't guess,' said the poet. 'You see, no mortal has ever been where you're proposing to go. Or at least never gone and come back. Therefore, reliable data is a bit thin on the ground.'

'Ah, the hell with that,' Jason said, striving to sound cheerful. 'Nobody had been to America before Columbus.'

Virgil looked at him and leaned forward. 'Have you ever considered,' he asked, 'how many people before Columbus tried to get to America but failed because they fell off the edge of the world?'

'But that's . . .'

'You can say that,' Virgil interrupted him, 'because you don't know what you're talking about. And,' he added, 'I'm buggered if I'm going to waste my time telling you, because very shortly you won't exist any more. Or at least, if I tell you, then you soon won't exist any more, because you'll leave the train. Whereas if I scare you shitless about what's out there instead of telling you the truth, then you won't leave the train and therefore you won't die. Clever, isn't it?'

'I don't know,' said Jason, 'you lost me quite early on, I'm afraid.'

'It's a bifurcation,' Virgil said. 'To be precise, it's an Impossibility Frontier. It's impossible for a mortal to know

354

what's out there and live to tell the tale. You have to follow
one of the two alternatives – know and die, stay ignorant
and live. There is no third choice.'

'Isn't there?'

'No.'

Jason grinned disconcertingly and lashed out at the
window with the Sword of Glycerion, still in its canvas
bag. The glass smashed, and the train vanished. So did
Virgil, the light, the Sword and – agonisingly – the sandwiches. The only thing that didn't vanish was Jason.

'Good dog,' Pluto lied.

Cerberus, the triple-headed Hellhound, ignored him
and growled again. The guard went white but stood his
ground.

'Sorry, mate,' he insisted, 'but unless it's a guide dog,
you can't take it on the train. Rules is rules.'

Pluto shrugged. 'Do you contain bone marrow?' he
asked.

The guard gave him a bewildered look. 'I suppose so,' he
said. 'Why d'you ask?'

'It said on one of those commercials,' Pluto replied. 'It's
good for dogs, apparently. How about calcium? They're
supposed to need a lot of calcium.'

'Here . . .'

'I know,' Pluto said miserably, 'I don't enjoy it much
either, all this threatening and menacing and so on. It's this
damned dog that causes all the trouble. I'd leave him
behind, but if he sees me going out and I don't take him
with me, he grabs the lead in his mouths and jumps up at
me and barks. I don't actually like dogs much, to tell you
the truth.'

The guard swallowed hard and tried not to look at the

six small, round red eyes that were fixed on him. 'Are you sure,' he said quietly, 'that it *isn't* a guide dog?'

'Positive,' Pluto said.

'Looks like a guide dog to me.'

'Does it? Oh I see. Yes, it's a guide dog all right.'

'Fine,' said the guard. 'Now go away, please.'

Pluto shook his head sadly and walked over to the escalator. There was a sign saying that dogs should be carried on the escalator, but it had clearly been put there by someone who hadn't considered all the possibilities.

'Next,' said Ms. Fisichelli, 'you take the patera in your right hand . . .'

'Like this?'

'No. I mean yes. Then you pick up the simpulum in your left hand, dip it in the sacred barley meal . . .'

'What sacred barley meal?'

'Drat,' said Ms. Fisichelli. 'Oh well, never mind. I usually use muesli anyway. It's not quite right, sure, but the worst that happens is the prophesy turns out ten minutes fast. Now place the simpulum on the patera and count to ten.'

Mary closed her eyes. 'One two three four . . .'

There was a sudden roar, and a cold blue flame sprang out of the sacred tripod, much to the surprise of Ms. Fisichelli, who was leaning on it. There was no harm done, however, since the flame didn't seem to know that fire is supposed to burn. It simply played up and down her sleeve a couple of times and then subsided to something like Gas mark 4.

'However did you manage that?' said the Pythoness.

'I don't know,' Mary confessed, 'it just sort of happened. Why, isn't it supposed to?'

'Well, yes,' Ms. Fisichelli confessed. 'Only it never has

when *I've* tried it. I usually end up having to use meths and a lighter.'

Mary smiled, slightly embarrassed, and murmured something about beginner's luck. Then, as directed, she placed the patera over the flame, sprinkled more of the sacred muesli, and poured a libation from the small silvergilt cornucopia. The flame started to rise again, only this time it lifted the patera up with it.

'Zippy,' said Ms. Fisichelli, impressed. 'You've done this before, haven't you?'

'No,' Mary said, looking away. 'What now?'

'Strictly speaking,' said the Pythoness, 'we should now sacrifice a kid, a lamb and a white dove. However, I have the neighbours to think of, so I generally skip all that. Sometimes, though, I do pop in a casserole. Less blood and saves me having to cook an evening meal.'

Mary shrugged. 'Sounds reasonable to me,' she said.

'Usually, though,' said Ms. Fisichelli, 'I don't bother. I've never noticed it make a blind bit of difference. You know how sometimes you can't be bothered sacrificing just for one.'

'Fine,' Mary said. 'So what do we do now?'

'We wait,' said Ms. Fisichelli. 'Sooner or later the god will manifest himself, and then we can . . . Oh hell!'

The flame flickered, rose up, crackled and went bright green. The patera bobbed on the crest of the flame and started to sink slowly down onto the tripod. There was a foul smell of sulphur.

'What's up?' Mary asked. 'Have we got something wrong?'

'No,' said Ms. Fisichelli, 'that's just the busy signal.'

'Oh.' Mary raised an eyebrow. 'Does that mean we have to start all over again?'

Ms. Fisichelli shook her head. 'Not any more,' she said. 'It used to, in the old days. But now there's a sort of Redial facility. Watch.'

She leaned forward and pressed an embossed lion's head on one of the legs of the tripod. The flame became blue again and the patera started to climb back.

'Look,' Ms. Fisichelli said, and pointed to the heart of the flame.

'Where?' Mary said. 'I can't see any . . .'

The words died on her lips. In the very centre of the flame a man's face was slowly becoming visible; first just the eyes, then the lips, nose and chin. Then the fire seemed to mould itself into the shape of a head, the flames curling up from a fiery neck and flickering wildly to form the thick, curly hair. Mary gasped. The lips parted and the fire spoke.

'Hello,' it said, 'this is Apollo speaking. I'm sorry there's no-one here just now to take your call but if you'd care to leave a message I'll get back to you as soon as possible. Please speak clearly after you hear the tone. Thank you.'

Ms. Fisichelli scowled. There was a sudden blare of trumpets that seemed to shake all the brains up inside Mary's head.

'Thia is Betty-Lou Fisichelli calling,' the Pythoness said. 'Er . . . Oh, dammit, I hate talking into these things . . . Look, would you please very kindly sort of descend or send down a messenger or a dream or something, when it's convenient, of course, because we've had, well, it's rather hard to explain, some very funny things have been happening and perhaps you should know about them, so please do call back, thank you. Message ends,' she added.

The fiery head nodded three times and slowly became nothing more than a random pattern of flames. The patera sank back. The fire went out.

'Well,' said the Pythoness, 'that was a complete waste of time, wasn't it?'

'It was the most amazing thing,' Mary whispered, as much to herself as to the Pythoness. 'He was so . . .'

'And if he does call back,' Ms. Fisichelli went on, 'you can bet your shirt it'll be while I'm in the bath or washing my hair or something. I really hate that, you know, having this great big burning face pop up at you while you've got your head over the washbasin. Still, there it is.' She started to clear away the sacred implements.

'Betty-Lou,' said Mary, after a while.

'Yes, dear?'

'What exactly is happening?' Mary asked. 'I mean, I know it must be important, because of what the entrails say, but . . .'

'I'm not so sure,' Ms. Fisichelli replied. 'Maybe the entrails were wrong. I've never been entirely happy about divining with frozen chickens anyway, but I'm in enough trouble with the Residents' Association as it is without killing chickens all over the place. Probably all a storm in a teacup.'

'Yes, but . . .'

'I think something funny happens to them when you defrost them in the microwave . . . Sorry, dear, what were you saying?'

'I was thinking,' said Mary. 'Maybe we could work it out for ourselves. What's happening, I mean.'

'I don't think so,' said the Pythoness stiffly. 'Best leave that to the experts, don't you think?'

'Yes,' Mary replied carefully, 'sure thing, but don't you think it's meant as an omen?'

'Absolutely,' said Betty-Lou. 'That's why he's got to be told.'

'But surely the whole point of an omen is that it's a sort of coded message,' said her apprentice. 'Which means that whoever sent it expected us to be able to understand it. So I thought . . .'

'Fine,' said the Pythoness with unwonted irony. 'So you just tell me what it means when a red plastic nose suddenly materialises on the sacred image of Apollo.'

'Well . . .'

'Or how a whoopee-cushion managed to find its way onto the Throne of Prophesy.'

'I thought maybe . . .'

'Or,' said the Pythoness, 'why the three heads of the Eikon Triceraunion are all suddenly wearing brightly-coloured paper hats. I mean,' she said, 'any fool can answer that, no point in bothering the god, is there?'

'I'm sorry,' said Mary, humbly. 'I was only trying to help.'

The Pythoness clicked her tongue in a not altogether unfriendly manner. 'I know, dear,' she said, 'and it shows initiative and all the rest of it. But it's not our place to go guessing at things; and besides, he'll have to know sooner or later. It might be important.'

'I suppose you're right,' Mary said. 'But the message . . .'

'That,' said the Pythoness, 'proves my point, surely. I mean, it could be highly significant, or it could just be kids climbing in through the ventilation shaft again. Really, we have to leave that sort of thing to the Chief. Now, give me a hand washing up these last few bits and pieces, and then I think we've earned ourselves a drink, don't you?'

Mary nodded and Ms. Fisichelli tried to dismiss the whole business from her mind, but as she dried the patera and put it back in the Holy Chest she couldn't help thinking that somewhere there was a simple explanation for it all, particularly when you considered the message which had appeared, cut into the rock of the lintel of the Treasury of the Athenians, that same morning. After all, it spoke for itself:

'WISEACRES OF THE WORLD UNITE,' it said. 'YOU HAVE NOTHING TO LOSE BUT YOUR CHAINS.'

About thirty thousand years ago, when telepathy was the only readily accessible form of mass entertainment, there was a popular game-show on the main brainwave channel called *Read My Mind*. A panel of guest celebrities had to guess what each of the contestants did for a living, and if they failed they were torn apart by wild dogs. It was good middlebrow family entertainment.

On the show in question, a panel consisting of two river-gods, a wood-nymph and the Queen of the Night were asked to guess the identity of a more than usually enigmatic character, who turned up wearing a loud check suit and a red nose, and answered all their questions by bursting into fits of laughter. The panel had got as far as the fact that the mystery guest was something to do with entertainment, but there they stuck. Time was running out. The mind-camera was playing lovingly on the slavering jaws of the dogs.

'He's a tax inspector,' guessed one of the river-gods wildly. The compere grinned, shook his head and made woof-woof noises. The Queen of the Night started to have hysterics.

'He's . . .' said the wood-nymph desperately. 'Oh God, it's on the tip of my tongue. Whatsisname. Whatchamacallit . . . Um, you know, er, thing . . .'

The mystery guest looked up sharply and scowled.

'Someone told you,' he said.

Then time ran out and there was an advertisement for soap powder, and so the telepaths at home never discovered the whole truth; namely that the mystery guest (whose name was Gelos) was in fact the personification of Laughter, the sworn enemy of the race of gods; in his previous incarnation one of the original Three. Another point which didn't get out was the fact that Gelos is the only force in the cosmos who stands between the gods and total universal domination, because only laughter and a sense of the absurd makes it possible for human beings to dismiss . the gods as a figment of the imagination; whereas if Gelos ever finds a hero brave and strong enough to protect him from the gods, he will be able to rule the whole of creation.

Pluto stopped, took a plastic bag from his pocket and opened it, revealing a sock.

'Here, boy,' he said nervously. 'Find!' He placed the sock in front of each of the dog's three noses in turn. The dog growled ominously, and two of its heads started snuffling at the ground. The third ate the sock and, shortly afterwards, was sick.

'C'mon, good dog,' Pluto muttered, and the ex-Hellhound suddenly lurched forward, heads down, and dragged his master into the corridors that led to the Piccadilly Line platforms.

It is often held that two heads are better than one, and so Cerberus should have represented the optimum in scent-following efficiency. However, after five minutes of enthusiastic baying, tracking, tail-wagging and snapping at the ankles of women with small children, he stopped opposite a fire-bucket, pointed like a gun-dog and sat resolutely down. Having emptied the bucket and found no trace of the missing Hero, Pluto began to lose patience.

'Look, you bloody animal,' he said, 'far be it from me to get heavy with a dumb beast, but unless you pack in the clever stuff and get back to work, you'll be up the vet's so fast your paws won't touch. Got it?'

That, Pluto later admitted, had been a mistake. Cerberus gave him a foul look in triplicate, snarled very convincingly, and bit through the lead. Pluto toyed briefly with the idea of blowing gently up the dog's nostrils, as recommended by the lady at the obedience classes, thought better of it, and ran for his everlasting life.

Cerberus, however, didn't follow. Having satisfied itself that its master was out of sight, it grinned widely and trotted off down the corridor in the opposite direction. A wall against which it paused briefly to cock its leg collapsed shortly afterwards into a pile of fizzing lime.

Cautiously, Jason Derry lifted his left foot, moved it approximately a metre forwards, and tried to put it down.

He immediately regretted it. There was nothing there; his foot simply continued moving, finding nothing on which to rest. The thoroughly disconcerting thing was that his balance was not upset, and as soon as he stopped applying pressure with his leg muscles, his foot stopped. He wasn't standing on anything, he discovered; he was just standing. Floating. Whatever.

The important thing at times like these, he told himself, is to stay calm. This environment may be decidedly hooky, but as yet it has exhibited no overtly hostile symptoms. You could probably get to like it in time. Let's be terribly laid-back and cool about this, and just take it as it comes. Who needs gravity, anyway?

'Help!' Jason said.

He listened as the word he had just spoken flopped

aimlessly about in the darkness, slowly growing fainter and fainter and finally dissolving into a clatter of disjointed consonants. He breathed in deeply (there was no air, but fortunately he didn't know that) and tried moving his right leg.

'Woof,' said a voice behind him.

He froze, and after a few moments his heart began to beat again. He turned his head and stared; but there was no light.

'Woof.'

'Woof.'

Three different voices. Either I'm going potty or there are dogs down here. Given the choice, I'm going potty.

'Hello?' he ventured. 'Anybody there?'

'Woof.'

'Woof.'

'Woof.'

Three dogs. Jason muttered something under his breath and speculated about whether the person responsible for all this had got his priorities right, exactly. Dogs are all very fine and splendid in their way – absolutely nothing against dogs, either as pets or as part of an integrated sheep control system – but what we really need most of all right now is a floor.

'Here, boy,' he ventured. 'Who's a *good boy*, then?' he added.

'Woof,' said three voices, and there was just a hint of ennui in them; as if they knew from experience that when somebody addressed them as Good Boy, it would soon be time to start retrieving sticks from freezing cold ponds. Jason plucked up his courage and extended a hand into the darkness behind him. 'Heel,' he murmured.

Almost at once, he was aware of something large and

364

hairy brushing up against his leg and a violent rasping sensation on the back of his hand, consistent with it being licked by three very sharp tongues at the same time. It wasn't pleasant; but compared to a number of alternatives that suggested themselves to Jason at that moment, it did very nicely, thank you very much.

'Now then, doggies,' Jason quavered, 'you and I are going to be friends, aren't we?'

Three voices said Woof in such a way as to suggest that a temporary alliance might well prove expedient at the present moment, but any more of this mushy anthropomorphic crap and the deal was off.

'OK,' Jason replied, 'suits me. Have you got the faintest idea where in hell we are?'

A trio of voices said Woof in such a way as to indicate that if Jason knew, he wouldn't like it terribly much, but if he insisted on a clue there was a pretty nifty one in his own last remark. Jason grinned nervously.

'I don't suppose you know how to get the hell . . . to get out of here, do you?'

'Woof.'

'Thought not.'

'Woof.'

'Sorry.'

Jason wiped his hand carefully on his trousers; then, for the first time in his life, he listened hard in the back of his head for the sound of three dots. Nothing. Marvellous.

'.' said a canine voice beside him.

'.' said another.

'.' remarked a third.

'Oh come *on*,' said Jason despairingly. 'Let's all stop pissing about here, or I'm going to give the whole thing up on the grounds of complete incomprehensibility.'

There was a long silence. Then the dog spoke; all three voices, but speaking as one.

'We,' it (or they) said, 'are the dog.'

'Well yes,' Jason replied cautiously. 'I had gathered.'

'We,' the voice(s) went on, 'would like you to consider what you get if you spell our name backwards.'

'What, now?'

'Yes, now.'

'All right,' said Jason, after a short pause, 'you get god. So bloody what? If you spell moon backwards you get noom, but right now I'm more interested in getting back to Piccadilly Circus, if it's all the same to you.'

'Think,' said the dog.

'Oh no,' Jason replied. 'I tried that, and look where it got me. Look, thanks ever so much for dropping by, but perhaps we'd all get on much better if we went our separate . . .'

'We,' said the dog, 'are merely Speakers.'

'Barkers.'

'Speakers,' said the dog coldly, 'for the Thought in your head. You called for us. We are here.'

Jason opened his mouth and then closed it again, waiting for some words to drip through from the filterpaper of his brain. Some time later he said, 'You're *what*?'

'We are saying out loud what the Thought in your head would be saying if it could speak out loud,' said the dog.

'Really?'

'Yes.'

'You mean to say,' Jason said, 'that I'm actually thinking all this garbage?'

'No,' said the dog.

Jason whimpered ever so slightly. 'Oh be fair, please,' he said. 'I can cope with gibberish just as long as it's *consistent*. I thought you just told me . . .'

'The Thought is not you,' said the dog. 'The Thought is the god-turned-backwards. Previously I have spoken to you in the quiet of your mind. Here I am speaking to you through the dog.'

'Why?'

'Why not?'

There was another very long silence.

'Had you going there for a minute, didn't we?' said the dog.

Stuff it, Jason said to himself, enough is enough. He made a careful estimate of the position of the dog's rear end and kicked hard. There was a triune yelp and a sharp stabbing pain in the back of his head, but he really didn't mind about that. He felt better now.

'Oueh,' said the dog.

'Serves you right,' Jason replied. 'You had it coming.'

'Can't you take a joke or something?' growled the dog.

'No.'

The dog growled ominously; and was that a very faint breath of moving air Jason could feel on his cheek? 'Would you care to rephrase that?' ventured one of the dog's heads.

'Why should I?'

'Because,' said a different head, 'in the circumstances that wasn't the cleverest thing you've ever said, that's all.'

'So what?' Jason snarled. 'You can have too much of being clever if you ask me. Right now I fancy being mindlessly violent.'

'Keep your voice down, for dog's sake,' whispered all three voices (but not simultaneously). 'This is not the right time for aggressive posturing.'

Jason shook his head. 'I don't care,' he said. 'I've had enough and I want to go home. Failing that, I want an explanation. My final, fall-back option is a heavily-mangled dog, but perhaps we can sort something out if we work at it.'

'You want an explanation?' said the dog.

'Yes.'

'Then you shall have it.'

Jason suddenly became extremely still, as if someone had just unplugged him. 'Did you say something?' he asked.

'No,' whispered three very nervous dog-heads.

'Somebody said something.'

'We know.'

'Who?'

'Woof.'

'*Woof?*'

Then Jason felt something in the back of his head; not felt as in an emotional response; more like felt as in there being a large, heavy weight behind his ears which was swinging in a semicircle, taking the head with it.

'Come here,' commanded the darkness. But a tiny spark of courage flashed across the contacts of what remained of Jason's personality, and he stayed where he was. Fear of death, the unknown, darkness and the Devil were one thing, he decided; bad manners were something else.

'Only if you put the lights on,' he replied.

The darkness laughed. 'Sure?'

'Sure.'

And there was light.

CHAPTER EIGHT

On his way back up Virgil was stopped by a hairy old man with long fingernails whom he recognised at once. He shuddered and tried very hard to look like somebody else.

'Excuse me,' said Pluto, 'but have you seen a dog?'

'Frequently,' Virgil replied. 'So thank you all the same, but . . .'

'No,' Pluto said, 'what I mean is, have you seen a dog *recently*?'

Virgil considered for a moment. 'Can't say I have,' he said. 'Not for ages. But I'm trying to give them up, actually, so it's no skin off my nose. Good Lord, is that the . . .'

Pluto looked at him carefully. 'Here,' he said, 'I know you, don't I?'

'Me?' Virgil shook his head vigorously. 'That's highly unlikely, isn't it?'

Pluto frowned. 'I do know you,' he said accusingly. 'You're dead.'

'Well yes,' Virgil said, 'If you want to be biologically exact I suppose I am, but I try not to dwell on it too much. Clearly where you come from, tact is held in roughly the same esteem as personal appearance. And now I must be . . .'

'Then what are you doing here?'

'Where?'

'Here,' Pluto said, 'in the land of the living. You should be in . . .'

'And the same to you too,' Virgil said quickly. 'Must rush. Bye.'

It was fortunate for the poet that Pluto had other things on his mind, for the ex-God of the Dead has never, despite his best efforts, completely retired, and he has extremely strong views on dead people who wander about topside, fiddling about with the Great Chain of Being and startling old ladies. Instead of taking the matter further, however, Pluto simply shrugged and carried on following the dog.

It wasn't difficult, actually; in many places, the tiles on the walls of the corridors were already starting to bubble, and the smell was unmistakable. He might be three-headed, immortal and capable of human speech, but Cerberus was very much a dog.

Down past the normal, everyday levels now, and Pluto began to feel that familiar feeling of uneasiness, together with a certain very faint nostalgia. It had been years since he last visited Hell (or, as he had always tried to think of it, the Autumn Leaves Rest Home); and – well, you can never completely let go, can you?

My God, Pluto said to himself as he wandered through the endless passageways, what *have* they done to the old place? All right, it had never exactly been what you'd call cosy – too many souls-in-torment for that – but at least he'd tried his best. You can do a lot with the odd pot plant here and framed print there, the occasional lick of paint and roll of woodchip when the budget could run to it; even just little things, like a table, a couple of chairs and a few old colour supplements, made a great deal of difference to

370

the guests (Pluto always thought of them as guests). After all, a lot of people have to spend a lot of time here, and the least you can do is try to encourage them to think of it as their *home* . . . He shook his head sadly and tried to remember where the laundry cupboard used to be.

He arrived on the platform just as the train was pulling in and jumped nimbly through the doors, stepping over the crushed bodies with the ease of long practice. The train was always pretty full at this time of day, he remembered, but he found one of those corner seats which have a little blue notice above it saying *Please give up this seat if an irrevocably damned person needs it*, put a damned expression on his face, and sat down. He was just starting to wonder where the dog could have got to when he became aware of someone standing over him.

'I said, Tickets please.'

Pluto looked up into what he took at first to be a pair of blue industrial lasers, and nearly jumped out of his skin.

'Look,' said the spectre, 'have you got a ticket or not?' Pluto twitched slightly and the spectre glowered at him, if yellow-fanged, goat-headed monsters can glower; the point has never been properly researched, understandably.

Pluto pulled himself together. 'Well, no,' he admitted. 'You're new here, aren't you?'

'If you haven't got a ticket,' said the spectre – how, Pluto asked himself, does he manage to avoid skewering his own upper lip every time he speaks? – 'you'll have to buy one now. That or I put you off at the next stop.'

Pluto, who knew what the next stop was, rummaged vigorously in his pocket for change. Being a god is all very well, but one doesn't like to push one's luck. Mercifully, he found some money.

'How much?' he asked, and the spectre told him. While

it was writing out a ticket, Pluto laid the two coins across his own closed eyelids and waited.

'Here,' said the spectre, 'haven't you got anything smaller?'

Pluto apologised, took his ticket and his change, and started breathing again. Spectres were definitely new since last time, although he remembered that there had been demons. State-registered demons, naturally. They had been pretty horrible, true; but at least they were polite and had their watches pinned to their frontal scales.

The panic over, he leaned back in his seat and watched the stations go by – Lechery, Gluttony, Wrath (change here for Murder, Parricide and Regicide), Sloth, Sloth Circus, High Street Sloth, Sloth Central, Sloth Broadway, Greed (escalator link to Simony), Pride and Being Found Out . . .

Being Found Out? Yes, thought Pluto, I guess I really am out of touch. He shrugged and started reading the advertisements.

'Ah,' Jason said, 'hello there.'

Me and my big mouth, he said to himself. Who was it insisted on having the lights on, then? Old Mister Dickhead, that's who.

'Hello yourself.'

There was a long pause, and Jason took a cautious look at his new companion.

Say what you like about Jason, he is not one of those idiots who takes against people just because of the colour of their skin. But he does like them to have skin, and this chap palpably didn't. Instead, he seemed to have masonry.

Description is the lifeblood of narrative, so let us start with the furniture. The throne he sat in was made from some sort of very shiny black metal, and its four feet, carved in the shape of disconcertingly realistic dragons' heads, rested on nothing at all. The little light that there was seemed to be coming from the throne, but it wasn't as if there were little bulbs hidden discreetly behind the reliefs of writhing serpents and contorted bull-headed shapes. The light just seemed to ooze out of the metal, like acid from a very old battery. There were other things oozing out of the throne apart from the light, of course, but since they seemed to be turning into snakes and spiders and other nasty things as soon as they got clear of the throne Jason decided to do the sensible thing and pretend he hadn't seen them.

So much for the furniture. Now for the clothes. He wore a flowing black robe, heavy with glittering black gemstones; jet and obsidian, that sort of thing, although ordinary gemstones don't hurt your eyes so much when you look at them. The cloth – Jason assumed for the sake of a quiet life that it was cloth – was simply the colour and texture of the absence of light. On his feet he wore shoes in the shape of huge hooked talons, except that they weren't shoes.

We are pussyfooting, we know; but that is because since the Great Adjective Shortage of 1976, we simply can't get the materials. We will therefore leave it at Very Horrible and hope that you will bear with us and use your imaginations. Carefully.

'Have a sausage roll,' he said.

Jason grinned weakly. 'No thanks,' he said. 'I had something before I came out, really. Er . . .'

'Yes?'

'Well, it's . . . I mean . . . Like, don't let me keep you or anything, I . . .'

'You're not.'

'Oh, I . . .'

'I don't get many visitors. It's nice to speak to someone occasionally, even just a mortal.'

'Well, that's very kind of you to say so, but I'm sure you're very busy really, and . . .'

'No I'm not.'

'Ah. Yes. Um . . .'

'Are you,' he said, 'Jason Derry?'

That, Jason felt, was one of those trick questions, like *Was it you who broke the window?* He made a small, indecisive gesture. 'Er . . .' he said.

'You are, aren't you?'

'Um . . .'

'Your dog seems to think you are.'

'My dog?'

'I take it that's your dog? Who's a *good* boy, then?'

Jason looked round to see Cerberus nodding all three heads at once. Not for the first time, Jason remembered that he didn't much like dogs.

'Yes,' he said.

'Ah,' he said, 'that's all right, then.'

There was a blinding flash of multi-coloured light and the throne and its occupant vanished. The sheer force of so much light knocked Jason clean off his feet (not that he was exactly on them to begin with) and he fell headlong onto nothing at all.

Or, to be pedantically accurate, a carpet. Quite a nice carpet, in fact. Woolly, deep-pile, the colour of spilt tea.

'Sorry about that,' said a voice above his head. 'That was clumsy of me.'

Slowly, Jason looked up, and his eyes met the toes of a pair of slippers. Blue, slightly scuffed, comfortable-looking.

'Pleased to meet you, Jason,' said the voice. 'You don't mind if I call you Jason, do you?'

374

Jason managed to detach his eyes from the slippers and looked up further still. The throne and the living statue had gone; however, the floor had come back. Also the walls, the ceiling, the Sword of Whatsit (but not its name), and the bag of sandwiches. The latter two exhibits were on a coffee-table beside an armchair in which was seated a very nice, apparently quite friendly old gentleman in a dressing-gown and blue slippers. He had a plate of the most delicious-looking sausage rolls on his lap, and he offered one to Jason.

'Sorry about all the black stuff,' he said, 'but in my position you can't be too careful. It's supposed to scare the crap out of people. Of course, I've never actually seen it myself so I don't know if it works. Does it?'

'Yes,' said Jason with his mouth full. For some reason, which he couldn't quite fathom, he felt a strong urge to burst out laughing at this point; being possessed of semi-divine willpower, however, he managed to keep it to a discreet snurge.

'Oh good,' the nice man replied. 'Now, let me introduce myself, and then we can have a cup of tea and a chat. My name's Gelos. I gather you wanted to meet me.'

'Your economy,' said Diana carefully, 'and raise you fifty.'

Apollo nodded listlessly. Diana muttered something under her breath and rolled the dice.

'More fool you!' she crowed. 'We're welching on our National Debt, so sucks to you.'

Apollo hardly seemed to notice. 'That's nice,' he said distractedly. 'Look, tell me when it's my go, will you, I'm just watching something over here.'

Diana scowled. 'Pol,' she said, 'I've just wiped out three of your major clearing banks. Aren't you interested?'

'Sorry?'

'Pol!' Diana banged her goblet of ambrosia sharply on the table. 'Will you please pay attention to the Game!'

'Mmmm,' Apollo replied. 'Could you just bear with me a moment while I just nip down to Earth? Perhaps you could just ask Ma or someone to play my hand for me while I'm away.'

Diana was now seriously worried. Asking a fellow god to take your go for you was like offering the Big Bad Wolf a job in a crèche. 'Is it, er, important?' she asked.

'Quite,' Apollo answered, 'yes.'

'Shouldn't I call Min, then?'

'No,' Apollo said firmly, 'decidedly not.'

'Why?'

Apollo considered his choice of words carefully. 'For the same reason,' he said at last, 'why you shouldn't remove rings from coffee-tables with coarse grain sandpaper. Won't be long.'

Diana watched as he disappeared into the far darkness, shrugged, and tentatively moved the Chinese army into Nepal. As she did so, a single golden rose leaf drifted slowly down from above her head, twirled gracefully and settled on her knee. She picked it up and saw that there were tiny letters picked out on it in fire.

I saw that, they said.

'Ah nuts,' Diana said, and removed her army.

'What do you mean,' said Ms. Fisichelli, 'there aren't any?'

'I'm sorry,' Mary replied ruefully. 'The jar's empty.'

Ms. Fisichelli scratched her head. 'That's funny,' she said. 'There were plenty when I looked this morning.'

'I know,' said Mary.

'Pardon me?'

'I ate them,' Mary explained.

Ms. Fisichelli suddenly became very still and cold, like a mammoth in a glacier. 'You ate them,' she repeated.

'Well, er, yes.'

'Apollo's sacred olives.'

'Yes. I . . .'

'I see,' said Ms. Fisichelli. 'Well,' she went on, 'that's fine. Thank you so much for letting me know. I suppose Mr. A is going to have to make do with tinned olives from the deli just this once but I'm sure he won't mind.'

'I . . .'

'And now,' Ms. Fisichelli continued remorselessly, 'provided always that you haven't eaten the altar and the sacred tripod I think it's time we made a start. Pass me the simpulum, please.'

Mary bowed her head and handed the Pythoness the simpulum without comment. Nuts, said a voice at the back of her head. I was just hungry, that's all . . .

Ms. Fisichelli, meanwhile, had turned on the Sacred Gas and was just trying to get the Sacred Lighter to work (guess who forgot to change the Holy Flint again) when the Sacred Flame suddenly leapt up of its own accord, nearly taking her eyebrows off.

'Goddamnit, you clumsy . . . Gee, I'm *sorry.*' In the presence of her god, Ms. Fisichelli's aggravation dissolved. 'I wasn't expecting.'

The divine head nodded on its neck of flame. 'Okay,' it said, 'my fault, sorry. Look, can we do without all this mumbo-jumbo for once? I've only popped out for a moment, and I don't want Min . . . I mean, this can only be a brief audience. I've got to, well, see a man.'

'Master?'

'About a dog.'

'I see, Master.'

377

'So,' said the divine head, 'if it's all the same to you girls, I'm just going to slip into something more comfortable. Back in a tick.'

The sacred flame went suddenly out and the patera, deprived of its support, dropped like a stone and shattered on the rim of the tripod. Apollo materialised next to it just in time to be hit on the back of the hand by a flying potsherd.

'Ouch,' he said.

'Master!'

'Betty,' said Apollo irritably, 'let's just leave all that stuff, shall we? As a matter of fact, I'm perfectly capable of getting here on my own without having to be conjured up, dematerialised, transmuted into the Spirit, sucked up through eight yards of narrow copper pipe and set fire to, so in future I'll trouble you just to leave a message with Reception, all right?'

Mary giggled very slightly, thinking of the olives. Ms. Fisichelli, if she noticed her disciple's lapse, ignored it.

'I'm terribly sorry to have bothered you . . .' she said.

Apollo sighed, removed a back issue of the *Journal of Byzantine Studies* from the armchair, and sat down. 'That's all right,' he said wearily. 'Can we get on now, please?'

Ms. Fisichelli flushed and sat down on the sofa. For her part, Mary folded her legs gracefully and kneeled on the floor. Apollo noticed, reflected that he was old enough to be her great-grand-father, and looked firmly at the Pythoness, who became suddenly flustered.

'It's nothing really,' she stammered. 'It's just, you did say to let you know if I came across anything unusual about the Derry boy, and there have been other things too, and you

378

know how sometimes even things that don't seem important at the time . . .'

The gods can be cruel, terrible, illogical and heartless, but sometimes they can be patient too. Apollo smiled reassuringly. 'I'm sure you're right,' he said. 'Please tell me all about it.'

Ms. Fisichelli swallowed the large clot of mud that had apparently formed in her throat and said 'Well . . .'

'Yes?'

'It's like this. Er.'

Apollo smiled even more, until Ms. Fisichelli could feel little flakes of skin detaching themselves from the tip of her nose. 'Perhaps,' she said, 'you should see for yourself.'

Apollo frowned. 'How do you mean?'

The Pythoness twitched nervously. 'In the Sacred Bowl,' she said.

'The Sacred Bowl?' Apollo looked puzzled. 'You mean that thing still works?'

'Well . . .'

'Well, I never,' Apollo went on. 'I thought it had packed up in the fifth century, when that clown Amaryllis IV used it for frying anchovies. Have you got it working again?'

'I cleaned it,' Ms. Fisichelli murmured, 'and it seemed OK. You don't mind, do you? Only it can be a great help sometimes and . . . Well,' she said quickly, 'actually, I've been using it to watch the baseball. You can't get the baseball on Greek TV, not even with a satellite dish, and Chicago have got to the Rose Bowl this year, and . . .'

'It works, then,' Apollo said.

'Seems to,' said Ms. Fisichelli. 'I'll fetch it.'

She jumped up and scurried off into the kitchen. While she was gone, Apollo tried hard not to look at her new disciple out of the corner of his eye. To the gods, Homer

379

was fond of saying, all things are possible. He was wrong.

'Er,' Apollo said.

'Sorry?' Mary smiled, warmly but respectfully. Apollo suddenly felt a bit tongue-tied.

'Um – are you, well, doing anything tomorrow evening?' Mary continued to smile.

'Only,' Apollo went on, 'I happen to have two tickets for the open air Bad Vibes concert in Central Park, and I thought . . .'

'Sorry,' Mary said, 'only I'm washing my hair tomorrow night.'

'Oh.'

Mary smiled again.

'Another time, then, maybe?'

Smile. And then Ms. Fisichelli came back with the Sacred Bowl and Apollo wrenched his attention back to far less important things. More important. *Damn.*

'I'm all out of holy water,' she said, 'so I used Perrier. It's generally okay, I've found.'

She put the bowl down on the tripod, fumbled in her pocket for her sistrum, and started to hum the incantation. Apollo (who is also ex-God of music) winced, thanked her, and hummed it for her.

At once, a pale golden glow filled the room, while the electric light quietly went away and found something else to do. There was also a strange, mysterious fragrance, but that had more to do with the fact that Ms. Fisichelli's lemon curd was boiling over on the gas-stove than anything particularly divine. Apollo stood up and peered into the depths of the bowl.

'Hey,' he said, 'this is good.' Ms. Fisichelli simpered.

On the meniscus of the still slightly effervescent water there was an image. There was a dog.

It was lying on a carpet gnawing three bones.

It was doing this at the feet of a man who was sitting in a very comfortable looking chair in an almost unbearably cosy looking room eating what appeared to be a slice of exquisitely yummy chocolate cake. Opposite him sat what could only be described as a very nice, friendly looking old gentleman who tended to wave his hands about a lot, making his companion laugh with his mouth full.

'Well,' said Apollo, 'I'll be a son of a thunderbolt. How do you turn the sound up on this thing?'

'Um,' said Ms. Fisichelli.

'Sorry?'

'You can't.'

'Oh,' said Apollo. 'No sound, then.'

'No.'

'Never mind . . . Hey, now what's happening?'

Ms. Fisichelli flushed. 'It does that,' she said.

The picture of the nice room had vanished as suddenly as it had come, and in its place was the image of another man, a man with long hair and long fingernails. He appeared for all the world to be standing up in an Underground carriage. Now he was walking to the connecting door between the carriages. He was opening it, and getting out . . .

There was a terrific hiss and all the water in the bowl suddenly became steam and flew upwards. The bowl overheated, cracked and shattered into splinters, one of which hit Apollo on the nose.

'*Ouch!*' he said.

Ms. Fisichelli looked as if she'd just gone into deep shock, and Apollo, as soon as he had recovered himself, helped her to a seat. 'Is she all right?' he asked, nervously.

'I think so,' Mary replied. 'She's a bit highly-strung, you know.

Apollo nodded. 'I wonder what made it suddenly do that?' he said, to himself but aloud.

'Too much current,' Mary replied.

Apollo nodded and then turned round quickly. 'Sorry?' he said, and stared at her.

'I'm just guessing,' said Mary modestly, 'but maybe you put too much strain on it, making it look down into the Forbidden Regions.'

Apollo's divine brain told his divine heart and divine body to stay cool and let it handle this. 'Just out of interest,' he said, as casually as he could, 'how did you know that was the Forbidden Regions?'

Mary caught her breath, gave Apollo a look of pure poison, turned into a huge eagle, and left the room.

In the dry heat of a Betamax sun, a column of Roman soldiers stopped in the market square of Tiberiopolis, until recently known as Jerusalem. A young man was led forward and made to take up a large wooden cross. As he did so, he instinctively examined the workmanship.

'Huh,' he said. 'Call that a mortice and tenon joint, 'cos I don't.'

The centurion snapped an impatient command to his troops, but they refused to budge. On his enquiring as to why this might be, they told him that Good Friday was a Bank holiday, and if they were expected to go around crucifying people, it was going to have to be time and a half.

The centurion fumed for a moment, said, 'Oh, bugger this for a game of soldiers,' and stalked off to the wineshop on the corner. After a long silence, the three condemned prisoners edged quietly away and went home, the soldiers lifting not a finger to stop them.

That was why it was a Betamax world, after all.

Unlike most Betamax worlds, however, this one survived the inevitable ensuing possibility crisis and remained extant. This was because of what can only be described as a spatio-temporal cock-up, involving the arrival of a team of interplanetary missionaries from the neighbouring Betamax world, where interstellar travel had been developed before the discovery of printing.* Soon after the mass conversion of the Betamax-human race to Methodism, however, the severe possibility problems caused thereby were all solved at a stroke by the timely intervention of a huge meteor, which smashed the planet into rubble.

The reason why possibility errors are treated so seriously by the authorities, however, is because once they start they tend to continue. It therefore came as no surprise to the Incident Room staff at Possibility Police HQ when particles of incandescent matter released by the destruction of Betamax 9567432 burst into the atmosphere of the world which originally sent out the missionaries, landed on the roofs of all the churches and burned them all down. The embarrassing result of this was that the majority of the population at once abandoned Christianity (thus cancelling the projected nuclear religious war against the Eastern Heretics which should have ended the planet) and set about persuading the remaining faithful of the error of their ways, inventing printing as a necessary method of information dissemination. The world thus created was so perilously close to the Absolutely Possible that the police were compelled to intervene, in the interests of Possibility Preservation, by planting a few absolute impossibilities in

*Which meant they could send probes to the moon but the astronauts were unable to sell their stories to the tabloids afterwards.

383

rarely-visited areas of the planet and then coming back next day and atomising the entire planetary system under Article 47(1) of the Sirius Convention.

Even then, however, their problems were far from over, since the force of the explosion of Betamax 5609765 was so violent that Planet VHS – our planet – was temporarily rocked on its axis, with the result that at a crucial moment a buckshee Thursday was suddenly introduced into the week; the Thursday, in fact, when Jason Derry went down to the Underground to find Gelos. More important, it meant that an extra day had been introduced which had not been foreseen when the Order of Play was drawn up at the very start of the Game. As a result, at the vital point of the story which follows, it was nobody's go at all.

'You mean to tell me,' Jupiter said, 'that all this time we've had a mole?'

Apollo wondered whether it was worth pointing out that it had been an eagle rather than a mole, but decided no, probably not.

'Yes,' he said.

'I see.' Jupiter had this knack of asking questions he already knew the answers to; a common mannerism among the omniscient, but aggravating nevertheless. 'And this mole has been collaborating with . . . with That Person all this time?'

'Yes.' Why is it, Apollo asked himself, that just because I'm the one who tells him, it's suddenly all my fault? There, I'm doing it now; I know exactly why. Because I'm a mug, that's why.

'And nobody noticed, is that it?'

'Yes.'

'And you lot,' Jupiter went on, 'call yourself gods, do you?'

'Yes.'

Jupiter laughed, and black clouds scurried guiltily across the skies of Earth to the positions they should have been in ten minutes ago. It can be tough, being a cloud.

'And now,' Jupiter said, 'that you have at last found out, may I ask what you're proposing to do about it?'

Apollo recognised that this was a question that couldn't be answered with Yes, and searched his divine mind for an answer. 'I don't know,' he said.

'The old brain a bit slow today, is it?'

'Well . . .'

'GET IT SORTED OUT,' said Jupiter – when you're the Great Sky God it's no problem at all to shout in capital letters. In fact, when he was really upset, he could shout in bold face, italics and pitch ten.

'Yes,' said Apollo, 'we . . .'

'NOW.'

'Yes indeed,' Apollo said, 'But . . .'

For all his omniscience, Jupiter didn't seem to understand the implications of But. He just frowned, with the result that race meetings on four continents were washed out. Apollo backed away, tripped over a self-propelled footstool (which apologised in Latin) and ran.

Not long after leaving the presence of the Father of Gods and Men, he bumped into Mars. To be exact, he trod on his foot.

'Watch it,' said the ex-God of War, 'I've had enough of it today with Claymore mines without you as well.'

Apollo apologised – he had often reflected on the aptness of his name – and stopped running. Mars looked at him.

'What's up, Pol?' he asked. 'You seem a bit flustered.'

'Flustered.' Apollo turned the adjective over in his mind.

385

A bit on the weak side perhaps, but it was in the right ball park, so to speak. 'Yes,' he added, from sheer habit.

'Why?'

'There's been a bit of a cock-up,' said Apollo – everyone else was having a go at understatement, he said to himself, why not me too? – 'and I've got to sort it out, apparently.'

'Hard luck,' Mars said sympathetically. 'Now what's happened?'

'You know Prometheus's eagle?'

Mars nodded, making the shrapnel-shredded plume of his helmet nod.

'Well,' Apollo went on, 'apparently it turns out that that bloody fowl's gone and changed sides on us. It's been working for You-Know-Who all along.'

'Really?'

'Yes.'

Mars thought for a moment. 'I wouldn't call ripping someone's liver out for him every morning and evening working for him exactly,' he said. 'Cheaper than a dialysis machine, I suppose, but . . .'

'It's not that,' said Apollo. 'It seems that that dratted eagle's been running errands for him. Subverting Heroes. Spying on us.'

'Spying?'

'That's right,' Apollo grunted. 'Been dressing up as a human and passing itself off as the apprentice Pythoness of Delphi.' Apollo reflected briefly on his brief infatuation with the feathered temptress, and shuddered. 'Which means that the Big P has known every move we make. Vexing, isn't it?'

Mars rubbed his chin, 'You mean like a sort of mole?' he asked. Apollo smiled. He could say it now.

'No, Ma,' he said, 'an eagle can't be a mole. Biologically impossible.'

386

Mars frowned impatiently. 'You know what I mean,' he said. 'Bit of a problem, that. You have my sympathy.'

'Also,' Apollo went on, 'though I'm pleased to say the Old Sod hasn't found out yet, he's also got Cerberus on his side.'

'Cerberus?'

'That's right. Bit poor, isn't it? Pluto's going to be in for a nasty shock any minute now, I can tell you.'

'He's down there?'

'At this very minute,' said Apollo, with just a hint of less than charitable feeling, 'looking for Jason Derry. He's the Hero who's been subverted . . .'

Just then, Minerva came in. She was somewhat red in the face and not in the best of moods. This was understandable, since she'd just had to tell Jupiter about a certain dog.

'There you are,' she said. 'You are a pair of idiots, aren't you?'

Mars opened his mouth to protest but Minerva ignored him. 'Anyway,' she went on, 'here's your orders from the Boss. Pol, you get down to Earth and deal with Prometheus. Nail that eagle and get a replacement, right?'

'All right,' Apollo sighed.

'And you, Ma,' Minerva said, 'you'd better pop down and see that Pluto's all right. And deal with the Derry boy while you're at it. He's getting out of hand and . . .'

'You're joking,' Mars said. 'I was listening to the Commentary just now, and it said he's armed with the Sword of . . .'

'Don't be such a baby,' Minerva replied. 'You are supposed to be the Driver of the Spoil, Ma, or had you forgotten?'

'Driving the Spoil I can handle,' Mars said rebelliously.

'Driving the Spoil is what I'm good at. Getting snipped up into tagliatelli by muscular youths with magic swords doesn't feature in my job description. Sorry, but . . .'

'Mars.' Minerva looked at him sternly. 'You don't want me to tell Pa about your trip to Greenham Common, do you?'

Mars sagged like a tent with no pole. 'You wouldn't,' he said weakly.

'He wouldn't like it, would he?' she said. 'A son of his climbing over the wire and daubing *No Nukes Here* in green paint on the missile silos. I think you'd better do as you're told for once, don't you?'

Mars inflated his lungs to speak.

'Language,' said Minerva pre-emptively.

'Anyway,' said the ex-God of War, 'what does he mean by Deal With? You might at least tell me . . .'

'Jupiter thinks,' said Minerva with an iceberg smile, 'that the constellation of Cassiopeia looks a bit lop-sided. Could do with an extra star somewhere in the middle. See to it, will you?'

Minerva turned, adjusted her owl, and walked serenely out. Mars drew in a deep breath, sighed and jerked his head at the space Minerva had just occupied.

'Daddy's girl,' he said.

'So,' said Gelos, 'that's more or less it, I think. Is there anything you'd like to ask me?'

Jason leaned forward in his chair until his elbows touched his knees and struggled for breath. When he had got some semblance of control over his body back, he removed the handkerchief from his mouth and gasped greedily for air. He hadn't laughed so much since the time the Nine-Headed Serpent of the Sun had tried to bite him.

Not, it should be stated, that Gelos had been in any way outstandingly witty, amusing or novel; it was, as far as Jason could make out, all in the way he told them. Otherwise, why had he nearly had a cerebral haemorrhage when the old gentleman had asked him if he wanted a scone?

'No,' he croaked, 'thank you, I think I've got all that.'

'The thing to remember . . .' Gelos paused politely while Jason rolled on the floor kicking his legs helplessly and making little wheezing noises. 'The thing to remember is that . . . Look, are you feeling quite all right? Would you like a glass of water or something?'

'No,' Jason shrieked, 'I'm fine, really.' He dabbed ineffectually at the tears in his eyes and rose unsteadily to his knees. 'Please do go on . . . I'm sorry, I'm not usually like this . . . I . . .' He collapsed into a private hell of giggles. Cerberus gave him a look. Three looks.

'This really only goes to prove,' said the old man equably, 'what I was saying. There's nothing in the world stronger than laughter. If it can have this sort of effect on someone like you, a Hero, son of Jupiter himself, just think what it could do to the ordinary man in the street, if only he came into contact with a strong enough dose. I could take over the world and be the One True God with no trouble at all. But I wouldn't want that.'

He paused while Jason ironed out the spasmodic convulsions in his chest and dragged air into his lungs. Sometimes, the old man was thinking, I don't seem to know my own strength. 'Look,' he said, 'perhaps it would be better if I changed back into the other shape – you know, the threatening statue stuff. Would that help?'

Jason managed to find just enough strength to nod his head, and immediately the cosy little room vanished and

389

Jason found himself lying on nothing again, looking at a pair of talons.

'Better?'

'Much,' Jason said. 'Go on with what you were saying.'

'I can cut out the hissing snakes if you like.'

'No,' said Jason, 'that's fine. Just so long as you lay off the jokes, that's all.'

'I don't make jokes, actually,' said Gelos wistfully. 'In fact, sometimes I wonder what a sense of humour is like. I'm disqualified from having one, you see.'

Jason nodded weakly. The risk of internal combustion, he supposed. Nasty.

'I wouldn't want to rule the world exactly,' Gelos was saying, 'not the world the way it is, you see. It's too – well, completely and utterly and irrevocably fucked up for my liking. All I could do would be take people's minds off it all, and I suppose that's better than nothing. It's what I do now, more or less. But that wouldn't be right, would it?'

'Wouldn't it?'

'No,' Gelos said. 'You see, I'd be making people forget about all the horrible things in the world, and that would mean they'd never do anything about them. And then, of course, something terrible would happen – a plague or a disaster at a power station, that sort of thing – and everybody would be so busy laughing about it that they wouldn't get around to actually doing anything to put it right, and then where would we be? In fact,' he added, 'that's exactly the possibility curve that I've calculated. You know about possibility physics and all that, do you?'

'A bit,' Jason said. 'But let's not get bogged down in all that theory stuff. What you're saying is that you want the world set right before you take over.'

'More or less.'

'And in the meanwhile, you just want to stay where you are and not be bothered by anyone?'

'That's it, yes,' said Gelos. 'People think I came down here, where it doesn't actually exist – you know, not as *such* – to hide from old Jupiter. Not a bit of it.'

'Really?'

'Really. You see, I'm a bit like radiation. I leak. If I was anywhere else in the world but down here, where it isn't actually possible to be, then great excess doses of laughter would sort of seep up through the ground and get into everything, and that would cause absolute chaos. As it is, enough of the stuff gets out to keep the world ticking over more or less, but it never reaches a critical level. And I think that's how it should stay, for now.'

'I see,' said Jason, nodding. 'So where's the problem?'

'Jupiter,' said Gelos. 'And all those other idiots too, of course. They want to kidnap me. Now they don't scare me, not one bit; if they were to come down here and try throwing their weight about, I could make them laugh so much they'd bust their heavenly guts. The trouble is, I'd have to release so much laughter it'd be bound to get out into the Topside and mess things up for people. That's why it's essential that things are kept under control, do you see?'

'I think so,' Jason said. 'You need someone to keep the gods off your back for the time being.'

'That's it,' said Gelos, nodding. 'Really, it's a case of making sure they don't get to me. That would have been all right, except that they've been looking for me a lot lately – I think the Betamax world where I don't exist is reaching critical level – and it was only a matter of time before they did their calculations and found out I was here. That's why I got Prometheus to bring you here.'

Jason raised his eyebrows. 'What can I do?' he said.

391

'Diversion,' said Gelos. 'You can fight the gods for me.'

Jason stared. '*Me?*' he said. 'You must be kidding.'

'I'm deadly serious,' said Gelos, 'if that's not a contradiction in terms. I want them to think you've rescued me or abducted me, and you've somehow got hold of me and want to take over the universe. Then they attack you, and you give them a good hiding, and . . .'

'Excuse me,' said Jason, 'but is that certain? Likely even?'

'Absolute certainty,' said Gelos. 'You see, I shall give you a secret weapon.'

'Oh good,' said Jason. 'I was hoping you'd say that.'

'Well,' Gelos added, 'more sort of lend, really. I was thinking of lending you one of the Three Jokes.'

'Three Jokes?' Jason's face must have fallen slightly, as if he had been expecting something a bit more tangible, like a tank. Gelos smiled.

'Let me explain,' he said. 'As any comedian will tell you, there are only Three Jokes. All other jokes are minor variants on the Three, they have to be diluted right down before people can take them, otherwise – well, they'd be fatal.'

'That funny, huh?'

'Oh yes. Now the first Joke, the strongest of them all, is called the Great Primordial. If you were to tell the first Joke, you would make the sun laugh so much it would trip and fall onto the Earth, which would be so cracked up with laughing it would fall into the sea.'

Jason nodded. 'Would that be the one about the three Scotsmen and the reel of cotton?' he asked.

'No,' said Gelos, 'though I know the one you mean. That's actually one of the Lesser Arcana of the Triple-Bodied Zephyr, and if properly told it can crumple up sheet steel like paper. The Great Primordial is rather better.'

'Wow,' Jason said.

'The second Joke,' said Gelos, 'is called the Celestial Labarum and involves an Englishman, a Pole, and a Goth. You've heard of the eruption of Krakatoa?'

'Yes.'

'My fault,' confessed Gelos. 'I have this habit of talking in my sleep sometimes, and one night the punch line – just the punch line, you understand – must just have slipped out. By the time it got out past all this nothingness and found its way through the magma layer to the South Seas there wasn't much left of it, I can tell you, but . . .'

Jason shuddered. 'Hot stuff, eh?'

'You could say that,' said Gelos. 'The third Joke,' he went on, 'is the weakest of the three. It's known as the Mighty Cloud Spirit Joke, and it's more of an anti-personnel joke, really. Knocks out people, leaves buildings standing, that sort of thing. And that's the one I'm going to lend you.'

'Um . . .'

'I know what you're going to say,' said Gelos. 'Too risky, you were going to say. You're quite right. That's why we needed the dog.'

Jason looked blank. 'The dog?'

'Quite so,' said Gelos. 'You see, what I propose to do is tell half the joke to you, and then send you out of the room. I shall then put two of the dog's brains to sleep while I tell one-sixth of the Joke to the remaining brain. And so on, until each of the dog's brains knows one sixth, and you know all the rest. It's a sort of failsafe system, really.'

'Well . . .'

'I know,' said Gelos, 'it's still a hell of a lot to ask, but I wouldn't take the risk unless I thought it was absolutely necessary. Trust me.'

'All right,' said Jason.

'Thanks,' said Gelos. 'You remind me a lot of me when I was younger,' he added.

Jason blinked. 'I do?' he said.

'Not surprising, really,' said Gelos, smiling. 'We are related, after all.'

'Are we?'

'Oh yes,' Gelos said. 'You see, although I am Gelos, spirit of Laughter, I wasn't always what I am now. Before I was Gelos, I was . . . well, never mind that. Here, doggie.'

Cerberus jumped forward, wagging his tail. Gelos made a slight gesture with his right hand and the dog was suddenly fast asleep.

'I put a long joke in his minds,' Gelos explained. 'Good as an anaesthetic, I always find.'

'A long joke?'

'Shaggy dog story, I think they're called. Now, are you ready to receive your half of the Joke?'

Jason nodded and braced himself. Although he was very frightened and not a little confused, he knew that the three dots in his mind had become words now, and the sentence was complete at last.

'Right,' said Gelos. 'There was this guy who went into this bar . . .'

CHAPTER NINE

Pluto reached out. Eventually, to his initial relief, his hand connected with something. It was wet.

'Yuk,' Pluto said, and reached for his handkerchief.

After a further period of exploration, however, he arrived at the conclusion that beggars can't be choosers, and set out to follow the series of damp, smelly patches on the walls of Nothingness to their eventual conclusion. If the dog came this way, he reasoned, Derry can't be far behind.

He had been feeling his way in this manner for perhaps ten minutes when he felt something that wasn't wet and smelly. If anything, it was rather worse.

'Don't mind my asking,' said a voice, 'but why are you holding on to my ankle?'

Pluto considered the cold, scaly surface he had just made contact with and shuddered. 'Beg pardon?' he said.

'My ankle,' said the voice. 'You appear to be holding on to it. Why?'

'Because it's there?' Pluto suggested. 'Whoever you are, might I trouble you for some light, by any chance?'

'Light,' the voice said thoughtfully. 'I may be able to manage that. Just bear with me for a moment, will you?'

A moment later there was indeed light.

'You've just missed him,' said the voice.

Pluto blinked. The same could not be said for the piercing eyes of the colossal obsidian statue, which seemed to be trying to see through the back of Pluto's head.

'Have I?' Pluto asked.

'I imagine so,' said the statue. 'He went that way.'

'Did he have a dog with him?'

Gelos made a show of thinking about this, and then replied, 'I believe he did, yes. And a man, too.'

Pluto drew his brows together in a frown. 'Did he indeed?' he mused. 'What sort of a . . .'

'Ah,' said Gelos, 'there you have me. Let's see.'

'Late middle-aged,' Pluto suggested, 'friendly looking, big smile, probably in dressing gown and slippers.'

'Now you come to mention it,' Gelos said, 'I think you could be right.'

'Thanks,' said Pluto. 'Er, how about the light? Do you think you could fix it to stay on for a bit, only I get a bit jumpy in the dark. You know how it is.'

The statue nodded its head. 'I'll do my best,' he said.

Pluto turned to go and then looked back. 'We've met before, haven't we?'

'No,' Gelos lied, 'I don't think so.'

'Ah well,' Pluto said, 'I've got a rotten memory for faces. Occupational hazard, I suppose. Thanks anyway.'

'My pleasure,' said Gelos. 'Go carefully, now.'

Pluto waved and soon was lost to sight among the shadows. For his part, Gelos sighed and shook his head. Of his three nephews, he considered, Pluto was probably (though only by a short head) the dimmest. He reflected for a moment on the fact that these same three nephews, idiots all, had castrated his brother Cronus, imprisoned his sister

396

Rhea and made him, Thing, the greatest of the three, hide out at the end of a sleazy underground railway line for most of the history of Creation. Fool's luck, he said to himself; or something like that.

There is an old accountant's proverb that it's no good the meek inheriting the earth if they end up having to pay tax on it at 40p in the pound. For his part, Thing (as Gelos should properly be called) didn't really mind being cheated of his inheritance just so long as none of the other members of his family got their grubby paws on it. Having reassumed his true shape, therefore, he reached out his mind into the World and made contact with his oldest and best ally, presently suspended from a number of mountaintops in the Caucasus.

'Pro?'

'Is that you, Gel?'

'How are things your end?'

A flicker of a shadow passed across Prometheus's thought-waves. 'I don't know,' Prometheus replied. 'I have a feeling something's going to happen.'

'You're right. Apollo is coming to get you.'

'I know *that*,' Prometheus thought back. 'The eagle told me. I've told it to lie low for a bit. Any suggestions?'

'None that spring immediately to mind, Pro. I'd send you the boy, but I need him here. Mars is on his way, and Pluto's just come through. I need the dog, too. Sorry.'

'That's fine. I'll think of something.'

'Look, Pro, if things get out of hand, call me, will you? I might be able to help out, you never know.'

'What was that? It's a very bad line.'

'I said I might be able to help,' Thing replied.

'Don't worry about me,' Prometheus assured him. 'But send the boy when you can spare him, I'll stall them till then, all right?'

'That's the spirit.'

Thing let the mental link subside and made himself a cup of Ovaltine; but his mind still moved on his comrade's dilemma. It was a pity he couldn't send the boy.

Of course, he said to himself, I could always send the next best thing.

At the very end of the corridor there was a door.

Like most doors in the Underground it had a very silly notice above it. It said *No Exit*.

Extremely silly. After all. if you couldn't go out of it, what was the point in it being there? Jason shrugged and tried the handle. It was locked.

'What do you think, dog?' Jason asked. It was a rhetorical question really, as he knew that the reply would be Woof, but asking gave him time to weigh up the pros and cons of the move he had in mind.

'Woof.'

'That's settled, then,' Jason said happily. 'What *is* the point, after all?'

He lifted his leg and gave the door an almighty kick. A door is just a door. It flew open, and a moment later Jason realised that the notice hadn't been so silly after all.

'Jason Derry.'

For someone who had led an adventurous life, frequently paddling in the backwaters of the paranormal and semi-divine, Jason hadn't quite managed to develop the proper attitude to apparitions. Contrast his reaction to Gelos in his statue persona, for example, with Pluto's, recounted above. Pluto, you noticed, just took a colossal talking statue in his stride. Pluto, after all, knows that something that looks like that can only be something else dressed up, since colossal talking statues are not, of course, possible.

'Er,' was all that Jason could find to say. Curiously enough, the apparition somehow managed to find it intimidating, because it crouched further down behind its shield and trembled slightly.

'Don't count on it, mortal,' said the apparition.

Jason took another look at the monstrous figure in front of him. Was it possible that this apparently divine and heavily armoured person was afraid of him?

'Don't count on what?' he asked.

'Look,' replied the apparition, 'I'm only doing my job, okay? I didn't ask to be sent. I just got volunteered.'

Time, Jason thought, to do a little essential spadework. 'Who are you?' he asked.

'Mars.'

'Pardon?'

'Mars.'

Jason didn't relax, but the quality of his tension improved. 'Really?' he said.

'It's not the sort of thing you'd lie about,' replied the ex-God of War. 'But if you don't believe me, I've got one of those little cards with my photograph on it. Hang on.'

The Widow-Maker leaned his spear against the doorframe, slipped off his shield and rummaged around in the inside pocket of his breastplate until he found a creased plastic folder. He opened it and Jason's eyes grew round.

'Wow,' he said.

'You what?'

'I mean,' Jason said, 'I've heard so much about you.'

Mars was so surprised he dropped his spear, which fell with a clang on the ground. At once Jason leaned forward and picked it up for him.

'Are you trying to say,' Mars asked, 'that you're actually pleased to meet me?'

'Of course,' Jason said. 'Hell, when I was at school I had posters of you all round the walls of my bedroom.'

'I . . .'

'You were my favourite,' Jason went on enthusiastically. 'I read all about you in the mythology books. I even had a tee-shirt printed with . . .'

Mars dropped the spear again. 'You're sure you're not thinking of someone else?' he asked. Jason shook his head, then blushed and produced a scrap of paper from his pocket.

'I wonder,' he said. 'I know this must be really boring for you, but could you just write . . . I don't know, *Best Wishes from Mars*, something like that. It's not for me, it's for my . . .'

'You do know,' Mars said, 'why I'm here?'

'Well, no,' Jason said. 'Is there anything I can help you with?' he added hopefully.

Mars swallowed hard. 'In a manner of speaking,' he said, 'yes.'

'What?'

Mars closed his eyes. Was this, he asked himself, yet another manifestation of his usual filthy luck? The boy's eyes were shining at him with the golden light of hero-worship; for the first time ever, he told himself, somebody is actually glad to see me. Oh nuts . . .

'You see,' Mars said, as gently as he could, 'I've been sent . . .'

'Yes?'

'I've been sent by Jupiter . . .'

'Yes? How is Dad, by the way?'

'. . . to kill you,' Mars grinned feebly. 'As it were.'

Physiognomists would have you believe that it is impossible for the human face to have no expression whatsoever; and if that is the case, then Jason was more divine than human. Mars bit his lip.

'When I say kill,' he went on, 'it's not as bad as it sounds. More translate you to the stars. Immortality. Apotheosis. Haven't you ever wanted to be a star?'

Jason said nothing.

'And,' Mars continued hopelessly, 'the apotheosis framework is designed for maximum flexibility, to cater for a wide range of individual aspirations. Red dwarf, blue giant, supernova, you name it. Just so long as you're not . . . well, alive, really.'

Jason said nothing.

'They tell me,' Mars whimpered, 'that it doesn't hurt a bit. It's not really death, you see, though of course death does come into it, peripherally. But really it's more a sort of *ouch*!'

Jason woke suddenly from his reverie and kicked the dog savagely on the rump.

'Cerberus!' he shouted, 'let go!'

Two of the dog's heads obeyed; the third needed a clip round the ears to convince it. Mars rubbed his ankle and then looked up.

'Thanks,' he muttered wretchedly.

'*Bad* dog,' said Jason. 'Mars, I'm so sorry, this bloody dog . . .'

'Look,' Mars said, 'don't worry about it, right? I mean, if someone should be apologising, it ought to be me. Except,' he added without conviction, 'really, it's more of a career move than anything else. And you don't actually have any choice, of course.'

'Sorry?'

'So am I,' Mars sighed, 'believe me. But when the Big J says that's the way it's got to be, then that's the way it's got to be. And . . .'

Jason looked at him. 'No,' he said.

'Sorry,' said Mars, 'but I'm afraid . . .'

'No,' Jason said again. 'Just because Dad says something doesn't mean anything of the sort. I thought *you* would have realised that.'

Oh, for crying out loud, Mars thought. 'Listen, son,' he said. 'I wish it didn't have to be like this . . .'

'It doesn't.'

'Yes it does.'

'No it doesn't.'

'Yes it does.'

'No it doesn't.'

In the very back end of his mind, Mars's memory nudged his consciousness and reminded him that in the old days, when he used to be the God of War, he didn't have to take this sort of shit from anybody, let alone a snot-nosed kid who thought the Widow-Maker was a more suitable candidate for a role model than, say, Mother Teresa. Enough of this, it said.

'Now you listen to me,' Mars said. 'I'm saying it does, and I'm the one who *ouch*!'

About ten seconds later, Jason helped Mars up again, handed him his spear, bent the chin-guard of his helmet back into shape, dusted off his cloak for him and apologised.

'Now get lost,' he added.

Mars, his divine head still swimming, tried one last protest. 'Look,' he started to say.

'. . . or I'll have to hit you again.'

'Right,' said Mars. 'Nice to have met you. Classy left hook you've got there, if you don't mind me saying so.'

Jason's face lit up. 'You really think so?'

Mars humped his throbbing jaw into a grin. 'You bet,' he said.

★

By a strange coincidence that would have had the Possibility Police round in ten minutes flat with a forged warrant had they known about it, Mrs. Derry was at that very moment removing Jason's Mars posters from the walls of his bedroom.

Part of being a mother is realising that one of these days, the fledgling is going to leave the nest for good. The sensible mother realises that this is perfectly natural, and also a heaven sent opportunity to give parts of the nest their first thorough cleaning for eighteen years.

She was just wiping away a tear while trying to scrape off a chunk of petrified Blue-Tack with the handle of a spoon when the doorbell rang. She muttered something, climbed down off the chair and went to see who it was.

'Hello, Phyllis.'

Mrs. Derry gave Jupiter that particular look that only female mortals can manage. It is a masterpiece of non-verbal communication, and says (*inter alia*) that you are not welcome to come into my house because of what has happened between us in the past, because you never even sent flowers or a postcard, and most of all because the kitchen floor hasn't been cleaned for a week. It is to Jupiter's credit that he managed to field it without falling over; but the gods, as Homer reminds us, are stronger by far than bread-eating mortals.

'It's about Jason,' Jupiter said. 'Can I come in?'

Mrs. Derry hesitated, even then. Because of Jupiter, her married life had been a cross between a Feydeau farce and one of Landseer's more exuberant productions; there was also the matter of the unwashed breakfast things. But in the end she nodded, and Jupiter walked past her into the house. As he did so, small clumps of incredibly sweet-smelling flowers sprang up where his divine feet left their print in the soft pile of the carpet. This is a common manifestation of a divine presence and Mrs. Derry could hardly fail to notice it.

'Oh for heaven's sake!' she said. 'Wait there.'

She darted off and returned with a bundle of old newspapers, which she arranged by way of a footpath leading from the hallway to the lounge. Having placed the final page on the seat of the sofa, she sniffed, sat down in the armchair, and folded her arms disapprovingly.

'Well?' she said.

'Yetch,' said Pluto, in fact. He had been reduced to drying his hands on his handkerchief, an operation which always made him feel seedy. Having put the now damp hanky away, he looked in the mirror, adjusted his tie and set out once again to find Jason Derry.

This time, he was successful, probably because Jason was now looking for him.

'Hold it right there!' said the son of Jupiter, 'or you'll taste the edge of my sword. You got that?'

Pluto turned round slowly and drew himself up to his full height.

'I'll trouble you,' he said, 'not to take that tone with me. After all, I am your uncle, so let's have a little respect, if you please.'

Jason's brows knotted. 'Respect?' he queried.

'Respect. And for pity's sake put that sword down, before you break something.'

Without quite knowing why, Jason did as he was told. Pluto nodded severely.

'That's better,' he said. 'And take your hands out of your pockets.'

The explanation is, of course, simple for non-Heroes to

grasp. Having throughout his career been confronted with a succession of opponents who were bigger, stronger, faster, nastier or better equipped with limbs than he was, Jason had never developed the necessary techniques for dealing with people who were smaller, weaker or better mannered than himself. He had killed dragons, but he'd never had to jump a queue of pensioners in a post office.

'You *are* Pluto,' he asked.

'Certainly,' said the god stiffly. 'And I presume you're the Derry boy.'

'Well, yes.'

Pluto gave him a look, and Jason suddenly became painfully aware that his fingernails weren't as clean as they might be.

'In that case,' Pluto continued, 'I really must insist that you return my dog and stop making a nuisance of yourself.'

Jason shifted guiltily. 'Have I been?' he mumbled.

'Indeed you have,' said Pluto. 'Wandering off, encouraging the dissidents, disturbing the guests, not to mention being extremely rude to a god you haven't even been introduced to. You ought to be thoroughly ashamed of yourself.'

Suddenly and for the first time, Jason was; and it was a distinctly unpleasant feeling. Not only do Heroes not know the meaning of fear, they are also generally immune to embarrassment; otherwise, they simply couldn't do their job. You can't be expected to rush in where angels fear to tread if the opposition can make you feel six inches tall simply by reminding you to wipe your feet.

'The dog, please,' Pluto demanded. Cerberus looked up at Jason with six worried eyes, which Jason couldn't meet. Instead he made a vague Good-Dog-Go-To-Master movement with his head and then looked away.

The dog bit him.

Jason's first reaction was to retaliate. Although somewhat unfashionable these days, retaliation is a tried and tested human reaction to threatening and inconvenient events; and deep down, Jason Derry was a traditionalist. He had therefore raised his foot to give the dog a kick that would have propelled it back topside when it occurred to him that the dog might be trying to tell him something. Not that there aren't more civilised means of data communication these days than a full set of teeth in the calf of the leg; but when the audience is likely to be unresponsive, subtlety is likely to be counter-productive. Jason lowered his boot, confused.

'I said,' said Pluto, 'give me the dog.'

'No,' said Jason. (What he actually said was 'No . . .', but the three dots were silent, like the W in 'shipwright'.)

'I beg your pardon?'

'No,' Jason repeated. 'I don't think he wants to go with you.'

Pluto frowned magisterially. 'That's hardly the point,' he said. 'Now, if you don't mind, my time is not without value.'

This remark had an effect on Jason. 'Mine too,' he said. 'Push off.'

'How dare you speak . . .?'

Jason grinned. For the first time in his life, he was beginning to wonder whether there might not be just as much fun in beating up small, weak, defenceless people as in beating up mighty demons. Probably not, but he would never know if he didn't try. 'I said push off,' he growled. The dog nodded his heads, wagged his tail and even managed to scratch one of his ears at the same time. Dogs have powers of balance that defy orthodox scientific explanation.

Pluto, for his part, remembered that he was a god, and

a high-rolling, time-served god at that. He drew himself up to his false height* and folded his arms grimly.

'Impudent mortal . . .' he began to say. Then he became aware of an agonising pain in his left big toe, and looked down.

'Ouch!' he said, and hopped up into the air. Jason pulled the sword clear of the deep incision he had just made, and laughed unkindly. A drop of ichor – god's blood – sparkled on the blade.

'Now clear off out of it,' he said, 'or else you'll get this up your . . .'

Pluto, now withdrawn to a relatively safe distance, scowled horribly and called on the Legions of the Damned to assist him. There are perks to being a god, and instant access to a large number of semi-divine heavies is one of them. 'Arrest that mortal!' Pluto cried melodramatically. From the shadows behind him, about ten or twelve muscular, well-armed figures stepped forward and advanced towards Jason, truncheons out.

At the risk of spoiling the impact of what follows and interrupting the narrative curve, a word of explanation would seem called for. Although at one time service in the divine cohorts was regarded as a supreme honour, ever since the evacuation of Olympus the gods have found themselves with a serious recruiting problem on their hands. The sad fact is that the pay is so much better in the private sector, and the prestige of being an instrument of divine justice comes a poor second to flexible working hours, a company chariot and a free uniform, usually with a dragon logo on it. As a result, the gods have lately taken

*About fifteen feet six inches. Pluto's main fear was that one day he'd stick like it.

407

to recruiting from those inhabitants of Betamax 76249708 who have inadvertently sailed off the edge of the world in the course of an ill-fated attempt to find a shorter searoute from Leningrad to Kiev. This has resulted in an overall lowering of staff quality. In fact it is rumoured that the entire divine army could only extract itself from the proverbial paper bag with the aid of massed air support and covering fire from offshore naval batteries.

There was a blur, and not long afterwards a contingent of celestial men-at-arms picked themselves painfully off the ground, gathered up their severed limbs and limped away in search of something to stick them back on with.

Jason lowered his sword. 'Push off,' he said.

'You won't get away with this,' Pluto muttered. 'The mills of the gods grind slow but they grind exceeding small.'

'And cracked pitchers,' said Jason, 'have big ears. Hop it.'

Pluto is unusual among the gods in that he knows when he's beaten. But he had one last weapon in his armoury; and although he usually despised it as mere shallow mummery, there was nothing to be lost by using it. He shouted an arcane word, made a magic pass and snapped his fingers. At once he vanished, and was replaced by an apparition that Jason didn't manage to forget for a long time. Pluto changed himself into a skeleton.

No ordinary skeleton, at that, but a grotesquely large gaudily decorated and extremely animated skeleton. The general effect was designed to convey an impression of extreme and irreversible death, coupled with an urgent desire to impose a similar condition on anything in the near vicinity, and it worked. There wasn't the smallest scrap of flesh anywhere to be seen, and the bones looked like malevolent ivory; ivory that has never really got over being separated from a perfectly good, comfortable elephant. As for the eyes, you could have defrosted pizzas with them.

Jason, as has already been more than adequately recorded, didn't know the meaning of fear; but it is arguable that you don't need to know precisely what the word *Fischhändler* on a street sign means if directly under it you can see a shop with a slabful of dead cod in the window. He winced with his whole body and covered his eyes.

Not so the dog. He took one look at the biggest collection of jumbo-sized, yummy-looking bones ever gathered in one place, uttered a threefold yelp of pure pleasure, and broke for lunch.

In the newly-restored quiet of his study, Gelos was communicating with Prometheus. As usual, it wasn't easy – the thoughtwaves are horribly congested these days, and if you aren't careful you can end up getting a stray fax right between the ears – but despite interruptions they were in the middle of a highly serious discussion.

'And what about the boy?' thought Gelos.

'Don't worry about it,' replied Prometheus. 'It'll be the old, old story; boy meets eagle, boy loses eagle, boy finally gets eagle . . .'

'Supposing he isn't interested?' Gelos objected. 'I mean, he may think there's more to life and being a Hero than just . . .'

'Pulling a bird?'

'Well . . .'

'Leave that to me,' thought Prometheus. 'Back to business. Has he got rid of those two clowns for you?'

Gelos laughed, something he tried not to do if he could help it. 'Yes indeed,' he thought. 'Young Jason has learned quite a lot today, I fancy. About life, and disappointment, and coming to terms with the way things really are; and, of course, that when all is said and done the only really effective way to deal with people is to hit them. Oh yes, he's coming along nicely, for a youngster.'

'Actually,' thought Prometheus, 'I didn't want to worry you with this, but Eagle says that a Certain Person has been to see a Certain Person, and . . .'

Gelos frowned. Telepathy is hard enough to understand as it is without archness as well. 'What?'

'J-U-P-I-T-E-R,' Prometheus spelt out in a mental whisper, 'has gone to see P-H-Y-L-L . . .'

'All right, I think I see what you're getting at. Problems?'

'Possibly,' Prometheus replied. 'You see, we've been concentrating so much on the fact that Jupit . . . that You Know Who is the boy's father that we may have neglected the other side of the equation.'

'You think so?' queried Gelos. 'I'm sure she's a very nice lady, but . . .'

'All I'm saying is,' thought Prometheus, 'oh hell, someone's coming. I'd better think you back later. Ciao.'

A long shadow fell across Prometheus's face and a voice spoke somewhere above him.

'Traitor,' said the voice.

Prometheus twisted his neck round until he could see a pair of golden sandals with a PA monogram on them, which he knew stood for Phoebus Apollo. They were the relic of an ill-fated sponsorship deal between a major multi-national sportswear company and the most photogenic of the male Olympians – ill-fated because Jupiter doesn't hold with his family appearing in full-page colour on the backs of the Sunday supplements and took his wrath out on the company in question by turning them all into lizards.

'Hello, Pol,' Prometheus replied. 'I'd offer you a drink or something but I'm a bit tied up at the moment. Could you call back later?'

'Traitor,' Apollo repeated; not from any great depth of feeling in the matter but because he was embarrassed and couldn't think of anything else to say. Strictly unofficially, and then only outside the range of Jupiter's mental radar net, he had always considered the treatment meted out to Prometheus to be not only unjust but injudicious. The Titan, unlike the rest of the gods, was clever – wise, even – and it was surely only a matter of time before he pulled a stroke that would deal the divine prestige of the Olympians such a blow that thereafter they would be hard put to it getting work doing conjuring tricks for children's parties.

'You think so?' enquired Prometheus, mildly.

'Yes.'

'Oh.' The Titan shrugged. 'I'm sorry about that, Pol. One does what one thinks is right, you know.'

'I don't.'

'Sorry,' said Prometheus, 'I forgot. You're a god; you don't have to worry about that sort of thing.'

'Are you implying . . .?'

Prometheus chuckled. 'I never imply,' he said. 'Not any more. I occasionally implied a bit when I was younger, but at my age it takes me all my time to insinuate, let alone imply. Usually I just say things.'

'Are you saying . . .?'

'I'm saying,' said Prometheus, 'that since you're a god and effectively beyond any form of retribution, you can do what you damn well like. Absolute power; is that right?'

411

Apollo tried to look stern. 'Correct,' he said, and his eyes sparkled with pale blue fire. 'Absolute power.'

'Then how come,' said Prometheus quietly, 'you can't afford a new chariot?'

This took Apollo by surprise, as if he had sliced into a hard-boiled egg to find a baby chicken sitting in there looking at him. 'What?' he said.

'You heard me,' Prometheus replied. 'I could hear the wheel-bearings squeaking from here. Also, from the sound of it, your suspension is completely shot, your axle is about as straight as a bent corkscrew, there's enough body putty in your wings to fill in the Cheddar Gorge and if your offside front shaft makes it through another five thousand miles you have my permission to use my head as a basketball. So?'

'Well,' said Apollo, weakly, 'You can't get the parts these days.'

'So why not get a new one?' Prometheus answered. 'They tell me Vulcan does a very nice little two-seater, four-winged horsepower, ABS brakes, adjustable scythes on the wheels as standard, four thousand gold staters plus interest free credit.'

Apollo frowned. 'Where am I likely to get that sort of money?' he said. 'With no worshippers and no sacrifices?'

Prometheus made a mighty effort and nodded his head. 'Exactly,' he said. 'And whenever you try any little sideline, just for a bit of pin-money, the Old Fool puts a stop to it. You'll notice, by the way, that he never drives the same chariot two years running; and how many temples has he still got? Or Minerva? The last recorded sacrifice to Minerva took place in AD 512, but she isn't driving round in a Gamma reg Vulcan Popular with knackered brake-linings.'

412

'Look . . .'

'Or Venus,' Prometheus went on pitilessly. 'What's it she's got now? Vulcan XR7 GTS with front-dove drive, isn't it? Or Neptune, with that big new Valhalla Donnerschlag – *Vorsprung durch Zauber* and all that. Trust Nep to be the one to have a flash foreign chariot. Or Mercury – zippy little Vulcan Elite Turbo with a sticker saying *My Other Chariot's a Vulcan 696* on the rear sun-guard. Or Diana . . .'

'All right,' said Apollo, 'you've made your point.'

'Maybe,' said Prometheus, 'and obviously you really don't care about such demeaning things as status. I'm impressed, honestly. If I was in your position and had to suffer the indignity of being burnt off at traffic lights by part-time river-gods in souped-up Vulcan Firebirds . . .'

'All *right,'* said Apollo. 'Look . . .'

'. . . with furry dice hanging from their rear mirrors . . .'

'*Look* . . .'

'Yes?'

'I . . .' Apollo had forgotten what he was going to say. He scowled ferociously and scratched the back of his neck.

'All I was trying to suggest,' Prometheus went on, 'is that you must be in it for the job satisfaction, not the material rewards. I'm right, aren't I?'

'Well . . .'

'I can understand that,' said Prometheus. 'You're a god's god, Pol, if you don't mind my saying so. Or you were, at any rate, before Jupiter decided to pack it all in and retire. Nice, is it, up there in the sun?'

'Very.'

'Playing the Game all day, so I hear. That must be very . . .' The Titan paused, as if mulling over his choice of word '. . . fulfilling, mustn't it?'

'Well . . .'

'Admittedly,' said Prometheus, 'there's not as much averting plagues and redressing wrongs as there used to be, but at
least you can lie in of a morning. Now you couldn't do *that*
when you were driving the chariot of the sun, could you?'

'I . . .'

'That must have been fun, I bet,' Prometheus said with
a chuckle. 'Out of interest, what could the old bus do? On
the flat, with the wind behind it?'

'Oh, a million and five, million and ten,' Apollo said
dreamily. 'Nought to two hundred and fifty thousand in
four point seven two, I once got out of her.' He stopped
and made an impatient noise. '*Look* . . .' he said angrily.

'Whereas now,' Prometheus murmured, 'there isn't
really any reason to get out of bed at all, is there? You
could sleep in all day and nobody would either know or
care. Still, if that's what you want out of everlasting
life . . .'

'Prometheus . . .'

'But I was forgetting,' said the Titan. 'You may not get
to drive the sun or answer the prayers of cities, but you do
get to run little errands for the Big J. And Minerva, of
course; I expect she keeps you pretty busy, doesn't she?'

'It's . . .'

'Odd that,' Prometheus mused, 'the way she bosses you
about, when strictly speaking . . . But that's none of my
business. Forgive me, please; I don't get many people to
talk to these days, except the eagle. You've met the eagle,
haven't you? Nice girl – it's a she, you know. In fact, more
she than eagle.'

Apollo couldn't help asking what Prometheus meant by
that, exactly.

'Didn't you know?' replied the Titan. 'I thought they'd

have told you – how strange. No, Eagle isn't really an eagle at all.'

'Isn't it?'

'She,' Prometheus corrected him. 'She's actually a wood-nymph, name of Charionessa. Nice name, don't you think? Jupiter turned her into an eagle as a punishment.'

'What for?'

'Unfriendliness,' Prometheus replied. 'Jupiter likes his wood-nymphs friendly, you see. Unlike Juno; she likes Jupiter's wood-nymphs decidedly hostile. In fact,' Prometheus went on blandly, 'that's why there are so few of them about these days, what with Jupiter turning them into things if they *don't* and Juno turning them into things if they do. Still, it's not for me to pass comments on the morals of my betters. Now, what's the little errand they've sent you on this time?'

Apollo struggled for some words and found a phrase that Minerva had supplied him with. 'I've been sent,' he said, 'to punish a traitor.'

'Really?'

'Yes.'

'Anyone I know?'

'Yes.'

'Are you going to tell me,' said Prometheus, 'or is it a secret?'

Apollo ground his teeth wretchedly. 'I think you can guess,' he said.

'Not me,' Prometheus replied. 'Always was hopeless at guessing. Do you remember all those games of Twenty Questions we used to play when you were a boy?'

Apollo remembered very well; he had had the misfortune to be a plump, querulous child with a tendency to burst into tears when rebuked, and the Titan was the only grown-up who could ever be bothered with him. 'No,' he said.

'Don't you? Ah well,' said Prometheus, 'never mind. Like they say, just because you're omniscient doesn't mean you don't forget the occasional birthday.'

Apollo suddenly recollected that today was Prometheus's birthday; his five-million-and-fifth. Now gods are very sensitive about such things, and the phenomenon that mortals know as the Milky Way is in fact the reflection in the Space-Time continuum of the seven million candles on Jupiter's birthday cake. It was therefore not unnatural that Apollo's somewhat soft heart should have been affected by this, particularly when he noticed, out of the corner of his all-seeing eye, a milk bottle with a single dandelion in it standing on an adjacent rock, and next to it a piece of plain card with *Hapy Birthday Pormeethius From Eegle* scrawled on it in crayon. In fact, a tiny tear lurched out of the corner of one sky-blue eye, until the heat of His gaze evaporated it into a tiny saline deposit.

'All right,' said Apollo with a badly muffled sob, 'if you must know, I've been sent to punish you.'

'Oh yes?' said Prometheus mildly. 'Why's that?'

'For subverting Heroes,' Apollo snuffled.

'Subverting Heroes,' Prometheus repeated. 'I see. And what are you going to do to me?'

'First,' Apollo sobbed, 'I'm supposed to flay you alive with a lash made of vipers; then I've got to hang you by your ankles from the Firmament and have vultures gnaw at your . . . Oh, Uncle Pro, I'm so unhappy!'

Apollo sank to his knees and subsided into a small, whimpering heap. Just like when he was a boy, Prometheus reflected, and Minerva and Diana used to take his golden bow away from him and put comets down his back. For a moment, he felt ashamed of taking advantage of the boy's kind heart (it was hard to think of Little Pol as anything but a boy); then he thought of the vultures and hardened his mind. It's a nasty world, he told himself; god eat god is the rule, and the one thing a superhuman being can't afford to have is humanity.

'It's all right,' said the Titan softly. 'Now then, what's the matter with you?'

Jupiter paused for a moment, searching for the right word, and looked out of the window.

'It's not as if,' he said, 'he's done anything wrong . . .'

'But you just said . . .'

'Well,' Jupiter replied, 'that's not quite true. He's been very naughty. Conspiring with prohibited persons. Duffing up gods. Can't be allowed to do that sort of thing. But nothing *serious*; nothing we can't deal with . . .' Jupiter's words tailed off and he squinted at something sticking up out of the ground between the rose bushes and the Arum lily. 'Excuse my asking,' he enquired, 'but is that the skeleton of a tyrannosaurus I can see out there?'

'Where?'

'There.'

Mrs. Derry looked closely. 'Oh that,' she said. 'Yes.'

'Where did he get that from?'

'I don't know,' said Mrs. Derry. 'I don't want to know, either. Hopefully, he's given up doing that.'

'Has he?'

'Well,' replied the Hero's mother, 'last month there were a couple of Rottweilers and a big sort of lizard thing, but apart from that there hasn't been anything since the mammoth. Just as well, if you ask me; it's a small garden and it was getting so bad we were having to double-bank them in places. And it only takes a shower of rain or something like that . . .'

'Yes,' said Jupiter, shuddering, 'yes, quite. Well, as I was saying, I really don't want to have to come the heavy father with the lad. It's really not my style at all. So if you could see your way to having a word with him . . .'

'I'll try,' said Mrs. Derry doubtfully. 'But you know what they're like at that age.'

'Not Jason,' said Jupiter. 'And I always knew that if you told him not to do it, then he'd stop. You know he always listens to you.'

'Well . . .'

Jupiter managed to restrain his grin of triumph. 'Just tell him,' he said, 'that you've heard he's been getting into trouble and how worried you've been and ask him to stop it; that'll do the trick, I promise you. He looks up to you, you know.'

'Well,' said Mrs. Derry again. 'If you think it's for the best . . .'

'Stands to reason, doesn't it?' Jupiter said. 'Not that I'd ever willingly let him come to any harm, you understand, but even I can't be in more than four places at once, and these people he's been seeing – Prometheus and Gelos and that crowd – really, they're no good. I mean that. Sooner or later they'll get him into real trouble, and it may well be that I won't be able to do anything for him. It's for his own good,' Jupiter added, recalling the phrase from the back of his mind. 'You'll see.'

'All right, then,' Mrs. Derry said. 'I'll see what I can do.'

Jupiter smiled. 'That's splendid, then,' he said. 'Right, well, it's been great seeing you again, Phyl, but it's time I wasn't here. Give my regards to . . . er, you know, your husband.'

'Douglas.'

'Quite so, yes, Douglas. How are things in the – what is it he does?'

'He repairs television sets.'

'Does he *really*? How very clever of him. Not that I watch much television myself, actually, but . . . well, do give him my regards, anyway.'

'I will.'

Jupiter's smile became slightly more glassy, if anything. 'And you take care of yourself too, of course. How's the back?'

'Painful.'

'Still? I *am* sorry. I must remember to get Aesculapius to fix you something for it.'

Mrs. Derry's eyes said *You promised me that the last time*, but she said nothing. She had a thin, crimped look on her face, and Jupiter felt very strongly that he wanted to go now. He went.

Halfway down the street, on his way to his rendezvous with his driver, he met a policeman on his beat. Being omniscient, he knew that the officer's name was Sergeant Smith and that he had acquired a wholly unjustified reputation for seeing things. Being possessed of a rather anti-social sense of humour, he transformed himself into a twelve-foot-high djinn with ten arms and three heads, stepped deliberately into the policeman's path, raised his three hats, nodded affably, and vanished in a cloud of opalescent light.

Jason stepped back, whipped the Sword of Glycerion from its scabbard, shouted his battle cry, and sprang forward.

The Hoplites of Hell grinned at him, clashed their swords on their shields, and advanced to meet him. There was a crunch, like a huge crab being run over by a lorry, and a number of thin screams.

'Next!' Jason demanded.

The Hell-Captain looked at his twelve decapitated warriors, shrugged disinterestedly, and felt in the pouch that hung from his belt. It contained dragon's teeth which, when scattered on the ground, turned into hideous and well-armed warriors. Warriors with no mercy. Warriors who knew no fear. Warriors who were insensible to pain. Warriors who didn't need to be paid. The Hell-Captain broadcast a handful of teeth, stepped back, and folded his arms.

Perhaps because he was getting a little bit tired, and this time there had been fifteen of them rather than twelve, it took Jason all of twenty seconds to reduce this contingent of draconian by-products to rubble. On the other hand, one of them had contrived, in his deaththroes, to tread on Jason's foot, thereby kindling his fury. For the first time, the Hell-Captain felt a trifle uneasy. He felt in the bag and found there were only another fifty or so teeth left. Being prudent rather than chivalrous, he sowed the lot.

'That's more like it,' Jason yelled. 'If there's one thing I can't stand, it's all this hanging about.' He flourished the Sword like a tennis player practising flowing backhand smashes.

A spectral warrior, taller by a skull than its fellow-demons, grounded its shield and scimitar with a clang.

'Right,' it said, 'that does it.'

Jason and the Hell-Captain both stared at it. It folded its arms defiantly.

'It's all right for you,' it said. 'You just look at it from our point of view for a second, will you?'

'Can we please get on now?' Jason interrupted. 'I haven't got all day, you know.'

'Stuff you,' said the spectral warrior. 'And don't you start, either,' it went on, turning and giving the Hell-Captain a filthy look through the eyeslits of its coal-black helm. 'We've had it up to here with the both of you, haven't we, lads?'

The other spectral warriors nodded their inky plumes in agreement. There was a small autumn of falling shields.

'I mean,' the spectral warrior spokesthing went on, 'just think about it, will you? We start off life in the mouth of a bloody great dragon, right? Now that's not exactly fun and games, what with the bad breath and the fireworks display sloshing round you every time the sodding thing sneezes. You wouldn't think it could get worse, would you? Only it does, because some nerd whips us out of it with a pair of rusty pliers, dunks us in a vat of magic potion, and the next thing we know we're a phalanx of doomed psychopaths getting smashed to buggery by some eight-foot jerk with a sword. Somebody tell me, for crying out loud, what is the point?'

The other spectral warriors clapped their fleshless hands and cheered. Jason frowned ominously. The Hell-Captain tried hiding behind his shield. This sort of thing wasn't supposed to happen, was it?

'All right,' he said. 'So what am I supposed to do about it? Explain it all away to Management while you lot all puddle off and become hairdressers?'

His words were drowned out by the clamour of furious serpentine dentistry. He closed his eyes and banged on the ground with his shield for quiet. Eventually, he got it.

'Look,' he said, 'believe me, I'm not unsympathetic. I know how you feel. It can't be easy, I know. But you've got to accept that in this life . . .'

The spokesthing made a rude noise. 'But we're not in this life, are we?' it pointed out. 'We aren't even human, that's the bloody galling part of it. We're just a job lot of recycled bridgework, and we aren't going to stand for it. You want this job done, you get some of your precious fellow-humans to do it. Right?'

The Hell-Captain went as red as a tomato. 'Who are you calling human?' he demanded.

'Oh yeah?' replied the spokesthing. 'Want to make something of it, do you?'

There was another crunch like a huge crab being run over by a lorry, and a number of thin screams. Jason leaned on the hilt of the Sword, scratching his head and wondering, as he did from time to time, exactly why he bothered. There was a quiet cough at his elbow.

He swivelled round, Sword uplifted, to find a small fiend with a pitchfork in one hand and a cellular telephone in the other looking up at him.

'Jason Derry?' it asked.

'Yes.'

'Call for you,' said the fiend and offered him the telephone. Jason took it, nodded and thanked him. The fiend didn't move, except to extend its hand meaningfully. Jason sighed, felt in his pocket and produced a fifty pence and two tens, the sum of his monetary wealth at that moment. Heroes rarely carry money around with them, as it spoils the line of their clothes. The fiend gave him a contemptuous look and withdrew.

'Hello?' Jason said into the phone.

'Jason?' said a female voice, 'is that you?'

'Hi, Mum!' Jason replied. 'How did you get my number?' he asked suspiciously.

There was a brief pause. 'I . . . I got it from your Dad,' said Mrs. Derry.

'Dad?' Jason asked. 'Which one?'

'Big Dad.'

'Oh,' Jason said. 'I might have known. What did he want?'

'Jason,' said his mother, 'I want you to come home right now, do you hear me? I'm very worried about you.'

'But Mum . . .' He ducked to avoid a severed arm. 'I can't come now, I'm busy.'

'Don't give me that, Jason,' said Mrs. Derry severely. 'You're to come home *right now*, or I'll be seriously angry. Do you hear?'

'But Mum . . .'

'And no buts,' said Mrs. Derry. 'I'll expect you back for tea.'

The line went dead, and Jason handed the phone to the dwarf. While he had been otherwise occupied, the Hell-Captain had reduced his fifty remaining myrmidons to a mound of battered and dismembered calcium, and his martial ardour was beginning to ebb slightly. That, he realised, only left him.

'Now, then,' Jason said, hefting the Sword and wafting a graceful square cut through the clammy air. 'Let's make this as quick as possible, because I really do have to go soon.'

'Suits me,' said the Hell-Captain. 'In fact, why not let's just leave it at that, shall we? Call it a draw or something.'

'A draw?'

'Why not?' replied the Hell-Captain. 'I make it fifty spectral warriors each. A tie.'

Jason shook his head and advanced crabwise, whirling the Sword above his head like an enchanted rotor-blade.

'Actually,' remarked the Hell-Captain, backing away, 'on reflection I find that you win, on higher scoring-rate. Congratulations. You played a fair match, hard but fair, and the best man won.'

423

'Will win,' Jason corrected him. 'As soon as you stop moving about.'

'Did I happen to mention,' said the Hell-Captain, 'that I've done my shoulder? You can't expect me to fight you with a dicky shoulder, now can you?'

'Shut up and fight.'

'Shan't.' The Hell-Captain sheathed his sword, dropped his shield and jumped on it. 'I yield,' he said. 'Got you there, haven't I?'

Jason considered this for a moment; then he sheathed the Sword and hit him.

'Nobody loves a smartass,' he remarked; then he marched off up the tunnel towards the distant crack of daylight.

About five minutes later, the Hell-Captain stopped shamming dead, picked himself up, and looked cautiously round. As far as he could tell, there was nothing there except the butchered components of a hundred spectral warriors, but he wasn't taking any chances.

'I,' he said, 'am dead. I was killed in the fight. This is just my astral body talking. Since I am dead, I am excused further duty. If you want any other Heroes catching, you can bloody well catch them yourself.'

He stripped off his dented helm, tossed it aside and limped off towards the topside, Piccadilly and a new life. For the record, he later became a successful and highly respected chiropodist. Further details have been suppressed at his own request.

CHAPTER TEN

'I dunno,' Vulcan said doubtfully. 'Tricky.'

'But you can do it?'

Vulcan scratched his head, walked three times round the vehicle, kicked the offside front wheel and said, 'Maybe.'

'That's great,' Apollo said. 'How soon can you start?'

'It'll cost you, though.'

'Never mind that.'

'It's all right your saying never mind that,' Vulcan replied seriously. 'First there's your parts, that's . . .' he made a few rough calculations on the back of an envelope. 'Plus your labour, at a hundred staters an hour, let's call that . . .'

'Just forget all that,' said Apollo impatiently. 'Expense is no object. Just get started, will you? We can discuss the rest of it later.'

Vulcan shook his head. 'Beats me why you can't be satisfied with something simpler,' he said. 'Look, I can do you a Vulcan Mustang Sports Turbo, alloy wheels, hot cams, hydraulic suspension, one careful owner, still in warranty, yours for . . .'

'Forget it,' Apollo snapped. 'It's this or nothing, OK? If

you can't handle it,' he added menacingly, 'I know dwarves who can.'

Vulcan scowled at him. 'You please yourself,' he said. 'It's your money.'

'Exactly,' Apollo said. 'I'll need it by the weekend, so get busy.' Then he left, thereby neatly guillotining the debate.

After he had gone, Vulcan spent about twenty minutes scribbling little sketches on the envelope. Then he looked at it, turned it upside down, shrugged, tore it up and summoned his assistants. His assistants are the Cyclopes, the monstrous one-eyed cannibalistic thunder-giants of Sicily. At that particular moment, they were sitting round the tyre-changing press with the transistor radio turned up to full volume, playing poker and ogling the Pirelli calendar (not easy if you're one-eyed).

'Brontes!' Vulcan called. 'Sthenos! Bias! Kratos! Gather round, we've got work to do.'

Grumbling, the Cyclopes abandoned their game and trooped through into the main bodyshop, their knuckles ploughing furrows in the dust as they came.

'Yeah, boss?' said Brontes.

Vulcan pointed to the thing on the hydraulic ramp. 'You see that?' he demanded.

'Yeah, boss.'

'What is it?'

Brontes scratched his head. Thinking, as opposed to overtightening bolts and hitting things with a mole wrench, was not his forte. 'Looks like a Volkswagen to me, boss.'

'Well done,' said Vulcan. 'Now listen to this . . .'

'Thanks, George,' Jason said. 'Call back at about half past nine tomorrow, okay?'

George scowled. 'You said that the last time, remember?'

'All right, all right . . .'

'Meet you here in about half an hour, you said.'

'George . . .'

'Fourteen hours,' George said.

'I lost track of time a bit,' Jason snapped. 'I said I'm sorry, okay?'

George made no reply. Instead he shook his head resentfully, put the golf cart into gear and drove away.

Jason fumbled for his key, opened the door and walked in. 'Hi, Mum,' he called out, 'I'm home.'

'Is that you, Jason?' came a voice from the kitchen.

Jason, as usual, mumbled 'No, it's the Pope' to himself under his breath and went through.

Mrs. Derry was making biscuits. There had not been a time, as far as Jason could remember, when his mother hadn't been making biscuits. And that was the funny thing; he was fond of biscuits and had eaten a great many. So was his father fond of biscuits. So was his mother. But the three of them, eating in shifts round the clock, couldn't possibly have stuffed away the infinity of Melting Moments, gingernuts, Maryland cookies and Viennese fingers that had poured out of this kitchen in the last fifteen years or so. Which meant that most of them must still be here, somewhere. In the cupboard under the stairs, the greenhouse, the tool-shed, wherever, one of these days, he would open a door and they'd all come pouring out . . .

'Sorry I'm late,' he said, 'I got – held up. Spectral warriors.'

'That's nice, dear. Your father came round.'

'I know,' said Jason, 'Big Dad, you said. What did he want?'

Mrs. Derry stopped kneading and dusted her hands off purposefully. 'He's very angry with you, Jason,' she said.

'So?' Jason said wearily. It had been a long day, his head was buzzing and his knuckles were sore. He wanted a cup of tea, a nice warm bath, and bed.

'Jason,' his mother said.

Now some names, as we know, have meanings. Dorothy means Gift of God, Winifred means White Wave and Stephen means Crown. Jason, to the best of our knowledge, doesn't mean anything. Except, of course, when said in a significant tone by somebody's mother.

'Mum,' Jason complained, 'I'm tired. Can't it wait?'

'Your father,' said Mrs. Derry, 'is very angry with you.'

'Tough,' Jason replied. 'But I really couldn't care less. I've had it up to here with him, and . . .'

'Jason,' Mrs. Derry said, 'you mustn't disobey your father. It's not right.'

'Mum . . .' Jason was on the point of pleading.

'Now you promise me you won't do it again,' said Mrs. Derry, 'and we'll say no more about it, all right?'

'Mum,' Jason said – it took a lot of strength of will to say it, too – 'I can't do what Dad says. It's wrong.'

'Jason,' said Mrs. Derry sternly. 'That's nonsense and you know it. He's your father.'

Jason wanted to object. He wanted to say that Attila the Hun had had a son, and so had Genghis Khan; that there was a flaw in the logic of her argument you could drive a very large vehicle through without even clipping your wing mirrors; that what Jupiter wanted him to do was as gross a betrayal of his mortality as it was possible to get; that Jupiter had sent a god – his own half-brother – to kill him today, and if that hadn't dissolved the filial contract, he wanted to know what would. What he actually said was 'Mum . . .'

'He's your father,' Mrs. Derry said again. 'And he's worried about you.'

That was almost too much – almost – for Jason. He was about to say that if he was worried about his son's safety, why was he sending divine assassins to have him forcibly stellified, but somehow he didn't. Instead, he said 'Look . . .' Which was a change from 'Mum . . .' but not an improvement on it.

When the gods first designed Heroes, they intended them to be a special reserve category of super-mortals with all the good mortal features souped up to competition standard and all the bad mortal features either sublimated or omitted. The design team assigned to the job had obviously enjoyed it, because they took a pride in their work that was notably absent from the standard production mortal. The everyday hatchback model, on leaving the showroom, has inbuilt design flaws: cowardice, greed, spite, frailty, appalling power-to-weight ratio and fuel consumption, and a tendency to measles. Not so Heroes; they are godlike in their strength and prowess, but most ungodlike in that they exhibit nobility, courage and altruism; seek to alleviate the sufferings of mankind instead of scoring five points (ten for a double Woe Score) for them; right wrongs; succour rather than sucker the weak; generally speaking, don't bicker like tired, spoilt children at every opportunity. In fact, Heroes are such a successful design concept that not long after the first batch were released, the gods realised that they'd cocked it up again and recalled the whole issue with almost indecent haste. Something had to be done.

What was done was this. Into each Hero, a tragic flaw was introduced, individually tailored to self-destruct the Hero just as soon as he began to show signs of getting too big for his seven-league boots. Achilles his pride; Oedipus his curiosity; Hamlet his indecision; David Gower his tendency to flap at deliveries aimed at his leg stump – each Hero has been deliberately sabotaged to prevent him making that final leap across the terminals of the sparkplug from imperfect to perfect. Jason, of course, was no exception.

'Mum . . .' he said.

'Jason,' said his mother, 'what is that dog doing in my kitchen?'

The words 'what dog?' froze on Jason's lips. 'Oh,' he said, 'yes. That's Cerberus.'

'Outside.'

'But Mum . . .'

'Outside.'

'But Mum . . .'

'Outside.'

Miserably, Jason grabbed hold of Cerberus by one ear and led him out to the garage.

'Good dog,' Jason said guiltily. 'Stay.'

Cerberus gave him a threefold look that reflected perfectly what Jason was himself thinking at precisely that moment, right down to the three dots. But Jason could only shrug his shoulders and look extremely silly.

'I *know*,' he said. 'But what can I do?'

He closed the door, locked it and went back into the house, trying to ignore the stereophonic whimpering and scratching noises coming from the garage.

'I don't mind your bringing them back dead,' said his mother. 'Alive is another matter. First thing in the morning you're taking him up the kennels.'

Jason could have said 'But Mum' again, but he felt it was beginning to lose its impact. So he tried sulking instead. Eighteen years of experience told him that it didn't work, but so what? They'd said the same thing about Edison and the light bulb.

430

'Now, then,' said Mrs. Derry cheerfully, 'now that we've got that sorted out, you can have a biscuit. I made some Melting Moments. You know how you like Melting Moments.'

Jason nodded resignedly. Yes, he liked Melting Moments and would do what he was told. Pity about the human race, but whoever said life was fair?

'Another thing,' said Mrs. Derry as she made more biscuits. 'Sharon's coming round for her tea tomorrow, so don't be late home.'

'*Mum . . .*'

Mothers since the creation of mankind have learned that the best way to stifle objections from their offspring is to stuff biscuits in their mouths. Nobody, not even Lenin, can preach rebellion effectively with a mouth full of Melting Moment. 'Six-thirty sharp,' she said. 'I'm doing lamb with pearl barley. You like lamb with pearl barley,' she reminded him.

'Yes, Mum.' In a sudden access of memory, Jason seemed to recall himself breaking into the Underground, conspiring to overthrow Jupiter, duffing up two gods and rounding it all off by pulverising fifty crack Hell-troopers. Or did he? All of a sudden he became aware that the memory can play strange tricks. Very probably he'd imagined it all.

'Goodnight, Mum,' he said.

'Mind you brush your teeth.'

'Yes, Mum.'

'Goodnight, Jason.'

' 'Night, Mum.'

When he got to his room, he noticed that all his Mars posters had disappeared and that someone, probably the Revenue, had been and impounded all his personal records. He found some of them later in a large cardboard box on top of the wardrobe, and the rest of them the next morning neatly packaged up in black dustbin bags outside the back door.

It wouldn't have been much of a consolation to Jason even if he'd known, but Hercules had had more or less the same trouble with his wife. The most notable occasion was on his return after the completion of the Twelve Labours, to find that in his absence Megara of the Fair Ankles had given half his clothes to a jumble sale, put a further quarter in the loft and washed and ironed the remaining quarter, thereby destroying at a stroke the carefully-compiled ambience of thirty years of blood, toil, tears and sweat. Mythology records that, at this point, Hercules lost his rag good and proper and settled his family's hash once and for all with several hearty blows of his club. This is all, of course, pure nonsense. Mythology, it should be remembered, is composed largely by men. What actually happened, apart from a few unheeded protests, was nothing at all, and the reason why Megara fades out of the Hercules legend at this point is that while Hercules was away killing monsters and averting evils, Megara had happened to meet a rather nice insurance broker who, although shorter, punier and incapable of dealing with any form of hostile wildlife bigger than a money-spider, was at least there at weekends and public holidays.

As Jason slept, a number of very insistent dreams came and stood beside him. He swatted them with a back issue of *Model Railway Enthusiast* and went back to sleep.

'Gel.'

'Here, Pro. Fire away.'

'Trouble.'

'What?'

'Big trouble.'

'All right, so it's big trouble. What?'

Telepathic communication is actually much faster than this. It belts through the air at a simply alarming rate, just like the new information technology that so nearly reproduces it, and so we can legitimately omit Prometheus's resumé of the scene between Jason and Mrs. Derry, logging back in at the point when Gelos says 'Oh *shit*!', without having abridged more than three seconds of actual time.

'Oh *shit*!'

'Exactly,' agreed Prometheus. 'Now what do we do?'

'Nothing for it, is there?'

'You mean . . .?'

'That's right,' thought Gelos gravely. 'The eagle has landed.'

In the sick-bay of the sun, Aesculapius was doing more business in one afternoon than he had done for the last fifty years.

'Right,' he said briskly, 'this may hurt a little.'

Nobody knows exactly why doctors say that. It can't be to set the patient at his ease, because anybody above the age of three knows from bitter experience that the words are the invariable prologue to agony, just as 'You may feel a little bit woozy for the next twenty-four hours' means that you're going to spend the next three days bumping into things and feeling like an LSD addict after a particularly bad trip, and 'It's just for a few routine tests' means that it's now too late to see about some life insurance. Perhaps they do it on purpose, just in case you weren't actually scared rigid to start with.

Mars shut his eyes and braced his few remaining rigid components. There was a click, a flare of therapeutic orange flame, and the noise of a god complaining.

'You can put your clothes back on now,' said Aesculapius.

'Want to bet?' Mars replied.

'That will do,' said Aesculapius. 'Next, please.'

Mars dragged himself off the couch and Pluto took his place.

'Now then,' said the heavenly physician, 'what seems to be the trouble?'

Pluto scowled at him. 'Did you do anatomy at medical school?' he asked. Aesculapius nodded.

'Very well then,' Pluto replied. 'Look at my skeleton and start counting the gaps.'

Aesculapius ignored him and started prodding him about. 'Hm,' he said at last, 'we've got a few bones missing here and there, I see. And what have we been getting up to to get ourselves in this state, then?'

'I'd rather not discuss it,' Pluto said. 'A dog was involved.'

Aesculapius, being a doctor, is at perfect liberty to ignore anything anyone says to him. 'We'll have to see what we can do about that,' he said briskly. 'Wait there.'

He went to the bone cupboard, picked out a number of bones from the stock, and tried them for size. They more or less fitted, roughly as an 11/16 inch bolt will fit a 15 mm thread if you ease it into place with a lump hammer. He fitted them quickly and fairly accurately and told Pluto to stand up.

'Ow,' said Pluto. Aesculapius helped him to his feet, told him to practise, and advised him that he might possibly experience some slight discomfort for the next forty-eight

434

hours. Then he shooed him out and sat down for a quiet half-hour with a cup of Bovril and a gynaecological journal.

Outside his surgery, Mars and Pluto compared notes.

'It's not good, is it?' Mars said.

'Distinctly worrying,' Pluto agreed. 'What I want to know is how that confounded Derry boy managed it.'

'Well,' said Mars, 'in my case he sort of drew back his left hand like this . . .'

'No, no,' said Pluto, wincing slightly, 'that's not what I meant. How did he get the power to fight with gods? Mortals can't fight with gods, not usually; it's just not possible, like wrestling with the wind. We're in a different dimension to them – unless, of course, they have help.'

'Help,' said Mars bitterly, 'isn't usually hard to find, is it? I have scars to prove it.'

'Oh, I agree with you,' Pluto said. 'In the past, one of us has always been only too glad to give his or her pet champion a helping hand against the rest of us. But not in this case, surely. We're all united; nobody has anything at all to gain from enabling Derry to fight with us. So, either he has the ability himself, without the need for any assistance which means that he's a bigger god than any of us – or else someone very big indeed is helping him out. And the only Person that big is . . .'

'Exactly,' said Mars. 'And Jupiter may be . . .' He looked anxiously around him, 'but he's not as crazy as all that. He's more worried by all this than any of us. That can only mean that the boy did manage to get through and make contact with . . .'

'Yes,' said Pluto hurriedly. 'It really isn't looking terribly good, is it?'

'Quite right,' said a third voice. 'And while we're on the subject, you both think I'm crazy, do you?'

435

The two gods looked round and saw Jupiter standing behind them. He hadn't been there five seconds ago, but really, that is neither here nor there. When you're dealing with an omnipresent supreme being, even looking behind the sofa and turning on all the taps is a complete waste of time.

'Anyway,' said. Jupiter briskly, 'I've solved everything, with no help from any of you clowns, as usual. All our troubles are over; you can get back to loafing about and looking decorative. Put your collar straight, Ma. You look like you've just been let out of prison.'

And Jupiter vanished. Mars turned to Pluto and shrugged.

'What we need right now,' he said, 'is a drink.'

Pluto nodded.

'Or two drinks.'

'Quite right.'

Having come to this eminently reasonable conclusion, they left the sick-bay and were crossing over the road to the bar when they were knocked down by Phoebus Apollo, who was test-driving a 1960s Volkswagen Beetle converted into a chariot drawn by four winged dragons.

Jason was woken from deep sleep by a sound uncannily like a large bird tapping on his window with its beak.

Being half-divine, Jason could sleep through most things, but not this. After a period of semi-consciousness, during which he was troubled with dreams involving huge thrushes knocking snails out of brightly-coloured shells, he pulled himself out of bed, groped hazily for the Sword of Who The Hell Cares, Anyway, and tottered to the window. He pulled aside the curtain and saw a large bird tapping on the glass.

'Shoo,' he said.

The bird refused to shoo. He noticed that it was in fact an eagle, and although one eagle looked pretty much like another to him, he made an intuitive assumption and opened the window six inches.

'What do you want?' he asked.

The eagle replied by thrusting a talon in the crack and shrieking. With a sigh, Jason opened the window fully and the eagle hopped in, shook the rain out of its feathers and turned into an extremely beautiful young woman.

'Hello,' she said. 'Sorry if I woke you. Have you got a moment?'

Jason nodded and waved vaguely at a chair. It had rather a lot of socks on it, some of them of considerable maturity, but the girl affected not to notice them.

'I'm Eagle,' she said, 'but you can call me Mary.'

Jason nodded again. He was fresh out of words.

'I'm a friend of Prometheus,' the girl went on. 'And Gelos. Gelos isn't actually called Gelos, by the way; or at least he is, but it's not his real name. Really he's called Thing.'

Jason nodded a third time, as if this was the most logical thing he had ever heard. The girl smiled at him, crossed her legs and went on.

'What they want to know is, would you do them a small favour? It's to do with what Thing – that's Gelos – was telling you about earlier on; you know, Jupiter and the diversionary tactics? I'm sorry to bother you with it now, but there have been gods watching the house most of the night, and I've only just managed to get rid of them.'

Jason's befuddled expression must have seemed to the girl like a request for an explanation of how she had managed that, because she coloured slightly. 'Oh, it was easy,'

437

she said. 'I just told each of them in turn that I'd meet them in ten minutes behind the . . .'

'Ah.'

'So,' said the girl, 'what they'd like you to do is . . .'

'No,' Jason said. 'Sorry.'

The girl stared at him. 'Sorry?'

'Yes.'

'No,' said the girl, 'I meant sorry meaning what was that you said.'

'I said sorry.'

'Before that.'

'No.'

'Oh.' the girl frowned. 'Why?'

'I'm busy tomorrow,' Jason replied. 'Another time, maybe.'

This seemed to have a strange effect on the girl. First she peered closely at her arms and then her legs; then she got up and looked at herself in the mirror. Having apparently satisfied herself that all was well, she came and sat down again.

'No, but seriously,' she said, 'what we'd like you to do is . . .

'Really, no,' Jason answered. 'No can do. Out of the question.'

'But . . .'

'In fact,' Jason went on, 'I hate to do this, but I'm afraid the whole thing's off. I've thought it over, and the fact is that I'm not going through with it. After all, Jupiter *is* my father, and it really isn't . . .'

'He tried to kill you.'

'Well yes, there is that,' Jason admitted. 'In a sense there's something in what you say, but . . .'

'He sent Mars, and Pluto, and a hundred Hell-troopers.'

'The Hell-troopers were just for fun, surely,' Jason said. 'I mean, you can't be expected to take an opponent seriously when he pops up out of the ground at you like one of those fast-motion films of a tree growing.'

The girl put her head on one side and nibbled absently at her shoulder-blade. 'You really expect me to believe you've had a change of heart?' she asked. 'Seriously?'

'Yes,' said Jason.

'No, you haven't.'

Jason felt a tiny green shoot of irritability thrusting its head up through the surface of his general bewilderment. 'What are you,' he demanded, 'a mind-reader or something?'

'Yes.'

Jason took that one in his stride. 'In that case,' he said 'you can see that my mind is made up. Now, if you don't mind . . .'

The girl recrossed her legs petulantly. 'Are you throwing me out?' she said.

'In a manner of speaking, yes.' Jason said. 'And you can tell your friends that if I've got to be bossed about by one side or the other, I might as well be bossed about by Jupiter. After all, he is my Dad and he is winning.'

'Bossed about?'

'Yes,' said Jason, with a sudden access of feeling, 'bloody well bossed about. Do this. Do that. Fulfil your Destiny. Chop the head off that serpent over there. Steal those golden apples. The hell with the lot of you. I'm sick and tired of being ordered around by people, and if you think I'm going to betray my own father just to be ordered around by you lot . . .'

'But Jason . . .'

'Don't Jason me,' Jason said. 'I've had all the Jasoning I

439

can handle tonight already. Now put your feathers back on and sling your hook, all right?

'Jason . . .'

'And it's no good you saying you're a protected species, because in this house the Wildlife and Countryside Act has no jurisdiction. Clear off before I stuff a cushion with you.'

'Jason . . .'

'I mean, you can say that Jupiter and his mob leave a lot to be desired, but what sort of a world would it be if there was a bunch of comedians in charge? Everybody would be so busy telling each other jokes, sooner or later someone would forget to plant any crops and then where would we be?'

'Jason . . .'

Jason Derry made an exasperated noise, grabbed the Sword and whirled it round his head, neatly but unintentionally slicing through the electric light flex. The girl squawked, grew feathers, and hopped onto the windowsill.

'Out!' Jason said. The eagle gave him a filthy look, spread its wings and vanished.

Trembling slightly, Jason closed the window, put the Sword away and climbed back into bed; and not long afterwards, he was asleep again. That, he realised in retrospect, was a mistake.

He had been sleeping quite happily for upwards of a quarter of an hour when a dream came to him. Since the window was shut, the dream had to squeeze in via the mains through the severed electric flex, and it stood at the head of Jason's bed for thirty seconds or so, getting its breath back. Then it gingerly inserted itself into his mind and got down to business.

It seemed to Jason as if he was standing in a queue. It was a long queue, and he couldn't see the end, and he didn't know what it was for. The people in front of him and

440

behind him had no faces; the fronts of their heads were blank and polished, with no openings on them.

The queue shuffled forwards and, because it was a dream, the whole sequence was able to fast-forward a bit, so that Jason was aware that he had been in the queue for an intolerably long time without that part of the dream taking more than a sixtieth of a second. Then quite suddenly he was at the front of the queue, and he saw Jupiter; and standing beside him, Mars and Pluto. They had big felt-tip marker pens in their hands, and as the people in the queue shuffled past them they drew in faces on the blank surfaces of their heads. Or at least they put in two blobs for eyes and an upside-down semicircle for the mouth; a sad face. Then they pushed each person over the edge of a cliff.

Well yes, said Jason's subconscious mind. Fair comment, I suppose. Allegory is all about value-judgments anyway and maybe I shouldn't have had that cheese sandwich before turning in.

Then he looked round and saw another queue, parallel to the one he was in. It was exactly the same, except that Gelos and Prometheus were at the head of it, and the faces they drew in had upright semicircles for mouths; smiling faces. And when these people were pushed over the cliff, they didn't fall. Instead, they drifted up into the air like space-walking astronauts, hovered for a few moments, touched down again and walked round to the back of the queue.

Heavy, said Jason's subconscious. If Sigmund Freud could see what was going on here, he'd have me in a padded cell so quick my feet wouldn't touch.

Then he suddenly found himself at the front of Jupiter's queue, and Jupiter – Dad – was drawing a face on him. A sad face. Then he felt a large hand in the small of his back and he was flying through the air over the edge of the cliff.

441

He opened his mouth to scream and could feel the ink smudging.

And then, as he fell (but slowly, since it was a dream), he saw three dots in the sky, very far away. The further he fell, the larger the dots became, until they turned into three eagles. Two of them flew straight past, but the third swooped down, caught hold of him in one talon and carried him back up. The other talon held a bag of chips, which it offered to him.

Then he was back on the cliff top again, and feeling extremely angry. He had a duster in his hand now, and he walked up to Jupiter, wiped his face off, and drew in a very sad face indeed. Then he picked the god up and tossed him over the edge. His subconscious mind started kicking up no end of a fuss but he ignored it. It felt good.

The dream grinned and stood up. The bit with the duster had been its own idea, and although it knew that Thing didn't really approve of ad-libbing, it felt that it was probably the duster which had turned the scales. Pausing only to blow deep sleep into Jason's eyes, the dream trickled back up into the light flex and vanished.

Half an hour or so later, Jason woke up, sweating. He could hear something.

He listened carefully. Nothing. He swore drowsily and tried to go back to sleep. Then he heard it again. It was the sound of a dog, or three dogs, or one dog with three heads, barking.

Indigestion woke up suddenly, gurgled, realised what was going on and made a grab for the alarm clock.

At the fourth attempt he made contact and prevailed upon it to stop ringing. That made things better. Slightly.

The various personifications of abstract concepts who

form the non-commissioned ranks of the divine hierarchy – Greed, Fear, Spring, Hope, Pennsylvania, Wealth and Appendicitis, to name but a few; Plato refers to them as the Forms, and why not? – have an arduous time of it. As their great spokesman Discontent put it on the occasion of the January Rising of 1979,* the Forms do all the work but the 'gods get all the gravy. This dichotomy between work done and status accorded was marked enough before the gods left Olympus; after the move, however, the gods delegated the entire management of their various portfolios to their respective teams of Forms – Mars handing over the conduct of war to Death, Fear and Victory; Minerva appointing as her attorneys Philosophy, Prudence and (curiously enough) Needlepoint; and so on – but neglected to raise their salaries, grant them the right to receive the worship of mortals or even let them use the Management Cloakrooms. Each Form remains answerable to his Head of Department for any errors or omissions, but receives little or no practical assistance with anything but the broadest and most far-reaching policy decisions. A certain degree of resentment was inevitable; and the final straw is believed by many to have been the so-called Form-busting measures introduced by Jupiter in the early 1980s. As a result of these, all Forms are now ultimately under the jurisdiction of the Great Sky-God himself.

As a Form Grade D in the College of Humours, Indigestion generally had little to do with Jupiter, and he was heartily glad of it. The work was bad enough as it was without having the Lord of Tempests to contend with.

*The direct result of the gods' refusal to allow the Forms to attend the Celestial Christmas Outing to Weymouth; now better known as the Winter of Discontent.

Only the previous evening, for example, Indigestion had been ordered to attend a reception for the Australian Ambassador in Moscow, with instructions to afflict no fewer than three hundred and twenty-seven guests. What with one thing and another, and in particular the Australian trade attaché's wager that he could drink the Secretary of State for Production under the table, it was well after half past three in the morning before Indigestion had finally got to bed, and now he found that he had woken up with something of a headache.

Having dealt ruthlessly with his clock-radio, Indigestion tried turning over and going back to sleep, but somehow the knack had left him. After a little fruitless cursing, therefore, the wretched Form got out of bed, put on his dressing-gown inside-out and went in search of orange juice.

Fortuitously, he found some in the fridge and drank it quickly. He was just starting to feel that he might, with the assistance of the best medical attention, eventually recover when the telephone rang.

It was a loud telephone at the best of times. Indigestion located the receiver and put it as close to his head as he dared.

'Lo?' he mumbled.

'Morning, Ind,' said a cheerful voice at the other end. 'How's tricks?'

Indigestion winced. 'Could you please speak a little more quietly, please?' he whispered. 'I have a slight . . .'

'My God, Ind,' said the voice, 'you aren't hung over *again*, are you? Beats me how you manage it.'

Indigestion scowled at the receiver until he discovered that contracting his brows made the rest of his head hurt. It was in the nature of Health, his immediate superior, to be rude; but just now he wasn't in the mood to make allowances.

'I was working late last night,' he replied coldly. 'And it is my day off . . .'

'Sorry, Ind,' Health said, 'all leave cancelled, by order. Be at the departure bay by nine sharp.'

'Hel . . .'

'Sorry, mate,' said his boss, 'that's how it is. All maladies and infirmities to report immediately; no excuses accepted.'

'Oh come on, Hel . . .'

'No buts, chum,' said Health. 'Oh yes, and you'll be in charge. You'll like that, won't you? Try not to cock it all up, there's a good lad.'

'Bloody hell, Hel . . .'

Health laughed. 'I know, I know,' he said. 'But I can't make it. Off sick,' he explained. 'Actually, I promised faithfully to take the old bag round the shops this morning, and if I don't she'll kill me. But that's just between you and me, right?'

Despite his annoyance, Indigestion could feel a slight flicker of sympathy for his superior. Health was, after all, married to Efficiency. Ruthless Efficiency, the lads in Vouchers called her.

'So what's so important that I've got to work on my day off?' Indigestion said resignedly. 'If it's just another 'flu epidemic . . .'

'If only it was,' Health replied. 'No, my son, there's something extremely mega happening upstairs. No idea what it is. But the order is that we've got to go and afflict Prometheus. ASAP.'

'I'm sorry,' Indigestion said, 'I thought you just . . .'

'Prometheus,' Health repeated. 'The coach leaves at

09.12, and remember to call the register. All absentees to be reported to me personally. Have a good time.'

The line went dead, and Indigestion knew how it felt. He climbed into his work clothes, retrieved his toolkit from behind the sofa, where it had fallen last night, and staggered off towards the bus depot.

He got there just in time to see a flight of winged chariots howling off overhead, packed full of heavily-armed Spectral Warriors. If there was a single dragon anywhere in the cosmos with a tooth left in its head, he reckoned, it would be something of a miracle.

Thanks to Mrs. Health's determination to do her shopping instead of her work, someone had made one almighty mess of the transport arrangements; and when Indigestion arrived at Bay 340, he was informed that the coaches intended to convey the Maladies to the Caucasus mountains had been commandeered by Vulcan and the Cyclopes to transport themselves and their mobile workshop. All the other coaches were spoken for, of course; and with all the winged chariots taken by the military, it looked as if Prometheus, whatever he was going to have to endure today, would be doing so in virtually perfect health. After ten minutes or so of running round arguing with irritable Forms with clipboards, Indigestion happened to bump into Venezuela, who was standing in a long queue behind the only telephone box on the concourse that didn't take phonecards.

'What are you doing here?' Indigestion asked.

'Standing in for Violence,' Venezuela explained. 'He'd got tickets for some poetry reading or other, so I said I'd help out. If I'd known what was going on, I wouldn't have bothered.

'What is going on?' Indigestion asked.

Venezuela grinned. 'Balloon's finally gone up,' she said.

446

'The word is that the Old Fool has finally flipped and put a contract out on You Know Who.'

Such is the level of paranoia in heaven that periphrases such as You Know Who are practically meaningless.

Indigestion sighed and asked her to be more specific.

'You know,' Venezuela hissed. 'Laughing Boy.'

Indigestion stared at her. 'You can't be serious,' he said.

'On the contrary,' Venezuela replied, 'if the Big J's to be believed, this is your last opportunity to be anything but serious. Twenty-four hours from now is to be VG Day, and the password is Killing Joke, if you're interested.'

'Look,' said Indigestion, 'what on earth is going on? What have I missed?'

'Well,' Venezuela replied, looking round carefully, 'I was talking to Rumour, and he reckons that that Hero who went off the rails and we all had to look for; you know, the Derry kid . . .'

'Yes,' said Indigestion, 'I know him.'

'Do you?'

'He's been eating a lot recently,' Indigestion explained. 'Go on.'

'Apparently,' said Venezuela, 'the Derry boy was subverted by You Know Who . . .'

'Look . . .'

'All right,' said Venezuela, 'by the person we don't talk about whose name begins with G and who makes people laugh. You know that old prophesy thing.'

Indigestion nodded; a mistake on his part.

'And then,' Venezuela continued, 'when the two of them – Derry and the Person in question – had broken out of wherever he's been holed up all this while – beating up Ma and Plu on the way, I might add – the Big J very cleverly managed to nobble Derry and make him change sides.'

'I thought he'd already done that.'

'Yes,' said Venezuela. 'I mean no. Look, he was on our side, right? Then he defects to them. Now Jupiter's got him to come back to us. Quite the human tennis ball, in fact.'

'Quite.'

'Apparently,' Venezuela went on, 'Jupiter fixed it by getting at Derry through his mother. Anyway, that's what Bliss told me a moment ago; but you know Bliss, dead ignorant. And so what that means is that the enemy's come out into the open but without a Hero. In dead shtuck, in other words. And so it's all hands to the pump time, to see if we can nail him before he gets back to his place of safety. Fun, isn't it?'

Indigestion breathed in deeply and sighed. Venezuela wasn't the sort of person one would choose to talk to when one has a poorly head, but he had caught the gist of it. 'Hang on, though,' he said. 'If we're supposed to be going after Gel . . .'

'*Shh!*'

'All right, after You Know Who, why did Hel say we were all being sent to afflict Prometh . . .'

'*Shhhh!*'

'. . . Whatsit?' said Indigestion. 'Surely we should all . . .'

Venezuela grinned. 'And who do you think the Great Smartass will go running to once he's realised his pet Hero's ditched him?'

'Oh,' said Indigestion, 'I see.'

'Particularly,' Venezuela added, 'when he hears that his old buddy and fellow traitor is being beset by maladies and Spectral Warriors and so forth. Be round there like a shot, don't you worry, and then we'll have him. Smart thinking, no?'

Indigestion nodded – slowly this time – and pulled a wry face. 'Oh well,' he said. 'I suppose it had to happen. Look, do you know where I can get hold of at least four large coaches? We should have been on the road about fifteen minutes ago.'

'Coaches are a bit tricky,' Venezuela replied, 'but if a winged chariot or so'd be any use to you . . .'

'Fine.'

'You could try OFT,' Venezuela said. 'Oh marvellous, the call-box is free. You got change for a twenty?'

Indigestion finally tracked Old Father Time down in the bar drinking Guinness, and talked him into a loan of his old but reliable Vulcan V12 Camaro. It would be rather a tight squeeze getting all the Maladies on it, he reckoned, but it was worth a try; and in the circumstances, if the worst came to the worst, it probably wouldn't be the end of the world if they left Tennis Elbow behind.

Once he'd found the vehicle, put the horses in the shafts, put the harness on the horses, checked the tyre pressures and wound back the in-flight movie it was nearly half-past ten. Fortunately, Old Father Time's chariot can cope with that sort of problem, and by a quarter to eleven Indigestion was coming in to land on the peak of one of the Caucasus mountains. Not that he was the first to arrive; not by a long way.

CHAPTER ELEVEN

It was raining.

'Aren't you going to take a coat?' said Mrs. Derry.

'No,' Jason replied, thinking of something else.

'Don't be silly, Jason,' Mrs. Derry said. 'Here, I'll get you one.' She disappeared and returned with one of Mr. Derry's anoraks. 'And you aren't going out in *those* shoes.'

Through the window, Jason could see George in the golf cart, looking at his watch. Was today the Serpent-Haired Gorgon of Sphacteria or the Hundred-Headed Hell-Dragon? Not that it mattered terribly much. Once you've slain one, you've slain them all. 'Look,' he said, 'I might be a bit late tonight, don't . . .'

'You aren't leaving this house till you change those shoes.'

Jason winced. 'Mum,' he said.

'This instant.'

There was a brief silence, charged with strong emotion. Then Jason let out a plangent sigh, leaned the Sword of Glycerion in its canvas case against the door-frame and sprinted up the stairs. When he came back he was wearing a different pair of shoes.

'Right,' he said. 'Now, if you don't mind . . .' He picked up the sword-case and reached for the door-handle.

'Hanky?'

'Yes,' Jason growled.

'Show me.'

'You what?'

'Show me that you've got a clean hanky.'

Jason turned slowly round and gave his mother a look that would have turned the Gorgon to stone and had the Hell-Dragon running in search of the nearest battered dragons' hostel. On his mother it had absolutely no effect.

'Hanky,' she said.

'I'm going beheading monsters,' Jason said, 'I don't think I'm actually going to need . . .'

'Hanky.'

My mother, Jason said to himself, a woman of iron will and limited vocabulary. 'Look,' he said, 'I'm late already, so . . .'

This time, Mrs. Derry didn't even say Hanky; she just looked it. That was somehow infinitely worse.

'All right,' Jason snapped. 'All right.' He hurried back up the stairs again. A moment later, his voice floated down over the bannisters.

'Mum . . .'

'Yes, dear?'

'Where are my handkerchiefs, Mum?'

'In the airing cupboard, dear, second shelf down at the back, where they usually are.'

'Oh. Right.'

'And don't run up and down stairs like that, Jason. It's not good for them.'

'Yes, Mum.'

Having proffered a spotless handkerchief for inspection

and picked up the Sword, Jason lunged for the doorhandle and rotated it. Even if it turned out that Jupiter had lined up the entire race of Titans for him today, he felt things could only get easier from now on.

'Jason.'

He froze. 'Yes, Mum?'

'Don't forget Sharon's coming over today.'

'Mum . . .'

So make sure you're back by quarter to six at the latest, because you'll need to have a bath and wash your hair.'

'Mum . . .'

'Have a nice day, dear. Go carefully, now.'

'Yes, Mum.' And so saying, the Seed of Jove crawled out of the door and slumped across to the golf cart.

'Morning, boss.'

'What?' Jason hurled the sword-case onto the back seat and sat down.

'I said Morning.'

'Be that as it may,' Jason replied. 'What's the old git want me to do today?'

'Shh!' George was cringing. 'Keep your voice down, boss.'

Jason shook his head. 'If I want to call the Old Git an old git,' he said loudly, so that a passing milkman nearly dropped a crate of gold-top, 'then I shall call the Old Git an old git, and if the Old Git doesn't like it, then the Old Git knows what he can do. All right?'

George nodded. Since he was hunkered down almost under his seat, all Jason could see was the top of his head, but from its movements he could extrapolate a nod.

'Fine,' said Jason. 'So what has the . . .'

'Nemean Lion,' George whispered quickly, 'followed by Storm-giants, then half an hour for lunch, followed by

452

wrestling with Time and ending up with stealing the Golden Pear of Truth from the Temple of the Nine Winds which is guarded by . . .'

'I know,' Jason said. 'Right, let's get on with it. And if I faint from boredom halfway through, don't forget to wake me.'

George put the cart in gear. 'Right you are, boss. Oh, and boss . . .'

'Yes?'

' 'Scuse me saying this, but it's good to see you back to normal, boss, after you went over all funny. I said to myself . . .'

'George.'

'Yes, boss?'

'Drive the cart.'

George shrugged and released the brake. 'Still,' he added, 'Glad to see you've put all that defecting crap behind you, boss. I could have told you no good would come of it.'

'George . . .'

'The lads were saying,' George went on, and Jason wondered why saying someone's name quietly didn't seem to work when *he* did it, 'he won't be able to keep it up, they said. Not once his mum's sorted him out. Right old battleaxe . . .'

'George!'

'Boss?'

'For crying out loud, George,' Jason hissed, glancing over his shoulder at the front door of the house, 'keep your voice down!'

The eagle banked sharply and dived, slicing through the cold air like a worried knife. Behind her, ten winged chariots

453

full of Spectral Warriors pulled up, wobbled in thin air, and changed tack. A flash of lightning narrowly missed the eagle's wingtip.

Nothing left for it, the eagle realised, but to climb. Try and outmanoeuvre them. G-forces, gravitational pull, power-to-weight ratios, Sopwith Camels, all that sort of stuff. It wasn't exactly her forte, but there it was. As the careers officer at theological college had told her, it is extremely ill-advised to overspecialise too early. She rose as sharply as she could, nearly pulling her own wings off in doing so, and soared.

'After her!' shouted the Captain of Spectral Warriors.

'But . . .' said his charioteer.

'No buts,' snapped the Captain. 'Follow her!'

'OK, boss,' said the charioteer.

Not long afterwards, ten empty winged chariots drifted away towards the ground, their crews having all fallen out when they tried to follow an eagle who was looping the loop. For a moment the eagle slowed down, exhausted, and rested on the crest of a strong thermal. Then she saw another ten winged chariots emerge from behind a bank of cloud, and jinked just in time to avoid a burst of lightning bolts.

Grimly, she started to climb; but the chariots didn't try following her this time. Instead they split up and spread out, rising in slow circles around her. Obviously, she decided, these were the teeth of one smart dragon. Wisdom teeth.

She reset her wings and dived, sending rabbits on the far-distant surface scurrying for cover in all directions. When it looked as if she was certain to hit the deck with extreme force, she pulled up as hard as she could – was that a bone in her left wing breaking, or just a few tendons? – and skimmed parallel to the ground. When she cocked her head over her shoulder, she could see that the chariots were following. Good. In a manner of speaking, of course; really good would have been if they had stopped following her and gone away, but this would have to do for the time being.

As well as making good starters for a dinner party, the eagle recalled, larks are good teachers. She slowed down slightly and zagged about, exaggerating the slight malfunction in her left wing. The chariots were gaining on her. They were coming up very fast now, the charioteers lashing the winged horses up to maximum effort. In fact, they were going so fast now that in less than twenty seconds they would have overtaken their quarry easily, if only they hadn't flown into a railway bridge first.

The eagle spread her aching wings and glided for a moment before looking round and seeing one winged chariot come out from under the railway bridge. With a squawk of furious despair the eagle flapped her pinions and rose up into the air; and the chariot, manned by fifteen Spectral Warriors, all minus their helmets, followed.

It didn't take long for the eagle to come to the conclusion that this bunch, unlike the others, had rather more intelligence than the average ex-molar. They declined to crash into the branches of trees when she led the way, and when she pitched on a low branch and sat tight, they hovered overhead for a while and then set the entire forest alight with thunderbolts, making it imperative for the eagle to leave. She had managed that, purely by dint of hiding between two large, slow-moving crows, and had been quietly sneaking off back the way she had just come when they'd spotted her and resumed their pursuit. Nothing flashy, you see, nothing clever; just plain, textbook stuff.

Her wings hurt like hell and her head was dizzy from too much climbing and swooping.

Meanwhile, the chariot was closing in; showing, it was true, a certain amount of circumspection, but nevertheless shortening the distance between them to an alarming extent. She'd tried looping a loop again, but they hadn't followed. They'd just waited till she came back straight and level again and resumed where they'd left off. When she'd hitched a ride in the undercarriage of a passing helicopter they had simply flown alongside throwing lightning-bolts, until the helicopter pilot had bailed out and his craft had gone spiralling away out of control. There really wasn't a lot left she could do, except maybe try smiling at them; and that probably wouldn't work, either.

'No,' said the Gorgon, 'not with a G, with a D.'

Jason frowned. 'You what?' he said.

'My name's *Gordon*, not *Gorgon*,' said the serpent-haired monster through the letter-box. 'You must have got the wrong address. Gor*gon* with a G lives – oh, a long way from here. Over the other side of those mountains over there, I think.'

'I don't believe you,' Jason said.

'Don't you?' The flap of the letter-box quivered slightly. 'Whyever not?'

Jason looked around at the large number of extremely lifelike stone statues that lined the drive of the house. Statues of postmen. Statues of milkmen. Statues of Jehovah's Witnesses. 'I just don't, that's all,' he said. 'Now are you coming out, or do I have to kick the door down?'

The flap snapped shut and Jason could hear a sound like a heavy stone statue being dragged against the door.

Probably, he reflected, a double-glazing salesman. He shrugged, strolled round to the back door, and kicked it in.

It was a curiously furnished house, to say the least, what with everything in it being made of stone and there being no mirrors or reflective surfaces; but Jason had a cousin who lived in one of those new developments in Docklands, so it didn't come as too much of a surprise to him. He made his way through the kitchen – there was a cup of coffee, literally stone cold, on the worktop; however did the poor creature ever manage to eat anything, he wondered; or did it live on nothing but gravel? – and arrived at the living-room door only to find it locked. He sighed and knocked politely.

'Hello?' he said.

'Go away.'

'I can't,' Jason said. 'Sorry.'

'No you're not,' replied the voice. Jason fingered the edge of the Sword and gave the surface of his brightly-polished shield a final rub.

'What I mean is,' he said. 'I'm not doing this for fun, you know. Left to myself, I couldn't care less. If you insist on turning people to stone, that's really a matter between you and your conscience. But I've got my job to do and I'm going to do it, so we can either do this the hard way or the easy way.'

There was a long silence. Then the voice said, 'So what's the easy way?'

'You come out,' Jason said, 'I cut your head off with this sword, that's it.'

'I see,' replied the voice. 'Let's give the hard way a shot, shall we?'

'I don't know what you're making all this fuss about,' Jason said. 'After all, I'm the one who should be scared. All

457

you have to do is look me in the eye and I turn to stone, right? Me, now, I've got to smash my way in, avoiding looking at you, of course, then fight with you, somehow keep myself from getting bitten by your hairstyle, cut your head off and wrap the bits up in a black velvet bag. Just ask yourself, where's the smart money going to be on this one?'

There was no reply. Jason considered this for a moment, then dashed quickly out through the kitchen and back to the front door. It was open.

'Oh bugger!' Jason said.

He lifted the shield and examined the reflection of his surroundings in it. There was a statue just by the door which hadn't been there before. He considered his next move carefully, while whistling.

'*Ouch!*' said the Gorgon, shortly afterwards.

'Don't blame me,' Jason replied. 'I gave you the choice, remember. Now, this may hurt a little.'

'You cheated.'

Jason drew his brows together, offended. 'I did not cheat,' he said. 'I just used my intelligence, that's all.'

'You cheated.'

'Rubbish.'

'If you don't call pretending to wander away and then rushing back and jamming a flowerpot over my head cheating,' said the Gorgon, 'then I do. A real Hero wouldn't have done that.'

Jason drew the Gorgon's attention to the fact that there were quite a few very realistic statues of real Heroes lining the drive, most of them with birds nesting in highly improbable places.

'Cheat.'

'You brought it on yourself, you know,' Jason said. 'Anybody else would have been satisfied with a couple of gnomes pushing wheelbarrows or fishing in the water-butt; but no, you had to be different.'

'So what's wrong with being different?'

'Nothing,' Jason said, 'so long as you don't leave large flowerpots lying about the place as well. You can do one or the other, but not both. Now, the next bit is rather tricky, so if you'll just hold still . . .'

A single snake's head pushed its way up through the hole in the bottom of the pot and hissed spitefully at Jason. 'Bully,' said the Gorgon.

'Sticks and stones,' said Jason. 'Now, then . . .' He pressed his foot firmly into the small of the Gorgon's back, swung the Sword up above his head, and made ready to strike. Then he saw something.

'Hey,' said the Gorgon. 'Just get on with it, will you?'

'Yes, all right,' Jason said. 'Just give me a minute, will you?' He was staring at the sky; or, to be more precise, at an eagle.

Not, let it be stressed immediately, that Jason was or ever had been a bird-watcher; whatever else he may or may not have done, his conscience was clean on that score. In the normal run of events, if a bird wasn't sitting on a plate with roast potatoes on one side and runner beans on the other, then he didn't want to know. But this bird was unusual in that it was being chased by a chariotful of Spectral Warriors, who were throwing bits of lightning at it. He lowered the Sword and stood watching.

'What,' said a resentful voice, slightly but not unduly muffled by a five-millimetre thickness of terracotta, 'the hell do you think you're doing?'

'Shut up,' said Jason, preoccupied. All eagles looked the same to him, but he could have sworn he'd seen that one before. Twice.

459

'Look,' he said, 'just wait there a minute, will you? I won't be two shakes.' Then he took his foot off the Gorgon's back and darted away.

For at least ten seconds the Gorgon simply lay there, too bewildered to move. Then it leapt to its feet, dashed its head against the flank of a life-sized marble effigy of an Avon lady, shook the fragments of flowerpot out of its snakes, and bolted. Compilers of dictionaries of mythology might like to note that the orthodox view that it was never seen or heard of again is not strictly true; it was, in fact, shortly afterwards offered a job by Fabergé staring at eggs and became a useful and productive member of society.

It was definitely the same eagle, and as he stood watching it struggling through the air Jason remembered that he owed it a hamburger. He sheathed the Sword, cupped his hands round his mouth and shouted, 'Hey!'

Aboard the winged chariot, the Captain of Spectral Warriors looked down at the figure on the ground below him.

'Hold it,' he said. 'That's the Derry kid.'

The charioteer turned his head and glanced quickly. 'So what?' he said. 'We're way out of range up here. Let's just keep going and . . .'

'What's he doing with that lump of *ouch*!'

Jason swivelled round, broke the other arm off the fossilised political canvasser who had at last proved useful to somebody, and let fly. The winged chariot banked violently and hurtled away across the sky like a frightened comet. The eagle fluttered for a few seconds, flopped to the ground and turned into a girl. Jason hurried across.

'Hiya, Mary,' he called out. Then he stepped back, looking puzzled. 'Or rather,' he said, 'Sharon.'

Betty-Lou Fisichelli polished her spectacles on her handkerchief, parked them on her nose and drew in a deep breath. She had never done this before.

Nobody now living – nobody now living and capable of death – had ever done this before. Partly because it was the most sacred of sacred mysteries; mostly because there just hadn't been any call for it. With a slightly moistened J-cloth she wiped away a thousand years of dust from the imperishable bronze of the statue's face, opened the manual on her knee, and looked for the place.

She was nervous. Apart from the perfectly understandable apprehension that anyone would feel about attempting the most sacred of sacred mysteries, there was also the fact that she was inside the vaults of the Delphi Archaeological Museum at half-past one in the morning without a pass. If she got caught, what with the Greek police being as they are, she doubted if even Apollo himself could save her.

CHAPTER ONE, she read, SETTING UP.

With trembling fingers, she took the two small, shining chips of metal from the matchbox in her handbag and pressed them carefully into the statue's empty eye-sockets. They fitted easily, and there was a faint click. At once, the broad bronze shield on the statue's arm began to glow, the verdigris giving off a bright green light. Then, suddenly, it went black, and a row of green lines materialised from nowhere. Once she had got her breath back, the Pythoness glanced down at the manual again.

Operating the Keyboard, it read.

The shield had stopped flashing green lines at her. Instead it displayed a message in sparkling green letters. It said: © *Copyright Olympian Software dlc. Unauthorised use of program material shall render the user liable to civil and criminal penalties.*

461

Then it went black again, and the statue said bleep, though without moving its lips. And then there were more letters on the screen, which read: *Hi!*

Ms. Fisichelli hopped that *Hi!* would disappear and be replaced by something rather less disconcertingly jovial, but it didn't. She dragged her attention back to the manual. Operating the keyboard.

Oh, very clever. Each of the fingertips of the statue's outstretched hands was a key, and to operate the upper case you stood on its toes. Tentatively she touched the left index finger. The shield flickered, and then read: *Error!!!*

Marvellous. She looked back at the manual and pressed the left middle finger. At once, a whole shieldful of words appeared, and a little green dot of light flashed on and off underneath them. That, the manual explained, was the Cursor. Ms. Fisichelli wondered idly what the Curse might turn out to be, and studied what the manual had to say about selecting a functions menu.

After a few minutes of bewildered concentration, she decided that what she wanted was Feedback Input Scan, and pressed the appropriate finger. The shield responded immediately. It now read: *Hiya!!!!*

Wouldn't it be easier, Ms. Fisichelli asked herself, to try and muddle through with a card index and a notched stick? Probably not. The manual now advised her to press the right ring fingertip and the left big toe simultaneously. She did.

Ouch!

Ms. Fisichelli apologised instinctively and looked down. No, she'd done it right. She glanced back at the screen, which now said: *Only kidding!!!*

Oh-for-crying-out-loud. If this was the state of the art in Olympian micro-electronics, perhaps now was the time to consider converting to Zen Buddhism.

Fun, this, isn't it!?

Painstakingly, Ms. Fisichelli selected the necessary fingertips to type in *No*.

The shield gave her a puzzled look and read *Error!!!* but she ignored it and went back to the right ring fingertip and the left big toe stage. She then remained aloof while the thing went through its tired little joke. Clearly you had to be something of a micro-electronics wizard if you wanted to input humour of your own into this gadget.

By this stage the shield read *Ready!!* which was apparently what it should do. Unfortunately, the next page of the manual was missing.

'Oh nuts!' said Ms. Fisichelli, uncharacteristically. She tried reading on, but it was hopeless. There was only one thing to do. Feeling slightly self-conscious, she stood on both the statue's feet and grabbed both its hands.

The result was incomprehensible but gratifyingly large-scale. The shield shimmered with a brilliant coruscation of messages in all the known languages and alphabets, alive, dead and intermediate. The statue said bleep, not once but many times. Its left ear began printing out.

After a while, things appeared to settle down, until there were only four words left on the shield. They were: *All right, you win*.

Ms. Fisichelli beamed, and then wondered what to do next. Fortunately, the shield told her.

Vocal input acceptable, it said. *Speak now*.

'Er,' she said.

The statue's lips quivered, then parted.

'Hi!', said the statue.

Ms. Fisichelli's jaw swung open and she forgot what she was going to say next. Probably just as well.

'C in a circle Copyright,' the statue went on, in a clear,

high monotone, like a Dalek newsreader. 'Olympian Software dlc. Unauthorised use of programme material shall render the user liable to civil and criminal penalties.'

'I . . .'

'Error!!'

'But . . .'

'Error!!'

'Scumbag!!'

'Ready!!'

'Oh.' Ms. Fisichelli wondered about that for a moment, and then decided that maybe you were supposed to lose your temper with the doggone thing. 'Look . . .'

'Input mode selected,' said the statue. 'Receiving,' it added helpfully. Ms. Fisichelli took a deep breath and started to talk, on the grounds that if the blasted thing said 'Ready!!' just one more time she would quite probably scream.

'Well,' she said, 'I'm terribly sorry to bother you like this, but none of the other divining instruments seemed to work, and I tried conjuring but of course you need an assistant for that really, and mine just turned into an eagle and left, so I wasn't able to get through that way and I was at my wits' end and then I suddenly thought, Wait a minute, I thought, there's always the Holy Icon, why don't I try that, and if you say "Error!!" at me I shall melt you down and have you recast as a bedstead, so be very careful.'

'Processing data,' said the statue, 'please wait.'

'Sure.'

The statue bleeped a couple of times, coughed and sighed. 'Input request command,' it said. 'Receiving.'

'Sorry?'

464

'What seems to be the problem?' said the statue.

Ms. Fisichelli relaxed and smiled. 'Right, then,' she said. 'It's sort of like this. You know I do prophesies, right?'

'Receiving,' said the statue. 'Oh, *sorry*, forgot. Yes?'

'Well, usually the prophecies come from Apollo, because, well, that's his job, OK? But the last couple of days I've been getting these prophecies, well, more sort of prophetic utterances, and I'm sure they can't be from him, because – well, I just sort of *know* they're not, OK? Don't ask me how I know, I just do. And of course, they're all like sort of riddles and I can't make head or tail of them and I thought perhaps, well, you might . . .'

'Input,' said the statue. 'Or rather, shoot, oh stuff this, input.'

'You're sure it's no trouble?'

'That's what I'm here for, receiving, continues, please wait, ready.'

'The first one,' said Ms. Fisichelli, 'came to me in my bath last night. I was just sort of, you know, sitting there, when suddenly I could hear myself saying this, well, *thing*.'

'Gee.'

'Sorry?'

'Error,' said the statue. 'Mine, not yours. Apology. Input. Open fire. Shit. *Shoot.* Sorry.'

'Er,' said Ms. Fisichelli. 'Oh yes. Well, what I must have said was . . .'

'Input?'

'Sorry,' replied Ms. Fisichelli. 'It's just a bit embarrassing saying it out loud. I mean, it all sounds so funny, if you see what I . . .'

'Correlates,' said the statue, sympathetically. 'Ignore error and continue.'

'Thanks. It went something like:

465

> *When that the Seed of the Pig conspires with the Door-*
>   *Half-Open,*
> *Then shall the Ducks'-Foe-Dwellers despair of their*
>   *humourless purpose,*
> *As Zippo, loosed from his bonds, devours a bacon sand-*
>   *wich.*

That's what it said, anyway,' Ms. Fisichelli added. 'Really.'

The statue bleeped thrice and burped. 'Computing,' it muttered. 'Data input up tree. Memory circuits active. Proceeding to foot of our stairs. Ready.'

'You mean you can understand all that stuff?'

'Confirming. Comparative values follow. Please wait.' The lights in the statue's eyes went out and then came on again. 'For Door-Half-Open, read When is a door not a door, when it's a jar, search, find First Joke, equivalents search to read, output equivalent Gelos Prometheus. For Ducks'-Foe-Dwellers, read Nice weather for ducks, find sun is foe of ducks, correlate sun-dwellers, output gods. For Zippo, read Fire-Producer, find Prometheus, correlates. For Seed of Pig read Jupiter is a Pig, find Jason Derry, correlates, bleep. Bacon sandwich does not copy, suggested correlation Prometheus is hungry, eats bacon sandwich, search completed, ready for new input.'

'Gosh,' said Ms. Fisichelli, 'aren't you clever. Well, the other one went:

> *Remember that Mother knows best how to deal with the*
>   *Smiter of Centaurs;*
> *That swords cannot cut what is stronger than steel that is*
>   *tempered in cocoa;*
> *Tough though the whites may be, the boil-wash may now*
>   *be dispensed with.'*

The statue made no noise of any description for a very long time. Then it sniggered, and said 'Computing. Offspring of canine female. Ready.'

'Yes. but . . .'

'Comparative values found,' the statue continued. 'For Smiter of Centaurs read Jason Derry, for difficulty rating read falling from chopped-down tree. For unit comparative value, read Jason Derry may be a right little tearaway but he's afraid of his mother, programme ends, exit.'

The lights in the statue's eyes went out, the shield ceased to shine, the little pieces of metal fell from the eyesockets and landed with a soft tinkle on the ground. Ms. Fisichelli stooped and put them back in their matchbox. That, it seemed, was that for this evening. She could take a hint. She put the matchbox and the manual back in her bag, switched off the lights and crept back up to the main gallery. Then she rummaged in her coat pocket for her skeleton key, unlocked the staff canteen door, and (ultimately) left the building.

A useful night's work, she said to herself, and just as soon as I can get hold of Apollo I'd better tell him all about it. Pity, though, she thought, that the statue hadn't waited to hear the third prophecy.

'Ungrateful little sod.'

'I am not an ungrateful little sod. Anyway, what the hell have you ever done that I should be grateful for?'

Sharon made a rude noise. 'Oh yes?' she said. 'All right, who was it warned you about the snakes in your pram, then? If it wasn't . . .'

'Nobody *warned* me,' Jason replied angrily. 'I just knew . . .'

'Bullshit,' said Sharon, who was not very ladylike, even

467

for an eagle. 'If I hadn't swooped down and made shrieking noises at you, you'd have been fast asleep. As it was, you nearly swallowed your sucker and I had to get it out of your throat with my claw. You bit me.'

'Good.'

Sharon raised one foot and made a sort of pawing movement with it before putting it back on the ground. 'And what about that time when you were three and you got stuck halfway up that big fir tree looking for phoenix nests . . .'

'I wasn't stuck,' Jason interrupted, 'just resting, that was . . . Hang on,' he said, as an unpleasant thought struck him, 'Are you trying to tell me you've been sort of watching over me or something ever since I was a kid?'

'Since before you were born, more like. Nasty little brat you were then, too.'

'I . . .'

'Talk about a messy little brute,' Sharon remembered. 'When you weren't up to your elbows in lion's blood you were all smeared with melted chocolate. Always stuffing yourself, even then.'

'Look . . .'

'When I remember the fuss you used to make whenever you had to have a bath! We could hear you in the next street; it was like someone killing a pig.'

Jason growled dangerously. 'Now look . . .' he said.

'And I'll never forget.' Sharon continued. either oblivious or unconcerned, 'that time when your mother left you in your pram outside the post office with the shopping bag, and when she got back . . .'

A true Hero, they say, will never strike a woman; so it was fortunate for Jason's blood pressure that Sharon was, at least to a certain extent, an eagle. If challenged, he reckoned, he could always say that he'd been aiming for the aquiline bits.

'*Ouch!*'

Jason lowered his hand, feeling that sort of furiously angry guilt that is usually reserved to small children. 'It's your fault,' he half-snarled, half-whimpered. 'You started it.'

'Didn't,' Sharon snuffled.

'Did.'

'Didn't.'

'Did.'

'Didn't didn't *didn't.*'

Jason was just about to rebut this line of argument when he caught sight of himself in the brightly-polished shield he'd used to fight the Gorgon with. What he saw, he recognised immediately as an idiot.

'Look,' he said gently.

'*Didn't!*'

'All right,' Jason shouted, 'you didn't bloody well start it, whatever it was. Only for pity's sake stop that bloody whimpering and tell me what's going on.'

'Shan't.'

Gods give me strength, Jason muttered under his breath, and then revoked the request at once. They'd already done that, and look where it had landed him. 'I'm sorry,' he said, 'all right?'

'You hurt me,' Sharon whined, and rubbed her ear vigorously. It would have been more effective if it had been the right ear, of course; but pain is an extremely transient condition for supernaturals, and in some areas they have extremely short memories. This can, in fact, be very inconvenient sometimes; for example, when they break a leg.

'Well, well,' Jason said. 'Something attempted, some-

469

thing done has earned a night's repose. Now, will you please tell me . . .?'

'All right,' Sharon said sullenly. And she told him.

She told him about the great plan to restore Gelos and thereby dislodge the gods for ever, and how he was an integral part of it, and how it was so important that he develop in the right way to fulfil his destiny that Prometheus had sent his own eagle to be born and grow up as the objectionable girl next door, where she could keep an eye on him nudge him in the right direction, drop heavy hints about hostile snakes in prams and so forth; how . . .

'I knew it!' Jason was furiously angry now, more so than he could ever remember being. 'Isn't that just bloody typical! That's my whole life, that is.' He toyed with the idea of drawing the Sword and splitting the Earth's crust with it, laying the Nether Kingdom open to the sunlight, out of pure pique. 'I mean, that's just bloody marvellous, isn't it? On the one hand, I've got Mum and Dad pushing me around, making me be a Hero and kill monsters and steal golden apples and all that crap; and now I find that Prometheus and your bloody lot have been doing exactly the same all along, only different. Why can't the whole bloody lot of you just bugger off and leave me in peace?' He jumped on the Gorgon-reflecting shield, denting it beyond economic repair, and kicked it away, Sharon folded her arms and looked at him, reminding him very much of his mother.

'All my life,' he went on, 'it's been nothing but do this, do that, and nobody gives a flying fuck what I want or what I think about anything. Well, that does it, I've had enough.' He looked around for something else to break, and eventually lit upon a life-size marble statue of a plumber, which he decapitated. 'At least that explains why Mum's been trying to push me off on you for as long as I can . . .'

Through the red cloud of rage that was fogging up his mind shone a tiny little ray of confusion. Did it?

'Does it?' said Sharon.

'Of course it does.' Doesn't it . . .?

Of course it does . . .

Oh no, not you again . . .

But . . .

Sharon seemed to melt suddenly. Her dumpy and exceptionally unerogenous figure blurred in front of his eyes, and grew taller and less broad. And then she wasn't there, but Mary was; and you could tell that Sharon had never really existed at all, just as a suit of clothes ceases to have any real meaning once the wearer has been removed from inside it.

'That's the spirit,' said Mary.

'Don't be so bloody patronising,' Jason managed to grumble; but his heart wasn't in it, being otherwise occupied.

'Sorry,' Mary said, 'I didn't mean to be. Look, Sharon's gone now, gone for good. She's served her purpose, you see. There's just me now.'

Just me, coming from her, was a contradiction in terms. Even so, that tiny little ray of confusion still glowed in his mind, like a distant lighthouse seen through dense mists.

'The reason for Sharon,' Mary was saying, 'was to get you nice and angry, just like you are now. That's what you had to do. Your mum doesn't have the faintest idea who Sharon was; neither did Jupiter. No, the whole point about Sharon was that one day you'd get so sick of the sight of her and her nasty, whining voice and her incessant fault-finding that you'd finally have the guts to break free from the power in heaven and earth capable of controlling you.'

Jason frowned. 'You mean Jupiter?'

471

'No.'

'Prometheus? Gelos?'

Mary shook her head. 'Your mother,' she said.

Jason thought about that. 'I see what you mean,' he said. 'Odd, I'd never seen it like that myself.'

'Well you wouldn't,' Mary said, 'now would you?'

'I suppose not.'

'That's the secret,' Mary went on. 'That's how Jupiter controls you. So, if you were ever to snap out of it and become a free agent, then you'd have to defy her, tell her to go boil her head; and the only thing we could think of that would make you do that was . . . well, a Sharon. And it's worked, hasn't it? Actually,' Mary admitted, 'it's gone and cocked itself up, because of course you found out about it before it could happen – before the final showdown, I mean – but the effect's been the same. Am I right?'

Jason considered. 'Yes,' he said slowly, 'I think you probably are. But,' – there was that little speck of light again; not three specks or dots of light, just one – 'there's something wrong with all this.'

'Is there?'

Jason scratched his head. 'Yes,' he replied. 'Most definitely. You see, I'm not a free agent, not a bit of it. I was right the first time. You are pushing me around, just as much as Jupiter's lot. And,' – Jason stood up straight, looked the girl of his dreams in the eye and saw nothing there that interested him – 'I'm having no part of it. Where's the point?'

'I'm sorry?'

'I said,' Jason replied, 'where's the bloody point? You aren't Mary, any more than you were Sharon. You designed Sharon expressly to get up my nose, and you've designed Mary to be the . . . the . . . well, anyway. What

472

you are, when you get right down to it, is a damn great eagle. And I'm very sorry, but I'm not selling my soul for something in feathers with a six-foot wingspan and little round yellow eyes. My profound apologies, but the deal's off.'

'Off?'

'Off,' said Jason. 'Go look for another Hero, because I'm retiring. Got that?'

'But Jason . . .'

'Don't anybody Jason me,' the Hero shouted, 'ever again. From now on, nobody tells me what to do. Nobody.'

He instinctively took a step back and put his hand on his sword-hilt. He was suddenly aware that he was big enough and ugly enough to do what the hell he liked, and the realisation was incredibly wonderful.

Mary smiled. 'You see?' she said.

Jason deflated like one of those balloons that people blow up at parties and then let go. 'You . . .'

'Exactly,' Mary said. 'It's worked. You've defied us, too.'

'Oh.' With what remained of his mental strength, Jason wrestled with the idea. 'Have I?'

'Looked like it from here.'

'Really?'

'Absolutely.' Mary came towards him and put her hands gently on his shoulders. 'We all knew you had it in you,' she said.

'So,' Jason said, 'I could tell you all to go and get stuffed, right now, if I wanted to.'

'If you wanted to,' Mary said, 'yes.'

'And nobody can tell me what to do?'

'Nobody can tell you,' Mary said softly, her lips close to his ear. 'But that doesn't stop them asking, does it?'

'No,' Jason said. 'I suppose not.'

473

Had Jason attended Professor Haagedorn's course at Wounded Elbow University, Wyoming, on predestination theory, he would have known that free will is perfectly possible, in the same way as a free lunch is perfectly possible. Just not very likely, that's all.

'And you wouldn't,' Mary whispered, 'want the gods to abolish laughter, now would you?'

'Well,' Jason said, 'no, I suppose not.'

'And you don't really think that Jupiter and Mars and Minerva and all that lot ought to be allowed to take the Universe over again, do you?'

'I . . .'

'Just think what a mess they made of it all last time.'

'Er . . .'

'So you will help, won't you?' Mary said. 'Please?'

CHAPTER TWELVE

'That's six and two makes eight, doubled for a free go, plus six penalty points because you revoked on the bidding, plus six above the line for a straight flush, plus fifteen for a clear round in Mercury, plus three bonus points for breaking service, makes . . .' Demeter had run out of fingers. 'Damn,' she said. 'Right, that's six and two makes eight . . .'

'Forty-six,' said Minerva coldly. 'Can we get on now, please?'

'Oh yes,' Demeter added, 'and another two for passing Novgorod. Forty-eight.'

Minerva gave her a look that would have kept milk fresh in the Sahara. 'Forty-eight, then,' she said. 'Now . . .'

'And,' Demeter said, 'another one for having two options in play during the same contract. Forty-nine.'

'Fancy!' Minerva replied. 'Now, if you've quite finished with the dice, perhaps I might have a . . .'

She threw, and the dice clattered on the marble floor of the sun.

'Oh hard luck, Min,' Demeter commiserated. 'That's the third time you've done that.'

'Yes,' Minerva said. 'I had noticed, thank you.'

'Not your day today, is it?'

'Indeed.'

'Now then.' Demeter scooped up the dice, blew on them (where did she get into that dreadfully common habit, Minerva wondered) and threw them, not omitting to shout 'Ha!' at the approved moment. 'Oh look,' she said, 'Double nine again. I am having a good day, aren't I?'

'If you throw double nine one more time in this turn,' Minerva said distantly, 'you go to Hades for three moves.'

'Well,' Demeter replied, 'that's hardly likely, is it?'

'It was hardly likely you'd throw it the last three times.'

'Fool's luck,' Demeter replied cheerfully. 'Well well, isn't that fortunate. You were just about to invade me and now I can invade you instead. Jolly hard luck, Min.'

Minerva closed her eyes for a moment, just long enough for a goddess to count to ten. 'Well, never mind,' she said, 'it's only a Game after all.'

The very thought of Minerva regarding it as only a Game was too much for Demeter. She sniggered. Then she invaded.

'It really isn't your day, is it?' she said. 'Look, all your armies have run out of petrol on the other side of the desert. Now if that isn't just the rottenest possible . . .'

Minerva stood up. 'How you can sit there wasting your time with this frivolous nonsense when there's important work to be done completely amazes me,' she said, and sniffed. Demeter looked up.

'Want to give it a rest for a bit, do you?' she said.

'I do think that in the circumstances . . .'

'You losing, you mean?'

'I am not losing.'

'Yes you are,' Demeter replied. 'But since it's only a

Game, what do you care? Actually, I wouldn't mind a few minutes' break myself. Cheerio.'

And, having ostentatiously noted the positions of the pieces on the board, Demeter wandered away in the direction of the kitchen. As she sat and stared at her stranded army in the flowing, trackless sands, Minerva found herself thinking, not for the first time, that it was a pity that Demeter had come into being several million years before Australia did. Otherwise, she felt, they would have been made for each other.

Frivolous nonsense, Minerva reminded herself. Instead, she would go and find out what was happening and do something about it.

Better to observe the passage of events, she climbed the spiral staircase to the Observation Saloon and sat in the Viewing Chair. From there, thanks to a freak refraction of light through the atmosphere of a profoundly bizarre Betamax world, it was possible to see the minutest details of what was going on on the surface of Earth. Minerva leaned forward in the Chair and concentrated on a certain spot in the Caucasus mountains.

What she saw was . . .

For the first time in a long time, a very long time, a very long time indeed, Mars was beginning to think that life wasn't such a pain in the neck after all.

Fighting he didn't hold with, but he was a born organiser, in the way that profoundly disorganised people often are. Without pausing to pluck the untidy desk and overflowing cupboard under the stairs out of his own eye, he delighted in sorting out the messes of others. Give him a clipboard, a box file and seven thousand little yellow stickers and he was as happy as a lamb in springtime.

'All right,' he was shouting, 'what's the hold-up? Get that lot unloaded and down to Base Camp 2 and look sharp about it. There's fifteen thousand tons of prefabricated girder bridge trying to get through . . . Oh, for crying out loud, you pillocks, not that way round. And who forgot to bring the butane cylinders?'

The Forms, stripped to their shirt-sleeves and sweating despite the cold, ignored him. In their opinion, in order to lynch one heavily-chained Titan there hadn't really been any need to bring one hundred and five thousand tons of pretzels, eight million forage caps, forty-seven million reams of white A4 duplicating paper, fifty-nine miles of three-core electric flex and seventy thousand soldering-irons. Someone, they felt, had got just the teeniest bit carried away. As for the piano . . .

Stupidity, promoted for the day to the rank of Staff Drum Lieutenant, tapped Mars gingerly on the shoulder.

'Sir,' he said, 'excuse me, sir.'

'Yes?'

'What should we do with the piano, sir?'

Mars glowered at him. 'Put it in the mobile officers' club,' he said, 'what do you think?'

'But sir,' said the Form, 'we didn't bring the mobile officers' . . .'

'You what?'

'It wasn't on the manifest, sir,' said the Form. 'Look . . .'

He thrust a clipboard under Mars's nose. The Widow-Maker groaned.

'Right,' he said. 'In that case, clear out one of those mobile field chiropody units, put in a few chairs and tables, get some bottles and some glassware and a few cut flowers and shove the piano in that. Whatever the hell happened to initiative?'

478

'Sir!' Stupidity saluted briskly, turned and wandered away, shaking his head sadly. Bloody amateurs.

For his part, Mars sat down on a half-empty packing case that had contained forty-six thousand pairs of tropical weight nylon undersocks, licked the tip of his biro, and started to write.

From: C-in-C, Caucasus Theatre
To: Divisional Commanders
Re: Centralised Stationery Distribution . . .

He was just getting nicely into it when a Colonel of Spectral Warriors came and stood over him, casting a shadow over his page.

'All ready to go, sir,' said the Spectral Warrior.

'Sorry?'

'All units deployed, sir,' the Warrior explained. 'Weapons checked, intelligence reports received and analysed, ammunition distributed, sir.'

Mars looked up. 'So?'

'So,' said the Spectral Warrior, 'do we go get the bastard, or what? Sir,' he added.

Mars wobbled nervously. 'Are you sure everything's ready?' he said.

'Positive, sir.'

'Don't you think it would be a good idea to have a final kit inspection and a general stocktaking at brigade level?'

'No, sir.'

'Lines of supply all in place, are they? Pontoon bridges all built?'

'Yes, sir.'

'Everybody returned their pink pension scheme questionnaires?'

'Yes, sir.'

Mars swallowed hard. This was the bit he didn't like.

479

'So,' he said, 'what you're saying is, there's absolutely nothing to stop us getting on with it.'

'Correct, sir.'

'Ah,' Mars replied. 'Fine. Well done, everybody. Well then, I suppose we'd all better . . .'

Just then, a tiny dot appeared in the sky. It was so small and so far away that you'd have thought nobody would have noticed it. Somehow, though, everybody did.

'Hold it a moment, Colonel,' Mars said. 'What do you make of that?'

The Spectral Warrior shaded his eyes with his hands. 'Looks like an eagle to me, sir. And a man. And a dog. Sir.'

Mars suddenly began to feel a very familiar feeling of being about an eighth of an inch away from the smelly stuff. 'Well don't just stand there,' he snapped. 'Get going. Nail the little sod.'

The Colonel saluted, then turned back, perplexed. 'By that, sir, do you mean the Titan or the eagle with the . . .?'

By then, of course, it was all too late. The dot had become bigger. It had also become three dots. Three dots streaming through the air. Three dots . . .

'Fire!' Mars yelled hysterically. Nothing happened.

Jason, meanwhile, had leapt from the eagle's back and was standing on a mountain-top, brandishing the Sword. At his feet, the Triple-Headed Hell-Hound was baying with two heads; the third was sniffing something on the ground directly under Jason's left foot – and overhead the eagle circled menacingly.

'This is asinine,' Mars yelled at his huge, silent, foot-shuffling army. 'There's twenty million of us and three of them. Pull your bloody fingers out, the lot of you!'

In the Spectral ranks, nobody moved. As for the Forms, they were all trying to turn back into figures of speech without anybody noticing. Stupidity hid behind the piano and, rather counter-intuitively, began to pray.

Then, from the Divine ranks, a single figure stepped forward.

'Hoo-bloody-ray,' muttered the Widow-Maker. 'Now can we please make a start, before the little jerk dies of old age?'

Nobody paid any attention to him. Forty million eyes were fixed on the one black shape strolling easily up the side of the mountain towards Jason, the eagle and the dog.

In the snooker-room of the Spectral Warriors Social Club and Institute one can, if one has the necessary degree of masochistic nerve, hear all the nastiest, most stomach-churning stories in the world's repertoire. Approximately seventy-two per cent of them share the same central character.

For example, there was the occasion on which Jupiter put out a contract on the King of Trasimene, who had incurred the Sky-Father's unquenchable enmity by wearing lemon socks with an Old Carrhasians tie. Owing to a complicated nexus of oracles, oaths and rainbow-sealed covenants, the gods were forbidden to offer violence in any shape or form to Gorgias II during his lifetime. So they sent for the one being in the whole of Creation capable of dealing with the problem, with the exception of the Air Traffic Controller at Athens Airport, unquestionably the most widely feared and hated being in the whole of the Universe. And sure enough, twenty-four hours later, Gorgias II had ceased to exist. Nothing was ever found of him, not so much as a trouser-button or a fire-blackened cufflink. A consignment of two dozen lavender silk cravats ordered by him from Gieves and Hawkes were found on arrival to have dissolved into their component atoms and soaked away into the wrapping-paper.

481

Some said that he had worked it by travelling back through time, hanging around Gorgias's mother shortly before she met Gorgias's father, and so preventing him from ever being born. Others pointed to the appearance of an unpredicted bifurcation in the fabric of possibility, closely followed by a violent eruption of molten logic in Macedonia measuring 34.76 on the Rictus scale, and the observation of a hitherto unrecorded star in the constellation of the Distributor Cap. Most people, however, just shuddered and tried not to think about it.

There was a silence you could have filled cracks with by the time he reached the top of the mountain, and Jason could hear nothing but the sound of his own heart pounding. It wasn't a very pleasant sensation, since he could tell that this wasn't just ordinary Let's-get-the-blood-moving-along-chaps pounding; this was the heart demanding to be let *out* . . .

'Hi.'

'Er,' Jason replied. Not the snappiest of answers, perhaps, and maybe Boswell wouldn't have jotted it down if Johnson had said it of a Saturday night down the Cheshire Cheese; but it is worth recording as one of the few replies that he has ever received from a potential victim.

'Nice up here, isn't it?'

'Well . . .'

'Good view.'

'I . . .'

'Apparently, you can see Stavropol from here,' he said, staring out in entirely the wrong direction. 'On a clear day of course,' he added.

'Er.'

'Stavropol,' he went on, 'is somewhere I've never been actually, but they say you can get a really authentic shish kebab at Jagadai's Café, down by the railway arches; I mean, you can really taste the little bits of burnt wool and everything. I forget who told me that.'

'Um.'

He turned round, swung his arms and appeared to do deep breathing exercises. 'Lovely air, too,' he said, and coughed. 'Sort of crisp.'

Jason squeezed a little of this highly recommended air into his chest, past the rather large blockage that had formed in his windpipe, but all he did with it after all that effort was say 'Um' again.

'Sorry?'

'Nothing.'

'Well,' he said, 'this is nice, isn't it?'

A tiny message wriggled up Jason's spine and clambered into his brain. This guy is scared, it said, and was immediately shushed by millions of nervous brain cells. That, presumably, is why it's known as the nervous system.

'Er,' said he.

They looked at each other.

Just as Jason felt his bowel muscles starting to give up – not, of course, that he knew the meaning of fear; it must have been something he ate – he made a slight whimpering noise, put both hands over his ears and started to run back down the mountain, as fast as his legs could carry him or maybe just a little faster. One little brain cell inside Jason's head smirked, said *I told you so*, and then wondered why it found it so hard to make friends. Jason, meanwhile, was dashing off down the mountain after him, and when he tripped over his flowing black robe and sprawled head-long, Jason wasn't far behind.

'Eeek!' he said and curled himself up into a tight, quivering ball, like a bald hedgehog.

'Come on out of it, you,' Jason replied sternly. It's remarkable what an effect the sight of a cowering enemy can have on one's vocabulary; if someone had asked Jason right then for a word meaning 'Painful emotion caused by impending danger or evil', he'd probably have replied 'Seasickness'.

'No.'

'All right then,' said Jason. 'Suits me.'

The ball uncurled itself quickly, and Jason could see two eye-sockets staring up at him from the recesses of his shroudlike hood.

'Please don't say it,' he said.

Jason blinked, but managed to keep his stern, remorseless expression steady and not giggle. 'We'll see about that,' he replied. 'Say what, exactly?'

'The Joke,' he replied. 'Whatever you do, please don't say it. Not that I'm saying you wouldn't do it terribly well, but . . .'

Jason remembered. The Joke, of course; Gelos's joke, the great joke, joke of jokes. So that was what they were all afraid of . . .

'There was this guy,' he said savagely, 'went into this hardware shop, right, and he said . . .'

'Eeeeeeeeeeek!'

'Don't panic. It's all right,' Jason said. 'Just kidding about. But you tell your pals down there that next time . . .'

'Yes. Right.'

'Got that?'

He nodded vigorously. If he'd had a tail, he'd have wagged it, and that would have been Jason's stern, remorseless expression gone for good.

'Fine,' said Jason. 'Now push off.'

He scrambled up, gave Jason a look of pure terror, and

then bounced away down the slope and into the serried ranks of Spectral Warriors, who retreated slightly. The eagle, who had been circling overhead, swooped down and pitched on Jason's shoulder.

'Ouch,' Jason said.

The eagle ignored him and put its beak next to his ear. Eagles cannot, of course, whisper, because of the bone structure of their beaks.

'Yes,' Jason said. 'Nice one.'

The eagle spread its wings and launched itself into the air. For his part, Jason straightened his spine, put his shoulders back, and faced the Divine Army, ranged below him in the natural amphitheatre formed by the mountain slopes. He took a deep breath and tried to imagine he was wearing a loud check suit and a red nose.

'Ladies and Gentlemen,' Jason shouted, 'a funny thing happened to me on the way to the Caucasus this evening. I was walking along, minding my own business, when this man . . .'

He paused and looked down. The Spectral Warriors Forms and gods had all gone, vanished into thin air, and he was alone. Except for the three-headed dog, of course; and the eagle, who floated over and nodded approvingly.

'It's the way you tell them,' it said.

'Look!' said the eagle.

Jason turned round. 'Where?' he said.

'There,' replied the eagle. Since eagles cannot talk, it naturally follows that they cannot have voices that are resonant with awe and reverence. So it must have been Jason's imagination.

'I can't see anything,' Jason said. 'Are you sure you're . . .'

485

'There, you cretin,' said the eagle. 'Oh, blow you.' It spread its wings and floated off on a gust of warm air that had no meteorological foundation whatsoever. Jason stared hard but couldn't make out anything. It was getting late and cold and he couldn't really see that he was needed here any more; and he was beginning to feel peckish. He thought of Baisbekian's Diner.

Then the mountain behind him cleared its throat.

Readers are asked to pay close attention to what follows, as the author cannot be held responsible for any sensations of disorientation or confusion which may result from careless reading practices.

'Jason,' said the mountain, 'are you busy for a moment?'

Jason thought hard. No, he decided, mountains can't talk, and neither can eagles, for that matter, let alone three-headed dogs. In a world such as this, there is much to be said for staying in bed with your head under the pillows.

'Hello?' he ventured.

'Yes, hello to you too,' said the mountain. 'Are you busy for a moment?'

'That depends,' Jason replied.

'On what?'

'On what you had in mind,' Jason said. 'And if you're a mountain, will you please stop talking to me, because I only have a very tenuous grip on reality at the best of times, and . . .'

'I'm not a mountain.'

'It's all very well you saying that,' Jason said, 'but how can I be sure? You look pretty much like a mountain to me.'

'What you're looking at is indeed a mountain,' said the mountain. 'I happen to be behind the mountain. Does this clarify matters for you?'

'Not really,' Jason replied. 'Who are you?'

'Prometheus.'

Little wheels went round in Jason's mind, and the result was three oranges and a Hold. 'Oh,' he said, 'yes. Right. Where exactly are you, then?'

'Behind the bloody mountain, like I just said.'

'Fine,' said Jason. 'Give me . . .' He made a quick estimate. 'Give me half an hour and I'll be with you.'

In fact, it took him just under twenty minutes to get within sight of the Titan, thanks to a short-cut through a narrow ravine, which fortunately didn't say anything to him as he clambered through it.

'What kept you?'

'Look.' Jason had turned his ankle in the ravine and accordingly he wasn't feeling at his most lovable. 'Would you mind just explaining . . .?'

'The chains,' said Prometheus.

'Yes,' Jason replied. 'Aren't they?'

'Aren't they what?'

'Chains.'

Prometheus raised his head, uprooting a large tree, and looked at him. 'Just cut them, will you?'

In the back of his mind – the only part still capable of function – the right question drifted to the surface and bobbed uncertainly.

'Why?' Jason asked.

'What do you mean, why?' Prometheus said. 'Because they're stopping me from moving, that's why. Get on with it, please.'

'But,' Jason said, 'what I mean is, why should I? I tried to go into all this before, but things kept happening and I never came to a satisfactory conclusion. Look, will someone please give me some idea of what's happening, because otherwise I'm going on strike.'

As it happens, there have been occasional strikes by Heroes, the most notable being the Withdrawal of the Labours of Hercules; however, they rarely last long and never achieve anything, perhaps because all Heroism is intrinsically unnecessary. When Hercules fell out with Jupiter following a breakdown of negotiations over unsocial hours payments, for example, Jupiter replied by drafting in contingents of Forms who were able to do Hercules's feats in half the time and without terrorising supernatural wildlife or stopping every twenty minutes to beget children. On the other hand, it is felt that Heroes marching up and down outside temples with placards looks bad, and in any event the demands of the average Hero are so modest that it would be mean minded not to agree to them.*

'You can't,' Prometheus said, however. 'The schedule's too tight.'

'What schedule?'

'Just cut the chains,' Prometheus replied. 'Come *on*, will you?'

'Oh for crying out . . .' Jason hefted the Sword of That's A Silly Name For A Sword, Anyway, whirled it round his head, and sliced through the nearest chain. The shock of the metal biting into the adamant jarred every bone in his body. The chain fell in two.

'Ouch!'

'And the next one.'

'All right, keep your hair on.'

---

*It is a little-known fact that all Heroes really want out of life is power, glory, victory, wine, sex, money, respect, adventure and chocolate, not necessarily in that order. The celebrated Bellerophon, who tamed the winged horse Pegasus and killed the murderous, death-dealing Chimera, wanted jam on it as well; but so what, jam's cheap.

'It's not my hair I'm concerned about.'

'If I cut through the next chain, will you tell me what's going on?'

'If you don't cut through the next chain, I won't tell you what's going on.'

'Ouch.'

'Two down, two to go.'

'Look . . .'

'You'll find it over there, at the top of that mountain. It won't take you a quarter of an hour if you run.'

'But . . .'

'I see,' Jupiter said.

Big chief speak with forked tongue. It was obvious, to Mars at least, that Jupiter didn't see, one little bit. Whether in the long run it would be worth making one last effort to enlighten him was something that Mars (who, unlike Apollo, is not a prophetic deity) could only guess at. He guessed safe.

'All those Forms,' Jupiter continued, 'all those Spectral Warriors, all that overtime, and you ran away. Because,' said the Thunderer, his eyebrows coming together, 'one mortal offered – I'm sorry, threatened – to tell you a joke.'

'Well,' said Mars, 'yes.'

'A joke.'

'Exactly.'

Jupiter stroked his beard, and the static electricity thereby generated would have removed the need for nuclear power in the industrialised nations for a century. 'Don't you think you might have been a trifle over-cautious, all things considered? Played it just a little too safe?'

Mars straightened his back and shook his head. 'No,' he said. 'Definitely not.'

489

Jupiter raised an eyebrow. Nobody ever said *Definitely* to him unless they were absolutely convinced of something or else had a great desire to be a frog. 'Perhaps,' he said, 'we ought to have a board meeting.'

Mars, feeling like a turkey on Christmas Eve who hears that everyone has been converted to Jainism overnight, nodded and hurried out of the Presence.

He found Minerva in the sun-lounge, lying on the sofa with her shoes off reading *Harpers & Goddess*. She looked at him over her spectacles.

'Well?' she said. 'Where's the fire?'

'Board meeting,' Mars replied. 'In ten minutes in the Great Hall.'

'Board meeting?' Minerva swung her legs to the floor and put heel to slingback. 'What's happening, Ma?' she said. 'There hasn't been a board meeting for eleven hundred years. He's not on about privatisation again, is he, because I went through the figures and . . .'

Mars frowned. He had thought it strange that Minerva had been lying around reading at a time like this anyway. 'It's the Prometheus situation,' he said, 'what do you think? Look, I've got to dash. Ask someone else, all right?'

'What Prometheus situation? I thought you'd . . .'

'It was a wash-out,' Mars replied quickly. 'So now . . .'

'You messed it up, you mean?'

'Yes.'

'How?'

'Flair,' Mars replied. 'Either you've got it or you haven't.'

'Right.' Minerva stood up briskly and marched out of the sun-lounge. Oh dear, said Mars to himself, it's going to be one of those meetings.

He found Apollo in the library, Diana in the gym and Neptune beside the swimming-pool, and then rushed off to find Demeter, who wasn't in the kitchen. Instead he found Pluto, making himself a cup of tea.

'Board meeting,' he announced.

'You don't say?' Pluto replied. 'Well, well.' The spoon writhed between his fingers, hissed and slithered away behind the sink.

Demeter turned out to have been in the kitchen garden, weeding the sunflowers. 'What's a board meeting?' was her reaction, and when he explained she asked if this would be a good time to raise the issue of rainfall allowances for the cloud-shepherds. As he chased off to round up the rest of the quorum, Mars found himself speculating as to why he bothered.

'Ye gods!' he muttered under his breath.

Clang.

'*Now*,' Jason said, 'Will you explain?'

The Earth shook. Slowly, very slowly, painfully slowly, the Titan flexed muscles that hadn't moved since before the destruction of Atlantis. He wiggled his toes, scattering topsoil in a whirling cloud.

'Only,' Jason went on, 'so many downright weird things have been happening lately, with me all mixed up in them, that unless someone lets me in on it all pretty soon . . .'

Imagine the sound – the last thing we want is endless product liability lawsuits, and so we will only tax one area of sensory perception to its uttermost limits at a time – the sound of a glacier scoring its way across a landscape at forty miles an hour instead of its usual mile every four thousand years. That's Prometheus getting to his knees.

The next sense we will dislocate with sheer vastness is sight. Imagine a mountain rearing up in front of your eyes, stretching, complaining, and then standing upright. That's Prometheus getting to his feet.

And finally, imagine the sort of earthquake you'd get if some gigantic and malevolent deity squeezed the Earth like an enormous spot, sending molten magma spouting out of all its half-healed volcanoes, faults and fissures. That's what it felt like to be standing in the Caucasus when Prometheus landed after he'd jumped up, punched the air and yelled 'Yo!' at the top of his voice.

'When you've quite finished,' Jason said.

The Titan looked down at the tiny dot below him, and grinned. 'Sorry,' he said, 'I'd love to stop and chat for a bit, but I have to get going. Ask the eagle, she'll tell you.'

Then, with a stride that arched over mountains, the Titan walked off. Far away, Jason could hear a sound like someone very tall and strong punching the palm of his hand with his fist and saying 'Right!'

'Be like that,' Jason said, and started to walk down the mountain. He had gone about thirty yards when a foot the size of York Minster landed beside him.

'Jason Derry?'

Metaphor is tricksy stuff. It is not actually possible to jump out of one's skin; but it is possible to try. Jason tried.

'It is you, isn't it?' The voice was slightly muffled, but that was because the words had to travel through a lot of thick cloud before they reached Jason's ears. 'Has he gone?'

Jason looked up. By craning his neck until he felt something give, he could just see, far up in the sky, a belt buckle. 'Sorry?,' he said. Then, for no reason at all that he could see, his lips arched into a grin and he felt a laugh creep cough-like across his lungs. No need to ask who the tall person was.

'Prometheus,' said the voice of Gelos. 'Has he gone yet?'

'Yes.'

'Which way?'

Jason blinked. 'I'd have thought you'd be able to see him from up there.'

'You know how it is,' said the voice. 'My eyes aren't what they were, I can't pick out little tiny details any more. Look, time's pressing rather; we've only got five minutes before the orbits are lined up, so . . .'

Jason may have been small compared to Gelos, but by now he was so fed up that mere size really didn't matter. 'Right, Buster,' he said grimly. 'Tell me what's going on or I'll . . .' He stared up at the mountain of toecap that rose high above his head. 'Or I'll give you a chiropody session you'll never forget. You hear me?'

Gelos chuckled. 'I won't tell you,' he said, 'but you can watch.'

A hand – we can tell it was a hand because we're far enough away to see it all in proportion; to Jason it was just a very big pink thing – reached down and very gently flicked Jason up into its own palm. 'Which way?' the voice repeated.

With a monumental effort Jason hauled himself up out of a ravine that was in fact Gelos's life line. 'Straight ahead,' he said. 'Head for that tall mountain over there.'

The enormous thing lurched forward. 'Which mountain?'

'The one you just trod on.'

'It's all right,' said Gelos, 'I can see him for myself now. Hey, Pro!'

Far away, Jason could see the Titan. He seemed to have grown; so, in fact had Jason. Actually, all that had happened was that his brain had adjusted the field of view and proportion registers of his brain to enable him to cope with the scale on which he was now operating. Under normal

493

circumstances this would have taken several million years of evolution, but we can only assume that Jason was a quick learner. Anyway, he could see Prometheus, and above him he could see Gelos, and below him very much below him – he could see the world. There was just about enough room on it for them both to stand, although very soon there wouldn't be.

'Hold tight, Jason Derry.' It sounded as if both giants had said it at the same time; and that wasn't as remarkable as it might have been, since now that Jason could see them both clearly, he noticed that they looked extremely alike. Sort of like twins; or reflections in a mirror. No, let's stop pussyfooting. They are *exactly* alike.

And now there was only one of them.

'Excuse me,' said Jason.

'Yes?' There were two voices; but both speaking in perfect harmony and coming from one throat. The two giants had merged.

'Oh,' said Jason. 'Nothing.'

'Excuse us,' said the giant(s), 'but we need our hands free, so if you wouldn't mind . . .'

Jason felt himself travelling through the air at devastating speed; and then what he could now perceive was a hand put him in what he was able to recognise as a shirt pocket. The pocket of a very big shirt; so big that the gaps between the weave of the cotton were large enough to fly an airliner through. Fortunately, the fibres of the cotton were as wide as the average motorway, and so there was no danger of falling through; and through the weave, Jason had a splendid view of what happened next.

High above his head he could see the stars; not as little points of light but as huge balls of fiery gas. The planets of the solar system were so big that he felt he could reach out and touch them. But what he mostly noticed was the other Earths.

We know them to be Betamax worlds, but Jason didn't. He just thought they were a lot of identical – fairly identical – copies of the thing he remembered having seen on globes. One of these globes was swinging down through the firmament, dragging a moon behind it like a very fat lady with a very fat dog on a lead. The giant(s) reached out a hand, grabbed hold of it, closed his/their fingers round it and said, 'Gotcha!'

'Excuse me.'

'Yes?'

'What are you doing?'

The giant(s) smiled. 'Saving the world,' he/they said.

'Ah,' Jason said. 'Right.'

'Not this one, of course,' the giant(s) went on. 'The other one.'

'Fine.'

'This one,' said the giant(s), tossing the Betamax world up in the air and catching it, 'is a right little tinker.'

'Really?'

'Here,' said the giant(s), 'look for yourself.'

'No, really,' Jason said. 'I'm quite happy to take your word for it.'

The giant(s) laughed. 'You wanted to know what was going on, you look and see for yourself. Here, catch.' And the giant(s) threw the planet to Jason.

Who, to his everlasting amazement, caught it.

According to ancestral belief, Delphi is the dead centre of the world; or, as the ancient Hellenes so quaintly put it, the earth's navel. On a hot day in high season, however, armpit might be a more fitting description.

Betty-Lou Fisichelli plodded from her office across the road from the museum up towards the temple site to post the day's messages in the usual place. Not that there was anything much: *Is this a good time to invest in Far Eastern unit trusts?* and *Congratulations! You have been selected as a lucky finalist in our prize draw* didn't seem to her to be crammed with arcane significance and could probably wait. Nevertheless, a good Pythoness doesn't take it upon herself to edit; only to relay.

When she finally reached the Treasury of the Athenians, she found it deserted except for forty-six French tourists, a three-headed dog and an eagle. Oddly enough, the tourists didn't seem able to see the dog or the eagle, but nothing tourists failed to notice surprised Ms. Fisichelli any more. What did surprise her was that the eagle was there at all.

'You!' she said.

The eagle looked down at its talons and made a very slight but deprecating gesture.

'How you've got the nerve to show your beak here,' Ms. Fisichelli went on, 'after the way you . . .' She tailed off. The dog was looking at her.

In fact, there was no anthropomorphic message in the dog's stare; it was just a doggy stare, plain and simple. But Ms. Fisichelli was nervous around dogs at the best of times, and a doggy stare in triplicate was not her idea of good vibes.

'Be that as it may.' She pulled herself together. 'Well, if you've got anything to say, I'd be grateful if you got on with it. My time is not without . . .'

The eagle gestured with its head towards the tourists, who were staring at her. They seemed uneasy, and none of them had asked her to take a photograph of them beside a pile of fallen-down masonry; in Delphi, this is tantamount to ostracism. Ms. Fisichelli sighed, and led the way up the hill.

On top of the hill at Delphi there is a large Roman race-track, trimmed tastefully with bushes. There, Ms. Fisichelli sat down heavily on a stone (did we mention that the hill is steep?) and said, 'Well?'

The eagle looked at the dog, who wagged its tail as if to suggest that it was incapable of speech and none of this had been its idea anyway. It's amazing what can be communicated with a few inches of mobile fur-covered appendix.

'Hi, Betty-Lou,' said the eagle.

'Mary,' replied Ms. Fisichelli, coldly affable. 'How've you been keeping?'

'Oh, fine, fine,' said the eagle. 'Look, I guess I owe you an explanation.'

'I guess you do.'

'Well,' said the eagle. It shifted its grip on the rock and winced. 'Look, would it be easier for you if I became human for a bit?'

'That's entirely up to you,' said Ms. Fisichelli. 'Far be it from me to dictate . . .'

'Thanks,' said Mary, shedding her feathers and donning a pale blue sun-dress with small pink flowers. 'My talons were killing me,' she explained.

'So then,' Ms. Fisichelli said. 'You were about to say something.'

'Yes,' Mary replied. 'Look, you've probably guessed or been told, I'm Prometheus's eagle. You know, the one who was given the job of ripping the poor guy's liver out every morning and evening as part of his punishment . . .'

'I'm a graduate of six universities,' Ms. Fisichelli interrupted. 'I do know my basic mythology, thank you.'

'Sorry.' Mary repressed an urge to spring into the air,

497

spread her wings and scream; she picked at her thumbnail instead. 'Well, Pro and I . . . When you've known someone as long as that, you can't help sort of getting to understand a guy, and besides, what the gods did to him was wrong. He was only trying to help the mortals, and they stomped him. The gods don't like us, Betty-Lou, they . . .'

'By us,' Ms. Fisichelli said, 'do you mean humans, or eagles?'

'Neither,' Mary said, 'only themselves. You know about the First Joke, don't you? And how they want to do away with comedy and take the world over again?' Ms. Fisichelli nodded. 'And you don't think someone ought to stop them? Godsdamnit, Betty-Lou, can you imagine for one moment what that would be like? A world with no laughter in it? We just couldn't survive.'

Mary realised as she said this that Ms. Fisichelli had managed to survive for over thirty-five years in this cold hard world without having a lot to do with humour; probably she kept out of its way, and if she couldn't do that she sort of stepped over it. But that, Mary felt, proved her point.

'Well,' she went on, '*we* couldn't survive, anyway. So Pro asked me if I'd help him, and I said yes. And so I sort of became his assistant, did all the leg-work for him. It was fun; I enjoyed it. For one thing, he showed me how I could make myself human again; in fact, several humans. That's cool, except there's some of me give me a pain in the butt, but never mind. I don't have to live with me, after all.'

Ms. Fisichelli remained unimpressed. 'So?' she said.

'So,' Mary went on, 'we found this hero, an actual son of Jupiter, someone who'd actually have the nuts to defy the gods and cut the chains at the proper moment and . . . pardon me, have you got the right time there, please?'

Ms. Fisichelli showed Mary her watch-face.

'That's good,' Mary said, 'because any minute now, Pro's going to be set loose and he's going to put a stop to this down-with-laughter thing once and for all. And once that happens, Betty-Lou, there's going to be big trouble.'

'So I should think,' said the Pythoness, loyally.

'For the gods, I mean.' Mary shrugged. 'Me,' she said, 'I can't see what Pro's worried about. If you ask me, they've got it coming. But he says no, they're the gods, you've got to have them, so long as they don't interfere too much. Without gods, he says, who could we blame for things? He wants to save them.'

'Save them?' Betty-Lou gasped. 'What from?'

'Themselves, mostly,' Mary said. 'You see, right now, they're having a board meeting. Have you the faintest notion what that means?'

Betty-Lou shook her head.

'Think of the end of the world,' said Mary, 'with added bickering, and you'll get the idea. Once they discover what's happened, Jupiter is going to be very, very angry. He's going to want to start saying it with thunderbolts. Now these days, you can't do that; you start spraying thunderbolts about the place, you're going to set off all the nuclear early-warning systems the superpowers aren't supposed to have any more, and the next thing you know it'll be goodbye, Earth. And the gods will be so busy falling out with each other and accusing each other of cutting bits out of the Sunday papers and leaving the top off the toothpaste that they won't notice what's happening and stop it. And if the Earth ceases to exist, then so do the gods. This is the world they're tied to; when it goes, so do they. Not us,' Mary added, 'them. When all the dust settles, it'll be them who aren't there any more. We'll be all right.'

'Why?'

'Reality bifurcation,' Mary said.

Ms. Fisichelli frowned; for a moment she'd thought Mary had said Reality Bifurcation. 'Pardon me?'

'It says,' Mary replied, 'in Article Seven of the Universal Charter of Possibility that it's impossible for the gods to destroy the Earth – the Number One Earth – except at the ordained time and through the proper channels. There's, oh, forms that've got to be filled in, that sort of thing. Public enquiries. Notices posted up outside town halls. What I mean is, they can't just do it by accident. So what'll happen is that an alternative world will come into being on which they *do* manage to destroy themselves – and the world too, of course; pretty short-lived world, huh? – and then it'll just happen. Only they won't be here any more. The Probability Police will see to that. I'm telling you, those guys are *mean*. You think death's a tough baby, you wait till you meet Sergeant Kawalski.'

Betty-Lou sagged like an Easter egg on a radiator. 'You can't be serious,' she said. 'They're the gods, Mary; nobody can push the gods around.'

'Don't bet on it,' Mary said. 'Just think what happened to Woden.'

Ms. Fisichelli fell silent and gnawed her lip, for Mary undoubtedly had a point. One of the first things young astrotheological students are told is the story of how, shortly after Woden, chief god of the now defunct Nordic pantheon, offended against the Possibility regulations by restoring his dead son Balder to life on a Sunday without a resuscitation certificate in a residential area, he was abducted by three large, anonymous men in a blue and white chariot. His severed head was later found outside the palace of Offa, King of the East Saxons (who shortly afterwards abandoned the beliefs of his forefathers accepted Christianity and made a pilgrimage to Salt Lake City); the rest of his body was never recovered. The kidnappers were later identified as Possibility Policemen. Although nobody has ever been able satisfactorily to establish what actually happened to Woden, it is thought that they made him an Offa he couldn't refuse.

Ms. Fisichelli thought about it, and shuddered, until she resembled a brightly-dressed blancmange on a speeding trolley. 'But he wasn't a proper god, surely,' she said at last. 'And anyway . . .'

She fell silent; somehow or other she had contrived to run out of anyways.

'It's serious,' Mary said. 'That's what Pro thinks, anyway.'

Ms. Fisichelli frowned. 'So just what am I supposed to be able to do about it?' she said.

'Easy,' Mary replied. 'Just get Apollo down here before he has a chance to go to the board meeting.'

'Apollo?' Ms. Fisichelli's eyebrows shot up like share prices in April. 'Why him?'

Mary grinned. 'You'll see,' she said. 'Do you think you can get in touch with him? Quickly, I mean? Without all that fooling around?'

Ms. Fisichelli shook her head. 'No,' she said. 'You know as well as I do how we go about invoking him. If you're right, there just isn't time . . .'

Mary looked at her.

'All right then,' Ms. Fisichelli said, 'so there is a way. But it's more than my job's worth . . .'

Mary looked at her again. These things are cumulative. 'Betty-Lou,' she said, 'just what do you think your job'll be worth if Apollo ceases to exist?'

'Well . . .'

501

'Betty-Lou.'

The Pythoness hesitated just a moment longer; then she shrugged.

'What the hell,' she said, 'you can only be turned into a weevil once, I guess. You win.'

Mary smiled, as the Pythoness took a step to one side and prepared her mind for what was to follow.

There are many different ways of summoning gods. You can sacrifice goats, or burn incense, or say mantras, or any combination of the three. There are also complex invocation rituals, some of which we have seen; you can leave messages on the architraves of temples, or use the statue. By and large the gods don't really mind being summoned in any one of these ways, because the summons is not binding, and they can use the divine equivalent of leaving the phone off the hook. But if you use the one method which they have to obey, regardless of where they are and what they might be doing at the time, you are guaranteed to get a god, quite possibly a god in his pants and socks and without his teeth in, and almost certainly a very angry god. Nothing, after all, gets up the nose of an omnipotent being like being told what to do.

What you do is, you put two fingers in your mouth and you whistle.

Largely as a result of the enormous quantum increase in philosophical productivity caused by the introduction of the new technology, many of the fundamental maxims that make up the structure of the modern astrophilosopher's world model have required amendment and expansion. For example, Descartes' immortal conclusion *cogito ergo sum* was recently subjected to destruction testing by a group of graduate researchers at Princeton led by

502

Professors Montjuic and Lauterbrunnen, and now reads, in the revised version to be found in the *Shorter Harvard Orthodoxy*:

(a) I think, therefore I am, or
(b) Perhaps I thought, therefore I was; but
(c) These days, I tend to leave all that side of things to my wife.

Developments such as this have in turn served to make academics working in the divinity subjects more commercially aware, and many of them now retain the services of specialist ecclesiastical lawyers, accountants and, of course, agents. The leading firm of ecclesiastical representatives is, needless to say, Alfred Furbank of New York and London, whose Mr. Kortright represents (among many others) Betty-Lou Fisichelli. Mr. Kortright is, understandably, a very busy man, and when he received two simultaneous calls from clients in mid-flight on his way to the annual Theological Trade Fair in Frankfurt, he wished that he had been able to find a suitable assistant to whom he could delegate. However, the qualities required of a successful ecclesiastical agent are rarely met with.

'Who?' he asked again.

'The Pythoness of Delphi on red,' replied the New York switchboard, 'Aleister Crowley on blue. He's on a pay phone. They're both holding.'

Kortright shuddered slightly. Against his better judgment, the New York office had recently installed one of those gadgets that plays callers piped music while they're holding, and some fool of a managing partner had chosen the *Dies Irae* as a suitable tune. Something to put the fear of God into 'em, he'd said.

He pressed the button. 'Right,' he told New York. 'Put on Fisichelli, tell Aleister no, not till I get the money, and then no more calls until we touch down. If anyone else calls in with a burning bush, tell them to call the fire department.'

Click.

'Betty-Lou, hi there, how's the prediction business?'

'Mr. Kortright?'

'Here.'

'Mr. Kortright, can you get me access to all the major networks, please? There's something very important I have to tell the world. From Apollo.'

I didn't think it could get worse, Kortright thought, but I was wrong. 'Betty-Lou,' he said, 'we've all got something very important we've got to tell the world. Some of us do it by shooting the president, some of us take overdoses, some of us just make do with the phone-ins. The competition for air time is very great at all times.'

'But this is *important*,' Betty-Lou said. 'It's a genuine message from the gods. Or at least one of them,' she remembered. 'He's putting himself in jeopardy speaking out like this; you have no idea how much trouble he'll be in when Jupiter finds out. The least we can do is make sure people hear him.'

'Are you sure about that, Betty-Lou?' said Kortright. 'I mean, it sounds to me like it'd be a very bad idea, from his point of view. And yours,' he added. 'There's this thing called credibility, you know, and I've been working very hard to build yours up. One little slip, like you going on the *Johnny Carson Show* saying you've been hearing voices and you'll think Joan of Arc had it easy. It won't just be the English who roast you alive, it'll be *Newsweek* and . . .'

'Mr. Kortright,' said Betty-Lou firmly. 'You have to arrange for me to broadcast to the world. If not . . .'

504

'Yes?' said Kortright impatiently. 'Go ahead, worry me.'

'Well, I hate to do this, but you have to understand . . .'

'What?'

'If you'll just look out of your window, Mr. Kortright.'

Kortright glanced out of the window. In the air just above the wing of the Lear jet, he saw what looked remarkably like an elderly car with a team of four winged horses attached to it by means of a complicated arrangement of transmission parts and drive-chains. In the driver's seat was what Mr. Kortright instinctively recognised as a very angry Sun-God, who was aiming at him with a bow of burning gold.

'Mr. Kortright?'

'Here.'

'What do you think you can do?'

Mr. Kortright looked at his watch. 'Give me fifteen minutes, OK?' he said. 'We can syndicate it through one of the big agencies. They'll send someone over to do the actual interview. Oh and Betty-Lou . . .'

'Yes, Mr. Kortright?'

'Do you think you could ask your friend with the bow to back off slightly? Only one of his horses is trying to eat the wing of this jet, and if I crash there won't be any interview at all. You got that?'

'I'll see what I can do, Mr. Kortright.'

Kortright pressed the button, leaned back in his seat, screamed, and then pulled himself back together. When you started seeing god yourself, it was time to move over more towards the administration side of the business.

He called up London office.

'Get me Danny Bennett,' he said.

505

CHAPTER THIRTEEN

Jason looked about him.

Far above, he could just make out four enormous pink bars that seemed to be clamping the sky to the Earth. The Caucasus had vanished, and he appeared to be standing in the streets of a city, though not any city that he could recognise. It was snowing bitterly, but for some reason the snow didn't settle on him; in fact, each single snowflake somehow contrived to jink out of his way at the last minute and land somewhere else. He had the strange feeling that wherever this was, he was really somewhere else.

'Where am I?' Jason asked.

'You know,' said a voice beside him, 'I never expected to hear anyone actually say that. It's only people in books . . .'

'Yes,' Jason said, 'but where in god's name actually am I, and we'll leave the literary niceties till later. And who are you?'

'Prometheus,' } the voice or voices replied,
'Gelos,' } saying the names together,

'and you're on the world you're holding in your hand. It's hardly an original device, I we know, but there, it's your fault for wanting to know what's going on.'

'Ah,' Jason replied. 'So I now know what's going on, do I? Thank you so much.'

'Jason,' said the voices or voice, 'the world you are standing on is a world which actually exists. Its technical name is Betamax 87659807 and it is the same as your world in most material respects. It is your world; or it could be. Your world could be merged with it, and nobody would know. Now there are some differences, as you will shortly find out, but once the merger had happened nobody would remember them. It would be as if everything had always been like this, and anyone who remembered otherwise would be sent somewhere quiet and restful with high walls until he was well again. Now the gods want your world merged with this one, and they've been trying to bring the merger about for a very long time. I we would like you to have a look at this world and let me us know what you think of it.'

Jason shrugged. It was like, he decided, those offers you get from the timeshare companies where you go along and listen to their spiel, and afterwards they give you a portable television. The only element lacking, so far as he could tell, was anything resembling a portable television.

'Where are we now, then?' he asked. 'I don't recognise this at all.'

'This is the street where you live, or would have lived, or will live, in Anglia, which is, was or will be what they call England,' he/they said. 'And the date is December the twenty-fourth. Sorry if this all seems needlessly Dickensian, but we haven't got much time, so we wanted to get in as much culture shock as possible. This is a world where Prometheus never stole the Joke from Heaven, and where the gods never retired. Right, roll 'em.'

As Jason stood there recovering from the above con-

507

versation, which put him in mind of a multiple choice English grammar exam, he looked up and saw a small knot of miserable-looking people trudging up the street. They wore grey homespun overcoats and grey knitted scarves, and they were getting drenched in slush by a passing oxcart. The leader of the party was carrying a collecting tin, with *For The Gods; Please Give Fearfully* written on it. The party stopped outside one of the dilapidated thatched houses that made up the street and started to sing.

> 'We wish you a Saturnalia,' they sang
> '*We wish you a Saturnalia*
> *We wish you a Saturnalia*
> *And a pious New Year.*'

'No Christmas, you see,' he they said in Jason's ear. 'No Donations of Constantine, no Christianity, ergo no Christmas.'

'Huh,' Jason replied, and for two pins he'd have added 'Humbug.' Christmas always bored him rigid, partly because he was a Hero and lived on a higher plane of background experience, and partly because his family always gave him socks. Something about the song troubled him, however. 'Shouldn't it be "We wish you a happy Saturnalia," though?'

'No such thing as a happy Saturnalia.'

The singers had finished their song and the door of the house opened. A terrified-looking man poked his head round, thrust two gold coins into the tin, and slammed the door. The leader ticked a name off a list and they moved on down the street. Outside the next door they sang;

508

'Bad King Atreus looked out
On the slopes of Pindus.
Lightning came and rubbed him out,
Blowing him to cinders.
Atreus, the silly sod,
Came to Jove's attention.
People who offend a god
Don't collect their pension.'

There was complete silence for a while, broken only by the mooing of a distant cow; then the shutter of an upstairs window opened and a very old woman poked her head through.

'Piss off,' she said. 'I haven't got any money, do you hear?'

The leader shuffled through the papers on his clipboard. 'According to the priests,' he said, 'you've got two denarii five quadrantes left out of your pension.'

'But that's got to last me till January.'

'Tough,' replied the leader – not unpleasantly; he clearly wasn't enjoying this very much. He was just very, very determined. 'You shouldn't have spent it all on butter then, should you? One denarius you're down for. We haven't got all night.'

'Go away.'

'Look, gran,' said another of the group, 'we know it's hard, but we're only doing our job.'

'Is that you, our Timon?'

'Yes, gran.'

'Then you should be ashamed of yourself.'

'Steady on, gran,' said their Timon. 'It is the season of illwill, you know.'

Jason turned. He couldn't see his companion or companions, but he turned nevertheless. In the circles in which

509

he moved, if you wanted to talk to someone without someone else hearing, you turned, and that was that.

'Shouldn't that be the season of . . .?'

'No,' he they replied. 'Shut up and listen.'

'Look,' said the leader of the group, 'it's no skin off our
nose if you don't make your voluntary offering, right? If
you want to offend the gods and get blown to bits by a
thunderbolt and spend the rest of eternity on the wrong
side of the Styx just because the thought of going hungry
for a few days meant more to you than paying your respects
to the everlasting gods . . .'

'All right, all right,' said Gran, and shortly afterwards
there was a shooting back of bolts and a slight tinkle, such
as might have been caused by a small silver coin dropping
into a very full collecting tin.

'Bye, then,' said the leader. 'Have a pious Saturnalia.'

'Bog off.'

The party slouched off down the street, and soon Jason
could hear them singing about how, away in a manger with
a crib for his bed, the impious Thyestes was found very
dead. Snow fell. Jason's sensitive nostrils detected the smell
of totally inadequate drains; or more accurately, no drains
at all.

'A brief history lesson,' said the voice or voices. 'In our
world, the Roman Emperor Constantine declared
Christianity to be the State religion, and the worship of the
gods was suppressed. In this world, however, Constantine
never existed. There was never a Constantinian revolution.
Constantine's predecessor, Diocletian, remained in power.
Now Diocletian believed in a place for everybody and
everybody in his place, and also in the gods. He set up a
system of government along those lines and, in this world,
the system has worked. One thousand seven hundred years

later, things have not changed much, largely because no-one's seen the need. There is still an Emperor in Rome – Severus the Thirty-Third – and the science of urban sanitation died in infancy; you are presently standing in the main sewer of the town. Petrol is still a black messy substance that interferes with well-digging operations in Mesopotamia, penicillin is an unfortunate by-product of inadequate bread management, and electricity is something that comes out of the sky to let you know you've forgotten to sacrifice to Minerva. The only known cure for an abscess under a tooth is death. This is because people never learned to laugh at the gods, and so never realised that it's possible to tell them to get lost. Discontent cannot exist without laughter.'

'Was Diocletian the one who made his horse prime minister?'

'That was Caligula, and not on this world he didn't. It was a joke, you see, and here there are no jokes.'

'None at all?'

'Try for yourself.'

Jason thought about this, and as he was contemplating a man appeared at the top of the street. Jason had been wondering if he was in fact visible to the people of this world, and asked as much of his companion(s).

'No,' he they said, 'not as such. The Possibility Police wouldn't allow it. However, since this is a controlled environment and we can adjust things later, we can make you visible for a few minutes if you like.'

Once this had been dealt with Jason walked up to the man and stood in front of him.

'Excuse me,' he said, 'but what's brown and lives in the sea and attacks young women?'

The man stopped and thought about it. 'Good question,' he said. 'You've got me there. It could be Neptune, because he lives in the sea and he's a bit, well, like that, His name be praised, but I never heard that he was brown, particularly. There's the Old Man of the Sea, of course, but he just attacks everybody, thanks be to Him. Then there's Porphyry, I suppose, except he's . . .'

'Actually,' Jason said, 'it's Jack the Kipper.'

'Who?'

'Jack the Kipper.'

'Never heard of him,' said the man, after a moment's thought. 'Is that another name of Scylla the Hundred-Headed Sea-Fiend?'

'No,' Jason replied, 'it's a pun.'

'A what?'

'A pun.'

The man thought again. 'No, sorry,' he said, 'you've lost me there. You sure you're not thinking of the Old Man of the Sea, because . . .'

'All right, all right,' Jason said. 'Try this one. Why did the chicken cross the road?'

'Which road?'

'Sorry, forget I said that. How many dentists does it take to change a light bulb?'

'What's a dentist?'

'Ah. Well, thanks for everything, have a nice day.'

'What's nice?'

Jason shivered, not entirely because of the cold. Fortunately his companion or companions chose this moment to wipe the man's memory clean, and he hurried by without saying anything further.

'All right,' Jason said, 'you've proved your point. Can I go and have something to eat now, please?'

But the person or persons he couldn't see shook his or

their invisible head or heads. 'Not yet,' he they said. 'You wanted to understand what was going on, didn't you?'

'In a way, yes,' Jason replied. 'Not this way.'

'How, then?'

'More a sort of comfortingly meaningless truism sort of way,' Jason said, 'or, failing that, a detailed exposition over lunch. Do they have food here, by any chance?'

He they considered. 'They eat,' was the reply.

'Whatever it is they eat, could I eat it too?'

'No.'

'Oh.' Jason thought about it, and remembered the story of Persephone in Hell. 'You mean, if I eat any of the food here, I'll have to stay here for ever and ever?'

'No,' said his companion(s), 'but if you eat any of the food here you'll be ill. It's winter, remember. No fresh veg, all the meat is salted, and there's ergotism in the bread. If you're really hungry there's always rats, but . . .'

'I think I'll wait, thanks,' Jason said. 'Okay then, so what else have I got to see before I achieve enlightenment and you let me go home, because time's getting on and . . .'

'Not here it isn't.'

'Look . . .'

'Roll 'em.'

'I shall now,' said Jupiter, 'call this meeting to order.'

He looked around him and frowned. Either all the gods had suddenly gone deaf or else they had forgotten what had happened the last time.

'I shall now,' he repeated, 'call this meeting to order, and anyone who doesn't shut up will spend eternity as a dung-beetle. Thank you.'

In the resulting silence the Great Sky God looked round and counted heads. Someone was missing.

'All right,' Jupiter said, 'where is he?'

Silence.

'I see,' Jupiter went on. 'Solidarity. Right.' Jupiter cast eye across the assembly, muttering under his breath. By the time he got to Eeny-meeny-miny he was staring straight at Mars.

'He was called away,' Mars whimpered. 'An urgent summons from Delphi. He asked me to make his apologies for him, and . . .'

'Called away.'

'Yes,' Mars continued, sounding like a whole Wealdful of sheep bleating simultaneously. It is part of the Divine Code of Ethics that gods stick up for their fellow gods and try to conceal each others' cock-ups from the Great Eye. Other components of the Divine Code are fair dealing, honesty, justice, consistency and kindness to animals. It was last observed on October 16th, 1145. 'At least that's what he told me,' Mars continued. 'I said to him, I said . . .'

'Called away.'

'Um,' Mars quipped brilliantly. 'Yes. Exactly what I said to him. I said . . .'

Jupiter stroked his beard, producing enough static electricity to power all the food processors in New York. 'In that case,' he said, 'as of now Apollo ceases to be a member of this council. Mercury will convey this news to him after we have taken Any Other Business. In the meantime he shall cease to function as an independent entity. Moved and unanimously carried, I trust.'

The gods looked at each other. On the one hand it was a terrifying precedent. On the other hand it was just plain terrifying. They nodded.

'Moved, then,' Jupiter said smugly, 'and carried unanimously. At this rate, we'll have this lot wrapped up by teatime. Isn't it satisfying when everyone does as they're told? Right, next item on the agenda, the destruction of Earth . . .'

Something hopped into Mars's mouth and bumped up against his clenched teeth. He was horribly afraid it was a protest. 'Um . . .' he said.

'Sorry?'

'Um,' Mars said again. Something told him that his point required a degree of clarification and expansion if it was to have maximum effect. 'Er . . .' he added. Everyone was looking at him, and he suddenly realised how pleasantly restful it was when people were just shooting at him.

'I believe,' Jupiter said – why is there no word meaning 'said' but having lots of harsh, grating consonants in it? – 'that Mars wishes to address the meeting?'

'Well,' Mars said, 'I'm terribly sorry to interrupt, break the flow and so forth, but did Your Um just say something about the destruction of Earth? On a point of order, and so on.'

'Yes.'

'Ah. Thank you.'

'And the transfer,' Jupiter went on, 'of our entire field of operations to Betamax 87659807, ultimately to be renamed—' Jupiter paused melodramatically – 'New Earth. I leave the motion to the floor.'

If the floor had any opinions on the subject, it kept them to itself, as did all the gods sitting on it. The discovery that the Supreme Being has finally flipped his lid is always likely to cause disorientation, even among gods.

'If nobody has any comments to make,' Jupiter said, 'then I shall put the motion to the vote. Seconded and carried . . .'

'No.'

Everyone swivelled round and stared at Mars, Demeter going so far as to count his legs. Jupiter frowned.

'No.' Mars was standing up. 'You can't,' he added.

'Oh can't I?'

'No you can't.'

'Yes I can.'

'No you can't.'

'Yes I can.'

'Look,' interrupted Mercury, who was taking the minutes, 'do I have to put all this down, because if it's going to go on much longer I'm going to need a new notebook.'

'It's not going to go on very much longer,' said Jupiter, 'as dung-beetles have no *locus standi* to address a meeting of the gods.'

'You still can't do it,' Mars said. His right hand was creeping upwards towards his mouth, with the general idea of tearing his own tongue out by the roots; but it was naturally cautious and had only reached chest height. In the meantime, Mars carried on. 'Because if you destroy Earth, we all cease to exist. There's no way out of that, and you know it.'

'He's right.' Minerva looked round to see who had spoken and realised it was her.

'Who asked your opinion?' Jupiter snarled.

'You did. You left the motion to the floor, and . . .'

'But you're not a floor,' Jupiter replied. 'Though that could be arranged,' he added.

'If you destroy the Earth,' she said, ignoring him – ignoring Jupiter is rather like trying to fly through rather than round a mountain, but to the gods all things are possible – 'then the laws of possibility require that we cease to exist, at least in our present form.'

Jupiter considered this before saying 'Balls,' and the

Olympians held their breath. Minerva continued:

'What will happen is that there'll be a reality bifurcation into a world where you decided to destroy the world – which won't be around for very long – and a world where you changed your mind at the last minute. Since that's impossible, because you never change your mind at the last minute, that world will quickly fizzle out, and all of us with it. On the world where you destroyed the world, we'll all be destroyed with it. Curtains.'

Jupiter scratched the tip of his nose. 'You're right, of course,' he said.

'I'm so glad,' Minerva started to say, 'and please forgive me for having the temerity to remind you of the fact, but . . .'

'Nevertheless . . .'

Apollo grinned nervously, straightened his laurel wreath and stared at the monitor.

'Six – five – four – three – two – one – on air!'

Danny Bennet switched on a smile that Amundsen could have driven a sled over, and leaned forwards.

'Your Majesty,' he said, 'is it true that the gods are conspiring to bring about the end of the world?'

Apollo opened his mouth to speak, and then something happened to his vocal chords. Difficult to say what, exactly; either they'd all fused together or someone had nipped quietly down his throat in the last five seconds and removed them. Something funny had definitely happened. In any case they weren't there any more. Meanwhile there were ninety billion people or whatever it was, all out there looking at him. Live.

'You know,' Apollo managed to say, 'I'm glad you asked me that question.'

517

'So what's the answer?' Danny demanded. 'Your Majesty,' he added.

When his agent had told him about this wonderful offer from the satellite TV people, Danny had taken all that stuff about the sky being the limit with a pinch of salt. You know where you are with the BBC, he had told himself, even if it is on the scrapheap. It had only been the promise that if he signed on the dotted line he could at last make the epoch-shattering documentary, based on shocking revelations by a renegade astrotheology don and provisionally entitled *Death of a Carpenter*, that had induced him to turn his back on the Corporation and hoist the Jolly Roger. And now here he was interviewing this strange, distinctly luminous person whom his producer assured him was the god Apollo. For approximately five minutes, he had panicked, before he had remembered the interviewer's golden rule: the bigger they are, the harder you hit 'em.

'The people,' he added, 'have a right to know.'

'No they don't.'

'You're admitting there's been—' Danny's lips caressed the magic words as they passed the gate of his teeth – 'a cover-up?'

'Of course there's been a cover-up,' Apollo replied. 'There's always a cover-up. That's what it's all about. That's not the point. Look, unless you want me to turn you into a frog or something . . .'

'Mr . . . Your Majesty,' Danny retorted, 'I think you'll find that threats are rivet rivet rivet rivet.'

Apollo blinked. Did I do that, he asked himself. Must have. Oh well. He unhooked the microphone from its stand and placed it on the chair beside the frog.

'Now I think you've put your finger on what I might call the nub of the problem, Mr. Bennet,' he said smoothly.

'Basically, when it comes down to it, in the final analysis . . .'

'Rivet rivet rivet rivet rivet,' said the frog. 'Rivet.'

'Quite so,' Apollo replied. 'Your point is, of course, entirely valid. But the message I'm trying to get across . . .'

Apollo fell silent. Hell, it was on the tip of his tongue. Something about something important. At that moment some words drifted down out of the air into his mouth, and he spoke them. They had come a long way, were slightly scorched and tasted disconcertingly of marzipan.

'Oh yes,' he said. 'The world is about to end.'

'Riv . . .'

'There is,' Apollo went on, 'absolutely no cause for alarm. The situation is under control, and even as I speak negotiations are in hand to attempt to reach a settlement that will be satisfactory in the eyes of all parties.' Just then, a cloud passed over the sun, and Apollo drew himself up short. Why was it, he wondered, that sitting in this chair being stared at by a camera made you say all sorts of silly things you didn't mean? 'They'll all fail, of course,' he added. 'Absolutely bugger all *you* lot can do about it, anyway. It's all up to the Derry boy and the dog and the eagle. And Prometheus, of course, and Gelos too, if he's turned up yet. But all I can say is they're cutting it a bit fine, because, well, there's a board meeting going on right now up in the sun and pretty soon they're all going to start chucking thunderbolts about and then it'll be you lot for the chop and why have you switched the cameras off, I haven't finished yet.'

'Now look,' said the producer's voice, 'I've had some nut cases on this show in my time but if you think I'm going to put my job on the line letting you say things like that over the ark ark ark ark . . .'

Apollo turned slightly in his chair and smiled at the camera, smiling as brightly as the sun (which had just emerged from the clouds overhead). The camera was being operated by a natterjack toad in a leather jacket and designer jeans. Do what you like to him, a television cameraman will always basically remain the same.

'Ladies and gentlemen of humanity,' Apollo said. It was easy once you got the hang of it, which was basically bearing in mind that if you let your brain register the fact that there are *ninety billion people out there staring right at you* then you're inevitably going to dry up, but if you just don't think about it then there's no problem, no problem at all. 'This is the god Apollo speaking. Throughout history it has been my pleasant task to pass on the messages of heaven to mortal men. Well, all good things must come to an end. The world's been a good thing, by and large, hasn't it? Well, it's got to come to an end, too. Now I know that's going to be hard on some of you, perhaps even all of you, but in the final analysis you'll all have the satisfaction of knowing that it's part of a divine plan that stretches back many thousands of years to the time of the creation of mankind itself.'

Apollo paused for a moment, rallied his mental forces, and tilted his head slightly on one side as if he'd been doing this sort of thing all his life. After all, he reasoned, PR is PR, whether it's done by television broadcasts or the entrails of sacrificial animals or posters on the sides of buses.

Now some of you,' he went on, 'will be saying to yourselves "Now hang on, that's a bit thick, isn't it?" And let me assure you that the Divine community as a whole has a great deal of sympathy with this view. We know only too well how hard it is to make sacrifices – or in our case, how to go without sacrifices. We understand, and we're going to do everything in our power to make what I would call the transitional period as painless as we possibly can. But . . .'

At that moment, a large eagle smashed its way through a skylight and pitched on Danny's chair, with the result that about nine hundred thousand viewers who had just come back from the kitchen with the tea got the impression that it was one of those ventriloquism acts that never quite ring true on television.

Apollo frowned, trying to remember who he'd turned into what, and while his mind was temporarily engaged in this fashion, the eagle spoke to him.

This statement simply cries out for qualification. The eagle didn't speak as much as transmit telepathic messages direct from its brain to his; and the messages were in fact being relayed via the eagle from a huge composite brain presently in possibility orbit round the entire concept of Earth. To complicate matters, there was a mild thunderstorm in the vicinity and the composite voice was transmitting on a rather popular mental frequency, with the result that there was a lot of crackling and a few distant snippets of a conversation between two CB Radio enthusiasts driving Leyland Roadmasters round the M25, but the messages were more or less intelligible.

'What the hell do you think you're playing at?' he they said.

'I beg your pardon?'

'Come on, Pol, pull your finger out. Have you heard what you've just been saying?'

'I . . .'

'Listen.' The entire interview so far was played back through the eagle's brain. Telepathic communication is very rapid indeed; compared with two seasoned telepaths thinking quickly, words are second-class letters to

Penzance posted in Dundee on a Sunday. 'Is that what you intended to say?'

'No,' Apollo replied, puzzled. 'Far from it.'

'What were you going to say?'

'I was going to say that the gods were about to betray humanity, and the only way out of it was for everyone to believe in them as quickly and as sincerely as possible. I was going to help by doing a few miracles.'

'Do you know what's happened?'

'I've been got at.'

'Who by?'

'Jupiter.'

'Correct. He's just passed a resolution that you aren't a god any more.'

'He's done what?'

'You heard me. You've been reduced to the ranks. As soon as the meeting's over, they're going to snatch you back to Olympus, and then it'll be a career in the real estate business for you. Meanwhile, he's using you as a mouthpiece, beaming signals down from the sun into your brain. Fortunately, I we have just put a green baize cloth over the sun . . .'

'How . . .'

'Don't ask. I we reckon that gives you about three minutes. Whose side are you on, Pol?'

'Reduced to the ranks!' Divine wrath filled Apollo's mind. He fizzed slightly, and the tubular steel arms of his chair were transmuted into pure gold. I'll show that jumped-up son of a concept exactly where he gets off . . .'

'That's the ticket, Pol. Now, why don't you tell the folks at home the truth?'

'Roll em.'

It seemed to Jason as if he were flying, and also standing

522

still at the same time. Air appeared to be rushing past him, but he wasn't conscious of any movement on his part. He was standing still and the world was turning very fast. You could get travel sick very quickly this way.

There was a click; the world jolted to a halt, paused for a stomach churning fraction of a second, and rushed back in the other direction. Then another click.

'This looks like it,' he they said. 'Right. Watch very carefully.'

The world was moving yet again, but this time at its normal pace; in fact, Jason wouldn't have noticed the motion if he hadn't been aware of the lack of it in between clicks. This was time running on playback speed.

He had apparently moved in space as well as in time, for he was inside a building of some sort now; a dark building, not particularly cheerful. Despite his innate optimism, Jason couldn't quite bring himself to believe that it was a restaurant. Which was not to suggest that it wasn't a place designed at least in part for eating in; it was just that a human being standing there would be justified in wondering on which end of the fork he was ultimately going to wind up.

'The temple of Jupiter in Londinium,' he they whispered. 'Not everybody's cup of tea.'

'Talking of . . .'

It was only then that Jason became aware that the place was full of people; thousands of them, but they were so extraordinarily still and quiet that they simply hadn't registered in his mind. They were all dressed alike, in rather threadbare homespun jackets and knee-length kilts. The women had their heads covered. All of them had that air of nervous resignation that you usually only find in doctors' waiting rooms and tax offices. Jason wondered what they were all doing there.

523

'Having a good time,' he they whispered.

Jason frowned. 'Are you sure?' he asked.

'I we use the term loosely,' he they replied. 'Actually there's no such thing as a good time here; the nearest equivalent is a pious time, and I we suppose you could say they're having that. This is popular entertainment, Betamax style.'

'What is it, exactly?'

'It's a game show,' he they replied. 'Listen.'

Jason was on the point of applying for further and better particulars when two huge curtains parted at the far end of the hall and a procession entered. At the head of it were two enormous men with black masks and very large axes, followed by a third man carrying what looked startlingly like a chopping-block; then came three very sour-faced young women in extremely decorous costumes – in Jason's world they would have been dentists' receptionists – carrying silver vessels of indeterminate use. Finally there was a tall, white-haired man with a beard like a silver doormat, dressed in the most outlandishly ornate robes Jason had ever seen; the sort of thing Louis XIV would have gone in for if only he'd had the money.

The procession halted in the middle of a sort of raised dais, and the masked men grounded their axes with a crash. The overdressed man stepped forward, stood for a moment and then spoke.

'A pious evening to you all, worshippers and females; my name is Godfearing George Maniakis, and I'm your host for tonight, when we're all going to play God's My Witness. Now before we begin, let me tell you all about a very spiritually uplifting thing which happened to me on the way to the temple tonight . . .'

Jason looked round nervously. The building was almost

as ornate as Godfearing George's costume; it had butresses, archetraves, roodscreens, pilasters and what Jason failed entirely to recognise as a narthex, but no doors. Pity.

'"Thy Will be done?" I said, well you could have knocked me down with a simpulum, so I turned to him and I said . . .' Godfearing George was getting steadily more solemn as his routine continued, and some of the congregation were starting to quiver slightly. Any minute now, Jason felt, some idiot was going to shout 'Hallelujah!' He did his best to ignore the rest of the story, which had something to do with everlasting punishment and the transmigration of the soul. Finally it ground to a halt, and there was a deep, respectful silence.

'And now,' said Godfearing George, 'it only remains for me to welcome tonight's first contestants, who are going to join me in playing God's My Witness. Mr. and Mrs. Constans; many are called but tonight, *you've* been chosen!'

There was a shriek from the second row of the congregation. Not that sort of shriek. A real shriek. For a moment nothing seemed to be happening; then the two axemen sprang forwards and returned shortly afterwards with an elderly couple, who were struggling with them in a spirited but entirely pointless way. At last the remaining dribble of fight evaporated and they stood facing Godfearing George with all the light-hearted exuberance of rabbits caught in the headlamps of a rapidly approaching lorry.

'And your name is?'

'Mmmmmmm.'

'Could you just speak up, Mr. Constans? The gods can hear you, of course, but we can't.'

'Flavius Constans,' the man whimpered.

525

'And you're a retired executioner?' Mr. Constans nodded feebly. 'That must have been a horrible job, Flavius. Didn't you ever wonder whether the people you executed might actually have been innocent?'

Mr. Constans snivelled. Clearly the thought had occurred to him, once or twice. Godfearing George turned to Mrs. Constans, who was somewhat belatedly trying never to have been born, and gave her a smile that would have stripped paint.

'And how about you – Domitilla, isn't it?' Mrs. Constans made a very small, very shrill noise, like a fieldmouse in a blender. 'How did you feel about all this, Domitilla, sharing your bed with a man who made his living by killing people? Didn't you sometimes wonder, Domitilla? Anyway, worshippers and females, how about a good, fervent prayer for the souls of our two contestants, who are going to play God's My Witness here tonight.'

There was a confused mumbling, like many angry bees. Mr. and Mrs. Constans tried to cling to each other, but the axemen parted them with the shafts of their axes. Godfearing George took a bundle of cards from a cedarwood chest which one of the stern young women had presented to him. Someone somewhere dimmed some lights. There was absolute silence.

'Now,' Godfearing George intoned. 'I'm sure I don't have to remind you of the rules. This first round is all about religious knowledge. For each question you get wrong, you get the opportunity to spend five thousand years in the Bottomless Pit Of Sulphur – that's after you're dead, of course, although I'm sure you don't need me to tell you that life is but a dream. For each correct answer, you get five denarii, which you'll be entitled to offer to the god of your choice when we play Sacrifice of the Century –

always supposing you live that long, of course. Right then, Flavius, you have the choice of answering questions on Myths, Orthodoxy or Heresy.'

'Myths, please,' said Mr. Constans.

'You've chosen Myths,' said Godfearing George, 'and you have five seconds in which to answer the following question.'

The lights dimmed ever so slightly. You could have built tower blocks on the silence.

'Tell me, then, Flavius,' said Godfearing George, and Jason could feel the palms of his hands becoming distinctly moist, 'in the legend of the Seven Against Thebes, what were the names of King Adrastus's daughters?'

Mr. Constans seemed to freeze. A great drum somewhere offstage marked the passing of the seconds: one, two, three . . .

'Deipyla,' Mr. Constans croaked.

'And?'

'Aegeia.'

'Correct!' The congregation sagged with relief, and someone actually did shout 'Hallalujah'. 'Heaven be praised, Mr. Constans,' said Godfearing George, 'Deipyla and Aegeia is right. Now, Mr. Constans, your second question is . . .'

To his utter astonishment, Jason knew the answer to this one (who removed the bones of Orestes from Tegea?), which was plainly more than could be said for Mr. Constans. On the fifth drumbeat he gasped out 'Mercury,' and the silence in the hall solidified still further. A wild guess. Jason shuddered to think what you got for a wild guess. It almost certainly wasn't a souvenir cheque-book and pen.

'I'm sorry,' said Godfearing George, 'but your sins have

found you out, Mr. Constans. The answer is, of course, Lichas. I expect it was on the tip of your tongue, wasn't it? Well, you'll have five thousand years in Tartarus to reflect on that, won't you? Now then, Mrs. Constans, do you want to answer questions on Myths, Orthodoxy or Heresy?'

Mrs. Constans squeaked pitifully.

'Heresy it is, then. Now, in the accursed rituals of the Paphlagonians . . .'

Mrs. Constans didn't do terribly well.

'Oh dear,' said Godfearing George, 'that's two incorrect answers, Mrs. Constans, and as I'm sure you're aware that means immediate decapitation. Never mind, let's have a really heartfelt prayer for the soul of Mrs. Constans, worshippers and females. She's been a truly wretched contestant . . .'

And that was more or less all that Jason could take for one day. There were some people, he knew, who didn't believe in the gods; not these gods, not any gods. That had always amazed him; it was like not believing in cholera. The two certain things about human life are, first, that there are gods; second, that pretty well all the gods would benefit enormously from a good hard kick in the head. With a yell that should have caused serious damage to the structure of the building, he unsheathed the Sword of Thingummytite and hurled himself at the dais . . .

Only to find that it wasn't there. And neither was he.

CHAPTER FOURTEEN

'Well, then.'

Jason considered his options. He had, within the space of a relatively short time, defied the gods, been to Hell, beaten up the Driver of the Spoil and the Grim Reaper, been made to feel about twelve years old by his mother, discovered that he had Free Will, discovered that, on the contrary, his entire life had been planned out for him from the start by the personification of laughter and an eagle, acquired a three-headed dog, mislaid a three-headed dog, been taught most but not all of the funniest joke ever, routed a divine army, spent a long time in his own shirt pocket and tried without success to murder a game show host. More or less the only thing he hadn't done in the last few days, in fact, was have a decent meal.

But there is that within a man that drives him ever onwards, just as the power of the seasons drives the roots of flowers into the hard earth; and so he decided, against his better judgment, to open his eyes and find out what was going to happen to him next. He was, after all, a Hero whether he liked it or not, and when he had been offered the choice between the path of Luxury and the path of

Glory he had chosen the path marked Diversion. Although he was no expert, he had an instinctive feeling that that came under the heading of Asking for Trouble. Anyway, he opened his eyes.

'So?'

He looked round, and the first thing he saw was sandwiches. Ham, beef, cheese, sardine and prawn sandwiches; also a pork pie, a plate of sausage rolls, two Cornish pasties and an iced bun.

'This,' said the voice above his head, 'is not a bribe.'

'No,' Jason replied, torn with indecision. 'Of course it isn't.' It had been difficult, but he had made up his mind. To start with, the beef.

'And since it's not a bribe,' the voice continued, as the sandwich jacknifed out of his hand and skittered away like a frightened kitten, 'it would be best if you didn't eat any of it until you've decided on your verdict.'

'I just did,' Jason said. 'I thought the beef first, then a bit of that pie, then . . .'

'About the future of the human race.'

'Oh, that. Well, I know for a fact that some of them aren't allowed to eat beef, or pork, so they really won't mind if . . .'

'About whether the gods should be allowed to destroy laughter.'

Jason remembered. It had been nice when there was just the food to think about, but clearly his destiny, the world's destiny and the destiny of the beef sandwiches were all somehow interlinked; how, he had no idea, but that was all right, he had never claimed he was Marcus Aurelius. Ah yes, the world. He considered the matter with the small area of his brain not mentally eating beef sandwiches, and after a short while he delivered the following judgment.

'Well,' he said, 'if that place, or world, or whatever you want to call it, that I saw just now was what the world would be like if the gods did away with comedy, then I don't think a lot of it and personally I wouldn't like to live there. On the other hand, I wouldn't like to live in Florida, but a lot of people are very taken with Florida, and who am I to say they're wrong? I mean, one man's meat . . .' Meat. Ham. Beef. Pork. Chicken. Turkey. Veal. Lamb. Sausages. 'One man's meat,' he forced himself – salami! Dear God, was there anything in the whole of creation as wonderful as a salami and mozarella salad, with fresh white bread on the side and – he forced himself to continue, 'is another man's poison and all that. I could just fancy a poison meat casserole, as it happens, but never mind. What I'm getting at is . . . Are you still there?'

'Yes.'

'What I'm getting at is . . . Will there be any mustard? Eventually, I mean?'

'Quite possibly.'

'What I'm trying to say is that I refuse to make a judgment, one way or another. I know what I want and what I'd do, but I'm blowed if I'm going to lay down the law to anybody else. Please stop me before I finally drift over the edge into complete incoherence, but I don't hold with deciding things for people. My dad does that, and I don't respect him very much for it. I don't think it's right to decide what other people's lives are going to be like. Personally, when I think of the hash browns, corned beef hash, no, the hash, the cock-up I've made of my own life, I can't really say that I'm in any position to shape other people's. By the way, exactly why is all this up to me, anyway?'

'Because.'

'Ah. I might have guessed. Well, if you want me to decide between you and the gods, then, bearing in mind all the experiences I've had over the last few days, what I've seen of you and the various insights I've had into the way the gods go about things, and also bearing in mind the fact that Jupiter has always bossed me about and apparently you've been manipulating me ever since I was born and I always seem to find myself doing what my mother tells me to do, my decision is that I choose whichever side will make it possible for me to eat all this food at the earliest opportunity. Satisfied?'

'No. Like I said, it's not a bribe. More a sort of – what's the word? Torture, that's it. Until you make up your mind and reach a decision, citing good reasons, you can't have any. Now get on with it.'

Jason scowled and, with the speed of a cat pouncing on a trailing ball of wool, hurled himself at an Eccles cake, which promptly scuttled away down a rabbit-hole.

'Are you Prometheus?' Jason asked.

'I am,' Prometheus replied.

Jason looked around; he had no idea where the voice was coming from. 'Where are you?' he said. 'I can't see you.'

'I'm not surprised.'

'Why's that?'

'You're not looking in the right direction.'

Jason scanned through three hundred and sixty degrees. Nothing; well, lots of sandwiches and pies and pasties and cakes – and, he noticed, a Black Forest Gateau and some cheese straws which he'd previously overlooked. He loved cheese straws. Not that he was averse to cocktail olives, crisps, cashew nuts, Ritz crackers with little bits of fishy carnage on them and baby frankfurters, and right now he could eat the stale bread left out for the birds. Yes, lots of food. But no Titans of any description whatsoever.

'Why me?' he asked. 'Because will not be acceptable as an explanation.'

'Why not?'

'Because it's meaningless and patronising and . . .'

'No,' Prometheus replied, 'Why not is the answer to your enquiry. Now, if you don't mind coming to a decision . . .'

'No.'

'The pasties are going cold.'

'I'm not hungry.'

'Now look here . . .'

'No.' Jason folded his arms, and there was a scream of pain and terror. He looked down and saw Prometheus in his shirt pocket, pinned to the wall of his chest by a gigantic forearm. He quickly removed his arm and apologised. 'What on earth are you doing in there?' he added.

'Damn you, Jason Derry,' said the diminutive giant. 'Why must you always be asking questions?'

Calmly, Jason lifted Prometheus out of his pocket and sat him down on the palm of his hand. 'Because,' he replied. 'Now, either you can tell me what's going on, properly this time, or else you can be put between two slices of bread and eaten. The choice is yours.'

'Where are you going to get two slices of bread from, then?'

'I can do without bread,' Jason replied, 'at a pinch.'

'It would be cannibalism.'

'Very probably.'

'I taste horrible.'

'How would you know?'

'I can't explain what's happening,' Prometheus said furiously, 'until you've made the decision.'

'I can't make the decision,' Jason shouted back, 'until you've explained.'

'What's so difficult, for crying out loud?' Prometheus shrieked. 'It's us or them, don't you understand?'

'Which is which?'

Prometheus didn't reply; instead, he tucked his head between his knees and started to hum at the top of his voice. Jason swore and then put him gently down on a slice of anchovy toast, which immediately lifted into the air like a magic carpet and whisked him away into mid-air.

It was then that Jason came to a decision and the decision was that he'd had enough. He stood up, and as he did so he became aware of something round and hard, like a cricket ball, in his trouser pocket. It was uncomfortable, and so without looking at it he pulled it out and hurled it away with all his strength. Doing that was meant to make him feel better. It did. Much better.

'Oh,' he said, 'I see.'

'I thought you would.'

Prometheus was standing beside him.

'Hello Prometheus,' he said. 'You've grown a lot since I saw you last.'

And indeed he had. He was now about eight feet tall and still going strong.

'And what do you see?' Prometheus said.

'Hang on,' Jason said. He made a sideways lunge at a cream horn, which stayed very still and let him catch it without a trace of a struggle. He ate it. Served it right.

'Now then,' he said, licking cream off his upper lip. 'What do I see? I see that the thing I just threw away was the world I was just in, the one where there were no jokes and the gods were in control. I see that I threw it so hard that it's shortly going to punch a hole through the wall of the space/time continuum and vanish for ever.'

'Very good,' Prometheus said. He snapped his fingers and a guided eclair hopped up from the ground and piloted itself neatly into Jason's mouth. 'What else?'

'I see that I subconsciously decided to do that because I don't hold with the gods. They exist all right, but there's no point in encouraging them. They're quite big and strong enough to take care of themselves. As it is, they run the world as a huge game, scoring points for all the horrible things they trick us into doing. But it's we who do them, of our own free will (if you'll pardon the expression); they just persuade us into it, like Dad persuaded me into being a Hero. No, stuff the gods. And the only weapon we have against them is laughter, because once there is laughter then nobody, however serious-minded or humourless he may be, will be able to take a bunch of clowns like Jupiter and Minerva and Mars and Neptune seriously for more than five minutes. Am I right?'

By way of affirmation a sausage roll hopped up onto his shoulder and slid down his chest into his hand. A moment later a salt-cellar appeared, running frantically along and puffing. Late as usual.

'On the other hand, laughter itself cannot rule the world because it is a force of anarchy – did I just say that? Where do I pick these expressions up from, I wonder? – it's a force of anarchy and cannot assert itself or exert authority. You can dissuade people from invading the country next door by making jokes, but you can't make them do it. Thus Gelos can never rule.'

'Actually,' said Prometheus, as a doughnut snapped itself into two and one half floated towards Jason's face, 'you've got the right conclusion but for the wrong reason. Hence only half a doughnut. But do please carry on.'

'Finally,' Jason said, 'I make this decision of my own free will, and I'm the only person in the history of the world who can, because . . . Hang on, that can't be right.'

'Don't think about it,' Prometheus urged. 'Look, have some profiteroles.' Profiteroles like chocolate-sauce-drenched cannonballs obligingly bobbed in the air in front of Jason's eyes, but he ignored them.

'No, but seriously,' Jason said. 'A couple of pages must have fallen out here or something, because . . .'

'Stay with it, Jason,' Prometheus said, 'and don't talk with your mouth empty.' He turned to make impatient gestures at a cheesecake which had overslept and was now dashing towards them, yawning and struggling into its kiwi-fruit as it ran.

'I make this decision of my own free will,' Jason repeated slowly, 'and I'm the only person in the history of the world who can, because . . . Look—'

'Just say it.'

'*Because it is fated.* Now just look here, will you?'

'There now,' Prometheus said soothingly, between sighs of relief, 'that wasn't so bad, now was it? Have a peach melba.'

Jason shook his head angrily. 'I don't want a peach melba,' he snapped. 'I want an explanation.'

'Oh don't start all that again.'

'How can I have free will if it was fated all along?'

'It was fated that you should have free will,' Prometheus replied. 'Brandy snap?'

'Bugger brandy snaps.'

'Cream slice?'

'Stop drivelling away about food and tell me what it means. I don't object to revelations as such, but I do insist

536

on them being intelligible. I mean, how would Saint Paul have felt if Someone had popped up on the road to Damascus, thrown him off his horse and then said "The cauliflower is mightier than the hairdryer"?'

'Apple doughnut?'

There was a long silence.

'What did you just say?'

'Would you like an apple doughnut?'

'Look . . .'

'Two apple doughnuts?'

'With fresh cream?'

Prometheus shuddered slightly. 'Of course,' he said.

Nature held its breath while Jason thought about it. After all, it wasn't as if it was entirely illogical, was it? Everybody else is predestined, but it is foretold that one day a Hero will arise who is able to choose for himself. *Apple* doughnuts. Oh, sod it, yes, why not?

'Since you're offering,' Jason said, 'yes.'

'Yes what?'

'Yes please?'

'That's better.' Prometheus nodded to a waiting spirit, who hared off to Plato's ideal world to borrow a couple of apple doughnuts. Luckily he got the last two. He returned.

'Not bad,' Jason said, licking his fingers. 'Is that it, then?'

'Not quite,' said Prometheus.

Instinctively, Jason made a grab at the nearest plate, but missed by six inches. The food was playing hard to get again.

'Don't try to fight it,' Prometheus advised him. 'Think how embarrassing it would be going out to dinner and having the prawn cocktail leap out of the glass and hide under the sideboard until you've gone. Everyone else would be wondering which fork to use, and you'd be scooping in yours with a butterfly net.'

537

'If this is your idea of helping me stay unbiased and impartial . . .'

Prometheus laughed. 'Blow that,' he replied. 'You've made the decision. Now we need you on our side for the actual fighting.'

'Ah,' Jason said. 'Fighting.'

'Didn't I mention the fighting?'

'Not in so many words, no.'

'Well,' Prometheus said, 'when the gods find out that the world they had such high hopes for has been kicked into touch and is now entirely beyond their reach, there's a material risk that they might feel rather upset. Particularly,' Prometheus added, 'as they have now sworn to destroy this world so that they can move everything and everybody onto the other one. And you know how it is with gods; once they've sworn to do something, then it's just got to be done . . .'

'Balls,' Jason replied.

Prometheus shook his head, startling a flock of lemon meringue pies that had pitched in a nearby tree. 'You're thinking of promises to mortals,' he said. 'That's different.* I'm talking about a promise Jupiter has made to himself. He can't break that.'

---

*Promises made by gods to mortals are binding on the gods, but the gods reserve the right to interpret the terms of the promise.

Promises made by gods to other gods are also binding on the parties concerned; but this is effectively a dead letter, since a god can always point to the relevant Betamax world on which the promise actually was fulfilled and thus justifiably claim to have carried out his pledge.

Promises made by gods to themselves actually are binding, partly because the Possibility Police insist, partly because gods, being immortal, have to live with themselves rather longer than the rest of us.

'Can't he?'

'No. So you see there may actually be quite a bit of fighting in the not too distant future.' Prometheus paused for a moment. 'That'll be nice, won't it?'

'Will it?'

'I'd have thought you'd have been pleased,' the Titan replied. 'You're a Hero. Heroes like fighting. It's what they're good at.'

'That doesn't always follow,' Jason replied. 'My mum's cousin Henry is a dentist, and people are always saying how good he is at it, and he doesn't enjoy it at all. Sometimes I think it's that way with me and Heroism.'

'Nonsense,' Prometheus said firmly. 'You'll enjoy it once it's started, I'm sure. And besides, you aren't supposed to know the meaning of fear.'

'Actually,' Jason confessed, 'I looked it up in the dictionary. Came as quite a surprise, actually. I always thought it was some sort of large bird.'

'All right, all right,' Prometheus said impatiently, 'I should have said you know no fear. Now can we . . .?'

'Maybe not fear,' Jason interrupted, 'but acute apprehension and blind panic I can manage quite easily. It's just practice, after all, and these last few days . . .'

Just then, Jason felt something cold and wet against the back of his hand. Something cold, wet and tripartite. He looked down.

'Hello, Cerberus, where the hell have you been?' he started to ask, and then he noticed that Prometheus was staring at the dog with a look of combined loathing and horror. Normally Jason wouldn't have thought anything of it, since he knew a lot of people who reacted to dogs in precisely that way; but Prometheus hadn't seemed the type. He looked again. In one of its three mouths, the dog was holding a small blue, green and brown sphere that seemed extremely familiar.

'Oh hell,' Jason said. 'He hasn't, has he?'

Prometheus nodded. 'Looks like it to me,' he replied in a hoarse whisper. 'You threw the Betamax world away; Fido here has fetched it back for you. Oh *hell*!'

The dog, sensing that man's best friend had cocked it up again, laid his ears back and wandered over to the shade of a boulder, where he proceeded to lodge the Betamax world between his front paws and chew it. Jason and Prometheus looked at each other.

'We'd better get it back from him quick,' Prometheus said.

'By *we* . . .'

'Don't stand there arguing the toss. Get the bloody thing.'

Jason shrugged and reached for the surface-to-air scotch egg. It shied away. Jason started to protest, and Prometheus apologised. 'What are you up to, though?' he added.

'Canine psychology,' Jason replied. 'I'll also need a Bakewell tart and some sausages.'

These were provided and Jason wandered over to the boulder, sat down and started to eat. A moment later, the dog was sitting beside him giving him that wistful, pathetic look that all dogs seem to have in common. Then it opened its mouth to make the quintessential doggy hopeful panting noise, and of course the Betamax world rolled out of its jaws and trundled along the ground. Prometheus swooped down, picked it up and shoved it inside the front of his robe. Jason popped a foodstuff into each of the three sets of jaws, collected the Betamax world and let fly.

For the record, the Betamax world didn't leave the

space/time continuum at all. The friction it encountered on leaving the Earth's atmosphere set it alight and it soon degenerated into a comet; given its unique genesis, however, it did not behave exactly as other comets do; that is to say, it combined the regularity of trajectory which is a characteristic of comets with the innate cussedness of all divine or semi-divine artefacts. For the rest of time, therefore, it circled through the galaxy, turning up with remorseless regularity exactly when it was least expected.

In any event, it ceased to be a Betamax world, and that was just as well. Because no sooner had it left Jason's hand than the sky darkened and the sun made a dash for the safety of a dense cloudbank, pausing only to glint significantly on the speartips of the vanguard of a huge divine army making its way rapidly towards the surface of the planet.

Religious revivals have been endemic on the Number One World ever since the gods retired and went to live in the sun. Nobody is exactly sure why. One view is that mankind has a desperate need to believe in something, preferably something so blatantly absurd that only blind, unquestioning faith will suffice – for example, the belief which sprang up in the late nineteenth century and was still widely current in Jason Derry's time and which held that human beings were not in fact created at all but were somehow the descendants of bald, mutant monkeys. The other view is that there is never anything much on television during the summer.

Never, though, has there been a religious revival as sudden and as widespread as the one which followed Apollo's first broadcast to the world. Perhaps it was simply his magnetic charisma – Apollo, after all, looked like a

541

young Greek god,* had a particularly appealing smile and a way of looking into the camera as if it had been the camera he had been searching for all these years – or perhaps it was simply the fact that what he was saying happened to be true. In any event, no sooner had he left the studio and wandered out into the carpark to reclaim his chariot than the entire world suddenly decided that it had seen the light. Those who had seen the broadcast immediately went and told those who hadn't and (being human) threatened to burn them alive if they didn't join in. So quickly, in fact, did the revival gather momentum that half an hour after the broadcast not only was there a High Priest of Durham but he was on TV asking for money.

Another aspect of this revival that made it different from most of its predecessors was the fact that although the gods were now universally believed in and revered, they were also intensely unpopular. Apollo had not pulled his punches. He had made it perfectly clear that the gods were not cuddly.

There had, of course, been religious protest groups before – one thinks automatically of the Guild of Merchant Plasterers Against the Crucifixion which enjoyed a brief prominence during the English Civil War – but none of them had expressly set out to believe the gods into oblivion. That, however, was what Apollo had achieved, simply by stating that it was ordained that if Mankind truly had faith, the gods would not be able to achieve their intended purpose. There was an oracle in precisely those terms, he had said. Which was, of course, perfectly true; as the god of prophecies he had seen to it personally.

*He was a young Greek god, which helped.

542

The eagle came swooping back just as he had got the winged horse back into the traces of the chariot.

'Well?' Apollo asked.

'Absolutely,' the eagle replied. She had been sent to check that the broadcast had achieved the desired effect, and had just flown round the world in thirty-seven seconds. 'It's worked like a charm.'

'Are you sure?'

'No problems,' replied the eagle. 'Everybody singing hymns and sacrificing like it was going out of fashion. If I was a white ram right now, I'd be very scared indeed.'

'Fine.' Apollo replied. 'Look, do you have to do that?'

'Do what?'

'Sharpen your beak against my spoiler. I've only just had this chariot resprayed, and . . .'

'Sorry,' said the eagle. 'Would it help if I assumed human form?'

Apollo remembered that he had seen the eagle in human form not long ago. 'Yes,' he said. 'Why not?'

The eagle became Mary, and sat in the passenger seat of the chariot. She adjusted the rear-view mirror and examined herself in it.

'The trouble with being an eagle,' she said at last, 'is, it does terrible things to your skin. Dries it out. It'll take three days in a mud-pack to get rid of these lines.'

'What's going to happen now?' Apollo asked. Mary looked at him and giggled.

'I don't know, do I?' she said. 'Who do you think I am, God almighty?'

Apollo frowned irritably. 'You seemed to have a pretty good idea just now,' he said, 'when you were telling me what to do. If this is some kind of practical joke . . .'

Mary assured him that it wasn't. 'If it was a joke,' she

said, 'the last thing it would be would be practical. No, I know what should happen now, of course, but there are no guarantees.'

'What should happen, then?'

'Jupiter,' Mary said, 'should set out to destroy the Earth. Halfway down, he will be met with a surge of faith in an essentially non-violent, ecologically aware carbon copy of himself who wouldn't willingly uproot a dandelion if there was any way of avoiding it. All this faith will get right up his spine and he'll be forced to pigeonhole the entire project.'

'Fine.'

'Well, up to a point fine,' said Mary, powdering her nose. 'The difficulty will be that he'll be very much aware that he wants to demolish the earth but can't, and this may make him resentful. And from what I can remember of the faith mechanics I learnt at college, there's nothing to stop him taking it out on someone in a big way, just so long as that person doesn't happen to be a planet. If I were you,' she concluded, closing her powder compact with a snap, 'I'd be distinctly edgy.'

'Me?'

'You,' said Mary. 'I don't want to worry you, but you are directly responsible for thwarting him. He should be arriving any time now.'

Apollo looked up at the sky; there was a thick bank of black cloud moving in from the east, and another from the west. Although he wasn't to know it, there was in fact another contingent trying to get in from the north, but it had got held up in a contraflow system over Finland.

'What can I do?' he said.

'Try and be dignified about it,' Mary replied. 'Well, it's been nice. Ciao.'

'Hold on,' Apollo said, grabbing her by the wrist.

544

'Oh, don't let's start all that again.'

Apollo blushed furiously. 'I didn't mean that,' he said. 'I mean, you've got me into this, now you'd better . . .'

'Nothing to do with me,' Mary said, 'Gods have free will, remember. And now I really do have to be going.'

'Where?'

'To meet the others. Prometheus and Gelos and the Derry kid. So if you'll just stop crushing my wrist for a moment, I'll be getting along.'

'Let me give you a lift,' Apollo said.

Actually, said a tiny voice at the back of Mary's mind, in a part of her brain that she had recently only used for operating some semi-redundant feathers on her left wing, he's quite good-looking, in a way. For a god. Nice smile.

'All right,' she said. 'Head for the Caucasus.'

'Why?'

'That's where the others are. Come on, hurry up.'

'We'll be safe there?'

Mary considered this for a moment. 'I always think safe is such a terribly subjective word, don't you?'

'What word would you choose, then?'

'Conveniently-situated.'

'Oh.' Apollo hesitated, his hand on the ignition key. The starter motor system had been one of the trickiest parts of the whole conversion job, and Vulcan had finally managed it by wiring the starter motor up to an electrode fitted to the lead horse's rump. When you turned the key, it gave the horse a severe electric shock. Being a divine horse, it was supposed to understand by that that the driver wanted to be taken somewhere; but even divine horses can only stand so much of that sort of thing before they start lashing out with their hind legs. Fortunately for his peace of mind, Apollo wasn't mechanically minded

545

and hadn't yet considered how the thing worked. 'Conveniently situated for what?'

'For a good view of the battle of course.'

Apollo was firmly of the opinion that the best view of a battle in which Jupiter was on the opposing or less friendly side was from the other side of space and, if possible, time, and said so. Mary replied by taking what later turned out to be a small sacrificial dagger from her handbag and pressing it, not unkindly, into the small of Apollo's back.

'I'm hijacking this chariot to the Caucasus,' she said. 'You know you're immortal but maybe I'm not convinced. Shall we go now?'

'I . . .' Apollo considered for a moment and then turned the ignition key. 'Are you sure you know what you're doing?' he asked.

'Yes,' Mary replied confidently. She was by inclination a truthful person, so it was for the best, she reckoned, that he hadn't asked her if what she was doing was sensible or not.

One of the leading drawbacks to travelling to battle in the heart of an inky black thundercloud is that you get very wet indeed. If you are carrying an ample supply of lightning bolts, there is also the risk of a serious short-circuit. Jupiter was therefore not at his most affable during the journey from the sun to Earth. The Captain of Spectral Warriors who had interrupted his light lunch with an enquiry about the possibility of overtime payments for the Forces of Darkness (it being daytime) and who was now buzzing sadly along behind the Host in the shape of a small bee, was generally considered to have got away with it lightly.

Minerva, as Officer i/c Destruction, North-western Sector, was sitting in her winged-dragon-propelled mobile command centre studying a confused bundle of maps and a dog-eared copy of Baedeker when Mars knocked tentatively at the door and stepped in.

'Well, Ma, what is it now?' Minerva took off her glasses and looked at him sourly. She tended to be impatient with failures, and the fact that after the previous debacle Mars had been temporarily suspended from his duties at War and put in charge of Troop Welfare and Entertainment made her less ready to waste valuable time on him than she would otherwise have been, which was not very. 'If you want me to sing in the Camp Concert, I'm afraid I'm far too busy.'

Mars, who had heard Minerva sing, assured her that he quite understood. 'No,' he said, 'what I really wanted was a quiet word about what's going to happen when we destroy the world.'

'We've been into that already,' Minerva said. 'And I do take your point, but there it is. You can't make omelettes without breaking eggs.'

'I don't want a bloody omelette, Min.' Mars gave her a despairing look. 'For crying out loud, we're all going to die in about twenty minutes and nobody seems to care a damn. What's got into you all?'

'We're trying not to think about it,' Minerva replied, putting her spectacles back on and returning to her paperwork. 'I can only recommend that you try to do the same. Close the door after you, please.'

On his way back to the Welfare Office, Mars met Diana. She had been given the post of Annihilation Liaison Officer, and she had been going round the army trying to find out what it meant.

'I don't know,' Mars replied when she asked him. 'I don't particularly want to find out, either. The whole point about knowledge, I always thought, was that you find

547

something out and then you remember it for the rest of your life. In the circumstances it all seems rather pointless, don't you think?'

Diana ignored him. 'I'm a bit worried about Pol,' she said.

'Pol?' Mars stared. 'You're worried about Apollo?'

'Well, he is my brother,' Diana replied defensively. 'I'm just hoping he's going to be all right.'

'How can he be all right?' Mars shouted. 'He's going to die in just under fifteen minutes, according to the schedule. So are the rest of us.'

'All right, yes, you needn't go on about it,' Diana replied. 'What I mean is, is he going to be all right till then?'

Mars left her and wandered off in search of the Officers' Mess. In his opinion, the description fitted the entire enterprise, but the part of it he was interested in was the small, tastefully furnished area selling intoxicants.

He finally tracked it down at the south-eastern corner of the cloud and went in. The only other customer was Neptune, who was sitting at the bar trying to drown his sorrows – a difficult undertaking for a sea-god.

'Siddown, Ma,' he said. 'Have a li'l drink. Think we just got time for a quick one.'

'What are you having?'

'Think I'll have a Gorgon's Revenge.'

Mars looked at him. 'Are you sure?'

Neptune hiccuped and grinned. 'Course I'm sure,' he replied. 'It's the only time in the history of the world a man can have five Gorgon's Revenges on an empty stomach and not have to worry about the morning after. Gesundheit.'

'You have a point there, Uncle Nep,' said Mars. 'Make mine the same.'

Soon afterwards the barman brought the drinks, and Neptune, by way of experiment, picked out a diamond from his dress crown and dropped it into the glass. It dissolved.

'I've always wondered what they put in these things,' he remarked, staring into the glass. The fumes blinded him for a moment.

'Best not to ask, so they say,' replied Mars. 'Well, here's health.'

Neptune looked round. 'Where?'

'No,' Mars said, 'it's a toast. Cheers.'

'Mud in your eye,' Neptune answered. They drank deeply and for a long time were silent.

'I think I'll have another one of those,' said Neptune.

'Why not?' Mars replied. 'That way, things can only get better.'

The cloud, meanwhile, had smashed its way through a very confused stratosphere and was rushing down towards the surface of the planet. It was just gathering momentum nicely when the prayers hit it.

Being hit by a prayer is no joke. The first thing that happened was that all the lights went out. When the backup power supply came on, Neptune and Mars found themselves looking at something quite unexpected.

'Here,' Neptune demanded querulously, 'what do they put in these things?'

A shaft of golden light had impaled the cloud like a skewer through a veal *souvlaki*. There were a lot of – well, it went against the grain to say this, but there was no avoiding the fact that they were angels. They were also holding flaming swords.

'How do they do that?' asked Mars.

'I dunno,' Neptune replied. 'Oven-gloves, maybe.'

549

As if the sunbeam and the angels weren't bad enough, there were other indications that something quite out of the ordinary was happening. There were a lot of quite unsolicited flowers, for example, and the air was heavy with strong, sweet, cheap perfume. Both Mars and Neptune suddenly felt an overwhelming urge to grant requests.

'I don't know about you,' Neptune said, 'but right now I'm feeling a bit funny. I think I'll just go and lie down for a minute.'

Mars nodded carefully. 'Good idea,' he said. "Which way is the door?'

Outside they stopped again and stared. Peculiar though the other manifestations had been, this was something else.

It was Jupiter. Jupiter standing in the middle of the cloud's parade ground. Jupiter smiling.

You could see at once that he was fighting it, with every fibre of his supreme being. And the harder he tried, it seemed, the harder it was to resist. The golden sunbeam had got him right in the navel.

'Do you think we ought to . . .' Mars's voice drained away.

'Help, you mean?'

'Well, yes.'

Neptune shook his head. 'Wouldn't do that,' he said.

'You wouldn't?'

'Certainly not,' he said. Twenty thousand years of sibling rivalry blossomed on his face into a grin the size of California. 'That'd be blasphemy.'

'Blasphemy?'

'Absolutely,' Neptune replied. 'To attempt to assist Jupiter would be implicitly to deny his omnipotence. No, let the old bastard sort it out for himself. I'm going back to the bar.'

'But . . .'

'My shout.'

Mars shot another glance at the Father of Gods and Men and headed back to the Mess tent.

'What's going on, Nep?' he asked.

'It's a prayer,' Neptune replied, hopping up onto a bar stool and eating olives. 'A biggy, too. In fact, that's the biggest prayer I've ever seen in the whole of my life. And Jupe's got it right through his guts. Champagne!' he called to the barman.

Apollo and Mary arrived in the Caucasus just in time to see the cloud grind to a halt, waver and slowly start to retreat back into the sun. The golden shaft gradually faded, until there was nothing left but a little sprinkling of silver filings, the residue of a few inappropriate prayers contributed by members of the Tokyo Stock Exchange.

'Thanks for the lift,' Mary said. 'Now, are you going to hang around and catch the fun?'

'Do I have a choice?'

'Of course you have a choice,' Mary replied, pressing very gently with the small knife. 'Weren't you listening to what I was saying about gods having free will?'

'I don't mean a choice between staying and getting knifed,' Apollo said. 'I don't really call that a choice, do you?'

'It's what you expect the mortals to put up with most of the time,' Mary started to say; but then she remembered what her mother had told her about not talking politics on a first date. Her mother hadn't mentioned the social effects of digging a small knife in the guy's back, so presumably that was OK.

'All right then,' Apollo was saying, 'so what's happening?'

'So far as I can see,' Mary replied, 'the gods have just tried to land and blow the Earth away, but all the prayers and faith you managed to whip up have forced them back again. That's it so far as destroying the Earth goes, at least for now. In about five minutes, I expect Jupiter will be back to kill somebody.'

'Fine.'

'Oh look,' Mary interrupted, 'there's Pro and Gel and the Derry kid. I think we should go over and have a word with them, don't you? They might be able to think of something to stop Jupiter killing us all. That'd be nice, wouldn't it?'

'Absolutely.'

Mary bit her lip indecisively. On the one hand, she knew it was totally counterproductive to go around throwing yourself at people; on the other hand, she had the feeling that unless she gave some sort of hint or indication at this stage, a promising relationship might simply fade away and die.

'I don't know if you were wondering,' she said, 'but there isn't anything between me and the Derry kid.'

'No?'

'No.'

'Well, there we go,' Apollo said. 'Do you think you might take that knife out of my back now?'

'There should be,' Mary went on. 'I mean, it was fated and so forth. But what the hell, just because a thing's fated doesn't mean to say you're stuck with it, does it?'

'Doesn't it?'

'And as for Pro and me,' Mary went on, finding it all rather harder work than she had originally anticipated but staying with it nevertheless, 'we really are just good friends. I mean, what there is between me and Pro is very special,

552

don't get me wrong, but really, there's the age difference, the size difference, the species difference. You've got to be realistic about things like that, haven't you?'

'Ouch,' Apollo replied.

'Oh hell, *sorry*,' Mary replied. 'I'm just so clumsy sometimes you wouldn't believe it. My mother used to say to me . . .'

Prometheus had seen them and was hurrying over. He looked the same, but there was somehow something different about him; if he had been a tune he'd be in stereo instead of mono.

'Pol, my boy,' he shouted, 'good of you to come. Just in time, too.'

'Hello, Uncle Pro,' replied Apollo resignedly. 'Look, if I'd known it was all going to get as messy as this . . .'

'Don't be silly,' Prometheus said. 'And anyway, everything is going to be fine. We've got the eagle, the dog and the Derry boy . . .'

'Hello,' said Jason, sheepishly. Meeting new gods for the first time always made him a little bit bashful.

Apollo nodded briefly and smiled a tight-lipped smile and then resumed his search for knowledge. 'Look, Uncle Pro,' he started to say; but Prometheus silenced him with a gesture of his hand.

'I know,' he said. 'But there's nothing to worry about. If Jupiter starts getting violent, Jason here will threaten to tell him the Joke.'

'What joke?'

'The Joke, idiot.'

Apollo's eyes widened like balloons in the course of being inflated. 'You mean to say *he* knows the Joke?'

'Most of it,' Prometheus replied. 'All of it except the punch line.'

553

'Ah. But even so . . .'

'It's all right, don't worry,' Prometheus replied. 'I made sure that neither part of the Joke would be volatile without the other.'

Apollo thought of something. 'How come you know the Joke, Uncle Pro?'

'Uncle Pro doesn't know the Joke,' said Prometheus, 'but I do.'

Apollo didn't understand at first; then the truth dawned on him. He backed away. 'You mean you're . . .'

'Thing.'

'Yes.' Apollo said, 'Begins with a G . . . On the tip of my tongue . . .'

'No, you fool, that's my name,' Prometheus snapped. 'It has pleased me to call myself Gelos and play at being a mere Form for a number of years, but in fact I'm your great-uncle, brother of Cronus and Rhea. Do you believe me?'

'Yes.'

'Well,' said Prometheus, 'just in case you don't . . .'

He narrowed his eyes and gave Apollo a good long stare. Suddenly Apollo started to laugh, until he could feel his lungs straining to bursting point. In fact he was just about to black out when the laughter stopped as suddenly as it had begun.

'Again for the sake of convenience,' Prometheus continued, 'I'm sharing bodies with my old friend Prometheus at the moment. Minds, too. We've always had similar tastes in minds, Pro and I, haven't we, Pro? Yes, ever since I can remember, except I like mine a bit less cluttered. Well, we won't go into that now; it takes all sorts. I was only going to say. Later, Pro, all right? Please yourself, then. Sorry, Pol, as I was saying . . .'

But before he could continue, his head snapped upwards. Apollo followed his gaze and saw something high up by the sun. He recognised it.

'What is it?' Mary said.

'Jupiter's coming back,' Prometheus replied. 'Right, everyone – action stations.'

'What might those be, exactly?'

'Er, you know, get ready and everything.'

'I take it,' Apollo said, 'that you do have a plan.'

'A plan, yes.'

'A plan of battle,' Apollo said. 'Stratagems and so forth.'

'Sort of.'

'And are you going to let us into the secret, or are we – ouch! For pity's sake, woman, mind what you're doing with that knife. You could do someone an injury.'

'It's all right, Mary,' Prometheus said, 'you can put it away now. Apollo won't desert us at a time like this.'

'Won't he though!' Apollo turned to make a dash for his chariot, only to feel the beginnings of another big laugh clogging his windpipe. 'All right,' he sighed, 'you win.'

'Let's hope so, anyway,' Prometheus replied. 'Now then, Pol, you and I and Mary and the dog will form the rearguard, and the rest of us . . .'

'That only leaves me,' said Jason.

'The rest of us will form the front line contingents. Ready, Jason?'

'No.'

'Here they come.'

Strictly speaking, of course, it wasn't necessary for Jupiter to come at all. But if there was one thing the Sky-Father loved it was melodrama, and if there was going to be a big fight, he wanted to be there in person, pitching in and

555

watching the bodies go splat. Sitting in the sun hurling thunderbolts was a poor substitute, he always felt, for actually getting to grips with an enemy's intestines.

His list of priorities was quite clear in his mind. Family first; Apollo and that ungrateful little git Jason Derry – he had something really hot in mind for him. Then, once the first flush of exuberance had worn off and been replaced with nice, grim resentment, he'd sort out Prometheus and that damn eagle. That would leave the highlight of the proceedings, his Uncle Thing, till last. Uncle Thing was the part he was looking forward to most.

As he roared through the air like a vindictive meteor, he quickly ran through the fundamentals of anatomy in his mind. A mental picture of his antagonists with little dotted lines and pairs of scissors drawn all over them draped itself across the retina of his inner eye and he made no effort to get rid of it.

Behind him streamed the selected elite of the divine special services unit. There was no point in cluttering the place up with rookies and idiots, not now that the demolition programme had been shelved indefinitely. For killing bolshy immortals you need quality, not quantity; and the Forms hurtling Earthwards in Jupiter's wake were the sort of abstraction that only a very powerful and extremely unbalanced mind could conceive of. Even he got the creeps just thinking about them, and yet they were merely personifications of the contents of his own head. Now that was scary.

Was he mad, Jupiter asked himself, as he zoomed through the Earth's atmosphere in a cloud of blue flames. He thought it over and decided that yes, he quite probably was. He only needed to look over his shoulder to know that his mind was so unhinged it was a miracle it didn't fall out of his ear.

Ah well. Too late to do anything about that now.

'And what,' Jason was asking, 'will the rest of you be doing while I'm . . .?'

And then he saw the flames, and Jupiter at the head of his unspeakable squadron, and realised that he was on his own. Only he could do anything about all this, fix things so that never again would Jupiter be able to command that the world be destroyed. And why? Nobody seemed to know. Because it was fated. Brilliant.

There was a screaming sound – it was just the air being torn apart by the violence of their passing, but it sounded much worse. Jason squared his shoulders, drew the Sword of – I couldn't give a toss what it's supposed to be called, he said to himself, I shall call it Freckles – and took one step forward. He wouldn't mind doing this sort of thing if only people would tell him what was going on.

'Hiya, Dad,' he said.

Jupiter stopped in mid-air, and the shock-waves caused by his sudden loss of momentum sent clouds scudding across the skies of four continents.

'Hi there, Son,' Jupiter replied. 'You're for it this time.'

'Am I?'

'Oh yes,' replied Jupiter. 'I mean, this isn't your parking in a no-parking zone. This is where you and life part company. Sorry, lad, but there it is.'

'Oh well,' Jason said. 'In that case, knock knock.'

'You what, Son?'

'Knock knock,' Jason repeated. 'You're meant to say "Who's there?"'

Jupiter felt as if the air had given way under his feet. 'Now steady on, lad,' he said. 'Let's neither of us get carried away and say things we might regret later.'

557

'Say "Who's there?"'

'Certainly not,' Jupiter replied. 'Got you now, haven't I?'

'Who's there?' Jason said. 'Cassivelaunus. Cassivelaunus who?'

And then he dried.

Any stand-up comedian will tell you it's a horrible feeling, and when your audience is a Sky-God with an army of very bad ideas at his back, it can get really hairy. Jason opened his mouth and nothing came out of it.

'Go on, then,' Jupiter said, folding his arms and tapping his toe on a wisp of water vapour. 'Cassivelaunus who?'

'Er . . .'

'Cassivelaunus who?'

'Do you know the one about the travelling salesman who goes into this, um . . .'

'I asked you a question,' said Jupiter. 'Cassivelaunus who?'

And then Jason remembered. He couldn't say the punch line because he didn't know it. The dog did. He turned, whistled, and called, 'Here, boy!' as loudly as he could. The dog stayed exactly where he was.

'Is that it?' Jupiter asked. 'Cassivelaunus Here-Boy? I've found funnier things in Christmas crackers.'

'Here, boy!' Jason yelled. 'Cerberus! *Bad* dog!' The dog stood there and wagged his tail at him. Then, very slowly, it faded away.

Jason turned round and looked at his father. He smiled, and while he did so his brain was improvising furiously.

'Well?'

'Er,' said Jason, 'Cassie, the lawn is badly in need of mowing. Um . . .'

'What?'

'You heard.'

'Cassie, the lawn is badly in need of mowing,' said Jupiter slowly, relishing every word. 'That's it, is it?'

'And let it be a lesson to you,' said Jason. 'Now, if you've quite finished . . .'

'Oh no,' Jupiter said. 'I haven't even started yet.'

The Sky-God grinned, and for some reason that was the final straw. All the aggravation that had been building up inside Jason ever since this whole tiresome business had started suddenly came to the surface and exploded. There was something about Jupiter just then, Jason decided, that didn't only get up his nose, it went right the way through and half way down his throat. With a yell so blood-curdling you could have made black puddings with it, he swung the Sword Freckles round his head and charged.

Jupiter didn't stand a chance. The Forms standing behind him recognised this before he did, and before Jupiter had so much as raised his arm in a fruitless attempt to shield his face, the slowest of them was ploughing through the cumulo-nimbus and motoring nicely. As it rushed sunwards it could just hear the sound of somebody very large a long way away saying 'Ouch!' It didn't stop to find out who.

Jason, meanwhile, was getting nicely into his rhythm. He had split the Helmet of Authority, sliced the thunderbolts into mortadella, shattered the Breastplate of Power and was just about to make an end of it when . . .

'Jason!' said a voice behind him. 'You stop that immediately, you hear me?'

Jason sighed very, very deeply and lowered his sword.

'Yes, mum,' he said.

'So now you see.'

Jason nodded. He supposed that it made sense, after a

559

fashion. Or at least, if it didn't absolutely make sense, it was at least less glaringly nonsensical than a lot of things which passed for components of that great pile of unwashed laundry known for convenience as The Truth. Perhaps a better way of looking at it was that if it wasn't true it was at least what all the protagonists believed to be true. In such circumstances as these, Jason was beginning to realise, an untruth tends to become indistinguishable from the real thing, simply through the action of protective mimicry.

'Well then,' he said. 'Did you get all that, Mum?'

'No,' said Mrs. Derry.

Jason sighed. He would have to explain.

'Look,' he said, 'what Prometheus was saying was that the reason why it was—' Language, Jason realised, was a large part of the problem, because words say what they want to say, not what you want them to say – 'why it was fated from the start that I'd be the only one who could, like, stand up to Dad and sort all this lot out . . .' He paused; somewhere his sentence had wrapped itself round his legs, like a fast-moving dog on a long lead. 'The reason why it had to be me,' he ventured, 'is that . . . Well, in the beginning, there was this word, right . . .'

'I think what Jason's trying to say,' Prometheus interrupted, 'is that Jason is unique in history because he has more of one particular quality than anyone else who's ever been, and it was this quality, this power, that was required in order to make the whole thing work.'

'Oh yes?' said Mrs. Derry politely. She had only the vaguest notion who this tall man was, and she wasn't sure she liked him. But he seemed to be saying that her son was a very special and important person, and she agreed with that. Like all mothers, she had known that from the very beginning, but it was nice to find someone who agreed with her.

'Let me put it this way,' Prometheus said. 'Some people say that love is the most powerful force in the Universe. Well, you can take it from me that it isn't. Others say, rather more plausibly, that it's fear, greed, hope or faith that makes the world go round. They're wrong, too. As for those who say that what fuels and drives the Universe is the laws of physics, all I can say is that they're living in a world of their own. No, the most powerful and significant force in the Universe, the one thing that gets things done and makes things happen, is aggravation.'

'Aggravation?'

'Aggravation. Why is it, do you think, that all the little atoms move about within their molecules, bashing into each other like so many Christmas shoppers and creating the effect known to scientists as Brownian motion? Is it love, do you think, or fear, or belief in the Supreme Being? Like hell it is. The plain truth of the matter is that if you put more than two or three atoms together in a confined space for any length of time, sooner or later they're going to get on each other's wick, and then they start hurling themselves about and colliding with each other. They also shout a lot, but since the science of physics is in its infancy, nobody has yet constructed an instrument sensitive enough to monitor the voices of millions of tiny atoms debating with each other whose turn it is to do the washing up. Probably just as well, if you ask me.'

'I see,' lied Mrs. Derry. 'But what's that got to do with . . .?'

'When Gelos and I,' Prometheus went on, 'came to the conclusion that something was going to have to be done about Jupiter if he wasn't going to get completely out of

561

hand, we realised that the only thing powerful enough to stand up to him was a really massive dose of raw aggravation. Faith wasn't enough. It would just about be possible, if the world was allowed to lie fallow, if you like, for a thousand odd years so that it could build its faith reserves up to the maximum, to generate a faith field strong enough to repel Jupiter once, but it could only be once; after that, he would be able to come back once he'd licked his wounds and found another Betamax world to replace the one Jason disposed of for us, and have another go. No, somebody was going to have to sort out Jupiter himself, and for that purpose, only aggravation would do. So we set about creating the perfect aggravation conductor. We designed Jason.'

'Well,' said Mrs. Derry, 'that's fascinating. And now Jason and I must be getting along. Come on, Jason . . .'

'The specifications,' Prometheus continued, 'were for a Hero who was at least as big and as strong and as brave as one of the old-time Big Three, Hercules, Theseus and Achilles – in other words, a son of Jupiter – but who had spent his entire life being put upon, shoved about and generally pushed around. That way, we could build up the necessary reservoir of aggravation, and then when the time was right we could prime it, so to speak, by letting him know just to what extent he'd been pushed around all these years, and further by giving him the impression that not just his mother and his father but everyone, on all sides, had been using him as a sort of human combination hammer, tin-opener and mole wrench. Finally we would put him in a position of enormous stress and fail him. That was what all that nonsense with the dog was for. There's no way we would have dared entrust the Joke or any part of it to him, let alone to a three-headed dog. We just let him think we had. We set him up good and proper. Sorry about that, Jason.'

'That's all right,' Jason said automatically. He had in fact been intending to pull Prometheus's head off and use it as a football ever since the truth of the matter had dawned on him, at that crucial moment when Cerberus had disappeared. Somehow, though, now that it came to it, he wasn't in the mood. So what?

'Anyway,' Prometheus said, 'we all saw what happened. Jupiter never knew what hit him. The combination of Jason's irritation and his own massive aggravation buildup, caused by the failure of his attack on Earth, led to the most almighty outburst of pure, undiluted aggro, and Jupiter just fused out. It was like putting a vastly excessive current through a five-amp plug. Jason, of course, is a superb natural conductor of aggravation, and so it just went through him like water through a pipe.'

There was a long silence.

'What you mean is,' Mrs. Derry said at last, 'our Jason saved the world.'

'Exactly,' Prometheus said. 'He lost his cool and thereby saved the world.'

'And what about Dad?' Jason asked. 'Not that I'm all that bothered, not after what he was going to do to me – well, to all of us, really, but . . .'

'You mustn't blame him,' Prometheus said. 'The sad truth is that Jupiter's been more or less off his rocker for a very long time now, pretty well ever since I stole the first Joke from heaven all those years ago. You see, unlike most of the gods he actually did care about the world, and – misguidedly, in my opinion – he felt very strongly that in order to survive, mortals need an unshakable faith in the gods. When I snookered him on that score, there was a huge

563

build-up of aggro inside him, and as we've seen he just can't handle it. Something gave way inside his head, and he's been missing on at least two cylinders ever since. What's happened today has, I'm afraid, finally done for the poor old devil. His supreme being days are well and truly over, I fear.'

'Then what's going to happen?' Jason asked. 'Does that mean that Thing is going to take over?'

'Perish the thought!' Prometheus replied. 'That would be a very serious mistake, and Thing knows it. He's going back into retirement, where he belongs. Going to write a novel, he tells me, and I wish him the very best of luck. No, what we've decided on is that Jupiter will carry on as Supreme Being in name only, with Apollo as a sort of Prince Regent. That way, Pol being Pol, the gods will spend all their time bickering with each other and they'll leave the mortals in peace. It'll mean the end of the Game, for one thing, and that can't be bad.'

'What Game?' Jason asked.

'And if Apollo ever does show any signs of getting above himself,' Prometheus went on, 'then we'll have Mrs. Apollo to keep him under control.'

'Mrs. Apollo?'

'Mary,' Prometheus explained. 'As you know better than anyone, the only thing capable of dominating a male with unlimited physical strength is a female with a comparable amount of mental strength. I don't think it'll take Mary very long to get Apollo properly trained, do you?'

'Oh,' said Jason. 'So Mary's . . .'

'Yes,' Prometheus replied. 'It's not what was fated, I know, but you take it from me, you've had a very lucky escape there. Bear in mind that Mary is also your Sharon.'

'Ah yes,' said Jason. 'That's a very good point. Thank you.'

'Well, then.' Prometheus yawned and stretched. The sun was starting to sink behind the Caucasus mountains. In the distance, Apollo and Mary were going for a quiet stroll, talking pleasantly of this and that. A couple of Forms in white coats were trying their best to persuade Jupiter that it was safe to come down from his tree. 'That more or less wraps it up, then,' Prometheus said. 'Thanks for everything, Jason. We couldn't have done it without you. Or rather, you couldn't have done it without us.'

'Will the world be a better place?' Jason asked.

Prometheus shook his head. 'I doubt it,' he said. 'It always amazes me, the way the old place quickly gets back to normal no matter what you do to try and improve it. No, you can make it worse, no problem, but it's virtually impossible to improve it. I tried, remember. I gave them fire, and yet millions of people are still cold. I taught them agriculture, and millions of them are still starving. I gave them laughter, and yet the majority of them are still as miserable as income tax. I can only imagine it's how they like it, deep down.'

'And what are you going to do?' Jason asked.

'Me?' Prometheus grinned. 'I'm going to have a holiday, what the hell do you think? After that, I don't know. I might have a shot at sorting out the gods a bit more, but I doubt it. Anyway, I mustn't keep you any longer. Thanks again.'

He smiled and then grew, until they lost sight of his head, then his body, and then finally his kneecaps in the clouds. And then he simply wasn't there any more, and Jason and Mrs. Derry discovered that what they were actually looking at was a mountain.

'Right,' said Mrs. Derry. 'Let's be getting home. I could do with a cup of tea, and you could do with a bath.'

'Mum . . .'

'A bath,' Mrs. Derry repeated, 'and no arguments.'

'But Mum, I had one this morning . . .'

'Jason,' said Mrs. Derry.

Just then, a helicopter appeared in the sky. In it were Betty-Lou Fisichelli and her agent, a camera crew, and a glass tank containing a frog. The frog seemed agitated, and Ms. Fisichelli was doing her best to comfort it by saying that it was all going to be all right, that Apollo would soon turn him back into human shape and then give him the most incredibly historic interview of all time, just so long as he minded his manners and promised never to coin the phrase Olympusgate as long as he lived. The frog lashed out at the glass wall of its prison once or twice with its hind legs, said 'Rivet' bitterly, and then nodded its head.

'It's been a long day,' said Mrs. Derry. 'Did you understand what that man was saying about aggravation and your Dad and all that?'

Jason considered for a moment. For the first time in his life he had a vague, shadowy idea of what was going on. It was the beginning of wisdom.

'No,' he said. 'Good, here's George with the cart. Come on, Mum, in you get.'

In his Lear jet, thirty thousand feet above Nebraska, Mr. Kortright was speaking to Nostradamus on Blue.

'It's a neat idea, sure,' he said, 'and I like it in principle. But you've got to ask yourself, maybe you're aiming your stuff at the wrong slice of the market, okay? I mean, do the people really want to know about Napoleon? Do they really give a two-cent fuck about the advent of nuclear war? That sort of thing just kind of depresses people, Nos, you know? Why do you always have to be so goddam *gloomy*?'

There was an agitated buzzing from the end of the wire. Kortright sighed, murmured something about maybe having lunch Thursday, and replaced the receiver. He ate a pickled onion.

'Odin for you on Red, Mr. Kortright.'

Kortright swallowed a few shreds of peel and picked up the phone. 'Odin,' he said, 'how's tricks? Afraid you missed the boat again this time, but we'll keep trying for you, you know that.'

The receiver turned into a serpent in his hand and Kortright put a broad, friendly smile on his face. Nobody likes having a disgruntled client.

'Look, I've been thinking,' he said. 'What we need for you is a brand new vehicle. You know, launch you from an entirely different angle. I mean, we've tried blood and human sacrifice and all that; how about making you, well, cuddlier? You know,' said Kortright, keeping a straight face in spite of himself, 'lovable. We could say you originally came here from another planet and you got stranded, and we're trying to fix it so's you can go home . . .'

The serpent glowed blue and sprouted another head. Kortright made a comforting gesture with his hands.

'Okay,' he said soothingly. 'We'll put that one on ice for now. What you really need,' he went on, 'is a Gospel.'

There was an interested hiss from the serpent.

Kortright thought for a moment, and then smiled.

'With a good Gospel,' he said, 'we could go places with you. We could get sponsorship, you know? Commercial backing. We could make the big time.'

The serpent coiled itself round Kortright's ankle and started to eat his shoelaces. This was, the agent told himself, a good sign.

'How about something like this?' he said. '*In the begin-*

ning was the Word, and the Word was Kawaguchi Integrated Circuits, and all rights in the Word were reserved, so that unauthorised publication thereof in any form of cover or binding or electronic data retrieval system other than that supplied by the publisher rendered the user liable to civil and criminal prosecution . . .'

The serpent bit him.

Jason Derry leaned back, wiped the soap suds out of his eyes and reached for the rubber duck.

On the one hand, he said to himself.